Saint Sullivan's Daughter

Claire Germain Nail

abbott press®

A DIVISION OF WRITER'S DIGEST

Saint Sullivan's Daughter
A Novel

Abbott Press books may be ordered through booksellers or by contacting:

Abbott Press
1663 Liberty Drive
Bloomington, IN 47403
www.abbottpress.com
Phone: 1-866-697-5310

Artwork © Melanie Weidner.

ISBN: 978-1-4582-0460-8 (sc)
ISBN: 978-1-4582-0461-5 (hc)
ISBN: 978-1-4582-0459-2 (e)

Library of Congress Control Number: 2012910678

Printed in the United States of America

Abbott Press rev. date: 10/23/2012

TO MY DARLING JIM

*For we are made for happiness, and any one who is completely happy
has a right to say to himself, "I am doing God's will on earth."
All the righteous, all the saints, all the holy martyrs were happy.*
—Fyodor Dostoevsky

We Meet Sullivan
Santa Barbara, California
June 17, 1960

Sullivan faced a hell of a fight. He hankered for a drink—anything to put off telling Dora he'd quit his job. Again. Time was their quarrels were sexy and led straight to bed. Afterwards, she'd lounge, wrapped in the bedsheets, her black hair tangled and damp, her olive skin pink with pleasure. Those crazy nights he'd riff on his clarinet and she'd hum along, lit with the joy of reconciliation. Any virtuosity he lacked in love, he made up for as a musician. "Guess I'll have to keep you, Barry Sullivan," she used to say, forgiving everything for a song.

That was before the kid, little Ceci, came into their world, big green eyes so like his own. His own gaze had darkened to an army green of late. He winced, wondering how long Ceci's sparkle could last, with a father offering so much disappointment and a barbed-tongue mother to nail it in. When angry, Dora could curl the snakes on Medusa's forehead. She didn't care if Ceci stood in the crossfire. Poor macushla, only six years old, and the things she witnessed when the Sullivans fought!

Anything not fastened down Dora threw, swearing in Spanish fit to embarrass a San Pedro stevedore. In the aftermath, exiled to the sagging sofa, Barry would lie awake, worrying what Ceci might have overheard. Even to get up for a piss, he'd have to navigate a minefield of broken brica-brac. Sure as clockwork, he'd step onto a shard and bleed all over the carpet on the way to the john. Come the morning, Dora would see his bloodstains, and the yelling would begin anew.

Still, he hoped they might recapture something of their former joy. He wasn't sure what had changed. Dora remained the tempestuous Fiesta Princess she'd been at nineteen. From the moment he had clapped eyes on her, Barry had fallen in love. She flashed like an opal. Unlucky jewels, opals, unless you're born under the right sign. He'd been taking a chance marrying Dora; his closest friends had warned him so, and he had known it deep down. Still, he'd hoped against hope she'd bring him luck, and he'd make her proud. To win her, Barry had promised the moon; Dora expected the sun as a chaser. All he'd given her so far was the kid.

Dora's ounce of patience was waning, just as her infatuation had already done. What she wanted now was glamour—and security. Her convent school friends from Santa Barbara had married into mink coats, alligator purses, and diamond tennis bracelets. Even the ugly ones, who didn't deserve their good fortune, pranced around in Paris fashion. Given half the chance she'd put them all to shame. Barry was no help at all.

Music gigs didn't earn enough for chicken scratch, so she insisted he teach music on the side. He'd landed a higher-paying job at a ritzy music school, but lost patience with tin-eared brats and spoilt geniuses. To satisfy Dora, he'd taken this ill-fated job selling band instruments. So far that month, he'd sold one set of drumsticks and a book of Sousa marches. Quitting was the manly way out. How to get that through to her?

Just that morning, she'd read aloud to him from *Photoplay* about Liz Taylor's Mexican divorce. He'd better start making some money, or she'd put on her high heels and walk out. She'd sighed, "I have to make the most of my looks, before I'm too old."

Before he faced her again, he'd have to find a job. After he quit American Band Supply Company, he called around for gigs, determined never to moonlight again. Like he told Dora that very morning, he'd be a pro musician—or nothing.

"Nothing, we've got!" She shrieked and threw her coffee cup, staining the faded wallpaper behind Barry Maxwell House brown.

"Quit my job today!" Barry plunked himself down on a barstool and breathed a sigh. How good to complain without being pelted with crockery! "What a bum racket! Couldn't sell a goddamn piccolo, Mac, not if my life depended on it. Man's got to do what he's got to do: what he's good at."

What Barry was good at was jazz, namely bebop. Los Angeles just wasn't hep to his style. West Coast jazz was too white, too heavily arranged, and too predictable these days. The surprise in jazz made it art, Barry told anyone who'd listen to him. Listeners were few. So Barry had begun to rely on bartenders, the best listeners a troubled man can find: reluctant to give advice and always refilling one's glass.

"I'm good at one thing—music! But will they give me a break? Like Ma always said, 'The tall nail gets hammered.' Well, I've been hammered, all right! Got the bruises to prove it."

Compromise? Not this cat! His one big break as studio musician, he'd overstepped by suggesting changes to a mediocre film soundtrack. The assistant music director admitted Barry's jazz arrangement might've won them an Oscar, but the producer fired him. Hollywood did not want him again.

A martyr to the unexpected blue note, a flattened third or seventh that could pick a man up and toss him heavenwards, Barry would stand for music, if for nothing else—jazz played right from the soul.

He ordered another whiskey, neat with no chaser, Irish. *"Macushla!"* he sang to the amber fluid, *"Your dear voice is calling."* With these words, he remembered Ceci. He had promised he'd pick her up at two o'clock! It was already quarter to four.

Part One:
Ceci Sullivan
June and July 1960

When Ceci was still five, magic leaked out of the sky, not really like rain, but just as quiet and regular. Nobody was there to help her catch it. So Ceci ran into the house to tell Mama and Daddy, "It's raining and the sun is shining! Come see!"

They were fighting about something, so they shooed her outside. That's why Ceci had stood out in the rain, the shining drops drenching her hair, tears stinging her cheeks. If Mama or Daddy had come out to see that shiny rain, things might have been completely different. Maybe they could have been happy.

Sure as the sound of her patent leather Mary Janes sticking together, as sure as dandelion fluff against her lips as she blew its tiny stars into the sky, Ceci knew how to wish. So she wished her daddy would hurry up and not forget his promise. It was her birthday, a good day for wishing—or asking the saints for favors. May they bring Daddy to her! And may the saints help her.

Great-aunt Pilar told Ceci about the saints when Mama wasn't there to tell her, "No Catholic mumbo jumbo, Aunt! Don't be teaching her

Spanish, either! California is part of America, in case you didn't notice! We're Americans, and we're modern. Even the nuns told me to speak English."

Whenever Mama said things like this, Pilar crossed her fingers behind her back. "All, right my niece—throw away your birthright—I wouldn't dream of interfering!"

When Mama wasn't there, Pilar did teach Ceci to pray before the altar with its statue, flowers, and candles. "It's the way of the saints, the blessed servants of God." Pilar would lift her grandniece onto her wide lap. "*Escúchame cariña*. Listen well, dear one. Ask for the right things and God will hear you. What you ask with a pure heart will come to you." Ceci loved praying with Great-aunt Pilar—lighting and blowing out the candles, like every day was a birthday. But Ceci didn't know what to ask; she wanted everything. It would be too much, even for the saints, to bring everything in heaven to one little girl. Even now that she had turned six, she didn't know what she needed most.

This birthday, Daddy promised they'd visit the Mission Santa Barbara. They'd see the place where her mother's grandmother married, where her mama once upon a time had been Fiesta Princess with a diamond crown and her arms full of roses. Fiesta Queen: so beautiful, she might have been a movie star, except Daddy, and then Ceci, had come along to get in Mama's way. She wished Mama would be happy, and Daddy—

Daddy didn't make enough money; so Mama had to sew, bent over the black Singer sewing machine, pins in her mouth and a yellow tape measure around her neck, the TV on to keep Ceci busy. Even when nobody came to have a hem pinned up, Mama always put on red lipstick and pearls. She looked like a movie star, everyone said.

On Ceci's sixth birthday—June 17, 1960—Mama stayed at home and sewed, so they could pay for rent. Daddy drove Ceci in their old blue car all the way to Santa Barbara, to Pilar's little house. While he was out trying to sell things, Great-aunt Pilar babysat, because Ceci was always monkeying around or asking questions nobody wanted to answer. Mama needed time without them around, Daddy explained, and made a sad but funny face.

"How can she miss us if we never go away?" He promised they'd eat at the drive-in with a roller-skating waitress and go to the movie at the Arlington. A real date, he said.

The Arlington was a movie palace Pilar always talked about; Ceci couldn't wait to see it. But Daddy was late—and they'd missed the matinee. Great-aunt Pilar kept looking at the clock on her big brown radio. "The late Barry Sullivan, that's your *papá*! Might as well eat our snack without him." Pilar laid the lace cloth over the kitchen table, and in the center of it set a jar of roses—so sweet and open Ceci wished she were a bee. Everything smelled of bleach and Ivory Snow. That was how Pilar liked things: clean, neat, and all in a row, like the shiny copper pots over her stove, like her prize roses in the garden.

"A birthday treat for you, *querida*." She held out a plateful of pink iced cupcakes.

"Thank you, Aunt Pilar." Ceci licked the frosting, watching the blue and white checked kitchen curtains lift in the breeze.

"*Chiquita*, I wish you'd call me *Tía*. 'Aunt' is a horrible word, sounds like a bug. Do I look like a bug?" Pilar took a small bite, just as a bug might do. "*Tía* is Spanish for aunt. I prefer you to call me that."

"But Mama doesn't want me to speak Mexican. We always speak American."

"American! Mexican! I don't care!" Pilar's eyebrows met the deep line over her nose. "At my house I want to be called *Tía*. I can ask that much, can't I?"

Ceci nodded. "Tía! Please, can you tell me a story? About the Princess Saint? The one on your shelf."

"First, let me pour you some *horchata*. Didn't your *mamá* ever tell you about our saint? *Santa Bárbara*?"

"Mama never tells anything!" Ceci swung her teacup in the air, sloshing horchata onto the table. "'Specially not about saints."

Pilar sopped up the dribbles and the crumbs from the table. "The old things, your *mamá* doesn't understand them. If I could just get her to—"

"*Tía, por favor*," Ceci patted Pilar's arm. "Please, the story!"

"Good girl—perfect Spanish. All right, owlet! The story." Tía Pilar brushed back a wisp of her white hair and smoothed her skirt. "It was a long, long time ago—before God even thought of your old Tía." She folded her arms over her big, soft belly. "That's when it happened. *Santa Bárbara* was a Christian, but her father, the king, was pagan. He wanted her to marry a man who—"

"What's pagan?"

"Someone who isn't Christian."

"Mama isn't a Christian. She says there's no God."

"Shh!" Pilar touched her finger to Ceci's lips. "Your mother says such things, but she can't mean them. She's just trying to be modern." Her eyes circled the room, as if the story had run away from her somewhere into the air. "Now, where was I? Ah, yes! *Santa Bárbara's* father was a pagan, and she, of course, was a Christian. She refused to marry a pagan. Her father put her in a tower to punish her."

"Is praying bad, then?"

"No, *chiquita,* it is what we must do every day."

"But her father punished her. And Mama doesn't like it."

Tía rubbed the back of her neck. "Let me tell the story, will you?"

Ceci nodded.

"*Santa Bárbara* didn't mind being in the tower. The quiet made it even easier for her to pray. Her *papá* couldn't stand it anymore. He threatened to cut off her head, if she still refused the marriage!"

"Didn't she want to get married and wear a bride dress?"

"No, she had bigger plans—she would serve God." Pilar's chin lifted. "*Santa Bárbara* is our family's protector." She patted the front of her yellow and black calico apron. "My mother, your *bisabuela*—when she came to California to marry your great-grandfather—she carried our little *Santa Bárbara* in her trunk, all the way from San Antonio. The *santo* was made a long time ago, in Spain. It was her treasure; that's why I'm so careful with *Santa Bárbara*." Pilar smiled, eyes closed, as if waiting for a lovely dream. "You must always treat the *santo* with respect. I remember—"

"What happened? Did she die? Did her father cut off her head?"

"Die?" Pilar opened her eyes. "W—what? Who? My mother? Oh, no, she didn't die—well, not for a long time. If she were alive, she'd be almost a hundred years old. Ah, well! You're far too young to understand. And look at you, you've got *horchata* all over your front! What a mess." She wiped at Ceci's blouse. "Did your *mamá* ever tell you this one?

Soy Chiquita, soy bonita.
Soy la perla de mamá.
Si me ensucio el vestido, garratazos me dará."

Pilar clapped her hands. *"Pom! Pom! Pom!"*

"What does it mean?"

"'I'm a pretty little thing—my mother's pearl—but if I get dirty, such a spanking she'll give.' Like this: *pom-pom-pom!*"

Ceci knew about spankings. Mama gave them all the time with anything she could grab, but Mama's spanking wasn't as bad as Mama's yelling—worse than sticks and stones for breaking bones. She'd choose a spanking over yelling any day.

"Just look at that sad face you're making! You'd think you'd lost your last friend," Pilar sighed. "I know, your *mamá* has a temper, just like Chiquita's mama. We'll have to make you more presentable, or she'll have a fit." Pilar fussed with Ceci's hair, clicking her tongue. Then she squinted at her watch. "Three o'clock! *Right to Happiness!*"

She cleared the table, rinsed the plates, and opened the refrigerator, removing a plastic bag full of wet clothes. "Turn on the radio, Cecilita, and I'll set up the ironing board. Time for my soap opera."

"Why do you put clothes in the fridge?"

"*Ay*, you are full of questions, *m'ija*! To keep them wet until my soap opera comes on. I love to listen and iron. Here, let me tune it in."

"Is it going to be a music show?"

Pilar waved Ceci's question away. "Shh! The news!"

"*California polls show Vice President Richard Nixon ahead of the Catholic Senator from Massachusetts.*"

"Mother of God, let it be Kennedy! Please, please—a Catholic in the White House! Imagine!" Pilar prayed to the kitchen ceiling and then spat on her iron. The organ music began. The old woman crossed herself. *"Ay, poor Grace, will the doctor ever marry her?"*

Not knowing the answer to that, or anything else about *Right to Happiness*, Ceci swallowed the last of her cupcake. No use asking any more questions, either, not till the Tide commercial. *Right to Happiness* was as important to Tía as church—the radio people might die without Tía to worry and pray about them.

Quiet as she could, Ceci pulled a stool up to the living room shelf, to Pilar's altar. Kids were not allowed to touch these beautiful things. Morning and evening, Pilar prayed the rosary before these tall glass candles, the glittering crystal vase of red plastic roses, brown photos of unsmiling people who had lived before Mama had even been born. Most interesting to Ceci was the wooden box with the glass door. Saint Barbara lived behind its glass door. Nobody ever touched her, except when Pilar dusted everything as part of cleaning the already clean house.

Great-aunt Pilar would lift the saint from the box, wiping the wooden face with loving care, kissing the top of its head. Once, when Ceci was a baby, maybe Mama had washed her like that. Nowadays, Mama scrubbed Ceci with a soapy washcloth, rough from the clothesline. Babies were so lucky—babies and wooden saints.

This might be a lucky saint, but she had the saddest eyes: two dots of dark brown paint. Saint Barbara's doll mouth was no happier, a pale red, like Mama's lipstick on the edge of her coffee cup. Maybe the saint was lonely—maybe she wanted someone to play with her.

Ceci opened the glass door and took the saint by the skirt to pull her out of the box. Bits of old lace crumbled into her hands, falling to the floor like dirty snow. She slid the doll back into the box, shut the doors, and brushed her hands on her sides. Her heart bumped against her chest like a trapped moth. A breeze snuck through the blinds; the candlelight flickered, but the saint did not blink. Ceci prayed.

"Santa Barbara, my mama is always mad and my daddy is—well, he's late—and it's my birthday. I just keep waiting." Ceci's hands tightened around the edge of the shelf, and she stared into the sad saint's eyes, until in one of them a teardrop formed. Down the side of Saint Barbara's nose it rolled and fell onto Ceci's thumb, cold and warm, like the wintergreen oil Pilar rubbed on her knees at night.

A shiver climbed Ceci's back and shook the teardrop off her finger. She was suddenly afraid. Never had she monkeyed with anything so important as a saint. But that was not all. Something was coming—something worse than being spanked or yelled at.

There could be very bad things in the world; she had watched the news with Daddy, seen the blurry movies of people crying about fires and earthquakes. The news wasn't as real as this feeling, balled up in her stomach, the size of an apple. Something was coming—what Tía called a catastrophe—a beautiful word Ceci had loved until she learned its meaning.

She searched the saint's wooden face. "Help me!" she prayed. "Help us, Saint Barbara!" She might have run to Tía Pilar, no matter that it was smack in the middle of *Right to Happiness*. She might have jumped into those fat, safe arms, but she heard the sound of the door opening and leapt down from the stool to run to the door.

"Daddy!"

And there he was, coming down the hall, his foot catching on Pilar's throw rug, laughing and whistling a song as he lifted her into the air. She loved his smell: whiskey, and the tonic he ran through his fine red hair every morning. Vitalis kept his hair neat and shiny as a new penny, but everything else looked rumpled and tired. Maybe the whiskey did that.

"Bean!" he sang out, his big hands tight around her waist, until her long hair flipped over onto his. "Aren't you a sight for sore eyes?"

His eyes did look sore; there were little red lines in the whites.

"Were you crying, Daddy?"

"Crying, macushlah? He set her down with a grunt. "On your birthday? I'd sooner eat my clarinet than cry on such a day!" He swept aside her hair, coppery like his, only curly like Mama's. "Today, you are the queen!"

He remembered! Ceci buried her head into the starchy cotton of his dress shirt, her left hand wrapped around the silky strand of his tie, and forgot about being afraid.

Pilar stood over the stove, stirring the rich chocolate sauce called *mole,* the Nahuatl word for sauce. She had taught Ceci some Nahuatl words—the language of the Indians who had worked on the hacienda for Pilar's parents. The Nahuatl people had lived in America, Tía said, long, long ago.

Pilar waved her wooden spoon at Daddy. "So, you finally grace us with your presence, eh, *malvado*! The child has been waiting for hours!"

"Sorry, I had some business to do. I hope Ceci wasn't too much trouble."

"Not my trouble, but your daughter's!" Pilar swatted his shoulder with her spoon. "Having to wait all day on her birthday!"

"Don't worry, Ceci knows I keep my promises." Daddy kissed Pilar's cheek. "Is that *mole* I smell? Wow!"

Pilar cracked just a hint of a smile. "*Mole, sí.*"

"*Mole,* the food of the gods! Maybe we could stay for dinner? Smells delicious!"

"You flatterer!" Pilar gave him another whack with her spoon. "You promised the child a hamburger, didn't you? You also promised to take her to the Mission. Now it might be closed. You'd better get going!"

"Closed? Really?"

"Maybe! Still, you could drive by and show Cecilita where her mother was crowned Fiesta Queen. Crazy child has been talking about saints all day. I even told her the story of our Saint Barbara." Pilar nodded at the window. "Still plenty of sunshine, if you get going." She flapped her apron after them, sweeping them out the door.

The faded blue Mercury waited in the driveway, the heart Ceci had traced in the window dust this morning still there. On the little patch of grass beside the car, Tía Pilar crouched to pull up a lone white dandelion.

Ceci made to catch the seeds that floated up from it. "You forgot to wish, Tía!"

"Wish—Pish!" Pilar brushed the dandelion fluff off her chest. "Now dandelions will come up every—look, your hair! People in town know you're my grandniece—oh—do comb her hair, Barry!"

"She looks fine. Like a little lion." He tousled Ceci's curls. "Get in the car, sweetheart."

Waiting for them to stop talking, Ceci folded her hands on her lap as they had taught her in kindergarten, wishing for Daddy to hurry up and go. She swung her legs, kicking the seat. Then she remembered. Like sucking on a Tootsie Roll pop, it didn't do to bite into a good thing all at once. It was best to lick it slowly, so it lasted.

"Wait!" Pilar leaned into the car window. "I almost forgot! Dora called, said you'd better be home by eight. She's in a mood, I tell you!"

"Dora's always in a mood." Even though he smiled, Daddy's eyes looked sad. "Just don't tell her about you and me, okay?"

"Ha!" Pilar fanned the air. "Go on, devil! Have fun—only get home early!"

As they drove the narrow, hilly road, Ceci glided her hand on waves of air. "It smells like flowers here. San Pedro stinks like fish. I wish we could move here. Is this where you'd like to live, Daddy? Tía says if we lived closer—"

"*Tía*, baby? I never heard that before."

"She told me to say *Tía*, because it doesn't sound like a bug."

"Good a reason as any, I guess."

"And, guess what—*Tía* is Spanish for aunt. Tía Pilar is teaching me Spanish."

"Oh, she is, is she? I thought Mama said no more Spanish, not till you're older."

"Why? Is Spanish bad for me?"

"Well, I don't think it's bad for you, sweetheart, but—"

"Can't I, just a little? I want to talk like Zorro."

"Well, I don't know—oh, why not? Learn Spanish. Live it up!"

Daddy was the most handsome man, except for Zorro, who had a sword, a cape, and a mask. If her daddy wore a cape, he would only look silly. Zorro didn't look silly, not ever. Still, Zorro could not play clarinet, and Daddy could. She'd always choose Daddy, but Zorro was interesting to watch, making zees with his sword on bad guys' shirts and galloping away on his beautiful horse.

"Keep speaking Spanish, but only with Pilar. Just keep it to yourself, Bean. We know how your mama is once she makes up her mind." He pressed his lips together tightly and stared straight ahead, frowning. "Don't we, though?"

Ceci pulled on his sleeve. "Daddy!"

"What, baby?"

"Would you like to live in one of these pretty houses? Not a regular house, like Tía's, but like that one there." She pointed to a big white house with purple flowers growing up its walls.

"How could I? Those houses cost a fortune."

"But if you had lots and lots of money—if you were a million, would you?"

"If I were a *million*!" Daddy laughed. "Sure! When my ship comes in, I'll moor her right here in Santa Barbara Harbor. We'll buy the biggest hacienda in town, with bougainvillea and jasmine vines all the way up to your bedroom window. Fat chance of that ever happening!" He stuck his arm out the window to signal. "Yeah, I used to think this town was magic. I met your mama here—a beautiful day, just like this one. I was playing for the Fiesta, and your mother was one of the Princesses, about to be crowned Queen. You should have seen her." He stopped talking, staring at the road as if he could see something both sad and wonderful crossing the street ahead.

Ceci looked where he was looking, but there was nothing.

"Do we have a picture?" Ceci waited for his answer, but he just stared at the street. "Daddy!"

"Huh?" He shook himself and turned to her. "Beg your pardon?"

"Do we have a picture?"

"Of what, sweetheart?"

"When Mama was a Queen—I want to see it."

"Ah! I used to. Don't know where it went." He made an eyeshade with his hand. "Look, there's the mission, Ceci!"

She saw a low tan building, church, trees, and a rose garden. Behind the gardens, tall white tree trunks caught the afternoon sun. The patchy grass was brown at the edges. "That place, Daddy, that's the mission? Can't anybody take care of it?"

"It's very old, sweetheart, that's why it looks like that."

Pigeons cooed in the shadows underneath the arches; blobs of their droppings whited the walkway. Sparrows swooped around the sky overhead, in and out of the bell tower. The corners of the buildings were round with wear. "Saint Barbara lives here, with the birds? Will we see her?"

"It's only named after Saint Barbara, like you're named after your mother's mother. Let's take a look 'round. It's part of your history, you know."

The stone path to the fountain gave Ceci a feeling like looking at old baby pictures—of places she'd been and could almost remember. She touched the water that overflowed its mossy bowl, making a little cup of her hand.

"Ceci, you stay here by the fountain. I'll see if there's a way we can still get in."

A breeze shook the leaves, and a cloud slid over the sun. Daddy was taking a long time. Sudden cold dropped through her like a stone. From her toes to the back of her neck, shivers stood up the little hairs. Ceci rocked on her heels, floating her arms like wings.

Through the rippled light came two brown women in long white dresses. On their heads they carried baskets of laundry. The younger woman, her long braids twisted with red ribbons, waved at Ceci. *"¡Buenos tardes! ¿De dónde vienes niña?"*

Ceci understood; the woman was welcoming her, asking where she was from. "I'm Ceci. I came in a car, all the way from San Pedro. Our old blue car, over there." She whirled around on her heels to point it out—no cars anywhere!

The two women set down the baskets before a wide, stone pool filled with greenish water. *"Vamos a lavar ropa aquí—en la lavandería."*

Ceci whispered the beautiful word to herself: *lavandería, lavandería, lavandería*—laundry. They were here to wash clothes in the long straight cement pool, the *lavandería*. Were they *Indias*—wild Indians? Good Indians?

Pilar often had told about the good *Indias:* women who had helped Ceci's great-great grandmothers. Once upon a time, the Indian women cooked, worked the fields, washed the clothes, and cared for people's children—even when their own got so sick from white people's germs that most of them died. The story had made Ceci cry until her eyelids stuck together, and Tía Pilar had put warm tea bags over them so they'd open.

Now the younger Indian took a shirt from her basket, squatting to scrub it with her balled-up fist. The old one kneeled and unrolled a white sheet into the water, brushing it with a bundle of twigs. Ceci splashed her fingers into the moving water. No smelly soap from an orange Tide box, but sea air and sunshine to clean—twig and rock to scrub.

When the old woman had filled her basket with wet laundry, she stood up, rubbing her bent back. She took Ceci's hands between her old ones, rough and knotty as the bark of a tree. "Take care, little daughter. Danger is coming, many dangers."

Ceci stared into the swirling water. Danger!

"Don't you worry; we will pray for you every day."

The younger woman stood and brushed Ceci's hair from her forehead. She held out a smooth, round white rock and placed it in Ceci's hand. *"Un regalo de Santa Bárbara."* A birthday gift from *Santa Bárbara*! Ceci closed her hand around the pebble and dropped it into her pocket.

"A birthday song, *en Nahuatl*, in our own language, the old one from before the *padres*." The women's song sounded like birdcalls, like the tock of water dripping into a hollow pot, like a creek turning pebbles. Lifting and twisting the white cloth in rhythm, their work was dance.

"Hey, Ceci!" From far away, her daddy's voice calling. "Sorry, baby, the mission really is closed. Want to look around outside?"

Still the women sang, and Ceci listened, tilting her head toward the music.

"Ceci! What are you doing? Ceci!" He squeezed her arm.

Ceci looked up at him, surprised. "This is a *lavandería*. Indians wash clothes here. See, they are using those sticks."

"What Indians? I don't see any Indians. What are you talking about?" Daddy jogged around the structure. "Well, look at this; here's a plaque!" He read aloud: *This lavandería, or washing basin, was completed in 1818. It served as the original mission laundry. The Indians soaped the clothes on the sloping sides and rinsed them in the center pool.*

"Wow! I didn't know you could read, Ceci."

"Just ABCs and my name."

"Then how do you know about the Indians, about the *lavandería*?"

"Those Indians, they told me."

"Those tourists?" He nodded toward some women smelling roses in the garden. "I don't think they are—well, I guess they could be Indians, if you pretend."

"Not them! These ladies, right here!"

"I don't see anyone, baby."

The two Indians picked up their heavy baskets. *"Cecilita,"* the older woman called, waving, "Go with God, little one. *Hasta luego.*"

Ceci waved back.

"Ceci, look at me!" He grabbed her shoulders. "Who told you about that *lavandería*? Who talked to you? Them?" He pointed again at the tourist women. "They don't look like Indians to me."

No one moved in the dusty light, no one but tourists smelling roses and cars swishing by. Ceci rubbed her eyes to keep from crying. "They're gone!"

"Don't cry." Daddy gathered her into his arms. "Silly girl!" He kissed the top of her head. "It's fun to pretend about Indians. Used to pretend I was the Lone Ranger, and Ma's broom was his brave horse, Silver."

"It's not pretend. I saw them. I did." The thump of Daddy's heart, his smell like clean wood, quieted her. She reached for his shirt pocket, toying with his ballpoint pen. "Daddy, I saw them." She clicked the pen open and closed. "They were right here. The old one told me—"

"Don't worry, my fey girl. I'll never begin to understand you, but you're an A-one girl! That I know for certain!" Daddy tousled her hair. "Let's skedaddle. I've an errand to run before we paint the town."

Lying in the back seat, looking up at the sky crisscrossed with telephone lines, Ceci felt her pocket for the little white rock. Though her pocket was slightly damp, the rock was gone.

A few minutes after they left the mission, Daddy parked in front of a pink building with a flashing neon cocktail glass above the door. "This'll take two shakes of a lamb's tail. Daddy will be right back."

"Can I go, too?"

"Oh honey, I don't know. Got to talk business with Mitch."

"Please? Please? Please?"

Daddy scratched his head. "Oh, all right; they're not open yet. But don't get into mischief, kiddo. This is my last chance: could make or break me."

The place smelled of stale cigarette smoke and the oranges the bartender was slicing. He waved, the knife still in his hand. "Hey, well, if it ain't Saint Sullivan, back from the dead! We missed you 'round here. Where you been?"

"Doing honest work, Douglas, my boy. Hey, can you do me a little favor and keep an eye on Ceci? Just for a minute? I have to check in with Mitch about a gig."

"All right," Douglas sighed. "Don't be too long. I've lots to do."

"Hi, Douglas," Ceci climbed onto the barstool. "I 'member you. You have a motorcycle."

A slow smile warmed his face. "Yeah, that's right. A Harley-Davidson." He swept the oranges into a jar, twisted on the lid, and began to stack clean square ashtrays on a tray. Shuffling around under the bar, he set a pile of matchbooks on it without standing up. Like puppets from behind a stage came piles of napkins, long plastic sticks, and more matchbooks. On everything, the same design in gold: a cocktail glass, about to tip out the olive.

"Know what?" Ceci pulled herself tall as she could to look over the bar and see Douglas where he squatted. "It's my birthday!"

Douglas stood up, rubbing his back. "Aren't you the lucky one?"

"Yeah! I'm not having a party—but if I had a party, I'd invite you. You could bring your motorcycle and give us rides." Ceci studied him, unsure. "You'd come to my party, wouldn't you?"

"I don't go to parties, kid."

"Not ever? Why?"

"This place kind of spoils me for parties." He stared over her head at the stage. "Never liked them much, but now I hate them." He started to mop the bar.

"Why?"

"Sick of people, I guess," Douglas sighed. "Days off I just want peace and quiet. And no parties."

Ceci spread her fingers out on the bar. Underneath each nail, a dirty gray moon. "You're just like my Tía. She hates parties."

"Who?"

"Auntie Pilar. She's always saying she needs some peace and quiet. That's why she always makes me take a nap. Peace and quiet."

"My kind of girl, your auntie. Want to give me her phone number?"

"Oh, gosh, she is probably a hundred! Too old, even for you!"

He threw back his head, laughing, until his eyes were wet, his basset hound cheeks red and shiny. A tear streaming down his smile, he patted her hand. "You I like. Maybe you and me could date?"

Ceci's curls crossed her face as she shook her head. "I'm too little. I won't be old as you for a long, long time."

"I'll just have to wait for you to grow up, won't I?"

"It's going to take forever. I can't even cross the street by myself yet. You better find someone else." She felt sad, wondering who would love old Douglas.

"Guess you're right. Don't worry, angel, your prince will come. In the meantime, how about a birthday Shirley Temple, my treat?"

"Can I have a cherry on a toothpick?"

"A cherry, and a slice of orange!" He bowed. "For the birthday girl!"

"Thank you!"

Douglas dropped another cherry into the drink. "My pleasure! You're a breath of fresh air." He turned to set a tray of glasses on the mirrored shelf, humming to himself.

Fresh air. Grownups said things like that. When she was five, Ceci used to ask what they meant, but only a few of them took the trouble to explain. Maybe being six was time to find out for yourself. She watched Douglas work on her drink, dangling the cherry before her eyes. It was glassy red, not like any fruit Mama ever gave her—wonderful! He placed the glass on a paper circle.

"To your good health, Ceci! Happy Birthday!"

"Thank you!" She popped the cherry in her mouth, and sucked the sharp, sweet juice until the cherry flattened on her tongue. Douglas was busy now, cleaning the glass behind the bar, too busy to talk anymore, and her daddy was taking too long.

Ceci slipped off the barstool and wandered to the side of the stage, finding an open door to an office. There Daddy was standing at a desk, talking to a man with silver hair and a suit to match who sat at a desk with a glass top. Behind the desk on the dark wall was a picture of a naked lady in high heels with feather wings: a bird lady. Daddy's back curled like a "C," his fingertips resting on the desk edge. Neither of them noticed her. She felt too shy to say anything so they would.

"But it was a done deal! What changed your mind? I'm good; you've said so many times." Daddy stood up from the desk, running his hand through his slicked-back hair. "Let me show you what I can do."

"It's not that you don't have the chops, Sullivan. It's just that—the clarinet-led band is, well, passé. Young people don't dig be-bop so much, and that's the clientele we want to bring in. Dick can lead on piano, and I'll hold out for a good horn, or better yet, a sax. College kids love—"

"I quit my day job for you, Mitch! What am I supposed to do?"

"You can still blow that clarinet!" Mitch smiled, flashing a gold front tooth. "Find yourself a big old dance band, playing oldies. The over-forty crowd—"

"Are you telling me I'm a goddamn has-been, at thirty? You good as signed—"

Mitch held up his hand. "Whoa! Look behind you, man! That your kid?"

Daddy swung around. "I told you to wait, Ceci!"

"I already waited and waited. Please, Daddy, can we go now?"

"Aw, honey, give me a sec here." He lifted Ceci into his arms. "Listen, Mitch, I need this gig. I've got mouths to feed!" He held Ceci out in front of him. "Exhibit A!"

"Yeah, cute kid. But I got nothing for you, Sullivan. The combo is not an option." Mitch shrugged. "Give it a rest, man. Take your little girl home."

"Please!" Daddy's arms tightened around Ceci. "At least give me a lead." Mitch came around the desk and tickled Ceci's chin. "Hiya, Toots!"

"I'm Ceci!" She hoped he'd never call her Toots again—a dog's name! She remembered Tía Pilar hating to be called an ant. "Ceci Sullivan!"

"Well, now!" Mitch laughed. "Red hair and olive skin! Rare, that!" He ran his hand through her curls. "Dynamite eyes! You'll have to lock her up when she's sixteen, if she's anything like your Dora. Now there's a gig I'd like to book myself—"

"Mitch!" Daddy coughed and shook back his hair. "Listen, could we get back to the job you promised me?"

"Relax, pal. In the long run, you'll thank old Mitch." He fished in his pocket, bringing out a skinny cigarette, holding it up like someone in a TV commercial. "Nothing personal. Just to show I mean well, how 'bout a reefer for later?"

"I don't smoke—*anything*!" Daddy shifted Ceci in his arms.

"Oh yeah, right!" Mitch put the cigarette in his mouth and clicked open his lighter. "I almost forgot. Saint Sullivan—you don't smoke weed, don't chase birds. Don't do anything us mortals do. You ought to loosen up, commit a couple of sins. Might help your music. Bring you down to earth."

"Please, Mitch!" Daddy was sweating; Ceci felt the warm wet coming through his nice white shirt. "Is there somebody you know who'll hire me? I'll do anything, long as it's music!"

Mitch held his skinny cigarette in front of him like a torch. He sucked that little worm of a thing until his eyes watered. "Ah, well, Sullivan, old saint, I can't let you go away mad, not with that kid staring at me like that. Swear to God, that kid has eyes like a cat: stares right through you!"

"You've got something for me, then?"

"If only you'd—" Mitch closed his eyes. "Well, I don't know. Well, maybe George Schwann. If only you weren't such a hipster."

"I can deal with whatever—"

"Well, that's more like it! This one, George Schwann and the Cobbs: here's his card. Gold embossed. Swanky!"

Daddy shrugged and handed back the card. "Never heard of him."

"Don't let that stop you, man. Nobody's heard of him, but he rakes in the dough. Very Glenn Miller, a square—but a pro all the way. Plays the swanky hotels, society weddings, Bar Mitzvahs. I'm talking steady gigs, man: telling you this 'cause you're a nice guy, with a kid and a real barnburner for a wife. Stop being such a sensitive artiste. You want to eat, don't you?" He thrust the card into Daddy's hand. "If you're ready to work, call George. Better a square gig than a day job, man!"

"All right!" Daddy took a long breath. "All right, you win! Just tell me one thing, will you, now?"

"Sure, Sullivan."

"What in the hell is a cobb? For crying out—"

"And you're a university man! Has to do with swans, highbrow play on his name. Check your Funk & Wagnalls!" Mitch stubbed out the skinny cigarette and checked his gold wristwatch, his diamond cufflinks glinting. "Got to scare Dick out of his apartment. The cat never fails to amaze me, even when he's strung out. Prop him up at the piano and he spins straw into gold." Mitch pushed past Daddy and Ceci, jingling his car keys. "Let me know how it goes with George."

"That man's cat—can I see him?" Ceci tugged her daddy's hand as she watched Mitch leave. "I want to see a cat play piano. Does he use his—"

"That's just the way Mitch talks. There's no cat."

"How about swans?" She skipped beside him to the car. "Are you going to play music with swans?"

Daddy sighed. "A gig is a gig, I guess."

He sounded so sad; Ceci had to pat his hand.

"I love you, Daddy—more than anyone in the whole wide world."

Without a word, he helped her into the front seat and slammed the door. He got in and just sat there, holding the steering wheel, his chin jutting out and lips pressed together, his chest lifting up and down with every breath. Ceci's heart squeezed hard; she felt she might disappear if she didn't say something to fill the quiet.

"Do you love me, Daddy?"

His eyes shut; he was shaking.

"Do you love me, Daddy? Because I—"

"God damn it, Ceci! What the hell kind of question is that?" He shot her a look, eyes hard and muddy, like someone had turned off the light in the sky. "Do I *love* you? Everything I do is for you; it's all for you! Why do you think I drove around selling crap all this year? I should have been out there making a name! Shit! What the hell more do you want?" He threw up his arms and Ceci ducked, her hands covering her face. He clapped his hand over his mouth, his eyes watering. "Oh, sweetheart, you didn't think—baby, I'd never hit you! Just letting off steam, that's all. Hell of a day I had. Just hell. What's your mother going to say? What'll she say?"

Ceci rubbed her eyes, trying not to cry.

"Oh honey, I'm sorry! I shouldn't be bothering you with this stuff." He fingered her curls. "Well, now, we'd better spruce you up. Your pretty hair's all tangled again."

Ceci shook her head. "It's not pretty. Mama wants to cut it off. She says my hair looks like snakes."

"Look at me, baby." He held her chin, turning her face. "Don't you listen to Dor—to Mama—when she says stuff like that. Sometimes, I—she's a little crazy. Had it real tough as a kid; that's why she's so tough on you—and me. She can't help it." He put down the sun visor. "Stand up so you can see yourself in the mirror here. See, don't you look pretty now?"

Though she tried to see what Daddy meant, Ceci could see no difference in her looks. Her red-brown hair still wild; squiggles stood up like corkscrews. Her face was like a cup of egg custard, her freckles just like the spice Mama sprinkled on it. If only her hair could be wavy and black and her skin coffee and cream like Mama's, then she'd be pretty.

"Come on, Bean, smile! There's my little movie star." Daddy tossed the comb onto the dash. "Hey, maybe I'm missing my calling. I could be a hairdresser somewhere in Beverly Hills, raking in the dough."

"Silly, you don't want to be a hairdresser!"

"No, you're right, but I want to see *Snow White*. How about you?"

"Really? Right now?"

"Shouldn't we get a bite to eat first? Then the movie."

"Can we go to the drive-in? Eat dinner at the beach?"

"Of course! Your wish is my command! The drive-in it is!"

Ceci's favorite drive-in was near the beach. With a swoosh of her short skirt, the carhop spun around on her skates, smoothed down her apron, and pulled out her order pad. "What'll it be, mister?"

"Just give us that Friday special fish thing—uh, number three—and a small vanilla milkshake. I'll finish whatever the kid leaves."

Ceci watched her skate away. "I like this place, Daddy."

"Well, I wouldn't call it the Ritz." He took a rumpled bag from his briefcase, unscrewed the cap, sipped, and afterwards breathed a wet, delicious sigh.

"What is that stuff, Daddy?"

"Just a little Dutch courage, baby. Takes the edge off the day."

"Can I have some?"

"No, baby, I don't think it's good for little girls; stunts your growth. Here she comes with dinner. Let's take it to the beach and check out the sunset."

They parked facing the harbor and rolled down the windows to let in the salty air. The orange sun hung like a ball over the sea; her birthday wasn't over, not yet. There was still the movie, and maybe there'd be a present.

"Here." Ceci handed Daddy her half sandwich. "I don't really like it."

"Let Daddy try it." He took a bite, winced, and washed it down with Dutch courage. He crumpled the rest into the bag. "Not worth eating. Ready for a movie? Ready for Snow White and all the dwarfs? How many are there, Ceci, sixty?"

"Seven, silly!"

"Seven dwarfs!" He revved the engine. "We're off! We'd better hurry, or we'll miss the cartoon."

Through a long Spanish courtyard with colored tiles and a fountain pool, they made their way to the Arlington's box office. A man in a gold and red suit checked their tickets and led them to their seats with a flashlight, just in time for the end of the cartoon.

Ceci rocked her seat as a sausage-string of wiener dogs chased Goofy 'round and 'round Mickey's backyard, snapping at Goofy's baggy overalls. Daddy sipped from his little bag, and the cartoon ended. All kinds of words Ceci couldn't read danced on the screen. The red velvet curtains closed and opened to the sound of beautiful violin music.

Then a castle filled the screen. Chubby bluebirds circled Snow White as she sang her wishes into the well. Ceci sighed with joy, squeezing Daddy's hand.

The Wicked Queen argued with her mirror, plotting her evil. Daddy snored, no louder than a purring cat, and the bag with Dutch courage in it fell to the floor.

The seven dwarfs welcomed Snow White to their cottage. Daddy snored through "Whistle While You Work," the poison apple, and everyone getting sad. Ta-daa—a magical kiss from Prince Charming, Snow White woke up, and Daddy still slept. His snoring sounded even louder once the music was over and the curtains closed again.

The lights came on, people filed out, and then more people came in. Ceci settled into her seat. "Coming to a Theater Near You!" a voice announced about a movie called "The Apartment." A repeat of the weenie roast cartoon, and Snow White's castle appeared again on the screen. Snow White and the bluebirds sang again, and Daddy snored louder and louder.

On the screen the Queen argued again with the mirror, while in the darkened theater the usher brought the beam of his flashlight up to Daddy's face.

"Sir, are you all right?" The usher shook Daddy's arm. "Sir?"

"Wh—what?" Daddy woke up. "What the hell? What do you want?"

"Sir!" The young man gulped. "You have to keep your—noise down, sir. Do you need some help getting up?" He offered his hand.

"No—let—I'm fine!" Daddy stood, tugging Ceci out of her seat. "We're just leaving! We don't need help, thank you!"

Daddy's ears were very red, and he almost ran up the aisle. Ceci's shoes slid on the carpet as he pulled her along. When they reached the car he let go her hand. "There's no way we'll be on—oh, God damn it to hell—a ticket!"

"Ticket for what, Daddy? Are we going to see another movie?"

"Dora will kill me." He wiped his eyes with the cuff of his sleeve. "It's way past time to be home."

"Don't cry, Daddy!"

"I'm not. I'm not gonna cry. It's just—not a word to your mother about the ticket! It'll be our little secret, okay?"

"Okay, Daddy."

"Had too much—I need to find a cup of coffee." He slipped the ticket back under the windshield wiper. "Well, at least we won't be getting another ticket."

He made to step off the curb. "Stop, Daddy! Cars are coming!"

"Oh, baby, I'm a real cad, aren't I?" He scooped Ceci up into his arms. "Great Zounds alive, you're getting big!" He planted a wet kiss on her forehead.

"I'm getting fat." Ceci patted her stomach.

"Who says?"

"Mama says I might get fat like Tía Pilar."

"You'll never be fat; you're a little bring stream. I mean string bean! My own little Bean!" He held her in one arm and patted her tummy. "Skinny, but just right for five—a five-year-old!"

"Six, Daddy! I'm six now."

"Six-year-old. Any way you look at it, baby, you're just right! Perfect!"

"And you're just right for a daddy." Ceci found the place she loved under his chin, the place where his neck met his ear.

Stepping into a coffee shop, Daddy called out, "Got any joe?"

"Sorry, bud, I'm closing in a few minutes."

"I need a little caffeine." Daddy leaned onto the counter. "Just a quick cup for the road, please?"

The man's eyes swept Daddy's face, then checked the coffee pot. "You might as well finish off the dregs." He poured the last of it into a heavy mug and slid it to Daddy. "Anything for the little girl? Pie?"

Ceci eyed the desserts circling slowly in a glass tower by the counter. "Can't I have lemon pie, Daddy? It's my birthday!"

The man behind the counter winked at Ceci. "Pie's on the house, and you should eat, 'specially if you're driving." He nodded to Daddy.

"That's really kind of you, but I can't accept charity. We're not needy."

"I'm telling you, bud, eat something. It'll soak up the booze." He set two plates of lemon meringue pie onto the counter and refilled Daddy's cup. "Ain't charity, anyhow. I'll throw this out tonight. Gets sweaty in the fridge."

Daddy eyed the pie. "I'm not hungry!"

"Come on, mister, eat." He poured a little more coffee into Daddy's cup. "It'll do you a world of good."

"To do me any good, it ought to be poison. My life is crap—absolute crap."

"When you get to be my age, you'll see. Nothing is as bad as it looks. You've got your—"

"Yeah, I know, I've got my whole goddamn life ahead of me. That's the rub!"

"You've got your cute little gal, was what I was going to say. What I wouldn't give for a kid! Me and Norma always wanted to have kids, but the good Lord didn't see fit to give us none."

"Yeah, I'm lucky. The rich get richer, and the poor have children." Daddy stared over the man's head at the milkshake machine and the stacks of plates and coffee cups on the shelf. "Well, it's late." Daddy's hand shook as he handed the man a quarter. "Keep the change. Might as well go home with clean pockets."

"Better keep it, then. Might need to make a phone call. Maybe your wife—"

"Not gonna trouble trouble, till trouble troubles me!" Daddy shoved the quarter toward him. "Never say a Sullivan left an establishment without tipping! C'mon, Ceci!"

Ceci shook her head. "I didn't finish my pie!"

"Never mind that." He lifted her onto his shoulder. "It's time we hit the road."

Daddy carried her all the way to the car. A salty wind had brought in the fog, misting the Mercury's windows. Before starting the car, Daddy wiped the clouded windshield with his sleeve. "Sometimes California is the coldest damned place on earth!" He fiddled with the heater, and the knob fell off onto the floor. "Goddamn piece of junk!"

He bent to pick it up, and when he did, bumped his head on the steering wheel. He sat with his head pressed against his hands. Ceci leaned against him, snuggling.

"For Christ's sake, I'm not a pillow! Move it, Ceci!"

With a little cry, Ceci slid away from him, up against her door.

"Aw, gee, now, you're not going to cry! I didn't mean to say that. Ceci, honey!"

Wriggling away from his touch, Ceci pressed her hot cheek against the car window and stared out at the inky sea. A few stars winked through the purple sky, and the full moon's yellow face broke into pieces on the waves.

☆   ☆   ☆   ☆

Finally, they bumped to a stop in their dark driveway. Ceci pretended to be fast asleep so Daddy would carry her inside, and she'd be put into bed without having to brush her teeth. The porch light was off, so he fumbled for the keys. The door opened from inside.

"Dora, baby!" Daddy shook just a little. "You're still up!"

Ceci opened her eyes just a crack to see her mama.

"So I am!" Mama pulled her black lace robe tighter around her. "Where the hell were you, you bastard!"

Daddy's arms tightened around Ceci, his voice high and strange. "Hello, darling, and how was your day?" Kissing the air by her cheek, he walked past her. Her high-heeled slippers clicking the linoleum, Mama followed them up the hallway to Ceci's room.

"I said be home by eight. Even called Pilar to remind you."

"I got held up at Mitch's."

Daddy laid Ceci on her little white bed and tiptoed out of her room. The grownups' voices echoed down the hall. Ceci listened, her hands in tight fists under the pillow. The usual fight.

"Mitch's? I thought you were through with that racket!"

"Shh, keep your voice down. It was about a gig."

But Mama didn't keep her voice down.

In the dark, Ceci felt around for Loli Bear. Burying her face in the bear's softness, she whispered. "We went to the movies—it was *Snow White*." She slid further under the covers. "And before that, I saw two Indians and they gave me a present, but I lost it somewheres." She cocked her head. Daddy was talking sweet-talk, trying to make Mama nicer.

"Oh, baby, if only you'd been there at the mission. Ceci was in great form, insisting she saw some Indians. Knew all about the place, even the Spanish terms. Gave me shivers, it did. Maybe she saw a ghost."

"Spare me the Irish hokum! Aunt Pilar probably told her some story about it. You can't shut the old biddy up about that kind of thing."

"Hey, show Pilar some respect!"

"Why don't you show *me* some respect? I told you to be home by eight—and you stagger home at midnight. You must've been drinking, and God knows what else!"

"Okay, okay, I'm a goddamn shit. You're perfect! Fight over!" he sighed. "Can we go to bed now? I'm bushed! I had a shit of a day. Had to talk to my two least favorite men in the world: the boss and Mitch."

"The boss? You weren't fired?"

"Well, no, but I—"

"You quit your job! Don't lie to me. You did, I can see it on your face. Val said you'd quit. And you went to see Mitch—"

Ceci rubbed her nose on her bear's tummy. She hated the way the house smelled. Mama had cleaned with Lysol again. Whenever Mama got mad, she started cleaning everything with Lysol—a smell that wouldn't go away, just like the fighting.

"I gave the boss my resignation. I've got a gig lined up."

"A gig! Oh shit, Barry! The last one Mitch found didn't even pay!"

Ceci plugged her ears and squeezed shut her eyes, making one last wish. "I wish we would move back to L.A. I wish it could be like before."

Before San Pedro, when they lived in the little apartment with the swimming pool, Daddy had jobs at hundreds of clubs. On hot days they'd get Chinese take-out and eat it down at Griffith Park, under the palm trees. Watching the world go by, that's what Daddy called it.

He'd play his clarinet and people would stand around listening, throwing money into the velvet-lined case. Ceci would dance sometimes, which made people clap and give more money. In those days, Daddy and Mama almost never fought.

"Barry Sullivan. You're going to be a big star!" Daddy had kissed Mama when she said that, right there in Griffith Park; the people had clapped and cheered. In L.A., when they had enough money for taxi rides and eating in restaurants, Mama used to laugh so much. She smelled like perfume, instead of Lysol. She never sewed, but bought their clothes from a big store downtown. It was so long ago, when Ceci was four-and-a-half, when they moved to San Pedro.

Since then, Mama had stopped laughing and never said, "Your daddy is going to be famous," not anymore, and Daddy didn't goof around the way he used to. He used to be so funny, like when he had made up her song: Ceci the Bean.

"Ceci the Bean, my little garbanzo:
Irish and Spanish, as ish as a fish is.
You know what my wish is?
To catch Ceci's kisses!
Play on your bongo, a beautiful song-oh!
You know we're so fond-o of Ceci Garbanzo.
Spanish and Irish, you know what the fish wish?
To make her their Queen, Miss Ceci the Bean!"

Once upon a time they'd been happy. Every memory formed a little rock, each one clinking against the other in her mind. The only thing to do was to shake them out by beating her head against the pillow. Then, worn out, she might sleep.

Ceci tiptoed into the living room where Daddy slept with both feet hanging over the arm of the couch. The nights he and Mama fought, he would sleep there, his coat for a blanket. She touched his forehead; his left eyebrow twitched and he rolled onto his side, making sounds like a bear licking honey.

She tiptoed down to the big bedroom and cracked open the door. Sun sliced between the curtains, lighting Mama's face. A black sleep mask covered her eyes, and a triangle of brown tape, something called a Frownie, kept her forehead still, so Mama wouldn't get wrinkles. Her long black hair spread on the pillow, and her arms were open across the bed, like an angel who had fallen asleep mid-flight.

Even in that eye mask, Mama was prettier than even Snow White. The only ugly thing was that black mole under Mama's eye, a little bit like a black bug, or a teardrop. Even though it was supposed to be a beauty mark, Ceci wished she could brush it off and make Mama perfect.

Then she sighed and turned away from Ceci, her arm over her face. It was as if Mama knew Ceci was thinking about touching her. She didn't like kids' sticky little fingerprints on anything, especially her face. So Ceci closed the door.

Back in her own room, she lifted the blinds and opened the window. Her friend Mickey was outside. He wore red overalls, his golden brown hair slicked up with butch wax, like the bristles of a toothbrush. She tapped the window with her knuckles. Mickey turned and waved. Just like that, the lump in Ceci's throat was gone. Mickey was a kid who ate sunshine for breakfast.

From Mickey she had first heard the words "sunny-side up." They were playing house in the sandbox. Mickey looked down at the pan full of sand she offered him and shook his head. "I like my eggs sunny-side up, Ceci! You have to have the yellow right in the middle." Ceci had to learn to shovel sand into a pie tin just right, if she were going to marry Mickey when she grew up. She loved him every time she saw him.

Even now, he made her laugh as he bent over for the newspaper, picking it up with his mouth like a dog. She ran out the screen door, yelling. "Hey, Mickey! Can you play?" Ceci crossed the lawn Mickey's daddy kept so perfectly green.

"You know what? I'm six now, Mickey, just like you."

"Yeah." Mickey nodded solemnly. "Happy birthday! Come on to my house. My mom's feeling pretty good today."

The house smelled like bacon and coffee. Mickey's mother, Mrs. Flicker, lay on the couch in her gray bathrobe. "Poor Ellen Flicker," the neighbors always called her. Mrs. Flicker was sick but didn't believe in doctors, or something like that.

"Hello, Ceci." Ellen smiled; the blue TV light glinted on her big front teeth. "Isn't it your birthday?"

"Yesterday was."

"Well, today is Saturday. Going to have a party?"

"No." Ceci blinked away the night before. "Well, maybe."

Ellen's smile faded. "Only maybe?" She took the newspaper from Mickey and tossed it onto the coffee table. "Thank you! Do me another favor, honey, and switch off the TV. I'm tired." She sunk into her pillow. "Well, happy birthday, Ceci dear."

In the Flickers' cool green kitchen, Ceci's eyes fell on a little plate by the sink, where two strips of bacon lay on a paper towel. Mickey pushed the plate toward her. "Hungry? Go ahead. Mom always makes too much." He pulled a chair out from the kitchen table, touched the box of fat crayons, and then scooted the pencil and scissors across the table. "You can use my stuff. I'm coloring a house."

Ceci crunched the bacon, watching him. "You're not coloring; you're drawing."

"Same thing."

"No, coloring is pictures in a book. Drawing is pictures from your head."

Mickey thought this over. "I'm drawing and coloring at the same time." He laid a ruler over the page and picked up a blue crayon. "First I make the lines, and then I color them."

"It's good. I wish I could make a house all straight like that."

"Daddy showed me to use a ruler." Mickey wrinkled his nose. "What are you doing? Why are you smelling them?"

She held a yellow crayon under her nose. "I like to smell things."

"Oh." Mickey picked up a red crayon. "Did you ever taste them?"

"Taste what?"

"The crayons—did you ever taste them?"

Ceci made some yellow whooshes on her paper. "When I was real little, I did. They taste like candles."

"Ha!" Mickey laughed. "Like candies? They don't taste like candies."

"I said candles, silly! Candles, like on a birthday cake."

"Did you have a birthday cake?"

"No." Ceci jabbed the crayon into her palm. "Mama forgot. Auntie Pilar made me cupcakes, though," Ceci nodded. "Maybe Grandma will make a real cake."

"Grandmas are good at remembering. Old ladies like kids better than regular grownups." Mickey took a black crayon from the box. Humming, he stuck out his tongue and licked at his cheek as he drew. Unlike Ceci, he always seemed to stay clean. Like polished seashells from the beach store, Mickey's nails shone: cut so short the tips of his stubby fingers bumped over them, pink and clean. He smelled like Ivory soap, baby powder, and bacon; everything Ceci loved about him filled her, until she had to tell him. "Mickey, you're my best friend in the whole world. My very, very best friend!"

And then, feeling shy to have said it, she grabbed a little bunch of crayons and drew a rainbow-beaked bird, pressing very hard so the colors would shine off the paper. She didn't want to look up and see how Mickey might be feeling about being her friend. They were quiet, both drawing their pictures. Then Mickey tapped her paper.

"Why is the bird so sad?"

Ceci looked up. "Sad?"

"See?" He pointed to a blob of white crayon just under the bird's eye. "He's crying."

She closed her eyes to think. "There's another place." She pressed the crayon blob down so it wouldn't fall off. "The bird can't remember how to get back there. That's why."

"Okay," Mickey nodded. "Where does he want to go?"

Birds always flew off; they always disappeared. But where? Ceci wondered. She shrugged her shoulders. "I don't know. He just can't. He can't remember. Like when you forget a dream. Easy to forget."

"I always try to remember dreams, but sometimes I don't."

"If he knew where it was, he'd go back." Ceci drew a round red tree for the bird to stand on. "He just doesn't know."

Rubbing the loose crayon flakes into the white places on the paper, she liked how these bits of crayon could still make color, just as pieces of dreams colored in the spaces of her day. Like yesterday at the mission: the little wet white stone so real that even after it was gone, it left her pocket wet.

"There!" Mickey had pressed so hard that the crayon was like waxy paint, filling a forest with green pointed trees, a blue river with purple waves. "Is this the place you mean?"

"Needs flowers." Ceci touched the tree trunk he'd drawn. "Flowers that grow up into the trees. Yellow fish swim in the river, too. Yes! Like that. And it's really hot."

"I'll make a big sun."

"No! Not orange. Their sun is gold."

'Mickey fished around in his pockets, pulling out a yo-yo, and then an almost new gold crayon. "I carry it for good luck." Then he drew a sun, with gold curls like a lion's mane, and leaned back to look at it with Ceci. "A safe place for birds, where nothin' bad can get them."

"Mickey, I love you!" Ceci leaned over and kissed him.

"Hey! Don't kiss!" Mickey placed his hand over his cheek but didn't wipe it off.

With the red crayon, she made an upturned smile on her bird's beak. With a pair of short scissors, she cut around it and set it down in Mickey's tallest tree. "Can you hear it? Like music?" Ceci whispered. "It's our bird singing."

He nodded. "Let's paste your bird onto my tree, right here. Then we can make some more pictures: houses, and cities, and all the bird's friends. We can make a whole dream world. Wait!" Mickey turned toward the kitchen door. "Who's that?"

Ceci heard Mama's high heels click, click, click into the Flickers' house.

"Cecilia Sullivan! You left without asking! It's too early to visit people."

"But Mama, you wouldn't wake up!"

Mama looked like a lady pirate in her tight Capri pants with gold coins jingling down the side of the legs. Ellen followed Mama into the kitchen.

"Don't worry, Dora. Ceci's always welcome here! They play so well together."

"Well, it's time to go now." Mama sniffed Ceci's hair. "Yuck! You need a bath."

"She doesn't," Mickey said. "She smells good! Let her stay."

"You have to go see your Grandma today." Mama combed at Ceci's hair with her fingers. "What will she think of me letting you look like a gypsy?"

"I want to look like a gypsy!" Ceci squirmed away, trying to paste her bird.

"Come on!" Mama took the paste jar from Ceci. "I need to wash your hair."

"No, Mama! Don't wash my hair!"

"You always throw a fit about your hair. I ought to cut it all off!"

"Oh, don't do that, Dora!" Ellen Flicker brought her hands together under her chin. "Such lovely hair! So lucky! I wish I had—I mean, she's beautiful just as she is!"

"Well she won't be, if she keeps this nonsense up." Mama crossed her arms, looking Ellen up and down, eyes flashing black. "I try to teach her good grooming, and it doesn't help if people keep telling her she's so—*beautiful!*"

"Don't mind me." Ellen took a slow breath and pulled her robe around her flat front, smiling a tight little smile. "I'm certainly not the one to give fashion advice. I wish I had half your style. I don't even—"

"Take it from me, Ellen—a good haircut would do you wonders." Mama reached up to fluff Ellen's hair, and a long tuft fell into her fingers. "Oh, God!" She breathed, dropping Ellen's hair like it burned her.

Ellen sighed, "It's the medicine, I'm afraid."

"We have to go! Right now!" Mama squeezed Ceci's shoulder hard. "We can't be bothering people when their hair is falling out!"

"Ceci can play with me!" Mickey trotted after them. "*My* hair isn't falling out! And my mommy is *beautiful!* Prettier than you!" Ceci was standing by the table, and Mickey took her hand. She squeezed it.

"Come on!" Mama kneed Ceci's bottom. "Let's go! Now!"

Soon they were out the door and crossing the Flickers' neat, peat moss lawn. "Phew!" Mama brushed back her hair. "Glad we're out of there! That Ellen sure gives me the creeps!"

Ceci folded her arms over her belly. "I like Mrs. Flicker."

"What's she ever done for you?" Mama stopped at their own back steps, her eyes blinking back tears. "You're not a very loyal daughter! You should have told Mickey that I'm prettier!"

"Than who?"

On the porch Mama had left the mop bucket, bubbles still floating.

"Than his mother, for Christ's sake!" Mama grabbed Ceci's hand from the bucket. "What's the matter with you! Don't touch that dirty water!"

Ceci stood up and wiped her hand on her shorts. "Sorry!"

"You're giving me a headache!"

"Sorry!" Ceci touched her mother's arm. "Sorry! Sorry! Sorry! Sorry—"

"Oh, my God, shut up, please! You're just making it worse!"

When they got to the kitchen, Mama poured herself a glass of water, washing down a pill. If they'd had a cookie jar, Ceci would've reached in right now and grabbed an Oreo, but they didn't ever have cookies, let alone a cookie jar. Cookies made people fat. Mama swallowed another aspirin. Her head must hurt a lot. Maybe Mama was sick, too. A headache must be a pretty bad thing, but at least Mama still had her beautiful hair.

"Mama, does it hurt Mrs. Flicker when her hair falls out?"

"How should I know? She should go to the hospital like a normal person, instead of lying around moping. For God's sake, that poor man—a wife like that—useless! I don't think you should play there anymore."

"But I love Mickey. I'm going to marry him."

"You love Mickey? Ha!" Mama's eyes narrowed. "You know, he hasn't a chance in hell of being good-looking, even. He's going to look just like that bucktoothed Ellen when he grows up."

Ceci wished she could explain to Mama that she didn't care what Mickey would grow up to look like. If they had a magic mirror, like the one the Wicked Queen in *Snow White* had, what would it tell Mama? That she was the fairest of them all? How could a mirror know this, looking only at one person at a time? Ceci wondered. Maybe Daddy knew. But she couldn't ask him now.

He was playing clarinet in his office, which was a corner of their garage behind a pile of boxes. Whenever he practiced, no one was supposed to bother him. Mama said he drove her crazy, playing a song until it was perfect. Daddy acted like a bear in a cave, disappearing for hours. She had better not ask him questions, not even through the door.

Mama called from the bathroom. "Come on, Ceci. Hurry up!"

Ceci trotted in, pulled off her shorts and tee shirt, stepped into the tub, and jumped out onto Mama's knees. "Hot!"

"Now I'm all wet! Why the hell couldn't you step on the bath mat?" Mama mopped up the puddle around Ceci's feet and added some cold water. "Get in, and get your hair wet. Now!"

Easing into the water, Ceci bent her head under the tap enough to wet just part of her hair. She sat back up and rubbed her eyes.

"More!" Mama pushed her back under. "Your whole head!"

Ceci sat up, banging her head on the faucet. Ceci screamed, "Ow! Ow!"

"What's all this?" Daddy laid his hand on Ceci's back. "No wonder she doesn't like her hair washed! Do you have to scrub like bloody murder? Be gentler."

"So, you're the expert now?" Mama stood up, shaking the lather from her hands. "All right, you're so great. You finish her hair!"

"Put this over your eyes." Daddy handed Ceci a dry washcloth. "Are you ready, sweetheart? Time to rinse."

"It'll get in my eyes!" Ceci shook her head. "No!"

"We have to rinse out the soap, honey. I'll be very careful; you put the washcloth over and close your peepers up tight."

Ceci peeked over the washcloth. "Peepers?"

"Your eyes—cover them up, okay? I'll make sure the water's not too hot. You make sure that washcloth is tight over your eyes."

"Okay, Daddy."

Soon her hair was rinsed. Ceci cried just a little, but she didn't scream.

"Ha!" Mama leaned back against the sink. "You remember the last time you did her hair? You took her to Kyle's birthday party."

"No." Daddy tilted his head. "When was this?"

"When I had the flu. Val told me she'd never seen Ceci such a mess!"

"Did anybody else say anything?"

"The other mothers were too nice—"

"There! I rest my case. Only Val would say something so mean."

"All right, you win, Perry Mason!" Mama grabbed the washcloth from Ceci, throwing it at Barry's chest, where it hit with a splat and wet half his shirtfront. "You get her ready! It's your mother—"

"I have to practice for my gig!" Daddy followed her out of the bathroom, their voices rising.

Ceci wrapped herself in a towel and tried to figure out how to comb the snarls out. Her hair a mess that stuck to her back, dripping a trail all the way to her bedroom, she flopped onto the bed and hugged her Loli Bear.

The door creaked open. Mama held the barber scissors and a comb, her red smile like a clown's: a scary smile. She sat Ceci down on the toy box and raked the comb through the snarls. "I am going to cut the snarls out of your hair."

There was no mirror to see the scissors coming. As the point of the scissors grazed her neck, Ceci shivered. "Don't cut it too short, Mama!"

"We can't have you going to Grandma's looking like something the cat dragged in." Mama's voice was calm, but cold. The scissors clicked; pieces of hair fell to the floor—wet, dark red corkscrews almost as long as Ceci's arm. She knew she had better stay very still, but she could feel the cold against her neck where her hair had been.

"Are you cutting *all* my hair off?"

"Shush! We are going to surprise your father."

"Daddy likes my hair long."

"He likes you neat and clean." Mama stood back a little. "It's not quite even." She snipped at one side, and then the other, standing back and shaking her head.

Ceci felt the point of the scissors poke. "Don't cut my ear!"

"Of course I won't!" Mama smacked Ceci's cheek with the comb. "Stay still!"

Like the statue of Cabrillo at the beach, even if pigeons sat on her head, Ceci would not wiggle. Nothing, not even the big wind that blew in from the ocean, could move her. Kids would climb her. They'd stick their feet into her face; they'd hang from her shoulders and yell, "Alley, alley oxen-free!" but she would not move.

"There! I'm done!" The scissors at her side like a cowboy's gun, Mama smiled that same cold, red smile. "Go show your father!"

Ceci wiped her itchy nose with the back of her hand and ran to the door that led to the garage—Daddy's office. She knocked. There was no answer. She knocked harder—still no answer. So she opened the door. "Daddy?"

He had his back turned to her, playing his clarinet so loudly Ceci had to yell.

"Daddy!"

Daddy spun around, his clarinet still in the air. "Ceci, I'm prac—Oh my God, what—what happened? Dora!" he yelled, and ran out, leaving Ceci standing in the garage. "What the hell did you do to Ceci's hair?"

Hands to her cold, wet head, Ceci felt nothing but short bumpy curls, like a poodle's. She ran to check herself in the bathroom mirror. She stood on the toilet and leaned over sideways to see her face in the mirror over the sink.

"I look like a boy! I look like a boy!" She threw herself onto the floor, crying, until Daddy scooped her up and kissed the top of her head.

He carried her to her room. "It's not really a boy's haircut, darling. It's a pixie."

Ceci rubbed the little curls on her head. "It's ugly!"

"Here!" He held up her shoes. "Put these on. When we get to Grandma's, ask her to tell you all about the pixies—how cute they are." He opened up the top drawer of her little white dresser. "We'll put this pink barrette on you."

"No Daddy, it won't help. I look like a boy."

"In that pretty dress? You look—"

"Like a boy in a dress!" She wiped her nose on her arm, staring down at the slippery trail her nose made on her skin.

Daddy wiped her arm with his handkerchief. "How 'bout you act like a young lady? Then everybody will forget about your haircut—and the fact you were raised by a pack of hyenas!" He gathered a bit of hair just above her bangs, clipping on the barrette, and shook his head. "Maybe not the barrette. Do you want to go look in the mirror?"

Her hair didn't move when she shook her head no. She might as well be bald. "I want to go to Grandma's. Are we going now?"

"Right now. She called to say she has a present for you."

Ceci sniffed, a little shiver in her smile.

"Knowing her, I'd say she made you a cake, too."

"Is Mama coming?"

"No," he sighed. "No, darling, your Mama is going over to Val's tonight. I made Mama mad again. Sorry, baby."

Ceci fell into his arms, without telling him how glad she was it would be just the two of them—and Grandma Katy.

☆　☆　☆　☆

In her little closet of a kitchen, Grandma was always baking: cakes, cookies, scones, and soda bread with baby bits of raisins, which she shared with her neighbors and any sick people in her church parish. She lived in a snug apartment in a building that formed a "U" around a straggly garden, closed in front by a brick wall and a rusty gate.

Everyone in Grandma's apartment house was old. Children weren't allowed to live there, only to visit. Grandma kept some puzzles and coloring books for Ceci, so she wouldn't make noise and bother the old people. It was hard to be so quiet. The apartment was a good place because Grandma lived there, and only because of that.

Even before they reached her door, Grandma was waiting out front, the tip of her long nose pulled up with her smile. "If it isn't the birthday girl! Come in, come in; we'll have us some tea." She stood on tiptoe to kiss Daddy's cheek, and then wrapped her arms around Ceci.

"Oh, Grandma, you smell like chocolate. Did you make me a cake?"

"Did I, indeed?" Grandma took Ceci's hand and let her into the kitchenette. "Will it do the trick? Can you force down a piece, just to please your Granny?"

"Oh, yes! Chocolate!" Ceci touched the purple flowers Grandma had laid all around the bottom of the cake. "Are they real, or frosting?"

"Real flowers they are; back home we called 'em heart's ease. Found them in the courtyard lawn this morning—just knew you'd like their sweet little faces. See, there's a little prince in there: the crown, the little beard—"

As Grandma pointed out the pansy faces, Ceci made to scoop a bit of frosting off the side and then, remembering her manners, thrust her hand into her pocket.

"Such self-control! You're growing up, Cecilia! Now sit yourself down, and I'll bring everything out to you, like a fancy restaurant. Barry, give me a hand?"

Ceci sat on Grandma's old saggy couch. The only picture Grandma had was of Mary, God's mother: a beautiful lady with a great, glowing, flower-ringed heart bumping right out of her chest. There wasn't much else to look at besides the brown armchair, the Bible where Grandma wrote everyone's names and birthdays, and the small TV. Daddy gave it to her to watch Art Linkletter and Lawrence Welk, while knitting wool socks for the brown barefoot children in Africa.

Once Ceci had asked Grandma to teach her to knit. The minute she touched them, the needles and yarn had tangled into knots. It was the only time Grandma had ever scolded Ceci, saying she had cat's paws for hands. Ceci knew she did; that's why she wore buckle shoes—anything like a string fought with her fingers. She just couldn't get it right, no matter what Mama, Daddy, or even Grandma tried.

At last Grandma carried in the cake, with six blue candles and one pink, all lit. "Happy Birthday to you," Daddy and Grandma sang. "Happy Birthday to you. Happy Birthday, dear—"

Bam! The wall behind Mother Mary shook. It must be that old man next door again, pounding. The last time Daddy had played clarinet for Grandma, the old man kept beating the wall until Grandma had taken off her shoe and pounded back.

"Keep singing, everyone! Happy Birthday, dear Ceci! Happy Birthday to you!"

"But Grandma, the old man—"

"Never mind that devil!" Grandma squeezed Daddy's shoulder. "Sing, boyo! You sing too, Ceci, top of your lungs!"

When they finally ran out of air to sing, Ceci blew out the candles, Grandma clapped, Barry hooted, and the old man hit the wall some more.

"Aw, Ma, why don't you invite him for a piece of cake? Maybe he's just lonely."

"Oh, I've tried that—invited him for tea. Thought I was making advances; told me so right in front of Cecilia! Slammed the—"

Another whack, and Mother Mary's frame tilted up like a ship tossing on a wave.

"That does it!" Grandma untied her apron. "I've had enough of the old coot!" She forced her black straw hat down onto her head, like a lid on a pan. "Let me at him!"

Daddy reached out his hand. "Now, Ma, calm down, please! He'll stop."

"Too late, my Irish is up." Grandma pushed up her sleeves. "I'll break that dashed cane right over his head!" She stomped out the door.

"Now, Ma—" Grabbing Ceci's hand, Daddy jogged after Grandma.

"Open up, reprobate! Open up!" Just like a policeman from Dragnet, Grandma knocked on the door. "I have some choice words for you!"

No one answered the door.

"Open up!" she cried again.

"Come on, Ma, maybe he'll stop now."

"No, he won't. Every time our Cecilia visits, he pulls this shenanigan." She pounded harder. "Open up! What's the matter, afraid of an old lady?"

"Let it go, Ma. We'll have some more of that delicious cake."

"Sure, and the roar of our chewing would rile him." Grandma swung back her arm to knock just as the door opened. A pale old man, his left hand gripping the crook of a metal cane, jutted out his chin.

"Who the hell are you, and what do you want?"

An odd look washed over Grandma's face. She dropped her arm to her side, still puffing like a steam train. Daddy tightened his grip on Ceci's hand. "Watch your language, Mister."

The old man squinted at Daddy. "Who's he?"

"My son! And you know me well enough! I'm Katy Sullivan, your neighbor!" She stopped to take a long breath, one hand on her chest. "Come to ask why you're beating my wall so! Our Blessed Mother nearly fell on the floor!"

"The blessed what?"

"The Lord's mother! She's on my wall in a nice gold frame, and that's where I'd like to keep her, if you don't mind. We were having us a little birthday party. Then, out of nowhere, you beat on the wall, like to wake the dead."

"Out of nowhere?" He crossed his arms over his chest. "What about all that damned racket? What the hell are you doing, strangling cats?"

Grandma crossed her freckled arms over her chest. "Most days, I'm as quiet as a mouse. You'd think I could sing Happy Birthday to my only grandchild!"

The man smiled; he did not look happy at all, as if he'd just won a game that he was playing with someone he hated, and the prize was a mud pie. "It says in the lease: no children, no pets, no wild parties."

"Wild party? Singing 'Happy Birthday?'"

"I'm going to report you to the manager for noise, harassment—and damages." He stroked the outside of his door. "You've dented the wood banging it like you did."

Daddy stepped forward. "Now, wait a just a minute, Mister! She didn't—there's not a dent on it. Come on, Ma, don't give this jerk the satisfaction." Daddy took Grandma's hand. "Let's go."

She pulled away from Daddy. "No son, I'm not done speaking my mind."

The old man wrinkled his nose. "I don't believe you have one! A mind, that is!"

"You listen, you! I've tried to be neighborly and to look the other way, but if you cause any trouble—I shall tell the manager about that dog you're hiding in there."

The man shrank back. "You wouldn't!"

A small yellow dog with a pointy nose, as if he'd heard her speak, came sniffing up to Grandma. He licked her hand.

Grandma patted the dog and sighed. "You're right, I don't think I shall. I feel sorry for the beast, living with the likes of you. I'll try to mind my own business, like a proper Irishwoman. How about you minding yours, too? Let us have our little party in peace, please!"

"If you keep on making a racket, I've the right to talk to the manager. And I will! You've been disturbing the peace!"

"So, that's the way you're going to be?" Grandma took a slow breath. "Then—then—" She pointed a shaky finger. "May your dog eat you, and the devil eat your poor old dog!" She marched off, Daddy and Ceci behind her, until they stood in her living room again. Grandma straightened the Blessed Mother's picture.

"The nerve of that man! I hope he gets a boil on his bum. Well, he's not going to ruin our day." She cut the cake, bending over the coffee table, licking the frosting from her fingers. "Cecilia, there's vanilla ice cream in the icebox. Won't you run fetch it for Grandma? And the big serving spoon, darling—the drawer next to the sink!"

"Who knew you had it in you, Ma?" Daddy fell into the armchair, laughing now. The old Irish curse and everything! Will you tell the manager about that dog?"

"What good would it do? There'll be no changing that man, you can bet on that. He'll be the death of me. How big a piece, Ceci?" Grandma drew a line with the cake server. "Big enough?"

"Bigger, please!"

"Your mother will have me flogged. But, why not?" Grandma shoveled a huge piece onto Ceci's plate. "Sure you can eat it all, macushlah?"

Ceci nodded. "We forgot to eat lunch. I had some bacon at Mickey's."

"Don't look at me like that, Ma." Daddy shrugged. "It's been a busy day."

"Sure, and the child will disappear if you keep having such days, boyo." She served Ceci a heap of ice cream. "Well, then! You've a new haircut, Cecilia. I noticed it early on but forgot to mention it."

Ceci scrunched up her face.

"Oh, dear, what have I gone and said? I shall miss the curls." Grandma stroked Ceci's bangs. "But 'twill be easier to have short hair, won't it?"

"I look like a boy."

"A pretty thing like you? Not on your life! You look like a pixie, be it a scowling one. Don't you want to be a pixie?" She drew Ceci close. "They're wonderful tricksters. Do me a favor, Barry; open the window a crack. Such a hot day!" With the back of her hand, Grandma wiped a trickle of sweat from her forehead. "Pixies move in and out of the fairy world, causing us all kinds of mischief. Sure, and they have more fun than other fairies, going about hiding our socks and handkerchiefs, making the grass and corn come up. I love them!"

"Are pixies pretty?"

"Pretty? Can't say as I know for sure. I do know with those lovely big eyes shining out of your little face, you're a very pretty pixie indeed. There's no mistaking you for anything but a little girl. Oh, your birthday present—I almost forgot!"

Ceci grinned.

"It's in my bedroom closet. I'll bring it to you while you eat your cake. Where did I put that bag?" It was taking Grandma some time: a shuffling of boxes, hangers, and crinkling tissue paper. "I know it's in here somewhere. I put it away for you a long time ago. It's already wrapped for you. Oh—"

There was a thud and a bump in the closet, some rustling and a choking gasp. Grandma lay on the floor on her side, her legs pulled up toward her. Her face had turned a bluish white. "My pills, right there—on the nightstand." She closed her eyes. "See them?"

Daddy helped her sit up, and she took a pill. "Nitroglycerin? Since when have you been taking these? You didn't tell me anything about this!"

"You've got troubles of your own, Barry." Grandma moaned, curling tighter into a ball. Ceci stroked Grandma's cheek.

"What's wrong, Grandma?"

"Just a dizzy spell." Grandma smoothed Ceci's hair. "All this excitement."

"Get Grandma a glass of water." Daddy wrapped an arm around Grandma and wiped her brow with his rumpled handkerchief.

Ceci ran to the kitchen, pulled a chair to the sink to fill a glass of water.

Daddy took it without thanking her, holding it up for Grandma to drink.

"Pill always does the trick." Grandma struggled to sit up, her face stretched with pain. "Ceci's present. It's right there—"

"Never mind that. Where's your doc's number?' I'm taking you to the hospital!"

"No, Ceci must have her present. See it, sweetheart? In a yellow bag?"

"Enough about presents! Get Grandma's purse, over on the chair. We're going to the hospital."

He tried to take her arm, but Grandma pulled away. "I'll walk on my own power!" She called out to Ceci, as she made for the door, "Never mind the purse—get the yellow bag, darling! The hospital will just send me right home."

"At least you've agreed to the hospital." Daddy helped Grandma into the back seat. He took off his shirt and rolled it into a pillow. "Put this under your head, Ma. Should I get your blanket? Are you cold?"

"Saints preserve us! Won't have you traipsing around shirtless!" She thrust the shirt into his hand. "I'll be fine, I tell you. The yellow bag! Can you fetch me my rosary?"

Ceci started toward the apartment, then turned back. "What's a rosary?"

Grandma lay down on her side, muttering. "Doesn't know a rosary, poor little heathen—the age for Catechism, and not even baptized. On the bedside table, darling, pink beads—"

"Save your breath, Ma. That's the least of our worries!"

"Nevertheless, I'll have my rosary."

Daddy sighed. "All right! Get the beads, Ceci, and latch the door on your way out. Hurry!"

Feeling scared but important, Ceci ran back with Grandma's bag and the rosary.

The Sullivans sped away in the old Mercury; Ceci prayed for all the lights to stay green till they got to the hospital.

The nurse set an orange plastic chair in the hospital hall near Grandma's room. "Sorry, dear, little girls carry big germs that might hurt Grandma right now." Ceci sat down in the chair and swung her legs back and forth, listening to the soft voices of the doctor and nurses, Daddy's questions, and finally, a little louder, Grandma. "Why can't my granddaughter come in? It's not like I'm dying."

"Please, Mrs. Sullivan, we must protect you from any germs that might worsen your condition."

"My condition!" Grandma's laughter turned to a cough. "Just some palpitations! Let me see my grandchild, please!"

Daddy brought the gift out to Ceci, and they stood together in the doorway, as the nurse pressed a button to raise Grandma's bed. "There now, Mrs. Sullivan. You can see her just fine from here. That's all the doctor will allow." She fluffed up the pillow and propped up the old woman's head. Grandma waved to Ceci.

"Do you believe it, darling? Stuck in here like a prisoner! Open your present, and Grandma will watch you from her jail bed."

Ceci pulled off the yellow paper. It was picture in a gold frame, like an illustration from a fairy tale. Two children at twilight crossed a bridge, a rickety one with broken boards over a hungry looking river. A fat angel in a nightgown flew above the children, big enough to lift them both out of danger with a flap of her feathery wings.

"Like it?" Grandma squinched up a little higher on the pillows. "It's the Guardian Angel."

Ceci gazed at the picture.

"You've an angel to protect you, like the children in the picture. Your Guardian Angel." Grandma's eyes begged the doctor. "Can't she just come near, so I can look at it with her?"

"I'm sorry, you've had quite enough excitement, Mrs. Sullivan. Nurse is going to give you a sedative."

"Please!" Grandma held up her hand, "Not just yet. I have to talk to my son a minute. Very important—"

"We can give you five more minutes." The nurse smoothed the blankets. "The child will have to stay where she is, mind you. Hospital regulations."

Unable even to thank her Grandma from such a distance, Ceci watched from the door, the angel picture tucked under her arm. After the doctor and nurses left, Grandma took Daddy's hand, patting it as if he were a little boy. "Now, I want you to pay attention. I have to tell you my last wishes."

Daddy winced. "Ma, don't!"

"Whenever I should die," she closed her eyes, waiting a moment, then opened them, smiling. "I want you to take me home. Not Los Angeles, but home. Especially if I don't make it—"

"You're not going to die! If you insist on being morbid, Ma, I swear I'll call that nurse to give you what for. Anyway, I thought you liked California better than Brooklyn. The climate, for one—"

"The climate! It's boring—and it's not Brooklyn I'm missing. I want to go home—to Ireland, Barry. Connemara. I want you all to come with me."

"How can I do that, Ma? I barely pay the rent these days."

She squeezed his hand. "I've got a little money put by. Not enough to amount to much, but it'd get us all there, including the child. It won't cost us much once we get there. We'll be with my sister, Moira. Take me home."

"Ma, we aren't really Irish anymore. We're Americans; this is home."

"America's not our starting place; I want to show Ceci her roots. And when I die, I want to be buried there—at Saint Brigid's."

"Let's not talk about dying. We've got a long time before we have to worry about that, Ma. You've had a small setback, that's all."

"I want to see Ireland again. I want to see it with you, Cecilia—and Dora, God bless her! You can show her off." She closed her eyes, gathering strength. "There's something else. The child needs—"

"Wait, Ma!" Barry put up his hand, as if to stop a car. "We're not going to baptize Ceci, Ma. I've told you before."

"And Dora set me straight years ago. Though I don't like it, boyo, that's not what's worrying me. It's you that I worry about—you and Dora. You've not been getting along. I can tell it. You seldom speak of her. When you do, you're all pins and needles. I remember the way you two used to look at each other. 'Tisn't the same."

As Grandma spoke, Daddy studied his left hand, smoothing each knuckle until he reached his wedding ring, turning the gold band around his finger.

"Am I right, Barry?"

He stood there very still, like a tree. When he finally answered, his voice was slow and sad. "Dora and I—she wants—there's no accounting for Dora these days. She can't be pleased."

"You're the husband! You're the one who must do the accounting. You have to lead the family. Show her the way."

"Like Da did? You want me to lead like he did?"

"Yes, I do," Grandma sighed, the lines between her eyebrows deepening. "Despite his troubles, Francis provided a good home—and I knew he'd be there when I needed him. All this running around with your bands, this traveling—you're inviting trouble. Dora's headstrong, and so very beautiful, too beautiful to leave alone. If you settle down, maybe she will, too."

Daddy took in a deep breath, and let it out slowly. "Don't you worry, Ma. I'll take care of Dora!"

"I'm praying that's so." Grandma searched his face, her mouth curving into a slow smile. "You're a good son, and I love you. Now go on and take the child home for some dinner. And don't forget about Ireland!"

Daddy bent to kiss her. "You concentrate on getting well. Then we'll talk about Ireland."

"It's a deal: I get well—and then we go to Ireland." Grandma laid her hand on Daddy's cheek. "While we're at it, couldn't we have the child baptized before we go?"

"Now you're milking it!" Daddy laughed. "Get some rest, Ma!"

"Be off with you!" Grandma laughed and waved him away. "Be the man I pray you'll be."

"Love you, Ma!"

Daddy held Ceci's hand so tightly on the way to the car, as if she might run away and get into trouble with the nurses. He seemed to forget she had been very grown up just a few minutes ago, waiting forever on the orange plastic chair.

Sitting in the car, Ceci held her Guardian Angel picture in her lap. When she was still five, she wouldn't have liked getting a picture for a gift, but this was her only gift—besides the Snow White movie and the white rock from the Indians that somehow had disappeared. Being six years old, it was probably time to think about things like hanging up pictures in her room, she decided—if Mama would allow it.

They passed the oil refinery that smelled like rotten eggs. Daddy had pointed it out enough times that Ceci knew it. Though it smelled bad, it was as beautiful as a castle: towers glowing with light. Grandma had told her about the castles in Ireland, made of stone.

Daddy coughed. "A penny for your thoughts, sweetheart."

"What will happen to Grandma?"

"The doctors will fix her up just fine, sweetheart."

"Are you going to take her to Ireland?"

"I don't see how I can, baby."

"She wants to go." She touched his sleeve. "She really does."

"Grandma wants things I can't give her." Daddy drove for a long time without saying anything more; Ceci felt the silence like water rising between them and hoped he was thinking of something to help Grandma get her wish. Maybe she should ask the other question on her mind. "Will Mama let me put up my angel picture?"

"I will tell her she has to, baby."

"Will that work, Daddy?"

"Grandma says it will. And Katy Sullivan is always right."

"She is?"

"Most of the time, yes." He smiled to himself, quiet again for a time. Ceci hoped he could keep the smile on his face when they got home. She hoped Mama's mood had changed. "Ceci, honey, what is it that would make your mama happy?"

"A million dollars?"

"Yes—but impossible to pull off!" Daddy laughed. "Try again, baby."

"A puppy?"

"That's what *you* want. The landlord doesn't let us have dogs, and neither does your mama. Hair on the sofa, that kind of thing."

Ceci nodded. The TV shows Mama watched were full of beautiful things: diamonds, fancy stoves, and cars—the kinds with the tops that went down so you could let your hair blow back in the wind. The things Mama wanted were shiny and fancy, like that. "Those shows where they give away stuff, like Queen for a Day—Mama always says, 'Oh, why isn't that me? What I wouldn't give for a car!'"

"Really? If only it were that easy. I show up with a new car and we'd live happily after."

"Mama wants a car, Daddy. Really! Truly! She's tired of taking the streetcar."

Daddy thought about this for a while. All at once he patted Ceci's shoulder.

"Why not? The grand gesture—a car! Ceci, you're a genius! I'm sure Ma would lend me the money. Now, not a word to your mama. I want this to be a surprise."

☆　☆　☆　☆

Three days later Daddy brought home the 1950 Chevy Fleetline. It was turquoise blue and white, prettier than the Mercury had ever been. Mama looked at it, chewing her lip. "How old is this thing?"

"Good as new. Ten years young—the last owner barely broke it in."

"Good grief!" Mama rolled her eyes. "The little old lady from Pasadena, eh? It's an old car. Admit it!"

"It's the best I can afford, Dora. Come on, get in and give her a test drive."

Daddy held up the key. "She has zip. You get more horsepower with the automatics."

"What do I care about horsepower?"

"Think of the freedom. These keys will jingle for you like the Liberty Bell."

Mama stroked the door handle. "Well, it might do—for a while, anyway."

"The guy who sold to me it kept it immaculate, and it has all the extras. Just check out the glove compartment; there's a light! There are mirrors on the passenger and driver side visors. You can check your pretty face at every stoplight."

Ceci climbed into the back seat, checking out the ashtrays in the padded door handles. "Look, these open and close! Come on, Mama!"

Still, Mama didn't get into the car; she circled it slowly, patting the shiny metal. "Are you sure it's an automatic?"

"I'm certain. Want to test her out?" Holding the keys in the air, he moved toward the car like a cowboy tricking a wild horse into the corral. "She's all yours!"

"Mine!" Mama slipped into the driver's side and pushed buttons until the radio came on. She turned the key and the car hummed. "Get in, Barry! We're taking her for a test drive."

"Purrs like a kitten, this one." Daddy beamed. "You like her?"

"Just wish it could be newer, that's all."

"Someday, my ship will come in, and I'll—"

"Stop!" Mama slapped his shoulder. "I've heard enough about your ship not to hold my breath waiting for it." She twisted around and backed the Chevy into the street.

After a while, Mama got lost somewhere downtown, so Daddy had to take the wheel.

"Like a dream on the freeway. Watch this!" Daddy turned off the radio and whistled. "A lot of pickup." He passed a station wagon. "Better than my Merc."

"Be careful, Barry! You're racing the engine!"

"You can't race an automatic transmission."

"Well, it's making a noise! You're hurting the engine!" She pulled his arm.

"Christ, Dora, we're in the middle of the goddamn freeway. Let go! You want to crash?"

"Pull over!"

"Where?"

"That exit—the gas station." Mama stabbed the air. "Right there!"

"Just remember who bought you this car."

"Your mother's money—"

Ceci plugged her ears, so that Mama's lips opened and shut like a lipstick-painted fish mouth. Finally, Daddy drove into the gas station with the flying horse sign and rolled the window down. "No gas today!" he yelled to the kid working there. "Sorry, we're just changing drivers." He tossed Mama the keys.

She slid her long legs out of the car, slipped the keys into her pocket, and traded sides with Daddy. Two guys sat atop a red Coca-Cola cooler, watching. One whistled so loud, Ceci jumped in her seat. "Damn, that's a hot tamale! I'd like to taste some of that Mexican dish!"

Ceci peered over the seat. Her neck pink, Mama gripped the steering wheel so hard that her shoulders shook. The car growled to a start, and Mama pulled out of the gas station like a TV cop, tires screaming.

Daddy put his arm around the back of the seat behind Mama. "I'm sorry that you had to hear that trash. I should've punched his lights out."

"Why didn't you? I'll tell you why, Saint Sullivan," Mama spit the nickname out like something bad-tasting. "You don't want to hurt your precious hands. You don't care about me, just your damned hands! God forbid you might miss a few days playing clarinet!"

"It's my livelihood, honey." He tried to touch her hair.

Mama shrugged away. "You love that clarinet more than me."

Daddy didn't speak. Ceci wanted him to tell Mama that it wasn't true, that he loved them both more than the clarinet. Holding her breath, she peered up through the oval rear window: black, black clouds blowing in like ghosts from the sea. The lighthouse circled its green lights and sounded its horn.

The lighthouse, like an angel guardian, wings of white cloud, had held up her green lantern over the harbor for as long as Ceci could remember. She had learned to count by it. The rhythm, one to thirty, and then the warning horn. One to thirty again, the sad horn once more. The foghorn drummed the heartbeat of this sailor town—the music under everything.

"Listen!" Daddy sighed. Looking out at the harbor, Mama sighed, too. "The only good thing about living in San Pedro is that lighthouse—the Angel's gate."

Ceci hadn't heard Mama speak so gently for a long time. It was as if she were sorry for saying that about Daddy's hands, about his clarinet. As if she were happy.

And Daddy touched Mama's shoulder, lightly, as if testing a stove burner. "I love a foghorn, too. It's mournful and hopeful at the same time. You know someone's looking out for us, for the sailors, like an angel." Daddy smiled back at Ceci.

"Enough of your blarney!" Mama spoke softly, her fingers tickling the back of Daddy's neck. "Just get us home. I'll make us some dinner."

That moment her parents were so beautiful, their faces soft with something Ceci hadn't seen for a long time. If Mama and Daddy could just stay happy, Ceci believed they'd be just like the families on television.

☆　☆　☆　☆

When Daddy broke the news of his tour with the new band, the Sullivans' kitchen smelled of *café española* simmering on the stove. It was still light outdoors, but Mama lit a candle to celebrate. There was supposed to be chocolate ice cream for dessert. Eager for the treat, Ceci watched the candle wax dripping down the sides of the candle, barely listening as Daddy talked about his new gig.

"You'd leave your mother, Barry? Don't you worry?"

"Ma's almost out of the woods."

Ceci tore her eyes from the candle—wasn't Grandma in her little city apartment? "Why is Grandma in the woods?"

Daddy shook his head at Ceci, mouthing, *"Not now!"*

Mama's fork clattered onto her plate. "You're not serious! You can't go now!"

"Our savings are running out, and Mitch did me a favor. I can't let him down."

"And me?" Mama wadded her paper napkin. "I suppose I'll be seeing to Katy while you're gone?"

"It won't be so bad. Ma doesn't need much anymore. She's even cooking for herself. Besides you've got the Fleetline—"

"Oh, you are something! The car wasn't a gift, was it? You bought it to make life convenient for you! I can now dedicate myself to taking care of your mother!"

"Be fair, Dora. Ma lent me the money for the car, you know! She was thinking of you. Said you needed to be able to get around when I travel."

"Did she?" Mama sighed. "I bet she did."

"It's a good gig. Union rates!"

"You could have tried to find a gig in L.A. Why San Francisco?"

"I did try, Dora. Apparently, I'm old hat around here, but Schwann—"

"It's too far away!"

Daddy closed his eyes, as he always did on the first sip of coffee. "Only going to be gone a couple weeks. It won't be so bad, and it'll lead to something better."

"Better for you! Everything will be on my shoulders, while you toot around!" Mama pushed her rice into a neat mountain with her knife. The look on her face made the dinner ball up in Ceci's tummy.

"Please, Mama, can I be excused?"

"No, you can't!" Mama pushed Ceci back into the chair. "Eat your broccoli."

"You're going to fight." Ceci held up her fork and gazed at Mama and Daddy through it; the fork made lines like jail bars. She wished she could block out what she knew was coming. "I don't like fights."

"We aren't going to fight, Ceci." Daddy mussed her hair. "I'm going to do this gig and make lots of money. We'll move out of this dump; maybe I'll start that music store, so I can be home all the time. Mama can buy new clothes, even a fur coat. She'll never sew another—"

"Ha, that's rich! You'll be out on your ear in a week or two. You always blow your chances, Barry. Always!"

His smile faded. "Let me keep a glimmer of hope alive!"

Mama began to stack plates, her face a puzzle. Ceci hoped the fight was over.

"What about ice cream, Mama?"

"Just go play!" Daddy said, and Ceci ran next door to Mickey's house.

☆　☆　☆　☆

A cloud coughed out of the sky, black, black, and blacker. At first just a dot in the distance, it grew into the shape of a dog. Ceci's feet stuck to the ground, a cold fear rising: first around her toes, then higher and higher around her legs. Cold. She wanted to run into her house, but when she turned to go, there was nothing but flat sand all around her and that cloud dog running at her—closer, closer, closer—too close for her to get away—

After the bad dream, Ceci sat up in bed, all sweaty and thirsty. The covers had slipped onto the floor, and after a moment she felt the cold. She leaned over to pick them up and pulled the blanket around her shoulders. A drink of water—that's what she wanted. Light reached through the curtains, drawing her to the window: the moon the only friendly face in the dark. The Mercury and the Chevy sat side-by-side in the driveway. Maybe Daddy and Mama hadn't kept on fighting. It must be very late; in every house, most of the windows were dark.

Turning from the window, Ceci could make out the little bed Daddy had made her out of orange crates and a crib mattress, her white dresser, and the child's tea table Tía Pilar won for her at Bingo. The new Guardian Angel picture hung over her bed—she could see only the frame shape, but it made her feel safe. She ran to the bathroom and cupped her hand under the faucet to drink. As she wiped her wet face on the hand towel, she smelled perfume. It wasn't the towel that gave off that dreamy smell, but the air, full of perfume, circling her with softness that she followed back to her bedroom.

A circle of light poured into the room from the window. For a few seconds Ceci watched it from the bedroom doorway, the blanket sliding off her shoulders. Then she jumped back into bed, unable to tear her eyes from the center of that spinning light. The brightness stilled, then gathered itself into a shape like a tree trunk.

Ceci crawled to the foot of the bed, fingers stretching to touch it, but as suddenly as it had appeared, the light faded. The dark that had felt so scary was now almost friendly. Ceci dove under the covers, feeling as safe as if the bright sun was shining, instead of a pale summer moon.

The smog screwed down over Los Angeles like a grubby jar lid, each day hotter than the last. Everyone was grumpy and tired. At night it was too hot to sleep, and Ceci and Mama sat up watching TV with the fan blowing over a tray of melting ice cubes. TV reruns—everything Lucy and Desi did last Christmas, with overcoats and long scarves wrapped around their necks—only made Ceci feel hotter.

Grandma was out of the hospital, and Barry had been on tour for days. Mama kept busy with her sewing, and Ceci spent her daytime in the Flickers' backyard. Mr. Flicker had set up a little wading pool, and

Ellen watched the kids from the screened-in porch in her bathrobe and a stocking cap, shivering as if it were January.

The last day of June came, a real hot one. After Mama and Ceci bought groceries, the Chevy stalled in front of Von's Supermarket. First fiddling with the key and pounding her fist on the dash, Mama finally tried looking under the hood. "Jesus! I can't open this thing! Ceci, look inside the glove compartment. Is there a manual?"

Ceci opened the glove compartment and stared at some booklets, maps, a comb, and a flashlight. "What's a manual, Mama?"

"Little idiot!" Mama pushed Ceci's hand aside and grabbed one of the booklets. "Here it is, right here." She read aloud, "*To release hood latch pull white lever under dash to the left of the foot pedals.*"

"You're lucky your mama is so smart!" Mama tried to open the hood. "Still won't open! Stay right here, Ceci." She tightened her belt and fluffed her hair. "I bet there's a man in the store who knows about cars."

Mama returned, wiping her forehead with her arm. "A tow truck is coming. We just have to wait." Mama put on more lipstick. The bright red woke up her face. Ceci wondered, was it lipstick that made women pretty? Fire and Ice was the brand Mama always wore—it made her lips look like Snow White's.

"Let me put some lipstick on, Mama!"

"Not now, Ceci! Here comes the tow truck."

A man leapt out of the shiny red truck. "You called for a tow?" He was handsome and strong as the guy on the Wheaties box, except browner.

Mama swung her long legs out of the car. The man smiled slowly, wiping his forehead with his red bandana.

"*¡Híjole!* Must be my lucky day!" He held out his hand, but Mama didn't shake it. Instead she just looked at him, her hands on her hips, like she was deciding something.

"Not so lucky for me." Her eyes sparkled under their long lashes. "If you'd just take a look and figure out what's wrong! I've got frozen food melting in the trunk."

He saluted. "Yes, Ma'am, Carlos Ramirez, at your service!" He clinked around under the hood and then came around to talk to Mama. "You got a sick car, lady."

Her hands came together at her chin. "That bad?"

"Let me check if I've got the part in my truck—"

"So you're a mechanic, as well as a tow truck driver?"

"Best around here. Maybe the best in the whole state."

"Not one of the humblest!"

"Listen, I've worked hard to get where I am. My brother and I built this business up from nothing. It's not easy for Mexicans around here."

"Ah!" Mama tossed her hair. "So, Mr. World's Best Mechanic, can you get us on our way?"

"Ought to give her a thorough going-over. Some amateur has been messing around in there. Who's your mechanic?"

"I don't have one. My husband has been tinkering with the whatchamacallit—"

"Excuse me for saying so, but he'd better give that up right away, Ma'am. With the right treatment, the car will last you. If you keep putting cheap oil in her and yanking things around—"

"Just what's wrong with it, anyway?"

"The carburetor—I'm almost positive."

"Is that major?" Mama frowned. "I'd better get home. The groceries—"

"I could take you home. After taking your Chevy to the garage, I mean."

"I guess I—well, I don't know how else I'll manage. Thank you!"

"My pleasure!" Carlos loaded the groceries into the back of his truck.

"Please?" Ceci tugged his sleeve. "Can I sit up front with you? *Por favor, Carlos!*"

"Well, listen to that!" Carlos smiled. "Little *señorita, ¿te hablas español?*"

Mama laughed. "She doesn't actually speak Spanish, not fluently. My aunt taught Cecilia a few words. I'm—we're Spanish Californians. Ceci doesn't even look Spanish, but she—"

"You do, though. You look like a Fiesta Queen!"

"I was, once, really."

"That comes as no surprise!" Finished hooking the car up to tow, Carlos wiped his hands on the side of his overalls. "I like it that the kid speaks Spanish. You should speak it with her; it's your heritage—and hers. You don't want her to be a *pachuca*."

"*Pachuca?*"

"You know, a girl who runs wild—rebels against her roots."

"Of course, I know!" Mama frowned. "But there's no danger of that ever happening. Ceci is crazy about roots! She'd love speaking Spanish all the time. I just don't want her taken for Mex—" She stopped herself. "I just don't want her confused in school, like I was. Please, don't take offense."

Carlos smiled. "No offense taken." He lifted them into the cab as if they were made of feathers, and he leapt into the cab like a rodeo cowboy onto his horse. "You go to school, Cecilia? My first grade teacher—her name was Sister Cecilia."

"You're Catholic," Mama nodded to the rosary hanging over the rear view mirror. "Aren't you?"

"Isn't everybody?" Carlos grinned at her. "All of us Mexicans, at least."

"I'm not—not anymore!" Mama sat up very straight. "Church never gave me anything but grief. I hate it. I married a Catholic, but if I had it to do over—"

"Well, I'm not devout. Never go to Mass, really. I believe in love, that's all: the only thing I really understand about religion."

"How very philosophical!" Mama arched an eyebrow. "What kind of love?"

"All kinds." He yanked his bandana from his pocket and ran it across his forehead. "Love's my religion."

"You don't need religion for that!" Mama crossed her legs. Carlos rested his right arm along the back of the bench seat, his hand so close Ceci could see the black line under each of his fingernails. His hands were wider, dirtier, and rougher than any she'd ever seen.

At the garage, Carlos lifted them from the cab, smiling like he'd never stop: teeth straight and white, his brown face so like the Indians at the mission. She thought Mama would ask him to take them home right away, but she just smiled at him as he stood there with his clipboard, writing things down and talking—and talking.

"By the way, Ma'am, what name should I write on the invoice—your husband's?"

"I'm not sure I'll tell him about the repair. Better put my name: Mrs. Sullivan. Dora, but I was baptized Doralinda."

"So, *Doralinda* Sullivan, what's your *apellido de soltera,* your maiden name?"

"You don't have to keep translating Spanish for me. Just for that I'm not saying." She gave his arm a little bump with her handbag.

"Come on!" He grinned wider. "Don't get sore; tell me your *soltera.*"

"I was—I am—an Alvarez-Montenegro. My mother was a Montenegro from Santa Barbara; my father an Alvarez from Ojai. Mother grew up on a rancho, with horses and acres of land all around her."

"Santa Barbara, eh? Nice place to come from! A beautiful rich girl!"

"Not rich, not anymore! My aunt's the only one who lives there now, and she's far from rich. But yes, like I told you, I was Doralinda Alvarez-Montenegro, Fiesta Queen—once."

"Wow! Honored to meet you, Your Majesty." He raised her hand to his lips. "Always wanted to do that, just like a fancy gentleman!"

"Suit yourself!" Mama handed him her dressmaking card. "And I always wanted to give a gentleman my business card."

"Well!" He looked down at it, reading it, and smiled. "Seamstress, eh? Honest work, that—a lady's job."

"Not really a *job.* It's what I do to help ends meet. Pays for clothes, the hairdresser to keep me presentable, that kind of thing."

"You don't need that stuff! You're beautiful."

"I try to look like a lady, to make the right impression. But you know, just a week ago, some punks called me vulgar things—in front of the child! I could've died!"

"Your husband must've blown his top. I would have punched their lights out."

Mama studied her feet. "If only he had!"

"I wouldn't let anyone call you anything but Queen!" Carlos flushed red. "No—I shouldn't have said that."

"No, it's all right. I don't mind. Kind of Burt Lancaster-ish of you!"

"Please, Mama!" Ceci pulled her mother's skirt. "Can we go home now?"

"Shouldn't keep you standing out in the heat." Carlos thumped the Chevy, just like Roy Rogers would his horse. "I'll get her fixed by tomorrow. In the meantime, I'll take you home."

"You've been so nice—a lifesaver. Why don't you join us for dinner?"

"What about your husband? Won't he mind me barging in?"

"He is out of town on some tour with his band. He's always somewhere."

"*¡Ay, Qué hombre tan flojo!* Real careless guy, your man, leaving treasure out for people to steal."

Mama laughed, way down in her throat. It made Ceci feel all crawly under her hair. The Chevy, left behind like old garbage, and Mama, so happy talking and laughing with a man who smiled at her like he was looking at a cake he was about to slice up for dessert.

☆   ☆   ☆   ☆

Carlos visited them every day, bringing Chiclets for Ceci or pink frosted Mexican pastries to eat with the sweet black coffee that Mama made when she asked him to stay. During these visits, each longer than the last, he worked a little on the Chevy and drove them around—to test the engine, he said. Each time he stayed until after Ceci went to bed.

The Fourth of July, Carlos brought red, white, and blue carnations and drove them down to the Port of Los Angeles to watch fireworks. Before it got dark Ceci begged them to walk down the pier to look at the small boats. Carlos took Ceci's hand and led her along the dock.

"Do you have a favorite ship, little one?"

"I like that pink one. What's its name?"

"Baby Dearie!" Carlos laughed. "Some baby!"

Mama gave them both a look that made Ceci wonder. "It must be a lucky ship, Ceci. Everyone has a ship they wait for, a ship of dreams."

"Daddy says we'll move to Santa Barbara when his ship comes in!"

Mama squeezed Ceci's hand—hard. Ceci pulled loose. "Daddy says—"

"What ship are you waiting for, Ceci?" Mama took up her hand again, but gentler. "That song, in that movie with Ginger Rogers. Do you know it, Carlos?"

Carlos shook his head. "An old song, is it?"

"Yes, well, one my mother liked; she played it on the piano.

My ship has sails that are made of silk
The decks are trimmed with gold—"

Mama sang; her smile was no longer Fire and Ice, but softer. Even her lipstick was pink, and that tight place between her eyebrows: gone. Carlos laid his arm over Mama's shoulders, and she gathered Ceci to her skirt.

Two old men carrying fishing poles and buckets nodded and smiled at the three of them as they passed. Mama nodded back, still humming the tune. Ceci remembered Mama's song; Daddy played it on his clarinet, sounding just like the radio. Her handsome daddy played Mama's song— Daddy, who often took her down to this very pier, who made up stories about the boats and talked about his ship coming in. Daddy should be holding Mama's hand right now.

Ceci ran away from Mama and Carlos up the pier and climbed onto the railing to look down at the dirty water. Three gulls bobbed like pond ducks; some candy wrappers and a smashed beer can floated near them. She breathed in the tar and bait odor of the pier. Everything as it always was, but still wrong. Mama was happy again; Ceci should not be sad. She jumped off the railing onto the pier and rubbed her eyes with her fists, but she couldn't push the tears back.

Carlos knelt down beside Ceci and held up a bag of salt-water taffy, still warm from the vendor. He looked into her face, pretended to pout, and then smiled like a clown, cocking his head. "Sweets for the sweet?"

Ceci wouldn't let him try to make her feel better; no, she wouldn't look at him.

"What's wrong?" He hugged her against his side.

She fought the warmth of him, holding tight to the splintery railing, her upper and lower teeth hard against each other.

"Come on, *chiquita,* what's wrong?"

"I want Daddy!" Ceci yelled into his face. "*Only* my daddy!"

"Oh, I see." He looked so big and sad, holding that little bag of candy out in front of him for Ceci to take. Mama clicked over in her high heels and looked from one of them to the other. "What's wrong with Ceci?"

"She's okay, Doralinda!"

"Sorry." He whispered to Ceci, "Gee, baby, I'm sorry."

"Where are your manners?" Mama caught her breath, gripping Ceci's shoulder. "Carlos bought you a treat! Did you say thank you?"

"Thank you." Ceci took the piece of taffy Carlos held out to her.

"Good girl! Smile for me?" Carlos tickled her chin. "There you go! There's a little smile, thank you. Never helps to cry."

He was wrong, Ceci thought. It would feel better to cry; it was telling the truth. Ceci unwrapped the lime green taffy from its waxy paper, tasting its fake fruit flavor. Eating it made her feel as bad as if she had stolen it, her heart pounding as she crumpled up the wax paper and tossed it over the railing. Watching the wrapper disappear among the beer cans and soggy feathers, she whispered, "Come home fast, Daddy!"

"Now I lay me down to sleep. I pray the Lord my soul to keep. God bless Daddy and Mama, Tía Pilar and Grandma Sullivan, Mickey, and please make his mama get well, and all the people—bless them. Amen."

Dora switched off the bedroom light. "Ceci?"

"Yes, Mama?'

"Who taught you that prayer, honey?"

"Tía Pilar."

"Do you believe in prayers?"

"I don't know, Mama, I think so."

She sighed. "You'll never understand why I hate religion, will you? Still, I—" She stroked Ceci's hair, something she almost never did, except if Ceci was sick. "Maybe Carlos is the answer to *my* prayers. I think I might love him. He's—"

"And Daddy—you love him, too, don't you, Mama?"

"Daddy—" Mama stopped stroking Ceci's hair, and folded her hands in her lap, sighing. Her voice was soft. "What would you think if you were to get a new daddy?"

"I don't need a new daddy. I have an old daddy."

"What if you had *two* daddies?"

"I don't know anyone with two daddies."

"It happens: two daddies to love you and take care of you."

"Would both daddies live in our house?"

"No, that isn't the way it happens."

"How does it happen?"

Mama stopped stroking Ceci's hair. "Never mind, I was just thinking. Forget it."

"Mama, please tell me. What were you thinking about?"

"Oh, nothing. Nothing! You just go to sleep, Ceci!"

"Could you sing your song again, Mama?"

"What song?"

"That one with the golden ship."

"No! You go to sleep now." Mama disappeared into the hall, her brand new perfume, orangey-cinnamon, settling around Ceci's sheets. It was not the perfume that Daddy had given Mama for Christmas, but a new one: too much like candy, and not enough like flowers.

The day after the Fourth of July, Ceci and Mama rode in Carlos's red Thunderbird with the white bucket seats, and everything so shiny that Ceci wished she had sunglasses like Carlos and Mama. The two looked just like movie stars. Ceci didn't look like a movie star, and she didn't feel like one, either. She felt sad. They were taking her to Val's apartment so they could go out. Ceci didn't want Val to babysit.

At the stoplight near her house, Ceci watched the DiPrinzio kids playing with sparklers on their front lawn. Mrs. DiPrinzio waved; she had a great big belly like Tía Pilar's, but from having so many babies. Her kids always looked happy. Ceci thought she could ask if Mrs. DiPrinzio could babysit her instead of Val, but the light changed and Carlos sped on. The Thunderbird whizzed past the Korean Bell, through the palm trees, past Harbor Park, to the Sea Gull apartments, Val's place.

Except for the sign, which had a statue of a seagull standing on it, Ceci hated everything about the place, especially the steep, cement staircase. The steps had wide spaces of air between them, and Ceci had to step up so high, she felt she might fall through them. Mama climbed three stairs ahead, the blue cloud of her skirt lifting a little with every step, her sparkled high heels drumming.

"Hey!" Val greeted them, a cigarette dangling between her long, orange fingernails, a drink in the other hand. "Come on in!" She plopped down on the couch, spilling a little of the drink. "Don't you look like a million dollars? How did you get such a snazzy dress on your budget?"

Mama swirled, showing off the ice-blue dress. Her black hair swung around in waves like the lady in the Breck commercial. She was perfect, from her shimmering hair to her clear plastic rhinestone-heeled sandals. "Made it myself. Leftover silk, from some bridesmaid dresses."

"Doesn't look like leftovers—and your hair looks good down—sexy!"

"Thanks, but is it too young?" Mama frowned, "Too ingénue?"

"Not for you—you can't be a day over thirty, Dorrie."

Mama winced. "I'm twenty-six!"

"Really? I wouldn't have thought it." Val puffed her cigarette. "Well, there you go, then—almost ingénue. Where's this Carl, or whatever his name is, of yours?"

"Carlos? He's down in the car, waiting."

"Don't want him to meet the competition, eh?" Val patted Mama's shoulder. "Now, Ceci, why don't you join Kyle in his room? He has his Tinkertoys all set up."

"I don't want to!" Ceci fell into Mama's skirts. "Mama, I don't want to stay here! Please!"

"Don't be rude, Ceci! Since Barry's been away I have—"

Val laughed. "When the cat's away—"

Ceci wondered what cats had to do with anything. Maybe Val's nails were kind of like cat's claws? "I don't want to be here. Can't I go to Grandma's?"

Mama shook her head. "No, Ceci, I—"

"Come on, kid!" Val took Ceci's hand. "Mommy has to go! Let's see what Kyle is doing. Bye, Dora!"

Kyle sat among a mess of Tinkertoys, cars, and army men. The bones of his bare white back poked out all the way up his center. Kyle was all jabs and elbows and skinnier than Ceci. He was much taller and stronger, though—and a lot older—old enough to ride all over town on a bicycle delivering newspapers.

"Look who's here, Kyle, your little friend."

"Ceci!" Kyle spat into the air. "She's not my friend; she's a girl!"

"Someday you'll be singing another tune. She's a little cutie pie."

"She isn't." Kyle shook his head. "She's ugly! She looks like Bozo the Clown. Who gave you that haircut, Ceci? The ringmaster?"

Val shoved Ceci toward him. "Go on, play! I've got stuff to do."

Ceci pointed to the Tinkertoys. "What are you making—a star?"

"It's not a star, dumbo!" Kyle rolled his eyes. "It's a bomb." He stared down, screwing the Tinker stick in, his jaw tight. "An H-bomb!"

Ceci paced the room, her hands behind her back. Through the dirty window, if she squinted—way down, between the brown house and the gas station—she could see ocean. "The sun's going down. Everything's pink!"

Kyle stared down at his bomb. "So?"

"Well, it's pretty." The sky turned darker pink until the sun dropped out of sight behind the palm trees. Just across the street, in front of the brown house, she spied a black dog, a huge one, chain stretched from his spiked collar to the front yard tree. He circled, his chain winding the tree trunk. He lay down, meeting her stare. Ceci flinched away from the window, rubbing the goose pimples on her arms.

"Hey!" Kyle coughed. "Don't sit on my bed—don't touch my toys, either."

"That dog across the street—"

"Big black one?"

Ceci nodded. "Is he dangerous?"

"Yeah!" Kyle grinned. "Almost killed Mrs. Lee's stupid little poodle."

"Oh, can he—can he—hurt *people*?"

"Him? He's always tied up! You *are* a scaredy cat, aren't you?"

"I'm not scared."

"Well, you sure act like it." He was making another H-bomb, cramming the Tinkertoys into the round holes with little grunts.

She waited a long time before she asked, "What can I do?"

"You can watch me. I'm going to blow up Russians."

"What Russians?"

Kyle didn't answer; he was setting up his green plastic army men in neat rows. Ceci reached for a *Casper the Friendly Ghost* comic book. The cover was Casper packing a picnic basket. Kyle grabbed the comic book from her.

"Do you have a nickel?"

Ceci felt her pockets. "I don't think so."

"You can't touch anything in my room, unless you pay five cents." Kyle turned away to set up another row of army men. Ceci made sure he didn't see her swipe some pennies from the dust under his bed.

"Five cents." Ceci held up the money. "Here."

He snatched them from her hand. "Hah! You are dumb! There's eight cents here." He went back to setting up army men, and Ceci picked up the comic book. Casper the Friendly Ghost was walking through the graveyard with a picnic basket over his arm.

Val called from the kitchen.

On the table, still in their foil wrap, were three TV dinners in tinfoil plates. Kyle ripped off the foil, grabbed a drumstick, and finished it before Ceci began to eat.

"Good grub!" he said, a little chicken dripping from his mouth. Val peeled off her foil, tossed it to the center of the table, picked up a cigarette, and opened her magazine. "Eat up, kids!"

Ceci stared at her plate until it cooled enough for her to pick an edge off the tinfoil. Everything about that TV dinner tasted like Reynolds Wrap. The little spaces in the plate didn't separate the food. An orange pool of butter ran off the mashed potatoes into the gluey creamed corn, which had slopped into the cherry cobbler. She turned a bit of corn over with the point of her spoon, wiping the cherry juice onto the side of her plate.

"You going to eat that biscuit?" Kyle grabbed the roll from Ceci's plate and gulped it down in two bites. "I'm done!" He burped and ran to his room.

"That's an expensive TV dinner, Ceci." Val pointed to the chicken leg. "Eat the meat! Just pick it up, that's right."

Ceci lifted the oily drumstick to her teeth, just as Kyle yelled, "Hurry up, the Russians are attacking!"

"Oh, well, then!" Val lifted her cigarette from the ashtray. "Take a bite of your meat, and then you can go play."

In no hurry to play, she listened to Kyle's exploding noises and the howls; Ceci guessed they were the sound of dying plastic Russian soldiers. The rubbery meat slid against her teeth. Grease oozed out of it, and she forced herself to swallow. If only she could eat every aluminum foil-flavored bite, she could put off being with Kyle.

"Kyle wants to play!" Val took the plate away from Ceci. "You're just pushing the food around, anyway. You're excused!"

Ceci sat in the middle of Kyle's room, just watching Kyle's war. The Russians lost; Kyle's bombs won, but only by crashing against Ceci's head as he dropped them. After putting on her nightgown, Ceci found Val slumped in a chair, watching *Have Gun Will Travel*. "Can I sleep in here? Then I can be ready when Mama comes."

Val blinked, and stubbed out her cigarette. "I'm watching TV."

"I can sleep with the TV on."

"Do you think I'm stupid? I'm not going to let you stay up and watch TV all night! You can bunk with Kyle."

Ceci shook her head. "I want to sleep here."

"No! Kyle will let you sleep on the top bunk." Val smiled, a blob of red-orange lipstick on her front tooth. "Come here and give your Aunty Val a kiss goodnight. Come on!" Val laughed. "Don't be shy. You like me, don't you?"

The saints hate thieves and liars, Tía Pilar had made that clear. Since Ceci had already taken the pennies from under Kyle's bed, she decided not to kiss Val, or do anything else that wasn't true. "Good night!" She ran down the hall.

Kyle did, to her surprise, let her have the top bunk. The television people talking and laughing in the next room kept her awake, but she wanted to sleep more than anything. Finally, she fell into a short dream of Tinkertoys and comic books. When she awoke, the ladder at the foot of the bunk was gone. She swung her feet over the side to test if the floor was too far away to climb off. It was.

Kyle sighed and stirred in the bunk below. She hung down from the top bunk to look at his face. He rubbed his eyes and yawned.

"Hey, Kyle, where's the ladder?"

He yawned again. "What?"

"I have to go to the bathroom. Bad. Where's the ladder?"

"It will cost you a nickel."

"I don't have a nickel." Ceci held her legs together to keep the pee inside.

"How about five pennies? Like the ones you stole—"

"No, I gave them to you."

"Right!" Kyle rolled over, so she couldn't see his face. "Too bad!"

"Please, Kyle!"

"Shut up, stupid, or I'll feed you to that dog 'cross the street."

"No!" Ceci's legs jerked, and some pee leaked out: first a dribble, then a rush. She rolled herself into a ball, pressing her knees to her belly, her nightgown and panties sopping, pee dripping onto the bed below.

"You peed on me!" Kyle switched on the light and ran down the hall, "Mom! Mom! Ceci peed all over my bed!"

"God damn it!" Val staggered in, her hair in rollers. "What the hell is going on?"

Ceci crouched in the bed, bunching her wet nightgown up around her legs, trying not to cry.

"Look, Mom, she peed all over everything!"

Val touched the blanket and jerked her hand away. "Christ! Never seen a kid piss so goddamn much! Look at you, soaked! You'll have to sleep in your birthday suit. Kyle, go get me some sheets from the closet. Wait a minute!" Val's eyes searched the room. "Where's the ladder?"

"That's why I wet the bed. I couldn't get down."

Val opened the closet, and the ladder fell out onto her shoulder. "Shit!" She leaned it up against the wall, shaking her head. "Goddamn kid—"

"Wow!" Kyle stood in the door, a pile of folded sheets and blankets in his arms. "She sure made a mess, didn't she, Mom?"

"You stupid brat! Hiding the ladder!" Val swung her arm back and slapped Kyle's face so hard he fell onto the floor. "Put that damned ladder back where it belongs!" Dry-eyed, he jumped up to follow her orders.

Val tugged at Ceci's sleeve. "Take off that wet thing!"

Dropping her nightie on the floor, Ceci climbed back to the top bunk, her heart pounding. She rolled her hands into two tight fists, rubbing her icy feet together.

"Now settle down and sleep, damn it!" Val threw a dry blanket up to Ceci. "I don't want to hear another peep out of either of you!" She switched off the light.

"'Night, Mom." Kyle's voice was calm, as if nothing had happened. Ceci was afraid to say a word until Val shut the door and stomped down the hall.

"Kyle, I'm sorry—sorry she hit you."

"Shut up!" Kyle punched his pillow. In the living room, Val turned the sound up on the TV. On the other side of the wall, from Val's TV, a comfortable clopping sound—horses—helped Ceci fall asleep.

When she woke up a while later, the TV was quiet. Kyle breathed beside her. Ceci cringed to the wall. "Why are you up here?"

"I'm scared."

"But you're eleven—almost twelve! You're too big to be scared of the dark."

"Not the dark. I had a bad dream, about bombs. Why don't we play?" His fingers slid over her belly.

"Stop!" Ceci sat up. "What are you doing?"

"You know where babies come from?"

Ceci held herself as close to the wall as she could. "Unh-uh."

"Pretend you are going to have a baby. I'm the doctor, and I need to check and see if it's in there—in your bottom. Come on, it's okay."

"That's not fun." Ceci drew her knees up to her chest. "No."

"It's a game." Kyle pried her arms from her legs, forcing his hand between them.

"Ouch! I don't want to play." She sat up. "Val!" Her voice barely croaked, "Val!" She tried to yell, but Kyle's face was so close to hers she couldn't.

"Mom's asleep; nothing wakes her up!" Kyle rolled over on Ceci, so she could not squirm, forcing his fingers into her with jabs. Never before had a pain so big come from inside her, from such a small place.

Everything pain: no sheets, no bed, no room, no apartment, and no seagull sign. Pain grew bigger and bigger, too big for her to stay inside her self. Ceci pressed her eyes shut. Mama wouldn't come; Daddy was far away. Then she thought of Grandma.

Grandma: her pale green eyes, her silver hair—the birthday cake with flowers and blue candles. Ceci counted: one, two, three. Grandma had taught her to count. She counted the candles: four, five, six, plus one to grow on, seven candles. Seven dwarfs. Seven days in a week. One, two, three, four—the sound of feet outdoors on those hollow open steps, the doorknob turning, and Val's front door opening. Kyle crawled under the blanket, next to Ceci's feet.

Mama! Ceci found her voice, loud and real. "Mama! Mama!" Mama! In Val's living room, Mama's laugh tinkled with happiness.

Carlos was the first at the bedroom door. "Cecilita? You called your Mama?"

"K-K-Kyle—"

Carlos tore back the covers. "Get off!" He caught Kyle by the scruff of his neck. "What in God's name?"

Kyle was blubbering. "I was just playing."

"The hell you were."

"Mama!" Ceci climbed down the ladder, crying, "Mama!"

Seeing Ceci there naked, Mama stood in the door, her face white in the shadows. "Oh my God. Where's your nightgown! Put it on!"

Ceci picked up the cold, wet nightie, holding it around her.

Kyle twisted in Carlos's grip, fighting like a fish on a hook.

"What's all this commotion?" Val grumbled in, her head wrapped in curlers and toilet paper. She took one look at Carlos clamping Kyle's wrists like handcuffs. "Lay off him, you—you goddamn Mexican!" She slapped Carlos across the face, so hard that he lost his balance, falling against the bunk bed. Val's face was red and puffy; a bristly curler flopped over her forehead. "So this is your new Romeo!" She turned to Mama. "This asshole?"

Free from Carlos's fists, Kyle giggled. "Asshole!"

And Mama just stared, her wet eyes wide open, like a cornered deer's. She turned toward the door, as if any moment she might dash out into the street.

Ceci squeezed her eyes shut, praying: *Stay Mama, stay! Turn around, pick me up and hold me! Mama!*

Val yanked at Kyle's pajama top. "What the hell happened?"

Kyle's teeth chattered. "N—n—nothing—Ceci and me were just playing."

"Playing?" Carlos shook his head. "Like hell! The little—"

"Wait just a minute, Spic! Kids play." Val tucked Kyle under her arm. "They play all kinds of things. Don't look at me like that, Dora*linda*. Your Ceci—the apple doesn't fall far from the tree. Why wouldn't she want to play doctor with Kyle?" She smirked at Carlos. "Guess you know what kind of woman you have there, don't you? No better than she should be.

Dora, your little flirt has been breathing down Kyle's neck all night. She brought this on herself."

Carlos lifted Ceci into his arms. *"Ay, m'ija,* You're shivering. Poor thing." He wrapped his jacket around Ceci. "You're so cold! *Pobrecita de alma."* He carried her to Mama. "Here, baby, here's your *mamá—"*

Refusing to take Ceci, Mama's hands flew to her throat, and she dashed to the bathroom across the hall.

"Christ on a crutch!" Val shook her head. "Retching her guts out! I hope she cleans up the mess."

"Dora's had a shock."

"She's shocked? You practically strangled my kid. For what? Playing doctor? He's a little kid, for Christ's sake."

"Little kid? Ceci's a little kid! What is he—twelve? Should know right from wrong by now."

"Don't you tell me about right and wrong! Looks like you and Dora could use a refresher course. Ever hear of adultery? That deadly sin?"

"I don't have to take your bullshit!" He made to go out the door.

"You can't just leave! You two owe me—for the babysitting!"

Holding Ceci on his hip, Carlos pulled a wad of money from his wallet, tossed it onto the floor, and marched out of the apartment. Mama waited in his convertible, crying into her handkerchief.

"Here you go, *chiquita.* You're safe now."

"No!" Mama shoved Ceci off her lap. "Don't touch me!"

"¿Estás loca, Dora? Have you lost your mind? She's terrified. Comfort her!"

"You shouldn't have let him do that, Ceci! You shouldn't, shouldn't let them!" Mama folded over onto her knees, her hands clasped behind her head. "Once they—if you let them—you're ruined! You're just like—"

Ceci could not hear the rest; Mama's crying was too loud.

Carlos swept Ceci into his arms.

"Cálmate Chiquita," he whispered. "Don't cry, please. We've got enough problems with your mama."

And Ceci did not cry. She wanted to, but the tears froze to ice inside her.

☆ ☆ ☆ ☆

The black dog: pulling and pulling on his rope, his black face closer and closer. Yellow light woke Ceci from the bad dream; she sat up in bed, heart fluttering, rubbing her eyes, the morning welcome and real. She heard—was it Daddy—someone laughing with her mother in the back yard? She heard music. It had to be Daddy! She ran into the kitchen, flinging open the back door.

Mama sat at the picnic table, Carlos's big brown hand wrapped around hers. Ceci closed the door, the joy leaking out of her. It was only Carlos's laugh, and Mama had taken the radio outside; the long extension cord led through to the patio. No Daddy. Ceci closed the door and searched the kitchen for breakfast.

Eggy pieces of *chili relleno* stuck to the cast iron pan and roasted pepper skins piled in the sink. In the green coffee pot thick, black *café española*. Flour tortillas they hardly ever ate. Mama preferred the corn. Maybe Carlos liked these better. The cold tortilla cracked between Ceci's teeth like a dry leaf. Spooning a great island of sugar into the center of a cup, she added an inch of coffee.

Seated at the table, she lifted one of the blind's slats to peek at Mama and Carlos. Carlos was kissing Mama, slow, like in the movies. She let the blind fall and picked up the *café*; it tasted bitter, even with all the sugar she'd put in it.

Carlos opened the kitchen door. "Hello, Cecilita! Did you sleep well?"

Ceci blinked, taking another sip of cold *café*. She didn't want to talk.

"*Chiquita*, how much do you remember from last night?"

"Val babysat me."

"That's all you remember, honey?"

She spooned more sugar into her coffee cup, deciding to lie. "Yeah."

"Good girl. I'm glad—you're okay." He patted her head. "That's good, *m'ija*."

"Hey!" Mama came in with their dishes. "It was a lovely day for breakfast outdoors. Too bad you missed it, kiddo. Early bird catches the worm."

Carlos sat down, facing Ceci. "Would you like to go to the beach today?"

"No."

"What the hell is the matter with you, Ceci? Apologize to Carlos!"

"Give her some slack, Dora! She doesn't have to apologize to me." Carlos leaned toward Ceci, patting her hand. "Maybe you'd rather do—"

"What's wrong with the beach? Of course she wants to go! Do her good to get her mind off herself. Go make your bed and get dressed, Ceci."

Ceci ran to her room, in case Mama and Carlos would kiss again, and climbed onto her toy box to check the driveway. Carlos's shiny red and white car, the top down, waited there. The Thunderbird was the kind of car men drove in the movies—the kind of men who kissed slow like they were eating the women's faces—the way Carlos kissed Mama. What would Daddy think?

This was trouble that hurt—like last night hurt—all the way through. Her bottom was still sore, but worse was the cold that balled up in her middle of her chest just remembering. Kyle's smell, like vinegar and soap, she remembered. She threw herself onto the bed and banged her head on the pillow, so as not to think of him—his smell or the feel of his hands. She thumped her head until the thoughts fell out.

Then she got up, dressed in a pink tee shirt and white shorts, found her flip-flops on the floor of the closet, and ran out to the driveway. They were waiting for her in Carlos's car. Mama wore a blue scarf tied over her hair, and big sunglasses spread across her perfect nose like jeweled butterfly wings. Carlos combed his fingers through his hair, his pinkie ring glinting in the sun. Ceci tried to hate him, pulling the feeling from her head into her heart like a tape measure. She wished Mama would hate him and love Daddy.

What was so good about Carlos? Ceci wondered. Was it his shiny car, his muscles like a man in an ad for suntan oil, the way he talked like music instead of locking himself in the garage to play it? Was that what Mama liked? Was it the fast way he drove, spinning the steering wheel with the heel of his hand?

When Carlos couldn't pass the big white Ford, he didn't say *Jesus H. Christ!* like Daddy did. He didn't drive behind it grumbling, like Daddy, but gunned the motor and drove right around, passing the Ford in a cloud of angry driving words, like singing bullets.

"*¡Ay, pendejo, vaya, vaya!*"

"What's he saying, Mama?"

"It's Spanish. Impolite Spanish."

"Why don't we speak Spanish, like Carlos and Tía?"

"I was taught not to speak Spanish—not in public. My parents didn't want people to think we were Mexican."

"There you go again!" Carlos hit the steering wheel with his fist. "What's wrong with being Mexican?"

"Nothing! It was just a very hard time. After what happened to my grandfather, my parents tried to hold themselves a little apart."

"I bet your grandfather didn't hold himself apart—not when he was hot, and your poor old grandma wasn't."

"What do you know about my grandfather?"

"I know what happened, and still happens, with rich hombres, always crawling into the *criada's* bed. I bet no maid was safe from him!"

"I'll have you know Grandmother was the most beautiful woman in all of Santa Barbara!"

"Mama, what is a *cree-ya-dah*? Is it some kind of dog?"

Carlos snorted. "Some people think Mexicans are dogs! God damn—"

"Watch your language! Ceci—"

"Little jugs, huh? Never stopped you from cussing, did it?" Carlos spat out the window. "Maybe you think Mexicans are dogs, Dora! Why do you always tell people you're Spanish? Why can't you say you're Mexican?"

"Because I'm not!"

"The hell you're not!"

Carlos pulled into the beach parking lot. He and Mama stopped arguing as a white-haired woman, carrying blankets and a picnic basket, passed the car. Ceci wished the old woman would just stay there, so the fight would stop.

Mama tightened the knot of her scarf, watching the old lady disappear down the hill toward the beach. "I'll have you know, I'm almost one hundred per cent Spanish!"

"One hundred percent!" he laughed. "I don't believe it!"

"You don't know my history, Carlos."

"Know enough to tell you, don't be ashamed." Carlos set his palm on her arm, as if to keep her from flying away. "You should be proud of being Mexican."

"My family is Spanish *Californio*! They had a land grant from the Viceroy—"

Carlos hooted. "Oh, the land-grant Spaniards! Stop trying to lord it over me with that bull crap. There's a little *mestiza* in you, for sure—look at those black eyes of yours—more Indian than mine, even! What's wrong with being mixed blood? Think you're too good for the rest of us?"

"I do not think I'm too good for you! You of all people should know that!"

"Just because you let me touch your fair Spanish ass—"

Mama slapped his face.

The black cloud that had been growing in Ceci all day felt like it would burst. Everyone was crazy, and she still hurt from last night. Carlos and Mama didn't stop yelling long enough to see as Ceci crawled out over the back of the convertible. She swung her legs over the left taillight and dropped down to the ground.

Sandals in hand, she ran to the top of the sandy trail leading down to the beach, looking back at the Thunderbird to see if they were coming. The wind whipped Mama's headscarf like a blue flag. Ceci waved, but neither grownup noticed she'd gotten out of the car. She turned away and ran down the hill to the water.

A shelf of cool morning mist hung over the ocean, but the sand was warm. Mothers in skirted bathing suits stretched out on blankets, shading their eyes to watch over children playing in the surf. What would it be like to be one of those kids? To sit down to eat whatever their mothers packed inside those picnic baskets—tuna sandwiches, potato chips, watermelon, Kool-Aid—to wipe your chin with a colored paper napkin, to smell of suntan lotion and chocolate chip cookies? Every day for such children would be like a drawing in a picture book, colored perfect.

Dropping her sandals, Ceci ran to the water's edge; it bubbled over her toes. Sand and wave worked together, giving her a little backwards ride. She searched the sky for something—anything that might make her happy. A trace of moon caught her eye.

Once, Daddy told her there was a thread between the moon and the sea, that the ocean was like a puppet in the hands of the moon, moving in and out at its say-so. Cut loose from the moon, far from its grandfather face, the ocean roared as loud as a freeway.

Whenever Ceci had stood in the sea before, Daddy had held her hand. Slick with Coppertone, stretched out on her towel, Mama had waited for them.

"Mama! Daddy!" she cried out, but no one answered.

Not one of those picnic basket mothers looked up from a magazine. Mama did not come. Daddy was somewhere far away. Carlos was trying to take his place, and even he made Mama mad now—everything crashing over, like the big waves in front of her, too big to stand.

Ceci walked up the beach until she made out a black shape coming toward her. As she backed away, it only grew bigger, until it became a huge black dog, his hair bushed up on his back in a hump, his eyes glassy and mean. White spit dripped from bared teeth. In her dreams, she'd seen this same dog, looked into his hungry eyes that told her he would eat everything in his way. He stood close; Ceci could smell him—no dream this time.

She could not take her eyes off him; she could only back away—away from the black dog—into the oncoming wave. The cold wave knocked her onto her face and dragged her into its deep cold. Seawater clinked, stinging metal in her ears, burning her throat. Trying to breathe—swallowing more salty wet, rolling between cold sheer walls—one side deep green, unclear, the other glassy and lighter.

A whip snapped through her. Tired—so tired—she rolled into the calling darkness. No more air, no light, no sounds, no up nor down. Nothing.

Then, warmth and safety. As if she were a baby again, velvety arms rocked her, "*Cecilita, mi querida, no es el tiempo.* Dear one, it is not the time. *Duérmete, duérmete, hijita.* Sleep, little daughter, sleep."

In the arms of this velvet mother, Ceci shrunk into a tiny bead inside herself, miles from her skin, only a grain of herself. No more cold, no pain, no, not, nothing, no things—she could live forever here, but—

Rip and slap of wave and cold: something lifted her into the air. Ouch, ouch, ouch, like wet paper pulled from her throat! Ceci grew bigger inside her skin.

Blurred colors, people: like trees, colored light leaking out of their legs and arms.

Voices.

Carlos?

"Come on! Wake up, *chiquita!* Live! Live!"

Far away as a slice of moon, Ceci heard Mama.

"Oh my God! Is she breathing? Please! This can't happen to me! No!"

Ceci shut her eyes to sleep again, shrinking into the sweet darkness.

Not the right mother. Not the right mother! I want the Velvet Mother.

Dreamtime rocking, wrapped in the comfort of velvet arms, then pain—breath forced into her—each breath forcing needles of light through her. She fought, clinging to the purple blanket of dreaming. She must stay here.

Through sleep's clouds, a ship sailed, all around it a halo of light. As the ship neared, Ceci saw a lady waving from the glowing deck. Under her crown of stars, she wore a veil the color of deep seawater. Rays of gold shot out from her head and shoulders. Behind the ship a great moon rose out of the sea, the sky but an outline, like the black in a coloring book. The lady waded into the shallows, Ceci in her arms. Her starry green veil fell around the two of them like a silky tent.

Ceci leaned into her softness. "Was it you? Are you the Velvet Mother, the one who held me in the water? Was it you who saved me?"

"Yes, I rocked you. Now you must go back."

"Why can't I stay with you?"

"You cannot stay in dreamtime, dear one. You must return; they need you there."

Far down the dark tunnel—Carlos? "Please, *chiquita!* C'mon, breathe, breathe!"

"No—no—she's not going to die! Don't let her die!"

Mama?

Ceci felt the bead of herself swelling. Blasts of pain so great that she howled—a wolf to the moon of the lady's light. "I won't go back! Let me stay with you! I will die there with them."

The Velvet Mother daubed at Ceci's tears with her fingers, touching them to her forehead, shoulders, and jeweled heart. "Tears are holy." She kissed Ceci's lips. "Breathe now, Cecilita—breathe and sleep. No more nightmares, my daughter. I am your Mother from Heaven—your comforter; everywhere and always, I am with you."

Part Two:
Pilar Martinez de Montenegro
July 1960

Ceci lay unconscious, hooked up to tubes and machines in the same bright modern hospital where she'd been born—Los Angeles General. The doctors were cautious about their prognosis; this is all Dora told Pilar. She summoned the old woman via telephone, sobbing between words. Dora seemed confused about the accident. All Pilar could get out of her was that Ceci had almost drowned, Barry was out of town, and would she come? Of course she would! Pilar laid down the phone, threw a toothbrush and her rosary into her purse, and boarded the first Greyhound bus to Los Angeles.

Perched like a broody hen, Pilar did not budge from Ceci's bedside, waving away the candy stripers' offers of coffee and donuts. She aimed her prayers at the specters hovering over her grandniece, praying for dear life. Hours crawled by, and nurses floated in and out to check the monitors, taking notes and whispering to each other. Slowly the phantom seemed to lessen its grip, and their worried but professional gazes softened. Still, Pilar did not waver, the clear blue beads of her rosary flowing over her knuckles like a waterfall.

One pale blond nurse slid the clipboard back into its niche at the foot of the hospital bed. She touched Pilar's hand, her fingertips cool and gentle.

"Your prayers must be working. Her temperature is dropping." The nurse swished out of the room before Pilar could ask whether the drop meant brain damage was no longer a threat.

Pilar lost track of the time, her only clock Ceci's breaths. Sun edged in, a slim shaft through the one stark window, unable to dispel the gloom that permeated everything. The clown portraits someone had hung on the gray-green walls for the sake of childish tastes—even these—had tearful eyes. Laying aside her rosary, Pilar studied Ceci's pierced hand, the gravity of the IV unnerving. She cleared her throat, dry from so many whispered rounds of prayer.

"Dora, did the doctor say if this is good? The temperature dropping—"

Etched by the lean light, Dora didn't respond, but paced, arms wrapped around her chest like a straitjacket. Intent on a point straight ahead, her mouth gathered in a pout, like a sulking child. She turned her back to her aunt, her posture defiant.

Thoughts raced in. *Angry with me, is she? She's angry with me, when it's probably her negligence that brought this all upon us?* Pilar's palm itched—she should have smacked her niece for letting this happen! Yes, that would be justice, she thought, and then flushed with shame, gazing at the rosary in her lap. *Lord, forgive me, a sinner!* Jesus almost cried out disapproval—the nails piercing His hands and feet, so like the needle of Ceci's IV. *Lord, I believe, forgive my unbelief—*

Christ's naked agony, the mystery of His meekness, Pilar prayed for faith, for patience, for wisdom—for her legs to stop aching—for Dora to say something, anything at all to break the miserable silence. Just as her dry throat stung for water, she thirsted for the truth. Pilar needed to know what had happened to the child. Dora's silence was claustrophobic.

Pilar was used to fresh air, to open windows and gardens. She hated to be cooped up in this room, would have liked a walk, a strong cup of tea—to feel easy again. If only she could go home, and water her prize roses—but duty required her presence.

Dora's last surviving relative, Pilar was now the matriarch and elder of the family. It was a *pundonor*, a matter of honor, to see this through.

She straightened, cursing the bones of her corselet. How had she gotten so stout? The young nurses flitted about her like tiny hummingbirds around a turkey. *God forgive you, Pilar, for thinking about your* panza—*such vanity*—*and Ceci at death's door!* Such thoughts were only distractions from the matter of confronting Doralinda.

What would she ask her niece first—about the accident, or what the sins were that led up to it? Every time she tried to speak a question, her tongue dangled like a clapper in a broken bell. Her elder sister, Cecilia, Ceci's namesake—now, she would have known what to say, and without getting cross. What a woman Ceci's Grandmother Cecilia had been!

Her much mourned sister, Cecilia, had been a saint while living. Long-suffering. God knows she had to be, with that husband to endure. Must be the reason Dora was so hard now—her father's gambling away the fortune and running around with ladies of ill repute. Impossible man!

Pilar would have hated and cursed such a husband. She would have kicked him out on his big, fat *culo*—but not Cecilia. Only a year or two before Cecilia had died, Pilar got up the nerve to ask, "How can you forgive him, when he's disgraced you like this, over and over again? You—living like a beggar in a hovel, taking in ironing to make ends meet—you say you still love him! How can you?"

"Little sister, if you will pray to the Blessed Mother, your heart will grow more like hers. Then you will understand."

Yes, Cecilia had been a saint, but not Pilar. Since then, she'd taken up her sister's habit of praying, but it hadn't changed her all that much. Even so, she was so weary of Dora she could scream. She stroked the crucifix of her rosary and began a Hail Mary.

Dios te salve, María. Llena eres de gracia.

So she prayed, her voice an audible murmur. Between each decade of beads she looked up, trying to engage her niece. Dora watched at the window, neck tensed like a doe listening for predators. Pilar laid her rosary on her lap. "Doralinda, are you expecting someone? What are you hiding? What's wrong?"

"What's wrong?" Dora spun away from the window, her face tense. "Isn't it enough that my daughter nearly drowned? That my—that—my boyfriend—"

"Doralinda!" Pilar leveled her gaze.

"Everyone looks at me that way!" Dora threw back her head, wincing. "Oh, please! Don't interrogate me. You make me feel like a criminal!"

Pilar counted to ten, then twenty. How trying the girl was! She clung to her beads, begging the Blessed Mother for patience.

Bendita tu eres entre todas las mujeres.

Blessed art thou among women.

"Auntie, I'm sorry." Dora heaved a sigh. "I shouldn't have snapped at you like that. I'm so tired. I'm just—I haven't eaten since I don't know when."

"Poor Doralinda!" Pilar forced up the corners of her mouth. Her head throbbed, as if someone were driving a barbecue skewer through her brow bone. "You're worn out. Go get something to eat. I'll stay here, in case the doctor comes."

"Yes, it might help if I took a little break." Dora's eyes thumbed through her handbag. "Oh, come on, where is it, that stupid thing?"

"What can't you find?"

"My address book; it's in here somewhere!" Dora slung her bag over her arm, and then hesitated at the foot of the bed, stroking the blanket. She lifted Ceci's hand to her lips. "I'm sorry, baby. I have to—go. Forgive me." With the back of her left hand, she wiped her eyes, the fingers of the right rearranging Ceci's curls.

"Doralinda! It's not like you're going to Mexico, or something!" Pilar clutched at her aching knees. "Better hurry now, and get some dinner. You'll have to call Barry after we talk to the doctor. You need your strength."

"Oh, Lord!" Dora sighed. "I don't see how I can call him. All I know is he's in Frisco, with some band called the Cobbs. He said he'd call home today, but I've been here—so how could he reach me?" She slipped her sweater over her shoulders like a cape. "Eventually, he'll find out; there's a phone number lying around somewhere."

"He'll want to come straightaway."

"That's all I need." Dora stopped at the mirror, flicked her bangs from her eyes, and rubbed at the little furrow between her brows. "God, I look like death."

"First, get something nourishing—none of that diet plate nonsense." Pilar kissed Dora's cheek, the rosary swinging between them. "Everything will be all right. You just have to do your duty."

"How would that help?" Dora held both Pilar's shoulders, wincing back tears. "All this trouble—everyone would be better off if I just disappeared!"

"Let's not indulge in self-pity!" Pilar crossed her arms. "Go on, get yourself something to eat. You'll feel better."

"Okay." Dora raised her hand to her cheekbone in a little curled wave. "Bye!" She turned to the door, her back shuddering. "Bye, Aunt!"

"Tía! Call me tía!" Pilar called out. "I'm not a bug!"

That new perfume of Dora's lingered a long time after she'd gone, an improper sort of fragrance—one that invaded the nose. That *tonta* must have bathed in it! The attar of violets Pilar's mother used to wear, how sparing she was with it! Now there was a lady—her beautiful *madre*. Pilar shook off the wistfulness. Time to pray. The little great-grandchild of such a grand lady deserved all the *Salve Marías* Pilar could muster.

Blessed is the fruit of thy womb—
Bendito es el fruto de tu vientre, Jesús.
Santa María, Madre de Dios, ruega—

"Er—Excuse me! Uh, Mrs. Sullivan?" A woman in a crisp brown suit nodded to Pilar from the doorway, thrusting her clipboard like a centurion's shield.

"I need you to complete some forms, Ma'am."

"Sorry!" Pilar slipped her rosary into her pocket. "Mrs. Sullivan went to grab a bite to eat. I'm Mrs. Martinez."

"Well, I need to talk to a parent about the billing. Apparently, the mother was too upset when the child was admitted to Emergency. How about the father, where's he?"

"Out of town. Can't I help you?"

She scanned Pilar, appraising. "I'd prefer a parent or guardian."

"Oh, I can go find her, if you like."

Furtively glancing at her clipboard, the woman sighed. "Maybe you'd better."

Pilar hoisted herself from the chair, smoothing the back of her skirt. "Who will watch over the little one? Can you stay a minute?"

The woman averted her eyes. "I'm not responsible for watching patients."

"Oh!" Pilar clasped her hands on her lap, rising a little in her chair. Her lip quivered. "There must be someone else, then."

"Maybe a candy striper is available." The woman shot out of the room, her clipboard clacking against the doorframe.

"I'll not leave you alone, little owlet." Pilar sought the slender reassurance of Ceci's pulse. The intricate blue veins on the little one's eyelids, the paleness of her dry lips, the fragility of her every breath mesmerized Pilar. How precious each detail weighed on her affections, now that the flame of the little girl's life flickered!

She had loved Ceci, yes, but less than she loved her own dear son, less than she imagined she'd love the grandchildren Eduardo could have given—had he lived. Now that Pilar had envisioned Saint Peter sweeping the child inside the Pearly Gates, how much dearer Ceci became! "God help me," she prayed aloud. "Let me love better than I have. Let me love this child as she needs to be loved."

As golden afternoon light pooled the room, Pilar's heart, like a great sea urchin, swelled open, unfurling its petals to a great wave of longing. She prayed, "Leave me just this one. Whatever you ask, I will give; just please, don't let her be damaged. Let her be healed!" And then the familiar words:

Santa Maria, Madre de Dios, ruega por nosotros pecadores, ahora y en la hora de nuestra—

"Hello, Ma'am?"

Pilar jerked upright. "You startled me."

"I'm a candy striper—I volunteer. You know, help out." She patted her pink and white apron. "Sorry to bother you. I just wondered if you needed anything?"

"Quite all right, dear." Pilar nodded toward Ceci, "My grandniece—I must go get her mother. Forms to fill out. I wonder if you'd stay a minute? I'd hate for her to wake up all alone."

"Sure!" The girl wiped her palms down the front of her apron and took her place at Ceci's bedside. "I'll watch over her. Don't worry; I just know she'll be fine."

"From your lips to God's ears—may it be so." Pilar folded her handkerchief into a little square and dabbed at her bleary eyes. "I shouldn't be long."

Stiff from sitting, Pilar hobbled down the corridor to the elevator. A little shiver traveled her spine. Too much air conditioning in these places: unease wafting down from the ceiling vents to prickle at her neck. No, it wasn't the air conditioning, nor was it her arthritis. Underneath her neat white chignon, her neck hairs rose. Pilar knew it then.

¡Mal Ojo!

The Evil Eye! She tapped the crucifix at her throat as she waited for the elevator. Evil all around in this place of death! Crossing herself, she stepped into the elevator. Canned music, the bell for the floor—Pilar strode out, her purse tucked under her arm, lifting her torso from the waist as her mother had taught her a lady should do. *Always feign courage; act as if you're in control and you will be.* But *Mal Ojo*—

Mal Ojo had taken hold of her family! Anxiety greased the weary gears of her thoughts; they turned so fast she could not follow them. What to do first? Yes, she must take control of the situation. She'd ask Doralinda—no, she wouldn't ask, she'd demand Doralinda call Rafaela and beg *la curandera,* the healer, to drive away the Evil Eye immediately. She took a comfortable breath, relieved to have a plan.

An orderly clicked by, pushing a wheeled apparatus, yards of plastic tubing looped around his hairy arm. What poor soul would the hospital torture with that machine? Not Cecilita, Pilar resolved. She had no more faith in doctors, their poisonous pills and beeping machines. Weary of speaking English all day, she longed for the familiar *velas, ruegos, y hierbas*—the candles, prayers, and herbs of her *curandera.*

White people in white—they treated her like a half-wit. These Anglos with clipboards and stethoscopes drove her crazy. She wanted her *curandera*, who spoke her language, understood her fears, and had known the family forever. When we need the familiar things most, Pilar sighed, we are forced into the company of strangers.

She lingered outside the cafeteria, scanning the tables. Where had Dora gone? She hoped her niece had mustered the courage to call Barry. Pilar's eyes searched the lobby. No Dora at the phone booths near the entry. Had she ordered a meal, then?

A tall black man in a clean white apron approached her, his smile a slice of moon.

"Can I help you?"

"Please, sir." Pilar pulled herself to her full five foot three. "I wonder if you've seen my niece? She might have ordered some food."

"When would you be talking 'bout, Ma'am?"

"Uh—about ten, fifteen minutes ago."

"Slow afternoon. We've only had a few customers. What's she look like?"

"Dark." Pilar blushed. "I mean, not so dark. I mean—"

"Not so dark as me?" he grinned. "Like you, you mean? Light brown?"

Pilar nodded, relieved. "Yes—Mexican. She's pretty."

"Ah, I think saw her. A stunner! She left a while ago. For her car—"

Pilar's hand flew to the side of her cheek. "She *what*?"

"I was just coming in from my break. At the front entrance—I almost bumped into her; she sure was in a hurry. Fifteen minutes ago."

"You must be mistaken. She was going to the cafeteria." Pilar gazed toward the door, as if Dora was due to make an entrance any second. She flashed a woeful little smile. "What was—what was she wearing?"

"A white shirt—tight black slacks." He dropped his eyes. "Yeah, she was beautiful, all right, like a movie star."

"Oh dear!" Pilar wrung her hands. It had to be Dora that he'd seen, but it couldn't be. Her joints ached, but she forced herself to jog to the entrance. She stared out the revolving glass doors for a sign of Dora. A nurse pushing a wheelchair approached, and Pilar stepped outside after her. No Dora, nor the Chevy in the parking lot. The Negro must be mistaken. He had to be.

Mustering her courage, Pilar asked the front desk to page her niece. The call resounded over the hospital intercom: *Dora Sullivan, please return to Room 237.* For what seemed at least a half hour Pilar waited, and then approached the front desk again. "I'm sorry to bother you again, but could you please call the nurses' station and ask if Dora Sullivan is back in the room?"

Dora was not in Ceci's room, nor anywhere on the pediatric wing. Pilar checked every waiting room, the women's restrooms, even the cafeteria again. Her black orthopedic oxfords clamped her toes like vises, and perspiration stuck her shirtwaist dress to her back and underarms. She leaned against the cash register counter dabbing at her forehead with her lacy handkerchief, wondering where else to look.

The same black man insisted she take a glass of cold water. She downed it in a few seconds and handed him the glass. "Thank you; you're very kind."

"I hope she shows up soon, Ma'am."

"Yes, of course she will! We just got our signals crossed."

She turned toward the elevators to try again. Maybe Dora had gotten herself lost and was in the wrong ward. With little hope of finding her niece, she searched every floor. Just one remained: maternity. The old rhyme they taught Catholic children: *Saint Anthony, please come around. Something's lost and can't be found.*

Alone in the elevator Pilar indulged herself, reciting Saint Anthony's prayer for the lost, turning clockwise three slow turns, and then leaning against the elevator wall, limp with exhaustion. The door slid open, and she gasped her surprise and pleasure. Someone she knew!

A young woman stepped into the elevator, her eyes brightening with pleasure—her slow smile, to Pilar, like sun breaking through clouds.

Pilar pulled her into an embrace. "Carmen! How good to see you!"

"And you!" The younger woman kissed her. Her white nurse's uniform redolent of soap and sunlight. "How are you? And your digestion, still suffering the *empacho*?"

"Now and then. I completely forgot you work here. How's your *mamá*?"

"Still going strong; I don't know if she'll ever retire."

"Oh, she can't." Pilar dabbed at her forehead with her sodden handkerchief. "People wouldn't know what to do without Rafaela's *remedios*. I wouldn't."

"Well, she's busy as ever, no doubt about that. What brings you here?" Carmen's smile faded. "You're not ill?"

Pilar hesitated, her distress flooded with shame. How to explain Dora's behavior? There was no way to do so. "It's my grandniece. She's had an accident. A serious one. I've not left her side since—I've just left her for a—little break."

"I'm so sorry, Pilar. Shall I get you something—a nice cup of tea? I'm on my break."

"Oh, Carmen, please don't trouble yourself."

"Nonsense, it's no trouble. You're like family!" Carmen led the old woman back to the cafeteria, where they sat opposite one another at a far corner table. "Mamita speaks of you often, of your beautiful garden. Speaking of gardens, have you been taking your *hierbas*? You look as if you could use them."

"I left in a hurry; Dora called, frantic." Remembering that phone call brought back tears. "She told me Ceci had nearly drowned. Very serious. Sorry—"

"It's natural to cry, *amiga*." She patted Pilar's hand. "You came straightaway?"

"Of course!" Pilar stirred her tea and set down the spoon without drinking. At last, here was someone trustworthy with whom she might confide. "Dora has run off. Left her own daughter!" She took a deep breath. "The Negro man at the cafeteria saw her leave the hospital. My grandniece at death's door, and her mother disappears! The shame of it! Like one of my soap operas!"

"People act crazy under stress. Dora's just upset; she'll come back."

Pilar stirred another spoon of sugar into her tea, regretting her daily devotion to *Right to Happiness*, to *Young Doctor Malone*—her delicious, scandalous soap operas. Was this God's punishment for wishing real life was as exciting as the radio?

Carmen leaned forward. "What about the girl's father? Where's he in all this?"

"Barry? He's away on 'business.' Business, nothing—a band tour! Musicians!" Pilar sighed, and shrugged. "He's not a bad man, but Dora has no respect for him. He's Irish—a Catholic, in name at least. But they didn't even christen Cecilita. I thought he'd insist, for his poor mother, if not for the child's sake."

"People are different now, less traditional." Carmen pressed the crease on her napkin with her thumb. "I didn't know Dora had married. How long ago?"

Pilar blushed—another matter of embarrassment for the family. "About seven years ago. They didn't have a wedding, not really, or you and Rafaela would have been invited. They eloped. No church wedding for Dora. Wouldn't have any part of it; she hates the Church." Pilar didn't bother to wipe her eyes again. "Especially priests. I don't know what's got into her. I just don't."

"We can never know everything, even about family. Maybe Dora has her reasons. Anyway, the world is changing fast; people are leaving the old ways behind. It's hard for you elders to understand, but we have to go with the times. I drive Mama to distraction with—"

"No, you've always been such a good daughter! Your *mamá* is so proud of you."

"I disappoint her, all the same. She wants me to follow in her footsteps, work with the herbs. I try, but I don't have the time to devote to it now. I have to make my own way, for my children's sake as much as my own—for my children's children."

Pilar's studied Carmen's sad smile. No lipstick—the dear didn't wear a bit of makeup. Didn't they allow nurses to wear makeup? Pilar always lightened her own coppery complexion with Coty's powder. She wondered if she should recommend this to Carmen; with a little effort she might be beautiful, even striking.

Meanwhile, Carmen was trying to loosen the last of the sugar from the dispenser, whacking it with the palm of her hand. Pilar handed her two sugar packets from a stash she kept in her purse.

"Thanks!" Carmen laid the packets on her saucer. "I probably should cut back on sugar, anyway."

"Oh, I don't see why. You're nice and slim. If I had your fig—"

"The diabetes killed my papa—that, and his heart."

"I'm sorry, dear. I forgot."

"Long time ago." Carmen rolled the empty sugar packet into a tube. "So what do you think is eating Dora? Why would she leave without telling you?"

"Don't know." Pilar shook her head. "I thought she'd settled down a little. She was a dutiful mother, though not the most affectionate. But I had no idea that she would desert like this, when the child needs her most."

"Maybe she didn't desert. Maybe she just slipped out for a magazine or something. When you go back to the room, Dora'll be there waiting."

"I hope you're right. The doctor is coming to talk to us—the prognosis." Pilar looked at her watch. "He's probably there right now, waiting." Pilar clasped both Carmen's hands. "My treat." She laid a dollar bill on the table. "It has been a pleasure—even with all this—to see you again."

"Same here!" Carmen kissed Pilar's cheek. "I'll check on you two after my shift's done, if that's okay. What's her full name?"

"Cecilia Sullivan. They moved her from emergency to pediatrics. Oh, the room number! I don't remember." She opened her purse. "It's in here somewhere."

"Don't worry, I'll find you. Is there anything else I can do?"

"Well," Pilar took Carmen by the hand. "Can you give me your *mamá's* phone number? I forgot my little book." She pulled Carmen closer. "I suspect *Mal Ojo*."

"Better than that, I can call her for you."

"If it's not asking too much—"

"Just see to your grandniece and leave the rest to me."

"You're a godsend, *querida*."

The candy striper looked up from her paperback, her eyebrows raised in question.

"No luck," Pilar sighed. "I couldn't find my niece, not anywhere. I thought she might've come back here. Did you see her?"

"No one, except for the nurse."

"Thank you for staying, honey. You're the best nurse on this floor."

"Thanks!" The girl blushed. "But I'm not a nurse."

"You have the heart for the job, though."

"Thank you. I do hope to be a nurse someday." The candy striper hesitated in the doorway. "Should I check in on you before I go home?"

"Please!" As the girl left, Pilar collapsed into the bedside chair. Ceci stirred just a bit, her lips quivering. Maybe there was a little more color in her cheeks. A mustard seed of hope sprouted in Pilar's heart. Soon Rafaela might come and bring the *hierbas* and candles, the remedies against *Mal Ojo*.

About an hour before sunset, a lull settled on the ward. Ceci snored softly, her eyelids trembling, and Pilar leaned her head against the wall, hovering between sleep and wakefulness. Accustomed now to the hospital sounds—machines, muffled voices, soft footsteps in the hall—Pilar felt her anxiety loosening.

A sharp scream—a child's—pierced the quiet. Pilar sat up, her nerves taut. About to check Ceci's charts, the pale nurse turned abruptly and jogged down the hall. Another childish wail echoed the first, and then a woman's urgent plea.

"Help! Somebody, quick!"

A buzzer sounded repeatedly at the nurses' station. Three men and women loped past, stethoscopes bouncing on their chests. Then a telephone rang down the hall, but no one answered it. The tension in the ward was as tightly wound and palpable as a noose.

"*Madre de Dios,* save us!" Pilar prayed fervently, hoping that the cries came from a child frightened by some routine procedure. Perhaps his mother had overreacted. She recalled Dora's hysteria that morning.

She had arrived to find Dora weeping in the hall. Dora clung to some Mexican man as a woman should only cling to her husband. The man, to his credit, tried to pry Dora off his chest, telling her, "Pull yourself together!" Finally, Dora had composed herself enough to introduce them, and then Carlos had excused himself. He must be going, he'd said; this was a family matter, after all.

"Don't leave me!" Dora had beseeched, her eyes desperate. The man's eyes had been distant, his demeanor cold. "God has given us this as punishment. I can't do this anymore. We're through."

Dora's wretchedness, the way she threw herself at that Carlos—the shame! She'd no business hanging on anyone except Barry—but this *gamberro*, with the dirty fingernails! Not bad looking, but coarse hands and mestizo features.

More screams echoed down the hall, then a guttural moan followed by gasping sobs that Pilar knew by heart—the first stabs of a mother's grief. The memory, decades old yet never far from the surface, recalled a summer day like this when she'd received the telegram.

That day she'd thought she was opening the door to a neighbor, but the tall man in his starched uniform, his practiced somberness as he thrust out that square of yellow paper—all these had told her otherwise. Her heart had fallen like a dove shot in flight.

"No!" She'd slammed the door in his face, had screamed for her husband, Diego, and he'd come running, his face rigid and white as death.

Yes, death!

Slow motion, frame by frame, as he opened the door, apologized to the young soldier and took the telegram, his arm wrapped around Pilar, who was already shaking even before she knew. She knew.

Eduardo.

All the time the California sun smiling, birds chirping, the kitchen radio playing *A Gal from Kalamazoo*, the terrible ordinariness of the day impervious to death. The sky should have gone dark; fire should have rained from the heedless, puffy clouds.

She still could see the horror in Diego's eyes when he'd looked up at her from the telegram. "Eduardo! *Querida*—he's—" He didn't have to finish the sentence.

"No!" A mistake. Not Eduardo! It couldn't be. Every night she had lit the *La Mano Poderosa*, trusting God's powerful hand, entrusting Him with her only son.

"Not Eduardo?" This time her eyes asking, not telling. "Eduardo?"

Diego stared at her as if trying to read her face, only nodding: *yes*.

She tore the telegram from his hand. "Omaha Beach—D-Day—we regret—died in action—a hero—a credit to his country—"

Then Pilar had screamed, just like that poor mother down the hospital hall; from the bottom of her soul, from the pit of hell the scream came— barbed wire cinching her heart: gut-piercing agony far greater than that of childbirth; hope ripped away with every paroxysm of grief. So she grieved even months later, as she waited for his Purple Heart.

Loss still twisting her innards, another knife had stabbed clear through. No medal, no recognition for Eduardo's sacrifice—for the son the country had taken and thrown away. The war ended—still no medal. The local Army office finally admitted the United States did not deem Eduardo an American—because his father wasn't a citizen; he'd come up before there was documentation. Pilar had no birth certificate, born as she was at home into the hands of a midwife when California was still a frontier. She'd insisted as a young woman on having her son at home as well. They asked, did she have proof her Eduardo had been born in this country—even written in the family Bible? One must be a citizen to receive a medal. Every Mexican an illegal till proven otherwise.

It all came down to a birth certificate—to something written in the front of a Bible? What did that matter now that Eduardo had died fighting Hitler? Pilar couldn't believe it; surely Uncle Sam would do the right thing for a hero, for the parents who had given their one and only. She had written the President a letter, but he didn't reply—and then he died, and that other President, the one she didn't like, took over. Pilar didn't give up, even after Diego came down with "the cancer," as he called it.

She had the hope he might rally, if he could just once hold Eduardo's medal in his hands. The candle of *Las Siete Potencias* of San Cipriano she lit at her altar, and she wrote to the Army again, still trusting that that Uncle Sam would make this right. She lit a candle to Saint Jude, the patron of impossible causes. Then she wrote to her congressman. No answer arrived. Diego's cancer worsened: no more time for letters and no heart for them. Everyone said it was time to let Eduardo go; it was just water under the bridge. While Diego died of grief, Pilar attended his sickbed during the day, staggering like a zombie after each tearful, sleepless night.

You must forgive and forget, Pilar. It's water under the bridge! Each time someone said this to her, outrage shook her awake again. *Water under the bridge!* Eduardo, nothing but a river flowing under the bridge out to the sea, used-up water flowing away? Never! Even now, the hideous thought yanked at her heart like a tow chain. Her one and only Eduardo, hair black as onyx and large, light eyes like—like—like Cecilita's! The poor little owlet!

Cold shooting through her, Pilar hugged herself and gazed at her grandniece through her tears. If only her grandniece would open her beautiful eyes! Eyes that saw into the next world as this one, like her only son's, like her sister Cecilia's—the eyes of saints who died too young. She would not give up! Oh, no, Ceci could not die!

With Eduardo long gone, and Dora so impossible, Ceci was the only hope left. One little girl who would not wake up—ay, the little owlet! Still gripping the rosary, the cross imprinting her palm, Pilar prayed:

Madre de Dios, ruega por nosotros pecadores.
Pray for us sinners, now until the hour of our death.
Ahora y la hora de nuestro muerte.

Twice, Doctor Jensen tried to explain to Pilar Ceci's improved prognosis. His thin, pale features swam before her tired eyes, and she could barely make sense of his jargon. The only things she clearly understood were that Ceci was going to live, and her brain would be fine. The news sang so loud in her ears, she forgot her English just for a moment—her joy so great.

He droned on. "Although she's out of the woods, there are still some concerns. So we want to keep her under observation . . . ."

Unable to concentrate, Pilar's attention drew toward some women's voices in the hall, offering the comfort of her first language—the language of her mother.

"Esté es el cuarto. This room."

The speaker peered into the room, her amber eyes surprisingly youthful in such a weathered face. *"¡Pilar, mi amiga! Hace mucho tiempo—"*

"Rafaela!" Pilar rushed to hug her friend, the tears now flowing. "Yes, it has been a long time! Too long!"

"Ahem!" The doctor pointed his pen at Rafaela. "Is this the grandmother, then?"

Pilar wiped away the tears.

"Ay, no, Doctor, this is Doña Rafaela, our *curandera!"*

"What?" He scanned the two women. "Curla what?"

"Curandera." Carmen entered the room behind Rafaela. "Hello, Dr. Jensen. Just so you know, a *curandera* is a Mexican healer." She winked at Pilar, extending her hand to the doctor. "Carmen Arroyos: I work here. We've met, remember, at Dr. Raymond's? My mother—Rafaela Aguilar."

Ignoring Rafaela, he stared at Carmen. "You're a nurse's aide, right? The nursery?" He let his fingers dangle before him, as if he weren't sure whether to shake her hand or slap it away.

"No, not a nurse's aide," Carmen opened her coat and tapped her badge. "Charge Nurse—Maternity—since Velma retired. Carmen Arroyos." She shook his hand. "At your service."

"No, really? Velma retired?" Dr. Jensen shrugged and turned back to Pilar. "So, if everything's clear to you, Mrs. Martini, I have to see another patient."

"Mrs. *Martinez."* Pilar forced a smile. "The great-aunt. So, doctor, when will Cecilita be well enough to go home?" Pilar forced another smile.

"A few days to a week longer, if she keeps improving, and should she regain consciousness. I expect her to do so very soon. I must say, we've done nicely, considering the gravity of her accident. Now, I really must go. Unless you have another question, Mrs. Martinette?"

"Mrs. *Martinez*."

"Yes, of course, as you say! I'll be back tomorrow."

The doctor sauntered out.

Pilar threw her arms around Rafaela again. "Finally, someone I can trust! How I want to kick that doctor's skinny behind! When Ceci wakes up, I bet he won't even let us give her *gordo lobo* tea."

"In time the *gordo lobo*. Let the doctors do their work; we'll do ours. I'll take a look at her now." Rafaela set down her oversized patent leather purse and slipped the covers from under the mattress, exposing Ceci's feet and shins. Cradling one foot at a time, she surveyed each toe, the arches, and the ankles, stroking with her ropy brown fingers.

"From the feet we can learn almost everything. Almost wet with fever—"

Looking up from Ceci, Carmen shot her mother a glance, her eyes questioning. "*¿Susto?*"

"*Sí*," Rafaela sat on the corner of the bed. "*Susto y triste*," Rafaela sighed. "Fear and sadness!"

Pilar swallowed. "So bad? Will you do a *limpia*?"

"We'll have to do several, to cleanse her and restore her spirit." Rafaela massaged the small of her own back, eyes to the ceiling. "One must be done right away. If only Carmen will help us—she knows her way around this hospital."

"Of course, Mamita," Carmen sighed. "Of course, I'll help, but—"

"You will help." Rafaela lifted her palm; Pilar couldn't tell if it was a blessing or a dismissal. "If not for this child's grandmother, I'd have never gone away to school. I'd have never met your father, either. You're needed this time, *m'ija*. I grow old." She shoved her hands into the pockets of her flowered dress. "I need you!"

"Mamita, I have to work." She looked at her watch. "I'm on the clock."

"I know, I know—you are busy." The *curandera* laid her head on the child's chest, tapping and listening as if having a conversation with Ceci's heart in Morse code. The young candy striper appeared in the doorway, eyes wide with wonder at what she saw Rafaela doing. Pilar beckoned her.

"Come in, come in, child! She won't bite. It's just Doña Rafaela."

"See," Carmen took the girl's arm. "She's listening to the child's lungs. She's a healer: as much as the doctors around here are healers." Carmen chuckled, "More than some of them, I bet. Mamita, tell her—"

"Not much to tell," Rafaela bowed to the girl. "I am a *curandera*, as were my mother and my grandmothers before me. I work in the barrio with my own people, in my own old house. I make medicines from herbs and listen to people's troubles, helping however I can. That's what I was born to do, *mi destino.*"

"Mamita can deliver babies; she taught me how when I was a girl like you. She's a pharmacist, obstetrician, and psychiatrist rolled into one. We Mexicans trust our *curanderas* more than we trust doctors." Carmen guided the candy striper closer to the bed. "See how she checks the patient's vital signs, takes note of the color of her skin, even her odor. She's very careful in her diagnosis."

"She works miracles!" Pilar nodded. "She cured my *empacho.*"

"Not a miracle, that!" Rafaela shook her head. "I haven't cured you. I just taught you what to eat and gave you the *hierbas.*"

"You did better than my doctor."

Rafaela grinned. "That's because my boss gives me such good instruction."

"Really?" The candy striper studied Rafaela's face. "Is he a doctor, your boss?"

"Oh, yes, he is the best of all of them, the Great Physician."

"You mean *God*?"

"God our Father, Jesus himself, and his mother." Rafaela grinned. "They boss me around all day! I have to pay attention, or else!"

The girl laughed.

Rafaela pretended to be hurt. "Do I look like I'm kidding? Don't tell those nurses about my boss." The *curandera's* eyes glinted. "They will get jealous and cast spells on me. Even my own daughter will turn on me like a hungry she-wolf. See how she looks at me? If looks could kill—"

"Rafaela!" Pilar shook her finger at her friend. "Quit teasing the poor girl! I like her. She sat with Ceci when I had to look for Dora. She'll be a nurse someday."

"We need good nurses," Carmen smiled. "What's your name, dear?"

"Betsy."

"You see, Betsy, many people call my mother *abuela,* grandmother—they depend on her. She uses home remedies, time-proven medicines. You know what I mean, like grandmothers do? But more—"

"My grandma gives us cod liver oil," Betsy sighed.

Rafaela winced. "Horrible stuff!"

"Oh, is it bad for you?" The girl lifted her chin. "Please tell me it is!"

"Sorry, I can't, *muchacha.* It only tastes like it will kill you." Rafaela pressed two fingers on Ceci's neck.

Carmen leaned to Betsy, murmuring. "She's taking her pulse, checking how the *energía,* the life energy, is traveling through Ceci's body."

"She really is like a doctor!"

"I guess you could say that." Carmen's gaze rested on her mother. "Except her medicine is older—ancient, actually—thousands of years old."

"So interesting!" Betsy checked her watch. "Oh, rats! I wish—I wish I didn't have to go home so early." She lingered at the foot of Ceci's bed. "Is the little girl getting better? I hope so."

"She will get better. Now you better go home, dear." Carmen escorted Betsy toward the door. "I don't want you getting in trouble on our account."

"Sweet girl!" Pilar watched Betsy leave. "If there were more young people like that, I wouldn't worry so much about the future."

"Ah, so much worry! It doesn't serve you." Rafaela perched on the edge of Ceci's bed, her eyes hooded. She looked, Pilar thought, like a small brown hawk about to dive-bomb a mouse. "Worry—it's what brings on the *empacho.* You can give up worrying if you like, you know."

"How can I?" Pilar threw up her hands. "It's always been my way. I almost believe my worrying prevents bad things from happening. My only power, I really think." She sighed. "Oh I don't know what I think—not now."

Rafaela sat silent, holding Ceci's hand, her expression rapt, as if studying each irregular breath for information. She began to massage the child's palm. Pilar and Carmen stood in the little pool of light from the bedside lamp, watching Ceci settle back into her dreaming under Rafaela's ministrations.

"Well, then!" Carmen broke their reverent silence. "I must go, too." She kissed her mother's cheek. "Tito and Adelita will be wondering. All will be well, Pilar! See you tomorrow?" She kissed Pilar's cheek, then Rafaela's. "Bye!"

"She's a good daughter, Rafaela."

"Ah, I am fortunate—and she has given me two wonderful grandchildren."

"What's her husband like?"

"He left her—some woman down in Guadalajara. Stupid man."

Pondering all that had brought them to this very moment, Pilar took Rafaela's hand. *"Ay, Dios!* Hard for the little ones—and for her."

"It turned out all right. Carmen has made a good life. She is strong."

Ceci whimpered in her sleep.

"What's happening, Rafaela? Is she waking?"

"She prefers to sleep. She's afraid to wake up."

"The drowning has done this?"

"In part." Rafaela closed her eyes. "Something dark is chasing her: the sadness that brought on the drowning. Such sadness—no, I will not break your heart by telling you this."

"Spare nothing. Tell me all of it."

"Sadness chased her—she walked into the water on purpose. She had no choice." The *curandera's* eyes focused somewhere in the air over Pilar's head. "The adults around her—"

She took Pilar's hands. "There are some things I can't tell you, not yet, *mi amiga.*" She searched for the words, her white eyebrows knit. She took Pilar's hand. "There are things that would hurt too much."

"Is it something I did?" Pilar could hardly speak. "Did I hurt her?"

"Quite the opposite—your prayers have done much to save her. The saints are at work on her healing, too. You have been faithful."

"But she is not baptized; she never had a christening." Pilar's eyes flitted to the bed. "She doesn't even know the saints' names. She's in peril of hell."

"Oh, Pilar!" Rafaela smiled slowly, her face suddenly very young under her crown of white braids. "About this and some other things you are ignorant. No, don't be angry; listen. There is much more to faith than you realize. It is not about the Church, nor about the priests. It is about the heart." She continued massaging Ceci's palm. "The little one's heart called to the saints. They will not ignore her."

"How did this all come to be?"

"I wish I knew, *amiga*." Rafaela laid Ceci's hand on top of the sheet. "It would make our work easier." She began to pace the room, taking a little notebook from her skirt pocket, scribbling something with a stub of pencil. "She needs flowers. Why hasn't anyone brought some flowers to cheer the room?"

"Who would bring them?" Pink spread across Pilar's cheeks. "No one knows she's here—none of our friends, not even her father. And I left in such a hurry."

"Then I'll bring some from my garden. *Lavanda:* I have much of it, and *romero.* She will have a big jar of rosemary and lavender flowers—an altar right here by the bed. When she wakes up, the flowers will be there to greet her. Little girls like such things." Rafaela paused, thinking. "We'll do our first *limpia* at dawn, when the veil between the worlds is thin. I'll call the little pieces of her back from the ocean. When she is more whole of spirit, she will heal faster."

Pilar's breath caught; the *curandera* was going to perform the *limpia* in Ceci's room! Would the staff allow this?

"There are some things I need." Rafaela nodded. "I'll go home to gather them. Carmen will ask them to bring you a cot, so you can sleep a little. No, don't shake your head. We'll need you fresh for the *limpia*. I'll come back early tomorrow. Then, we must find the child's father. He's our best hope."

"What about Dora? What will happen with her?"

"Dora?" Rafaela squinted at the big men's Timex that dominated her wrist. "What do you think? It's very late already—"

Pilar shook her head, the knowing sharp in her stomach. "She is not coming back, is she?"

"Yes, *mi amiga,* Dora has gone. Gone to Mexico."

"But she hates the very idea of Mexico! She hates it so much, she pretends she's Spanish, or even Italian, sometimes!"

"Nevertheless, she has gone to Guadalajara."

"Why?"

"It is Dora's to explain, but I can tell you this: it has to do with her past. She has great wounds that are still open. *Ay,* such wounds!"

Pilar stared, her eyes like brown glass. "Wounds?"

"In her soul, *mi amiga.* Because of these wounds, she hurts others." Rafaela sighed. "But our focus must be the child. We must speak of urgent matters—about finding Barry. You must find him and bring him back to us."

"How?" Pilar slumped, overwhelmed. "How can I?"

"Ah!" Rafaela snatched up her gigantic purse and fished around in it, producing a glass votive the size of a jelly jar. "*San Judas de Tadeo!*" She balanced the candle on the palm of her hand. "Patron of Impossible Causes."

Pilar giggled, "You're like a woman on the TV, the way you hold that up, like a commercial." Her hand flew to her mouth. "I should not laugh when the *chiquita*—"

"Go ahead, laugh." Rafaela cleared the bedside table. "With laughter the heart heals." From the depths of her purse, she produced a red cloth that she spread on the table, set the candle in the center, and lit it with a large gold cigarette lighter. "Ask *San Judas de Tadeo* to help you find Barry."

"What about Saint Anthony? He always helps me find my glasses."

"*San Judas de Tadeo* is the one for this cause." Rafaela tapped the side of her forehead. "Not only *lavanda* is needed—I should bring the child some roses."

"Roses?"

"A child's soul likes the rose's fragrance." Rafaela paced some more. "Now, as for finding the father—"

Pilar nodded.

"Carmen will go with you. You will leave after the *limpia*. She's already asked for two days off, and the grandchildren will stay with me."

"I must go?"

"Who else but you?" Rafaela sat down on the edge of Ceci's bed. "Even if I saw this man, I wouldn't know him. Carmen is a good companion. She is very strong, and unlike me, she can drive. So you must go with her."

"But you could find him easily with *curanderismo*!"

"No, finding missing persons is not my specialty. Too bad La Caterina has passed away; that old *bruja* was like that dog with the long face—ah, yes—the bloodhound! La Caterina has gone to her reward. We'll have to depend on you, Carmen, and *San Judas de Tadeo*."

"What will the doctor think if I just get up and leave? Her mother has already disappeared."

"Why do you worry so much what people think? I'll be here to explain."

Pilar imagined how well Rafaela's explanations would go over with Doctor Jensen. "How will I find Barry? I have no idea where he is."

"Do you remember what Dora said about his plans?"

"She didn't know; she didn't seem to care."

"When she left, wasn't there something she told you?" Rafaela closed her eyes. "What did Doralinda say?"

"She was hungry; I told her to go eat. Then she—*ay*, I'm too tired!" Pilar covered her face. "I can't remember anything."

"Yes, you can. Why did you tell her to come right back? Did she say something that made you think she would be long?"

"Maybe, maybe." Pilar wrung her hands, scanning the room, as if the answer was somewhere on the walls. "She was looking for her address book."

"Oh?" Rafaela's eyes glinted. "She was going to call someone? Did she say?"

"No. I said she had better hurry. She had lots to do here."

"A lot to do?" Rafaela circled her head. "Here in this little room?"

"Well, no, not exactly." Pilar leaned forward. "I wanted her to call Barry." Pilar closed her eyes. "Wait! Dora did say something—something—about San Francisco!"

"Good." Rafaela laid her hand on Pilar's knee. "What else?"

"Only that he's in San Francisco." Pilar shook her head sadly. "It's no use. I can't remember anything else."

From the pocket of her dress, Rafaela took a gauze pouch. "Smell this and remember."

Its scent was pungent, but pleasant. "*Romero?*"

"Rosemary, for remembrance. The memory is still in you. The fragrance will draw it out."

As she took in the fragrance, Pilar thought of her mother, how she steeped a tisane of *romero* leaves and flowers for a hair rinse. Lovely, her mother's hair was—sleek as ravens' wings against her long neck.

The rosemary reminded her of barbecues long past: brushing on Eduardo's favorite adobo sauce with a branch of the herb. Also, Eduardo had loved sweet corn, barbecued in its husk, low over the embers. Wait, corn—corn cobs—something about corn cobs! Pilar smiled, a light dawning in her. "I remember, Rafaela. Something about corn—corn cobs!"

Rafaela lifted her brows. "Corn cobs?"

"That's right! The band's name has something to do with corn cobs." Pilar nodded. Must be my son, Eduardo, reminding me from beyond the grave. He did so like corn on the cob."

"A blessing, then." Rafaela grasped her chin, closing her eyes. "Then you'll go to San Francisco and look for this band: The Corn Cobs. It's not such a big city, no?"

"Yes, it is big, but not so big as Los Angeles. Maybe we can find him, if we're lucky."

"Now you are talking like a Montenegro! It's not like he's a tiny needle in a field of hay. He's a big man, somewhere in San Francisco, hiding in the corn cobs!" Rafaela threw her arm around Pilar's plump shoulders. "You will find him, right in the middle of a pile of *mazorcas*, just like one of Don Pascual's piglets!" She sniggered as she took Pilar's hands in hers. "Remember Don Pascual?"

"He was so fat! He made the pigs look skinny!" Pilar laughed. "Ha, I can hardly believe it: *mazorcas,* the corn cobs! Who would name their band such a thing? Only gringos. Crazy gringos!"

Rafaela slapped her knee. The two women leaned onto each other like drunken sailors, gasping and hooting, until Pilar wished she could loosen her corselet. Taking a long breath, Rafaela straightened, at once very serious.

"Tomorrow morning, before you leave to find him, the *limpia* to cleanse her spirit."

"You know what to do, *m'ija.* Can you fend off the nurses?" Rafaela nodded to Carmen, who held Rafaela's medicine basket on her hip. The three women gathered around Ceci's bed. Almost as soon as she said this, the nurse came in to check the IV. Carmen whispered something to her colleague, pointing to Ceci's chart. The nurse handed Carmen the chart and left with a nod.

"The sooner we start, the better," Carmen said as she scanned the pages. "No one's coming in for at least half an hour." She handed Rafaela the basket. "The eggs are in there: two extra, just in case."

"Good." Rafaela set the basket on the floor. "Ready, Pilar?"

"I think so." Pilar fidgeted with her rosary.

"Carmen, close the door, please." The *curandera* stood very still, eyes closed, hands crossed over her heart. "Let us begin."

Pilar and Carmen prayed their rosaries at the foot of the bed, while Rafaela lit the four tall cylindrical glass votive candles depicting San Martin de Porres, Santa Marta, Santa Bárbara, and La Virgen de Guadalupe. Over each she rubbed her fingers together, dropping flecks of copal incense that sputtered and sparkled in the flames.

"*Vengan, por favor, Santa Virgen de Guadalupe, Santa Bárbara, Santa Marta, y San Martin de Porres a rogar con nosotros.* I ask you to come, Holy

Virgin of Guadalupe, Saint Barbara, Saint Martha, and Saint Martin of Porres—come pray with us."

On her makeshift altar Rafaela set a slim vase of roses, rosemary, and lavender and four rough, colored stones, then she placed a glass bowl of water in front of the flowers. She circled the rim of the bowl with her finger, stopping four times at each cardinal direction. From her round basket, she pulled a rattle made of gourd and shook it at the corners of the room. All the while she sang in the language she'd learned from her Apache and Huasteca grandmother, the same song her house-servant mother had sung long ago, when Pilar's mother lay mortally ill. Pilar felt tears welling, remembering how this haunting chant had eased her mother's fear.

Rafaela took an egg, holding it up before her forehead, again invoking in Spanish the Virgin of Guadalupe, Santa Bárbara, Santa Marta, and San Martin of Porres. As she and Carmen continued praying the rosary, Pilar stole glances at Rafaela. She was rolling the egg in the sign of the cross over each one of Ceci's joints.

When the *curandera* had done this three times, she laid the egg in the hollow between the child's neck and chest. She shook her rattle around the perimeter of the room and began again to sing the ancient prayers. When she was done with her song, she prayed, cradling the egg in her hand.

"Saint Martha, Saint Martin of Porres, Our Lady of Guadalupe, and Saint Barbara, please, in the name of God, dear saints, take all that is troubling this child away. Remove the fear and sadness and make room for her soul, in Christ's name, and return what is lost. Amen!"

She lifted the egg to her forehead. "I open my ears and my eyes to what God will show me. *Aquí viene la verdad:* Here comes the truth!" With that, she cracked the egg and opened it in the center of the bowl.

From the door, there was the sound of someone clearing her throat. Pilar and Carmen looked up from their prayers. An older nurse approached them, her pale face very stern.

"What's going on, Carmen? I heard singing. What are all these candles for? These stones?"

As the nurse surveyed the room, Carmen snatched the bowl from Rafaela and covered it with her sweater.

"We are praying for Cecilita," Rafaela smiled. "Would you like to join us?"

The nurse glanced at the little altar Rafaela had made by the bedside. "But you can't light candles in the hospital. Carmen should have told you."

"I thought it would be all right just this once, Sarah. The women are scared for the child. They want to pray."

"I know, but we have rules."

"Just this once—if we're very careful?" Carmen glanced at Rafaela, who stood there grinning as if she'd just won the lottery, offering Carmen no help with convincing the nurse.

"No!" The nurse folded her arms over her flat bosom. "We can't have candles in here. Sorry."

Rafaela sighed. "Please, this is my religion, *señora. Por favor.*" She posed her hands prayerfully. "America is the place of freedom for religion."

Nurse Sarah's face softened slightly. "You can light candles in the chapel, if you want. That's how everyone else prays, as long as there's no service going on in there."

"The candle ought to be near the sick person." Pilar picked one up and showed the nurse. "These are very safe candles. I leave them lit all day at my house."

The nurse blinked, her lips pursed, her forced patience obvious. "I'm sure they are wonderful candles, ma'am, but the hospital has its regulations. Fumes—"

"I'm sorry, Sarah!" Carmen bent over the altar and blew out the candles. "I should have told them to go to the chapel."

"You'll remember next time. And by the way, don't close the door again. We want to keep our eyes on the little girl. It may seem like we're too busy to care, but we do." She gave Rafaela a tart little smile. "Even if we don't have time to pray with you." She turned and marched out.

With a sigh, Carmen pushed back her hair. "I'll hear about this."

"I'm a troublemaker," Rafaela chuckled. "So, let's go to the chapel."

"Will it work?" Pilar picked up her purse. "From a distance?"

"Mamita can heal from a distance—at least she used to."

"I will show you how it's done." Rafaela's grin faded, all business. "Where is this chapel, Carmen?"

"Downstairs, on the first floor; want me to show you, Mami?"

"You must stay here and pray with Cecilita. The nurses can tell us which way. Pilar, come; help me carry these things. Yes, take the candles, but leave the stones like I've put them."

"Mamita!" Carmen took her mother by the arm. "You can't carry a bowl of eggs around the hospital!"

"Why not? I will be careful."

"You just can't. They'll think you're nuts, Mamita."

"Why should I care what they think, *m'ija*?" Rafaela unfolded a handkerchief over the bowl. "There, I will cover up the evidence."

Carmen rolled her eyes. "If any one asks, don't tell them you're doing a *limpia*. Tell them you're going to pray, but please, don't—"

"You want me to lie?"

"No, not lie—just keep quiet. You have to fly low around here, or they'll tell you to stop."

"They won't bother me, daughter, no matter how I fly. At least I don't ride a broom." Rafaela laid one hand on Carmen's back. "Don't worry, I will behave." She nodded to Pilar. "Let's not waste any more time, *amiga*."

The chapel was a deserted room: ten short wooden pews and a plain wooden altar. Before the backlit crucifix, Rafaela genuflected, set up her saint candles, and went about lighting them. Pilar slid into one of the pews, her rosary dangling from her wrist. The *curandera* scooted in sideways next to her, balancing the egg bowl on her lap. She lifted the tissue.

"Here comes the truth."

They both stared into the bowl.

"Do you remember how I read the egg, Pilar? The yolk is Cecilita. The white represents others, how they are affecting her. What do you see, right there?"

"The white is separated from the yolk."

"Yes, right—she is all alone. See how the yolk is leaking out in little yellow threads? Those are the pieces of Ceci's soul. This swirl of white is Doralinda. See the wavy hair? She is leaving her family behind for something new. Our only hope is the father. He stands nearer the yolk—there. See?"

Pilar's eyes welled. "What can we do?"

"Like I told you: find her father. He has a heart that can open."

"What do you mean?"

"Dora's hurt has closed her heart. Something her father did—and that devil, the one who called himself a priest—terrible things have happened to her. Her heart is closed now. She's not ready to help."

"What priest? What about Dora; what will she do?"

"Dora has gone to Mexico, I believe. It is God's will for her. For once, Dora is listening to God. She must go so that the child can heal. Cecilita has been born with *un gran destino*—a great destiny. See that little white angel hovering around the yolk? Her angel tells us to fight for Cecilita. We must fight!"

"Fight? We will use violence?"

"No, wait—fight is not the right English word! In Spanish it's *luchar*—struggle. We must struggle for Cecilita's sake. What she has lost will not return easily. It will be hard work for me, for all of us, even Ceci. I hope I'm still strong enough."

"What do you mean?" Pilar drew her sweater around her. "You are the best *curandera* in Southern California!"

"I am old. Long before the day's work is done I get tired. I had hoped that Carmen would continue my work, combine it with her nursing, but she is so busy. The old ways—" Rafaela stared at her hands, smoothing down a raised vein with her forefinger.

"Yes, I know, I know. The only ones who want to carry on the old ways are the *migrantes* just up from Mexico. Dora doesn't even let me teach Ceci Spanish. It's like they're ashamed of their culture—Dora and Carmen."

"No, no, Carmen is not ashamed. If anything, she is too proud. But we'll talk about this later. Now we must think of Cecilita. I wish you would bring her to my house. There she can heal."

"Now? I don't know if they'll let us."

"We will wait till the doctor says she is well, that her body is safe. We will work on her spirit, you and I. It is love that she needs more than—"

"We: you mean you and me? The both of us?"

Rafaela put her arm around her friend. "Couldn't you stay at my house? Plenty of room for both of you, even Barry, when you find him."

"He has a place in San Pedro, but—"

"He can stay, too. She needs her papa there to heal. And when she's well enough, she can play with my grandchildren. We will give her roots: the stories and ways her mamita didn't. She will grow fat and happy."

"How beautiful!" Pilar leaned back in the pew. "Just like the old days, like the hacienda."

"Yes, except this time, *mi casa es tu casa:* my house is yours. I can repay the kindness your family gave me so long ago."

"No, *amiga,* my mother never wanted payment. Mamá loved you and your family." Childhood memories rushed at Pilar so fast, she was afraid she might burst into tears.

Pilar's father was the *dueño,* master of the Montenegros' Santa Barbara hacienda. Pilar's mother had come to California during the heyday of the ranchos, before there were many Anglos with their factories and freeways. Rafaela was the daughter of Conchita the cook and Pablo the head gardener.

So many Anglos had come to make their fortunes off the Golden State, that the old pioneers—the Spanish-speaking Californios who had owned acres of land and who once enjoyed wealth and privilege—had lost most of it by the time Pilar was a teenager.

Now many Mexicans lived in California, newly arrived and working in menial jobs. The days of entitlement for the hacienda owners were long past. By 1960, Pilar was poorer on her husband's post office pension than Rafaela, who led a very prosperous life healing Los Angelinos in the barrio.

Everything had turned upside down. Pilar would be beholden to Rafaela for this favor. A wave of shame heated her cheeks. The Montenegro family had always helped the mestizos and indios, not the other way around. Pilar shot a desperate look at the altar crucifix. Could she bear to accept Rafaela's gift?

"Pilar, *querida,* it is a blessing to me—a privilege to help a friend." Rafaela's grin softened. "Don't worry, *amiga,* I will never forget who you are, even when the whole world has forgotten. I remember your mother was a great lady: a saint and a leader. You, in every way, are her daughter."

Part Three:
Barry Francis Sullivan
July 1960

B umper-to-bumper on the freeway, his old Mercury close to overheating, Barry had been following Carmen's white paneled station wagon since San Francisco. As they reached Los Angeles, he lost it in a surge of traffic merging to avoid a pileup. Awake only by the grace of a quart of truck-stop coffee, he craned his neck out the window. He couldn't see the source of the delay. Heat rippled off the tarmac into a haze of smog, no station wagon in sight.

The truck ahead of him inched forward, Barry let up on the clutch, and the Mercury stalled. The driver behind honked. Barry struggled with the ignition, stealing a glance into the rear view mirror. The culprit, a black Lincoln Town Car, glinted in the sun, as if mocking the old Mercury's dilapidation.

"God damn it, go around me!" Sweat pooled under Barry's arms and forehead, sticking his shirt to the seat—his need for a shower, enhanced by the stench of last night's whiskey.

The engine was flooded; there was nothing but to wait. As he rolled down the window and signaled everyone to pass, Barry wondered. Did all his youthful promise come to this—a kind of metaphoric symmetry—a beat-up car and a beat-up life?

Was it only six years ago that he'd had been driving this same car down the same freeway, singing for joy? That sparkling June morning in 1954, he drove to Los Angeles General to pick up his wife and newborn daughter. A brand new tune had come to his head as he barreled down the freeway—a tender sprout rooted in the first glimpse of his daughter swaddled in pink flannel. Then the possibilities had seemed limitless; the freeway had led to the sky.

That happy day, he had driven to the hospital, thoughts drifting to planning Ceci's christening, thinking how he'd debut the song, gathering a combo of musician friends. He had thought he might arrange the melody as a jazz fugue, segueing into Amazing Grace and Saint Cecilia's Hymn. He'd imagined Ma, Aunt Pilar, the Connemara cousins, and their friends gathered into the pews in their pride and finery: their church veils and Sunday hats, their suits and ties ranging from Irish drab to Latino bright.

Then there'd be the party: Pilar's tamales and Ma's beef pasties, the centerpieces of a feast like no other. And such music! The staid linoleum floors of some parish hall would rattle with Irish and Mexican dances—reels, jigs, the merengue, and the cha-cha-cha. Uncles tipsy, weeping, and hugging each other, till the disparate Catholic families would be soon forgiving Barry and Dora's elopement. But, it wasn't to be. Not ever.

Soon after, Dora had put her foot down—hard. No christening, no First Communion, no Catechism, and no Confirmation. Nothing to do with the Church. Not ever.

Why, he begged her, why?

When he prodded, Dora clammed up, storming out of their apartment, all the while the newborn Ceci screaming in her bassinet. When Dora had returned, Barry handed her the baby, all repentance. That is when she made him promise: nothing in a church, not ever again, especially not for their daughter. Mystified, but eager to mollify, Barry had agreed to her demand. More hypocrites than saints fouling up the Church these days, he'd told himself.

Six years later, he was still of two minds about it, bouncing from one to the other with nimble agnosticism. Now, with Ma having been so ill, it all swam before him again as he waited in traffic limbo, pondering his predicament.

In the more Catholic of his two minds echoed Ma's teaching. Her Irish fairy lore mingled with his parochial school education. The Sorrowful, Luminous, Glorious Mysteries Ma believed without questioning. Everything Dora scoffed at, Ma more than believed: she lived and breathed, staunch as a Cardinal and yet soft as Irish moss.

In the sterner of Barry's minds his father's cynicism resounded. Barry had inherited more than his dad's love of whiskey. New York City Police Detective Frank Sullivan had always insisted, "Fact, not fancy, my boy, gets the job done."

Detective Sullivan met life square in the face, pulled no punches, letting whiskey cure the wounds it dealt him. He wore his gun in a chest holster even to Mass. After church the neighborhood kids would beg Da to show them his gun. Briefly protesting for modesty's sake, he'd open the gun, take out a bullet, and offer it as a prize to the first who could recite the American Presidents up to Franklin Roosevelt. Da strutted the Brooklyn streets like a B-movie hero, his path always the shortest distance between points.

Five years of familial neglect and grueling overtime advanced him from beat cop to plainclothes detective. Barry kept record of his father's successes with the same taut devotion with which he followed the Yankees. Ma was the source of all the warmth and music.

New York was but a temporary evil to Ma; she dreamed every night of her home in Connemara. Come bedtime, she'd plant herself in her faded brown chair, take Barry onto her lap, and roll out glorious yarns: of the *Tuatha Dé Danann,* Land of the Young, and the deeds of the bold Fenians. She'd enchant him with tales of half-human silkies rising from the Western Sea.

During the telling, her green eyes washed with mist, she assured Barry that her tale was, after all, "Truer than true, my boy, 'tis." Because Ma so believed in this world between worlds, Barry had believed in it, too—longer than he'd ever admit to any of his buddies, to Dora, to anyone.

Not to say that Ma wasn't an orthodox Catholic. While tucking the blankets around Barry, she'd croon a verse of Schubert's *Ave Maria* and, finally, kneel to pray an Our Father and a Hail Mary with him. Prayers and stories were all one cloth; Barry hardly differentiated one thread of thistledown from another. The magic of Ma's words, the lilt of her accent, shed stardust over everything.

Their young lives were so charmed that little Barry was sure there wasn't a kid in all of Brooklyn that didn't wish he were a Sullivan. So it remained for them until one Spring-cleaning day when Barry was but seven, and the Sullivan magic ended with a bucket of mop water.

Weary from scouring the apartment to prepare for the coming baby, Ma had plopped on the couch to rest her swollen ankles. "My legs are aching. Frankie, will you throw out the dirty mop water for me?"

His ear to the radio, Da glimpsed Katy's belly like a bowling ball under her white apron. With a martyr's sigh he switched off the ballgame, swooped up the mop bucket, and chucked the water onto a patch of weeds outside the back door, then back to his game he went.

"Jesus, Mary, and Joseph! You've thrown out the bucket without watching for *sidhe*! You should have called out to warn them, Frankie." Ma heaved herself up from the davenport, an anger in her eyes that Barry had never seen.

"*Sidhe!* Katy, darling, you've never seen a fairy in your life—nary a one!" Frank Sullivan teased, chucking her chin. "Neither have I, no matter how much whiskey I've downed."

"Even if you haven't seen them, you're supposed to look out for them. What if—oh, what if they take our baby?" Ma rubbed her belly, her eyes darkening with tears.

"Aw, Katy," Frank sighed. "You don't still hold with that stuff? It's the twentieth century; we're in America now. I'm sure we left the fairies behind us. The baby will be fine. Just you wait and see."

"You just don't care!" With the powerful dignity that only a pregnant woman can wield, Ma rose from the couch. She stomped to the bedroom, snatched her rosary off the bedpost, and slammed the door behind her.

Her murmured prayers seeped through the wall. Frank decanted the Old Bushmills to drown them out: a whole tumblerful, neat.

Through the afternoon, Barry kept eyeing that patch of weeds behind the house. Not a fairy in sight; Ma must be driving them away with her Hail Marys. Those were the days of children being seen and not heard. Barry kept his thoughts to himself, while Da slammed around their apartment—the radio blaring a Yankee's game no longer worth anyone's bother.

The more Ma prayed, the more whiskey Da downed, and the quieter Barry remained, shuffling his baseball cards like a fortuneteller at a fair. For supper Frank served up chipped beef on burnt toast, a cloud of smoke rising from the toaster, hovering over the kitchen table like a gray ghost of the argument. Barry would never forget that awful dinner or the tragedy that came after.

This episode might have been an anecdote that Barry could have shared with friends, a story to tell with a put-on Irish brogue and a wink. It might have been a laugh. It might have been so, but it was not. Less than a week later his poor baby sister arrived stillborn, after a difficult labor that nearly killed his mother. This event defined Barry's adolescence.

Everything changed thereafter; the heat of love between Ma and Da dwindled. Katy poured herself into her only child, taking in mending and ironing to fund his tuition at the Jesuit school and, later, Columbia University. Da poured himself larger and larger tumblers of whiskey.

The more Frank drank, the more the shine drained out of him, his swagger slowing to a shuffle, his dazzling reputation fading to glimmers of neighborly pity. Slaving away to expel her grief, Ma averted her eyes, staring down onto her ironing board as if it were the Oracle of Delphi.

No longer having truck with fairies, Barry begged his parents to rent a piano. Music became the one refuge mother and son shared. He'd learned all the old songs and copied everything new on the radio. Once in a great while, spurred on by the music, Ma still began a tale, then stopped herself and tousled his hair.

"Sure, and I cannot remember the rest. I've work to do, and you should be studying now, shouldn't you? Put your heart in it, boyo, and you'll get somewhere."

"Get somewhere? Not today!" Brushing a fleck of soot from his eye, Barry shook his attention back to the freeway chaos. The closer he got to Los Angeles, the more urgent his longing to get to Ceci. Carmen's car was nowhere in sight. A spasm of grief rose from his belly, until finally he let himself weep. If he lost the little Bean, he didn't know what he'd do. Worries had been tumbling on him like loose bricks, since Pilar burst into the Mark Hopkins Ballroom waving her fat arms, a messenger of doom in lace-up orthopedic shoes.

"Where's Barry Sullivan? It's urgent!" A titter had risen from the posh people gathered at candlelit tables. "Sorry!" Pilar's cheeks reddened as she spoke to the crowd. "It's an emergency."

"The band will take a little break." Schwann had dropped his baton and, thank God, he'd laughed. "What can I do for you, Ma'am?" he'd said into the mike, smirking at the Frisco sophisticates watching this drama. "George Schwann, at your service."

"Must speak to Barry Sullivan!" Pilar's chest had heaved with exertion. "His daughter's in the hospital."

Barry's embarrassment had turned to horror; everything blurred except Pilar's face. Slow motion: George in his white tie, his coattails swinging out behind him. "Take a break, long as you need, Sullivan. We'll play around you next set. No problem."

So Barry had waded through the air, as if it were mud, and fell into Pilar's embrace. She squeezed his hand and told him everything she knew about the accident and Dora's disappearance. "We're all Ceci has right now. You have to come home!"

Barry felt he'd never surface from the sea that had deluged him.

Amid the backstage clamor, Pilar had collapsed into a folding chair. She explained what she and Rafaela hoped for Ceci. Eyes grave and accusing, a younger woman who'd come with Pilar stood against the wall with her arms folded, her discomfort palpable. Finally, Pilar introduced her simply as "Carmen," and the woman nodded to him, still unsmiling. Why she had come was a mystery to Barry—one he had no interest in uncovering. He'd thanked them, but he didn't feel grateful. It had weighed on him like an anvil: shameful resentment of them for bringing the bad news, and then guilt about the resentment. He might as well kiss the Frisco gig good-bye. Sure enough, Schwann offered little sympathy beyond a brief, sad nod. Then he'd fired him. "God, Sullivan, you know I hate to do it, but I've no choice. The show must go on!"

First gig in a year and a half—he'd sat behind that godawful swan-shaped music stand, savoring the polite applause of ladies and gentlemen of means. First chair, playing schmaltzy show tunes for debutante balls and Bar Mitzvahs, but the band was okay. Schwann's trite arrangements left him cold, but the guys were good musicians. Nobody to jam with, but it was music. What a relief: to get a check at the end of every week—for playing music! And now—it was all over!

Nothing but Ceci mattered now, of course. There were realities beyond Ceci's recovery to face. How would he earn a living? How would he pay the hospital bill? He wondered how he'd care for a little girl and work, even a day job. If only Dora had stayed and played her part.

"God damn it, Dora, you're the *mother!*"

Someday she would be sorry for shirking everything. She'd come crawling back, her tail between those pretty legs. She'd last about five minutes without a man to take care of her. The thought pealed like a church bell—without a man! Barry slapped his forehead. That was it! Another man—that had to be it. Pilar hadn't said it, but he knew. Dora had left him—for a man. He gritted his teeth. He might as well face the music, he told himself as he turned the key another time, pumping the gas pedal.

The Merc started, humming like a top. The traffic knot slowly eased until Barry could shift into drive and make his way. Along the way to the exit ramp, he swatted at self-pity. *Quit feeling sorry for yourself, Sullivan!*

The kid had the worst rap; it was up to him to lift them both out of this bad luck. He wasn't sure he could, not without someone, something—he'd used up all he could muster and didn't know how to face what lay ahead.

At least he knew the way to Los Angeles General. Turning into the visitors' lot, he parked under a tree, swept back his sweaty hair, and rummaged his coat pocket for his tie, drawing it around his neck like a noose. He wondered who'd even care if he wore it? Pilar would, probably.

And there she was; Pilar's stout frame nearly filled the rearview mirror, revealing only a flash of Carmen several paces behind. "Time to face the music." He groaned and opened the car door. "Time to face the music—and it ain't jazz, either!"

"Bye, Barry!" Carmen waved. "Good luck with the doctors. I'll check in after my shift."

"Great, Carmen. Thanks for everything!" Barry hoped it would be longer till he had to face her again. Her disapproval got to him—what a holier-than-thou attitude! She might be good-looking if she ever really smiled. And then again, she might turn into a bitter old maid who cried over lost kittens, yet voted to send men to the electric chair.

Pilar tugged his sleeve. "The doctor won't stand around waiting for us, Barry." He trailed behind her, wishing he'd thought of bringing Ceci a gift. He dug a few coins out of his pocket, examining them in his open palm. A newly minted quarter might do the trick. Then again—

"Pay attention, Barry! This way!" Pilar grabbed his sleeve, dragging him like a miscreant schoolboy. At the threshold of the hospital room, Barry gripped the doorjamb, shocked by the sight of his daughter. Ceci lay awake, her eyes sunken and feverish. He stepped into the room, wiping his palms on his pants legs. "Bean!"

Ceci reached out to him, her eyes watering, then began to cough.

He lifted her from the bed; she weighed only a slight bit more than his clarinet. "Oh, sweetheart, you're so skinny!" He kissed her. "I came as soon as—"

Pilar cleared her throat. "Dr. Jensen, this is Barry Sullivan, Cecilia's father."

"Thanks for all your work, sir." Barry reached for the doctor's hand.

Dr. Jensen merely nodded. "That's our job, Mr. Sullivan. Now, if you please," he motioned to the door. "We have some paperwork your wife neglected to fill out."

Your wife! Barry winced.

"We'll need you to sign these before we can release your daughter."

"Won't she be going home soon? I understood that she'd—"

"Oh, yes, Mr. Sullivan, your daughter is doing much better, better than we could have expected."

At this, Pilar beamed at another old Mexican woman—someone Barry didn't recognize. He guessed, from the conversations they'd had, she must be Carmen's mother, the healer. He glanced back at the doctor. "When does Ceci get to go home?"

"Tomorrow morning." Dr. Jensen drew closer to Barry, his voice lowered. "Look, I need to talk to you. Right now. Let's go to my office."

Ceci coughed, and Barry turned to her. "But I just got here."

"It will only take a moment." The doctor patted Ceci's head. "I need to speak to your father—privately."

Behind his rich mahogany desk, enthroned in a posh leather chair, Doctor Jensen steepled his fingers. He scrutinized Barry—just like Father Dominic, the bane of Barry's high school career. Jensen wore the same taut, disgusted smile, the same beetled brow as the severe Jesuit. He spaced his phrases with the same immaculately pregnant pauses.

Barry was a Columbia graduate—a man of the world. Dr. Jensen reduced him to a recalcitrant pupil again! He wondered why the visitor's chair was always the least comfortable in these men's offices. Just as he would've done at sixteen, he bit at a hangnail, the sting of it oddly satisfying.

"Mr. Sullivan—"

It didn't pay, Barry remembered, to be impatient with the affected pauses. Instead, one must devote extra attention to conversations with the men in power.

As if about to dive off a bridge, the doctor breathed in and leaned over his desk. "First off—I want you to know—your daughter—is going to be—fine. No permanent damage—not that we can—clearly detect." Again, that chilly smile.

Before Barry could express relief, the doctor's smile melted to a horizontal line. "It's not her condition—that's not why—I arranged this meeting. Let me get right to the point."

Barry nodded his encouragement.

"We've had quite a sideshow from your family, Mr. Sullivan. Disruptive—to say the least—that woman—"

"Oh, my wife!" Barry squirmed, his back sweaty against the wooden chair. "She was very upset, I gather."

"Of course, she was—we're accustomed to such reactions. No, it's the old—er—medicine woman; she has given us quite a turn."

"Aunt Pilar?"

"No, the woman she brought in—the so-called—healer."

"Sorry, I don't know what you're talking about, Doc."

"The skinny old woman—don't you know her?"

"I only just got here. I saw an old lady whom I gather is Pilar's friend, but we haven't been introduced."

"This *friend*—she's supposed to have some sort of—ahem—miraculous powers." Dr. Jensen let that seep in, an eyebrow raised. "That's what your aunt told me."

The air around Barry grew yet cooler.

"It's pitiful to watch. She's been praying over the child. With candles! We could smell them all the way down the hall."

"Candles!" Barry laughed his relief. "Oh, they're all very devout, old school Catholics. It probably was some incense she got from a priest. Incense and candles are *de rigueur*. They're just praying."

"Look, Mr. Sullivan—you don't know the whole story. She prayed gibberish—and burned some kind of grasses or herbs—until the nurse had to come in and open the window. The woman was singing—at the top of her lungs—so loud she couldn't hear the nurse telling her to stop."

"Did it scare Ceci?"

"That's the odd thing—your daughter seems to like her—immensely—asks for her. The old woman is peaceful enough—when she's not sending—er—smoke signals. Despite their concerns—the nurses said she was most polite. At times—even helpful."

"Well, then, I can't see the problem—"

"You have to understand. This is an uneducated Mexican—you know what I mean—backward people. Good intentions—but—dangerous ideas.

The old kook told me Ceci's soul was lost—somewhere at sea—due to the drowning. She believes she can go get it. I guess she'll—dive for it!" He laughed mirthlessly. "Can you even imagine— what else she believes? The herbs alone—"

Barry sighed. So that was it? Dora had talked at length about the bad-tasting herbal remedies she had to swallow as a child, the little amulets against the Evil Eye her mother made her wear to school. Ashamed to be so different, Dora had hidden them under her shirt, so the Anglo girls wouldn't see. Barry maintained a fond tolerance for harmless relics of the old days, like Ma's belief in fairies. Still, it wouldn't do to scoff at the doctor. What if the woman gave his Ceci something toxic?

"Did this woman harm Ceci?"

"Well," Doctor Jensen sighed like a steam train entering a station, and Barry stiffened on the edge of the uncomfortable chair. "I hope not. It doesn't seem so. After we cleared her lungs—Cecilia woke up disturbed—disoriented. When she didn't see her mother—she called out for you. Oddly, the one person—who could comfort the child was that—crazy old hag! I have to give her that. Good psychology. But your aunt—she reads more into it." The doctor rested his hands on the desk blotter, palms down. He looked at them, speaking without raising his eyes. "Your aunt gives that woman all the credit for saving your child."

"That's unfair to you—and the nurses."

"Mrs.—er—Martinelli never had much faith in us, I'm afraid. It took—so long to bring Ceci round—it was touch and go for a few hours. We all worried. Then the old woman arrived—with her candles and mumbo jumbo—and Cecilia began to rally. Your aunt is sure that—that woman healed your daughter. You and I know better—of course. Coincidence—"

"I'm sorry you're not getting any credit, sir. But I can't see any real harm in Pilar's beliefs. Just like carrying a rabbit's foot in your pocket. A little luck never hurt."

"Seriously, Mr. Sullivan!" Dr. Jensen clicked his pen with his thumb, his eyebrows lowered as he glared at Barry. "I've seen children come into our Emergency room poisoned from the concoctions these quacks cook up. I hope if Ceci needs medical attention, you'll bring her into her regular doctor, and not rely on these, these so-called healers. They make our work harder in the long run."

Barry smiled. The doctor could speak quite rapidly when his dander was up.

"Listen, Doc, I'm an educated man. I'd never depend on some quack. If Ceci needs medicine, she'll always see a doctor just like she should. Promise!" He hoped he could afford to keep his promise. "I'm really grateful for all you've done for Ceci. You're a hero. I mean it!"

"I am relieved to hear that, Mr. Sullivan. With the progress we've been seeing, I should be able to release Cecilia tomorrow. Now, for the paperwork." The doctor tapped his pen on a pile of papers. "Who's your regular physician?"

"Regular physician?" Barry squeezed his hands together, ignoring an itch on the back of his ear.

"If you'd just tell me where I can send a copy of Cecilia's records. Your doctor's name and—"

"That's just it, doc; we don't have one."

"No family doctor—is that wise, Mr. Sullivan?"

"Times have been tough. We've had to let some things slide."

"I see." Dr. Jensen again forced a smile. "We had better check—just a few things. When they brought Ceci in, Mrs. Sullivan couldn't recall whether the child's immunizations were up to date. Did Ceci receive her boosters?"

Who were *they*, Barry wondered: the ambulance corps—or Dora and the mysterious boyfriend, of which Pilar had hinted? Swallowing his confusion, Barry nodded. "Of course, of course, Ceci has had her shots. To get into school—"

"Are you sure?" The doctor raised an eyebrow. "We can update her immunizations—before we release her, if you like."

Barry calculated the expense. How much was a hospital stay per day? If they'd brought Ceci in an ambulance—those things cost a fortune. He surveyed the doctor's handsome desk set: the gold and marble holder, the leather-bound blotter, the matching leather-framed photo of his well-dressed wife and a handsome, athletic-looking son in a college sweater. If only music paid as well as medicine!

Barry's low chair put his eyes a half-foot beneath the doctor's; he strained to meet the questioning gaze. "Do we have to take care of that today? We'll get her squared away soon as we can." He smiled, he hoped convincingly. "There's a lot on my plate, doctor. I gave up my job to come down here. I'm nearly broke."

"I see." The doctor blinked, as if considering, and then he set his pen down with a flourish. He shoved the papers forward. "Well, then! Just leave the completed forms at the nurses' station." He straightened his tie and stood, smoothing the front of his white coat. "One more thing, Mr. Sullivan—Ceci needs a follow-up appointment. I'll see her—in my clinic—Thursday. You can call my office to schedule. After that—I advise you to find a pediatrician." When Barry didn't answer, the doctor lowered his black-rimmed glasses and winked. "Or, if you prefer—call on the services of your aunt's friend—the kindly witch doctor. Maybe she'll vaccinate your daughter with her knitting needle!" He stood. "Now, if you'll please excuse me, Mr. Sullivan, I have an important meeting." The doctor was out the door before Barry could say good-bye.

"Important meeting—my ass!" Trudging back to the nurses' station with a fistful of forms, Barry pledged he'd rot in hell before he'd take Ceci anywhere near Jensen's clinic: Thursday or doomsday. Condescending bastard! He might be a doctor, but what a jackass! The old woman might be a quack, but Pilar seemed to love her—Ceci, too. He'd have to find a doctor he could trust in the same way.

After turning in the forms, he rushed back to the room to find Ceci asleep. How tiny she was! Her head seemed to disappear into the pillow. And so wan—her cheeks, once tawny, ashen under her red-brown crescent of eyelashes.

"Look how much better Cecilita is doing!" Pilar approached him, her eyes soft with joy. "I have to introduce you to my friend, Rafaela. She brought our Cecilita back from the dead. A miracle!"

Perched like a bird on Ceci's bed, Rafaela tilted her head, crowned with thick white braids. She was fingering a fat string of pearls circling her scrawny neck. Except for her coppery dark complexion, she might be one of the old dears in Ma's altar guild. She didn't look like a witch doctor. "It was not I, but God who gave her back to us. I am just a servant."

"It's good to meet you, Mrs. Aguilar."

"The same here! But, call me Rafaela, please!" She blinked her gold-flecked eyes and took his hands between hers. "I've something important to ask."

"Why don't we discuss it over coffee at the cafeteria?"

"Another time, *mi amigo*. I must go to another appointment. All I ask is this, please. After the doctors release her, let me take Cecilita to my house for a few days. Then she can heal completely."

"I'm going to take her home—to my house." Barry's scalp tingled, the doctor's warning echoing. "The doctor said she's well. She only needs rest."

"So the doctor said." Rafaela grinned, catlike; it seemed Barry had set a dish of cream before her. She let go of his hands, still staring at him with her feline gaze. "You will take her home. Then what will you do?"

"Uh, I'll take her home and—and—I'll try to get Dora to come back. I'll go back on tour, earn some money. Pay the hospital bills—"

"Ah, yes!" Rafaela began to gather her candles into a grocery bag, wrapping each one in a sheath of newspaper. "This band, the Corn Cobs, they will take you back?"

"Possibly." Barry smiled in spite of himself. "If I can get back to Frisco by Friday, I think they might."

"A problem with your plan, *amigo*—you will have to find someone to take care of Cecilita." She patted his arm. "Dora cannot help you." She turned to take the roses from the altar. "She has gone to Mexico, maybe for good."

Barry eyes welled, "But—"

"It is hard to hear, I know, but it gets worse. I believe she will divorce you there." Rafaela studied Barry a moment. "But Dora is the least of your worries. Think of Cecilita! She's lost too much weight, is eating very poorly. She will not step into water, even a bathtub. She needs more healing than this hospital has given. The nurses are beside themselves trying to keep her in her bed at night. She wakes up—sleepwalks. She is terrified of everything." Rafaela retrieved her purse from the bedside. She embraced Pilar and patted Barry's arm at the door. "I must go, *amiga*. I have spent two days away from my home. I have work to do. Carmen will tell me how the child is doing."

"Rafaela, thank you! Shouldn't I give you something for all your trouble—days away from home, and all those candles?" Barry thrust out a twenty-dollar bill. "I don't know if this is enough."

"No, thank you." Rafaela folded the twenty back into his fingers. "I offer my work as an exchange for a debt long owed to Pilar's mother. Now, I must be going."

"Wait!" Pilar took her friend's arm, pressing her toward Barry. "Please, Barry, listen to what Rafaela has to offer, for Cecilita's sake. The child's soul is in danger."

"You can't expect me to believe that—it's superstition." Barry winced at the hurt these words brought to Pilar's eyes. "I'm sorry. Your ways are—so new to me. I don't understand them."

"Not new, Barry—old. Older than all of us put together," Pilar sighed. "Old!"

Silence crackled between the three adults. Ceci slept, unheeding, her curls spread on the pillow like tongues of flame. Rafaela stroked the child's cheek. "When she wakes, she will need a cleansing. Please, bring Cecilita to my house, Barry. You can stay with me. I have room for everyone. Let me show you how we cure *susto y tristeza* in the barrio, not with tubes and machines, but with herbs, prayer, and kindness."

"Please, Rafaela—I don't understand. *Susto?*"

Rafaela smiled, as if heartened by his question. "*Susto* is fright, the fright of the ocean and other evils. *Tristeza*, that's sadness. Because she has been abandoned, Cecilita has much *tristeza*. So, good that you're here. She can see you care," she sighed, patting his arm. "You need some herbs and kindness, too. You're hurting, here." For a brief moment, Rafaela pressed the tips of her fingers on Barry's heart. Warmth emanated from her elderly fingers, and a little crackle of electricity.

Barry touched his chest after she removed her hand. The warmth lingered.

"I'm okay, Rafaela. A lot on my mind, is all. My mother had a heart attack last month. Damn it! Should've called Ma hours ago."

Grief flashed through him like lightning, and with it came tears. Rafaela dug a fresh package of tissues from her purse. Barry took it silently, pulling out one after another. He steadied himself, his fingers pressed on his brow. "It's been a hell of a day. Maybe I should wait before I call."

"No, call her now!" Pilar pressed a dime into Barry's hand. "She is stronger than you think, and so are you, *m'ijo.*"

As he trudged down the hall to the pay phone, Barry heard the two old women chattering their goodbyes. At the pay phone, he squinted at the coin slot like a far-off target, the dime poised between his fingers. At his periphery, something blurred white, and he glimpsed Carmen in her uniform and cap.

"Hey, Carmen!"

She smiled, a rosy blush coloring her high cheekbones. How had he missed that she was so striking? Too bad she was such a killjoy.

"Hi! You met my Mama, yes? She was supposed to meet me downstairs."

"Yeah, I guess they can't stop gabbing. Old hens!"

"They share so many memories." The warmth in her smile surprised him.

"Yeah, they must. I have good news: Ceci's completely awake and aware. She looks a fright, but the doc says she's going to be all right."

"Montenegro blood—stronger than they thought."

"Everybody is, according to Pilar."

Carmen raised one brow. "Oh?"

"They want me to call my ma, to tell her everything."

She nodded, her eyes very soft. "Will you?"

"Ma has a weak heart," Barry sighed. "God, she'll be broken up about it all. She thought Dora and I could make it work. I'm not the man Ma thinks I am. I mess everything up. Probably even this call."

"You'll do fine. I've got to—" Carmen gestured toward Ceci's room. "Well, tell me how it goes—with your phone call, I mean." She blushed again. "That is, if you decide to let Ceci come to Mamita's house, I hope." She shifted her gaze every time she met his eyes. "So, uh, I'd better go." Her hand slightly brushed his. "Bye!"

As she walked away, Barry wondered what secrets hid in the depths of Carmen's stillness. She had an athletic gait, nowhere as sexy as Dora's, but cute. Still waters run deep, Ma always said.

There was something refreshing about Carmen, her steady gaze like the pool at Bethesda: troubling but curative. Maybe she approved of him after all. He smiled to himself and dropped his dime into the slot. "Hey, Ma, it's Barry. Listen, something's come up. It's Ceci."

"Oh?" He could picture her worried face.

"She's going to be okay, but there was a bad accident."

He heard Ma's sharp intake of breath. "Oh, no!"

"I'm calling from the hospital—L.A. General. Ceci's been here a few days. A rough go at first, but she's all right."

"What happened?"

"They went to the beach and Ceci almost drowned. No, I don't know. I'm hazy on the details. Dora was there, not me."

"So, what did she say?"

"Like I said: the details aren't fleshed out yet. Dora, she—"

"Put Dora on, then; I want to talk to her."

Barry swallowed. "I can't. Dora left."

"Well, tell her to call me when she gets back, please."

"I don't know when she'll be back, Ma. She's really *gone*."

"Gone?" A long silence, then, "Where?"

He lowered his voice to almost a whisper. "She left me."

"Where? Why? I can't hear you, son. Speak up. Why has she gone?"

"She left me! I don't know why, Ma. You remember her Aunt Pilar, don't you?"

"Good woman she is, and devout."

"She's here. Dora left two days ago; she left Pilar in charge. They think Dora might be in Mexico."

"They? *They* think this?"

"Pilar and this—this friend of hers, Rafaela, say Dora's there. In Mexico. Now, Ma, don't cry. I know, I know—but right now Rafaela says I have to—"

"Who's this Raphael? How does he know so much about everybody?"

"Pilar's friend—Rafaela—she has what you call the second sight, Ma. Pilar swears by her."

"Whomever Pilar trusts, I would trust, Barry. She's a rock."

"She's been a regular Gibraltar, all right. But now Ceci's almost well. Doc says she can go home any day now."

"Jesus, Mary, and Joseph, what home? How will you manage without Dora? Oh, I wish I were up to—"

"No, you mustn't fret yourself. I'll find help. But Pilar, she wants this friend of hers, Rafaela, to help us. Rafaela's offered to take Ceci to her house to—er—work on her. She's a healer. She's really kind, but I don't know. I just don't know."

"What does Pilar think you should do?"

"She's gung-ho, but then she would be. To tell you the truth, Ma, I don't know. All these herbs and potions—Dora hated them."

"If it weren't for herbs and potions, the Irish would've been wiped out long ago."

"Rafaela told Pilar that Ceci left some of her soul in the ocean. It's something to do with sadness, and being scared. Can you believe that? Weird."

Another silence.

"Ma? Aren't you shocked? I mean—"

Ma cleared her throat. "What led them to think these things?"

"Things Ceci does, lots of things. She's afraid of water. Apparently, Pilar and Rafaela even have to hold her down so the nurses can give her a sponge bath. She isn't eating. Her color just doesn't look right to them. They say Ceci's not all there. Since the accident something is missing—in her eyes, they say."

"What do you notice, Barry?"

"I don't know. She's thin and pale. Coughs a lot. Sad eyes, like a refugee child." Not for the first time today he tried to swallow the lump in his throat. "But you can't believe that Ceci has lost part of her soul, can you, Ma?"

"I can believe, son. Back in Connemara we had wise women, blessed with the second sight. We listened to 'em, if we knew what was good for us. Just like your da you are—too quick to disbelieve what you don't understand."

"Aw, Ma! If you could've heard what they said!"

"I've met many a fool in my life, but Pilar has the sense God gave her. Listen to her, son."

"I didn't say I wasn't listening, Ma. I just can't be—"

"What would Dora think of the healer, Barry?"

"Ma, I can't talk about Dora now. It's too much," he sighed. "Please, whatever happens, pray for us. All of us—"

"Of course I will!" Ma's voice quavered, the way Barry knew it did when she was tearing up. "I'll pray. You get back to our Cecilia. Sure, and call me, one way or the other, when you decide."

"Yeah, I'll call. Bye, Ma." He dropped the phone in the cradle, just glimpsing Carmen and Rafaela strolling up the hall. Rafaela kept up a brisk gait for a woman her age.

Barry jogged to catch up with them.

Rafaela grinned. "Hello, *amigo!*"

"Look, I hope you're not sore I didn't snap up your kind invitation. I'm under a lot of pressure."

"Yes, you are!" Rafaela nodded.

"I try to be, you know, scientific, to give everything the benefit—to be—" He faded into a mumble.

"Modern." Rafaela nodded. "What does your mama say to you? Is she all right?"

"As good as can be expected. She's shocked at what happened. Of course, she wishes she could—come be with Ceci."

"Your mama is trying to regain her strength."

"Yeah. Like I told you—her heart—"

"She wants to be strong, so you can take her home, to her homeland, to Ireland."

Suddenly chilled, Barry lifted his eyes to check if he stood under the air conditioning vent. "No," he lied, just to test her, "she hates Ireland."

"But it is a place in Ireland she wants to visit—Con-ne-mara?" Pronouncing the syllables with care, Rafaela closed her eyes. "To visit the place of a saint there, that is her wish, isn't it?"

Again, the cold assaulted Barry's neck. "You think, eh?"

"Saint Brigid—is it the place where her ancestors' bones remain?"

Barry shivered, forcing his careless smile. "I couldn't say exactly."

Carmen tugged Rafaela's arm. "Come on, Mami! The kids are waiting for me."

"Ah, yes!" Rafaela extended her hand. "Glad to have met you. May all go well!"

Barry took her hand, his hand numb and cold in the warmth of hers. "Likewise." He watched them disappear into the elevator, his cheeks now hot, and his heart pounding against his chest.

☆   ☆   ☆   ☆

That evening, Barry passed the time at Ceci's bedside, balancing the checkbook. Dora had withdrawn their savings, and the checking balance was minimal. He hoped that the paycheck from his gig with Schwann would arrive soon, or there would be no way to pay the rent. He might have to move their stuff into storage, but that would also require money. Maybe Ma had some space where he could stash the essentials. Everything else he'd just have to leave to the landlord's disposal.

"Daddy?"

"Eat your chicken, Ceci; then we can talk."

She pushed at the gluey mass with her fork. "Are we going to Rafaela's house?"

"You really want to go there?" Barry slipped the checkbook into his shirt pocket. "What's so special about her house?"

Her voice was just a rasp. "Rafaela has chickens and a turtle; she told me."

"Don't you want to go home to our house? Or to Grandma's?"

Ceci's eyes widened; it seemed she was torn deciding. It hurt him that she would have such reservations. "Okay," she said very quietly. "Okay." Her eyes flickered with wetness. She swallowed and then coughed. "Mama has to know where to find us when she comes home."

Barry brushed a few curls from Ceci's brow. "Your mama—"

"Rafaela told me where Mama went."

"Rafaela!" He didn't know whether to be angry or relieved. "She did?"

"Yeah, Mama went to Mexico. She said Mama is like a deer: beautiful and scared of things that hurt her."

"How did that feel—to hear that Mama is gone?"

"Sad, kinda. Are you sad, Daddy? Because of Mama—"

"I'm okay. Right now, I only care about you getting strong." He chucked her chin. "So, eat your dinner." He scooped some of the creamed chicken up onto the fork and held it to her mouth.

Ceci shook her head.

"Don't you want to get some meat on your bones, Bean?"

"I'm not hungry." Her eyes swept the room, coming back to Barry's face with a look of tenderness that reminded him of Ma. "Maybe she ran away 'cause she's scared."

Barry stared at Ceci, the muscles of his throat tensing.

"Mama told me; when bad things happen to me she's scared."

"Did she tell you why?"

"No," Ceci sighed. "I don't know, 'cept I—I get into trouble. I'm bad."

"Who says?" Barry took her hand in his. "Who says you're bad?"

"Mama does, sometimes." Her chin quivered, her mouth crumpled, and a tear slid down her cheek.

Barry felt rage he knew had to control. *Don't mind what she says, Ceci; your mother is a snob, and a slut—and not even in that order,* he wanted to tell her. He stopped himself, remembering how he had idolized Da. Even when the old man staggered home the worse for the whiskey, shouting obscenities, Barry would've punched out anyone who called Da a drunk. Ceci loved her mama. He measured his words.

"Mama had a terrible time as a child, Ceci. It did something to her. I think sometimes she's not—er—not right in the head. She's the one who's bad, baby. Not you. Maybe it's because she had tough knocks, and she's scared. But damn it, I can't let you believe you're bad. You're—"

"I know!" Ceci's face lit with an idea. "Maybe after Mama takes this trip, she'll be happy." Ceci rubbed at her eyes with her fists. "Like Snow White when she lived with the seven dwarfs."

Barry nodded. "Maybe."

She pushed her plate to the far end of the tray. "Can't eat this stuff—too thick. Rafaela gives me soup. She feeds it to me with a spoon. She's really funny."

"Funny ha-ha or funny weird?"

"Funny! She can crow just like a rooster. She sings this song about chickens." Her eyes lost some sadness, speaking of Rafaela. "Where is Tía?"

"Pilar went down to the cafeteria. Can't I feed you, like Rafaela does?" He spooned up a glob of creamed chicken.

"I'm too sleepy." She slid under the covers, closing her eyes.

It took her only moments to fall asleep. Barry let the checkbook slip off his lap and watched her, so stunned by the thought that dawned on him that he spoke it aloud.

"That old Rafaela just might know what she's doing."

"*¡Ay dios mio!*" Pilar puffed over to the hospital bed. "I ate the most terrible thing. I think it was supposed to be chicken. I hope my *empacho* doesn't act up." She eyed Ceci's tray. "Oh, there it is, again—like glue. I can't believe they gave it to a sick child." She grimaced, lowering herself onto the side of Ceci's bed. "Poor owlet— exhausted. Last night she sat up, fast asleep, weeping. Rafaela had to comfort her." Pilar yawned. "No one gets any sleep."

Barry's heart expanded, noticing Pilar's cheeks were slack with tiredness and her eyes baggy with sleeplessness. How had he not seen this earlier? "Take the chair, Pilar. I'll stand a bit." She settled onto the chair like a sleepy hen, adjusting her skirts.

He kissed her forehead. "I've been thinking. Maybe we do need Rafaela."

She stiffened, suddenly alert, her face a question mark.

"Ma said I should listen to you, that I should trust your judgment. So—"

"Thank God for your mother!" Pilar shook her clasped hands under her chin. "I'm going to call Rafaela right now!"

"Now, just wait a minute! I have to straighten out a few things. I assume Rafaela will want payment. We'll have to cover Ceci's room and board. Dora cleaned out our savings before she left. She left me broke, Pilar."

"Don't worry; I will pay for everything."

"I wasn't fishing for your help."

"Wait!" She lifted her hand. "I know. You're proud, but so am I. My niece caused all this trouble. She has dishonored the family. It's honor, not pity, which compels me."

"I will repay you, with interest."

"No, you will not." Pilar lifted her chin, her lips pressed together. "Ceci will."

"You can't expect her to—"

"All I ask in return is that she gets well. I'll call Doña Rafaela." She strode out, not bothering to wipe the tears that welled in her eyes.

Barry collapsed into the bedside chair. "God help me; what am I getting into?"

Barry sat at the wheel, and Pilar gave directions. "Turn right here—no, don't. I meant left, right here." *Do Not Enter, Not a Thoroughfare*, a sign read, and behind the sign a crowd gathered. A colorful array of outdoor stalls offered everything from piñatas to whirligigs. The smell of barbecue drifted in the car window, and at the far end of the lane a man led a donkey loaded with trinkets.

"¡Ay, ay, ay! This isn't the way!" Pilar threw up her hands. "Pull into that driveway and turn around." She twisted her neck to see behind her. "I forgot about Olvera Street—the *mercado*. It might as well be Disneyland, nowadays."

"Sure you know how to get to there?"

"Everything has changed since the freeway; nothing looks right. Not even the colors."

"It's colorful enough, Pilar! That yellow and red pushcart—and is that really a donkey, in downtown L.A.? I must be imagining things."

Ceci sat up taller in the back seat. "A donkey, Daddy?"

"A burro!" Pilar clicked her tongue. "He'll leave his droppings all over the street. There ought to be a law against—"

"I like the donkey, Tía."

"See that kid following the donkey with a shovel? I think your poop problem is solved."

"A good thing he's there!" Pilar turned to the back seat. "See, all the stuff they sell here is Mexican, Ceci. You can get delicious *churros* from that cart. See the church? That's where Los Angeles got its name: *Nuestra Señora Reina de los Angeles*—Our Lady Queen of Angels. This is the oldest part of the city, where everything began. It was people like your great-grandfather—those who started this town before the gringos took over." She sighed. "I wish I could have lived here then. A little town—"

"It's exactly as I imagine a street in Mexico City might look, except not a sombrero in sight!" They passed a group of men, musicians all in black-fringed sombreros and velvet suits, and Barry laughed. "Well, I spoke too soon!"

"*Mariachis!*" Pilar rolled down her window to listen.

The *mariachis* strummed their guitars and blared brass horns in front of a store. A crowd was gathering. Eyeing Ceci in the rearview mirror, Barry hoped that this spectacle could dilute the sadness in her face.

"Is there going to be a parade, Tía?"

"I don't think so, *chiquita*. It looks like a new restaurant is opening here. Pull over, please. I want to listen just a minute. Okay?"

"Yes, ma'am! I want to hear them." Barry found a place to park. "You like this music, Baby Bean?"

"It sounds so happy."

Pilar sighed. "Funny thing, he's singing about how sad he is—how he misses his homeland and the sweetheart that he left there. It's a sad song, really."

The trumpets bleated like joyful lambs at suppertime, and the singer danced during the instrumental bridge, waving a yellow handkerchief in the air.

"Sad? Come on, Pilar! Tell me that that guy with the hankie isn't the happiest cat that ever licked cream! Look at that shit-eating grin!"

"Language, Barry!"

"Tía," Ceci tapped Pilar's shoulder. "Why is he happy and sad at the same time?" Her eyes welled with tears. "Why?"

"Don't worry, *chiquita*. It's just a song." Pilar patted Ceci's hand. "Be happy, like a lark, instead of a sad little owlet who cries about *mariachis*."

As if Ceci could turn off her sadness like a water tap! Barry cleared his throat, impatience mounting. "Let's get back on the road!"

Pilar sighed. "Can't we wait for this one song? It takes me back to a happy time."

Shame overcame Barry's impatience. Pilar had survived more grief than he hoped he'd ever know. He idled the car as she stared out her window, apparently fascinated, until the *mariachis* brought the song to an end with a trumpet fanfare. He cleared his throat. "All right, now! Do I just keep on straight here?"

"Ah, yes! You'll turn right—no, left—right at the next intersection."

"Sorry? Left or right?"

"Yes!" Pilar craned her neck. "Aren't we almost to Arcadia Street? I can't make it out."

"I believe so. I'm not so familiar with this area."

"Is there a church up there? Your eyes are better than mine."

"Yeah."

"You're sure?"

"Yeah, there's a steeple, Pilar. So, where do you want me to go?"

"Oh, I don't know. Just turn right, and we can turn around if it's wrong."

"Why don't I pull into that gas station and ask them?"

"Just turn right. This time I'm sure; it's right." They passed the church. "No, no, I was wrong, it's left at the church." Pilar fluttered her hand at the window. "That way."

"Okay." Barry's patience stretched. "That way, then—if you're sure."

"I'm sorry. I usually take the bus when I get here, and I'm always crocheting something. I never look up until the driver says Olvera Street."

"But we passed Olvera; it can't be she lives on Olvera Street!"

"That's when I know to start paying attention—Olvera. It's almost to Chinatown, Rafaela's house, but it's still in the barrio."

"Okay, this is Figueroa Street. Look familiar?"

"Yes, that looks right: that little *taverna*, and the shop. There it is! Flower Street, turn right. The adobe house."

"She lives in an adobe?" Barry pulled to the curb. "A real adobe!"

Pilar grinned. "That's it!"

"That's one swell looking house—almost a mansion. I kind of thought she would live in a little rabbit hutch, like we do. Wow!"

"Oh, no, not Doña Rafaela—no rabbit house for her! Even if it hadn't been for her husband's money, Rafaela does well for herself." Pilar opened the car door and Barry helped her out. "The healing skill, the *curanderísmo*, has been good to her."

"Was Rafaela born with her—uh—curing skills?"

"Oh no, she trained for maybe ten years with her grandmother down in San Antonio. That was before she met her husband. When his father died, they moved into this old house. It's been in his family forever. He was a native Angelino—a founding family with a land grant—the Aguilars."

A wide veranda graced the front of Rafaela's whitewashed adobe. Hanging from hooks on the portico were pots of geraniums and petunias, and a magenta bougainvillea climbed the south-facing wall. All the trim gracing the porch and the upstairs balcony was roughly hewn, heavy wood that looked as though it would last several hundred years more. The door was carved oak, with a circular knocker of hand-forged iron in the center panel. Beneath the knocker was an inset painted—a Madonna in a green starry veil: the same image Barry had seen everywhere as they drove through the barrio.

Ceci pointed to the tile as they approached the front steps. "Daddy, that's the lady in my dreams."

He wrapped his arm around her. "The Queen of Los Angeles. She's all over the barrio, anyway. Maybe she lives here with Rafaela."

Ceci's eyes swept the house. "Really, Daddy?"

"He's teasing, Cecilita." Pilar struck the knocker. "But Rafaela is a devoted *Guadalupana*. She loves Our Lady."

Carmen welcomed them in. She wore a slim red dress under a red gingham apron, much prettier in these clothes than in her uniform. "You won't believe the feast awaiting you. Did you have trouble finding us?"

"No trouble!" Pilar embraced Carmen. "I know the way like the back of my hand."

"With a few detours, that is." Barry sniffed the air. "*Mole?*"

"Yes, it is, chicken *mole*! Come in and meet everyone." Footsteps clattered down the hall, and Carmen lifted Ceci into her arms. "I'm afraid my Tito will knock you down; he's so excited. He's been waiting to meet you. Oh—"

"Hi! Hi! Hi!" A small boy ran towards them. He leapt up and down in front of them, his shiny hair like an up-turned ebony bowl. "Come! You have to see! The *tortuga* has seven eggs!"

"Careful, Tito." She smoothed her son's bangs. "Our friend Ceci has to play quiet games."

"Aw, Mamita, the *tortuga* is quiet; she never says nothing!"

"*Mijo*, please—she never says *anything*."

Tito rolled his eyes. "That's what I said, Mami!"

"What a kid!" Barry squatted down to shake Tito's hand. "I'm Barry."

"What kind of berry? This kind?" Tito sputtered a raspberry into his fist and ran about, giggling like a hyena.

"Tito!" Carmen grabbed his shirtsleeve. "Don't be rude!"

"Sorry!" Tito blurted and ran off.

"He must have been watching Jack Benny, that one. He's pretty punny."

"I'm sorry; Tito's manners are terrible. Right down this hall—the kitchen." Carmen called down the hall, "Mamita, they're here!" She led them there.

"*¡Bienvenidos, amigos!*" Rafaela stood at the stove, her kitchen awash with yellow sunlight and the aromas of spices, chilies, and frying. A long, rough wooden table stood in the center of the room, already stacked with rainbows of plates, fruit in baskets, and sweating glass pitchers. A whitewashed corner fireplace, just like Barry had seen in pictures of old Mexican houses, held a pile of logs—but the rest of the kitchen had been modernized, the appliances gleaming, though old. Rafaela held a tortilla over the gas burner. "Pilar told me you like *mole de pollo*, Barry."

"It looks mo-licious!" He winked at Tito. "Mo-licious, eh?"

"Mo-licious!" Tito spun around his mother. "Mo-licious *mole!*"

Framed in the back door, a slight teenager, pale brown hair frizzing out from a tight braid, held up a sprig of some herb. "This enough cilantro, *Abuela?*" She blushed at the sight of the strangers. "Oh, hi."

"Do you remember me, Adelita? Pilar?"

"Yes, I do!" Adelita hugged Pilar. "You gave me that doll, the one with the First Communion dress just like mine. I still have her."

"A masterpiece. She made your dress, as well, *m'ija*." Carmen took the cilantro from Adelita. "The Montenegro women are known for their sewing."

"Adelita!" Barry held out his hand. "I'm Barry Sullivan, and this is my little girl—"

"I know: Cecilita. Abuela told me. Pleased to meet you, sir, and welcome!"

"Pretty manners." He glanced at Carmen. "Who taught her?"

"You won't believe it, but I did." Carmen smiled. "Adelita is my eldest."

"You can't be that old, Carmen!" Just as he said it, Barry wished he hadn't. "Uh, I mean I—"

"That's all right." Carmen hugged Adelita's slim shoulders. "Adelita is almost fifteen. We're already planning her *quinceañera*—a big party for her birthday."

So, Carmen had to be at least thirty-five. Barry was surprised by the pang that arithmetic caused him, compelled to change the subject.

"What's in all the jars? Spices?" He studied the handwritten labels: *malva, manzanilla, naranjo, sangre de drago, ruda, tlachichinole.*

"Herbs, roots, and flowers: some for cooking, some for medicine, sometimes both." Rafaela stepped up onto her kitchen stool and reached for a can. "Here is something that might interest you." She lifted off the tin lid, sticking the can up to his nose.

"Barry sniffed. "Intoxicating! Marijuana?"

"Ha! No, *amigo*, it is *lavanda de desierto*: desert lavender—for the hangovers."

"See here, just because I'm Irish doesn't mean I drink."

"Ah!" She tapped her chest. "And just because I'm Mexican doesn't mean I peddle marijuana." Rafaela punched his arm. "Come, sit down." She nodded to the refrigerator. "Carmen, please give our friends what they like to drink. I must see to the *mole*. Adelita, you and Tito will set the table for me?"

The family set about making everyone comfortable. Tito fetched the telephone book to boost Ceci higher in her chair. Adelita set out beer and iced *limónada*. Pilar and Rafaela carried dishes of *mole de pollo*, salad, rice, and beans to the table. Staring into the steaming bowls and casserole dishes, Barry let his troubles slide from his shoulders. It had been a while since he'd had a home-cooked meal, let alone a feast like this. Here was profound welcome, with abundance that even Ma's Irish stew couldn't match.

In the center of the table Rafaela laid a mound of warm tortillas alongside a crock of butter, a huge plate of sliced mangoes and grapes, a speckled blue bowl heaped with grated cheddar cheese, and a wooden bowl of crisp, green salad. Pots steamed on the stove, their spicy aroma rising in graceful arcs of steam. Tito sat beside Barry, a little bowl of stuffed olives in the crook of his elbow. Carmen took it, setting it near the center of the table. "Grace first."

Rafaela nodded to Barry. "Will you do us the honor, *amigo*?"

"Well," he swallowed. "I don't pray much these days."

Rafaela waited, her eyes closed over her folded hands.

"All right, then." Barry began, his voice almost a whisper. "Lord, for what we're about to receive may the Lord make us ever thankful. Amen."

"Short and sweet." Rafaela passed the tortillas. "Perfect."

Barry lifted a bowl of green food, garnished with a pepper and a cherry tomato. "Can you tell me what I'm about to serve myself?"

"They are *nopales*—cactus—we take all the stickers off."

"A lot of work, isn't it?"

"Valuable work." Rafaela pushed the bowl closer. "Sometimes it's the only green food out in the desert. I love them. This is *gazpacho:* the clear soup that Ceci likes. You put the vegetables you like—nopales, avocado, radishes, or these little green onions. Cecilita, don't you want to try anything else?"

"No," Ceci shook her head. "Just plain soup."

"*M'ija.*" Pilar patted her hand, "Say, '*No, gracias.*'"

"Just add this one thing, for medicine." Rafaela ladled up some *gazpacho* and dropped in a few leaves. "Cilantro, for your blood."

Ceci fished out a leaf, tasting and grimacing. "Tastes like soap."

"Don't spoil your soup, then." Rafaela spooned off the cilantro. "Tomorrow you can try cilantro as a tea."

Tito frowned. "What's wrong with Ceci? Why doesn't she eat?"

Adelita elbowed him. "Don't talk with your mouth full."

"I didn't." Tortilla flakes crumbled from his lips. "I chewed, then I talked."

"Listen to your sister!" Rafaela chuckled. "You have to swallow before you speak, Tito. How else will Cecilita know you are a prince of the barrio? You know what I always say. 'If you have the manners of a frog, you'll never venture out of the pond.'"

"So what? I don't want to be a prince. I want to be a cowboy like Roy Rogers and Dale Evans."

Adelita giggled behind her hand. "Dale Evans is a cow*girl, tonto.*"

"Ha!" Tito punched his chest with both fists. "Tonto is the Lone Ranger's helper. He's an Indian. I want to be him, too!"

"*Tonto* is also Spanish for silly." Adelita picked up her napkin to wipe some crumbs from Tito's mouth. "That's you, all right."

Tito sputtered behind Adelita's napkin.

"Hey!" Ceci stopped her spoon midair. "Why does the Lone Ranger call him Tonto? It's not nice. Doesn't he like him?"

"Cecilita, let the grownups speak! When I was a child we were barely permitted to talk at the table. If we were to talk, it would certainly be about something besides TV shows." Pilar glanced around meaningfully at the parents present.

"Ah, *mi amiga*," Rafaela dabbed her lips with her napkin, "that is only because we had no TV. We children would have watched Roy Rogers faithfully. I think he is—oh! Someone at the door—might be Guillermo, with the earache again. I'd better go see who's there."

The *curandera* returned with a crumpled bag in her hand, her face sad.

Adelita flew to Rafaela's side. "What is it, Abuelita?"

"The *brujo*—he has sent me a message."

Carmen whispered to Barry, "A *brujo* is a sorcerer. Black magic."

"Don Jiménez has sent me the feet of a chicken and a note. 'Your medicine is finished, you skinny old hen!'" Rafaela gave Adelita a tight little smile. "Now, children, don't be afraid. I won't let him hurt anyone."

"Gadzooks!" Barry shuddered. "Why would anyone write such a thing?"

"It's a long story." Rafaela tossed the crumpled bag into the trash and washed her hands, scrubbing them with a nailbrush. "Last year, I helped his youngest daughter, Felicia—very devout she is." She opened the refrigerator, removed a dish, and set it into a bowl of water on the counter. "Felicia wanted to join the convent, but Jiménez wanted her to marry. He locked her up like a—uh—"

"Like Saint Barbara!" Ceci's eyes glimmered.

"Yes, Cecilita, exactly like her, but he didn't cut off Felicia's head. Oh, no—he just made her life miserable and lonely. The girl stopped eating or going outside. Soon she was white as a ghost. Her mama brought her to me in secret."

Pilar leaned forward; her vast bosom quivered. "What happened?"

"With God's help, I healed the poor girl. But then, to make matters worse, Jiménez caught the influenza. He thinks I cast a spell on him when I took the sickness off the girl." She laughed, "I do not cast spells. Only I do what is God's will. But here's why he hates me. While he was in bed with the fever, his wife drove their daughter straight to the convent. Felicia has been with the Carmelites ever since. Even Don Jiménez doesn't have the boldness to kidnap her from there. Blames me, though—claims I'm depriving him of grandchildren." Rafaela stood twisting the strap of her apron, her eyes clouded.

Tito held up his plate. "Are we going to have *flan*, Abuelita?"

Carmen tapped his plate. "You must eat some vegetables first."

Tito glared at his mother, swinging his fork in the air. Carmen took the fork and laid it quietly on the table. "Tito, you must eat!"

"I'll run away like Felicia, to the nuns." He crossed his arms and pouted. "You're mean!"

"Hold it, feller!" Barry laughed. "You'd better stick with your ma. She's a damned sight nicer than any nun I met in school. Tough as drill sergeants, they are. You know, I'd even settle for a *brujo* over old Sister Parakeet with her full set of whiskers."

"Parakeets don't have whiskers!" Tito laughed.

"Well, this one had them, and she had a beak of a nose. Her real name was Sister Paraclete, and she taught me choir. She had this high chirpy voice, as sweet as sugar. But she'd wallop anybody singing off tune, upside the head with a ruler."

Tito's eyes grew rounder.

"Sister Immaculate is really nice, and she's pretty," Adelita sighed. "I'd like to be a nun like her."

"I'm with your *brujo*." Barry took in Adelita's shocked stare. "A pretty girl going into the convent is a damned waste."

Carmen cleared her throat. "I am careful with my language around my children."

Barry blushed. "I'm sorry!"

"Barry means well, Carmencita, but—" Rafaela eased the flan from its copper mold. A perfect, shivering mound, it landed on the plate. "Tito, will you bring some clean plates?"

"I will, Abuelita, but tell about the *brujo*. What else happened?" He handed her a little stack of blue saucers.

"Not much to tell." Rafaela began to serve quivering slices, spooning strawberries over each plate. "Even before Felicia entered the convent, Jiménez's intentions have been unfriendly. Most people prefer my herbs and prayers over his magic." A smile flashed on her lips. "He is not as rich as he'd like to be. So he tells everyone that my strength is fading, that I should retire. The first time I fail, he'll be ready."

"Him?" Pilar waved her hand. "Ready to do what? He's a fake. He just takes people's money. He has no power."

"Oh, I don't know about that, *amiga*. He must have great power; here we are talking about him when we should be enjoying our dessert."

"Well, I say we forget about him and eat *flan*!" Barry lifted a spoonful of the cold vanilla custard to his lips. "Man, that's wicked good! Rafaela, are you sure you aren't a sorceress yourself?"

"When I was a child, Rafaela's mother was our cook. We treasured her." Pilar took another spoonful. "This is even better than hers, Rafaela. What's the recipe?"

"A secret."

"Oh," Pilar chuckled, "it *is* magic, then."

"No, no!" Rafaela waved away the compliment. "Anyone can make a good *flan*. Just takes practice."

"Anyone?" Carmen shrugged. "Mine never comes out right, no matter how much I practice. It always plops out of the mold in a runny puddle."

"You have to slow down to make a good *flan*." Rafaela threw her arm around her daughter. "You go too fast, *m'ija*; even your dessert is running."

Morning sun had just begun to creep between the curtains. "Barry," Rafaela knocked at the door. "Wake up! Your *mamá* has come."

"W-what?"

"Your *mamá* is in the kitchen. Came on the streetcar." Rafaela stepped into the room. "Come down and see her. I will make you *huevos rancheros.*"

Barry pulled the covers up to his chin. "Huh?"

"Eggs and *chorizo*, and there's coffee." She scurried downstairs before he could answer. He shuffled to the bathroom and splashed his face, squinting into the wavy silvered mirror. Should he shave? No, he must hurry to see if Ma was all right. He jogged downstairs, buckling his belt as he went, stopping short at the kitchen doorway.

Ma sat at Rafaela's table, a mug of tea between her hands. How frail she looked, her shoulder blades poking out the cotton of her pink summer dress! His heart fell, but he mustered a cheerful voice. "If it isn't herself—bright eyed and bushy tailed!"

She turned to him. "Mornin', son. I just couldn't wait to see our Cecilia, so I took the streetcar." She took a lusty sip of tea. "You and your musician's hours!"

"But Ma, I would've come to get you."

"No fretting, boyo! Raffy-ella and I had ourselves a talk. She reminds me of Bridie Bannion back home. One and the same, I tell you. She had the same way with healing, Bridie. My da used to get this balm from her, for the cows' teats; cleared the sores in two days, it did." Ma winced. "You sure this tea will strengthen me, Raffy-ella? Tastes like the bottom of a bog."

"It thins and cools the blood. Good for the heart."

"Ah, well, then." Ma Sullivan took another sip.

"Where's our Ceci Bean?" Barry yawned and stretched. "Still asleep?"

"Yes, she had a bad night. Sleepwalking."

Ma touched Rafaela's wrist. "What do you do for sleepwalking?"

"She'll do a *limpia* for her, a cleansing, and you can help us."

"Me? Oh, I don't know how I could help."

"Would you pray the rosary?" Rafaela poured herself a cup of tea.

Ma fished a little white patent leather pouch from her purse and laid it on the table. "I always carry it."

Eyes on his mother, Barry rested his chin on his folded arms. "I don't suppose I'm needed for the ritual, am I?"

"Did you bring your rosary, son?" Ma winked at Rafaela. "We can hope."

He rolled his eyes. "Aw, Ma, I don't even own one anymore."

"If that is all that's troubling you," Rafaela poured Barry some coffee, "I can lend you one. I have many."

"Now look, Rafaela. I think it's fine that you and Ma have your, uh—your ritual together, but I don't really want to get involved with the specifics. Let's just get this over with. Okay?"

With a gasp, Ma covered her mouth. For the first time since he'd met her, Barry saw Rafaela's eyes truly darken: gold to brown. She turned toward the stove, making herself busy pouring beaten eggs into a skillet.

"The cheek, Barry! I can't believe you'd be so rude to someone who's making you breakfast! Raffy-ella's your hostess!" Ma pulled him by the sleeve. "Now you apologize to my friend before I have to box your ears!"

Rafaela's back trembled so that Barry feared she was crying. He leapt from his chair to her side. "Oh, God, Rafaela, I'm terribly—" He stopped when he saw the laughter in her eyes.

"Your *mamá* is right. I ought to poison your eggs." Rafaela reached over the stove for a string of tiny red peppers. "Or burn the evil out of your tongue with chilies!"

"Oh, sure, it's a fact," Ma nodded. "There's no mistaking. It's our tongues, not our hearts that get us in trouble. Remember, Barry when your da—"

"Let the poor man eat, *amiga*." Rafaela handed him fluffy scrambled eggs and *chorizo* on a plate. "You know what we say in the barrio? 'A closed mouth catches no flies.' Eat up and stay out of trouble! Tortillas?"

Barry nodded. "Please."

Ma leaned back in her chair, a touch of rose in her pale cheeks. "I'll be honored to say the rosary for your lim—limp—er—what did you call it, Rafaela?"

"Limpia—it means cleansing."

Rafaela placed a tortilla on Barry's plate. He loaded it with egg, slathered it with hot sauce, rolled it, and pushed it into his mouth. Ma watched him with pleasure. "He likes your spicy foods, my Barry. I wish I had his appetite, but try as I might, I just can't eat very much these days."

"I have medicines that might help your appetite." Rafaela laid a hand on Ma's shoulder, studying her face briefly, then poured her a little more tea. "I grow the herbs myself. Come, I'll show you the garden."

Barry stayed behind, savoring the coffee and cream Rafaela had served him. He could get used to such luxury. Dora had stopped cooking real breakfasts, convinced they were fattening. The thought of Dora turned his stomach—he stared down at the perfectly cooked eggs with despair. With a sigh he pushed away from the table and wandered through the screened back porch into the garden.

Large for downtown, Rafaela's yard was, Barry guessed, a quarter-acre or more. He stepped off the porch onto the wide brick pathway, around which grew plants that Barry presumed were the herbs for Rafaela's medicines. At the back of the land, a sizable vegetable garden flourished in front of a row of citrus trees and several animal pens. Chickens scratched around the sunflowers, and Rafaela tossed them handfuls of grain. Ma took a handful, scattering it with obvious pleasure. Her face invisible under a huge straw hat, Pilar lay on a chaise lounge, her hands folded on her belly, her legs stretched out before her like two stout logs. Rafaela and Ma were deep in conversation, even as they fed the chickens.

"Hey!" he called out, waving. "What mischief are you girls cooking up?"

"Just feeding the hens," Rafaela waved back.

Ma brushed the grain from her hands. "Don't you have roosters?"

"The crowing would bother my neighbors. As a girl I had one. He followed me everywhere."

"Did you have to eat him one day?"

"Oh, no, my mother never let Papá kill Paco. He was our alarm clock. But I have something better than a rooster to show you. Meet Lupita, my tortoise."

"Oh!" Ma stumbled, grasping Rafaela's arm. "Oh, sorry, feeling a bit—"

"Better sit a bit." Rafaela helped Ma to the stone bench under the eucalyptus.

Barry rushed to her. "Need your pills, Ma?"

Her hand at her collar, she smiled. "No, I'm fine. I'm just tired."

"Chest pains?"

"No pain. I'm just woozy, and a bit too warm—"

Pilar brought a glass of cool water and Rafaela crouched, massaging a little point on Ma's wrist, smoothing her hands upward toward her shoulder.

"I'm going to call the doctor, Ma."

"I feel fine, son."

"Well, then, we better have Carmen look at you."

"Who is Carmen?"

Rafaela laid her palms on Ma's shoulders. "My daughter—she's a nurse, but she's at work. May I listen to your heart? Maybe I can help."

"But Ma has a doctor, a perfectly good—"

"Posh!" Ma waved away his words. "I'd rather Raffy-ella check me out."

Barry helped Ma into the house. Rafaela spread a clean sheet over her kitchen table and asked Ma to lie down in the center. The old *curandera's* head pressed against Ma's chest. Rafaela glanced at Barry, shaking her head so slightly, he wasn't sure he'd seen it. Then she helped Ma up and off the table.

"What happened?" Pilar wrung her hands. "Is Katy going to be all right?"

"She will be, after she rests." Rafaela brushed Ma's hair out of her face. "We'll have to do the *limpia* without you this time, Katy. You had better rest."

Ma dabbed at her eyes with a handkerchief. "But Ceci needs me."

"Barry will help us," Rafaela slapped his back. "He's a good sport."

"Oh, will you, Barry?" Ma took his hand. "Will you say the rosary for Cecilia?"

Barry smiled sadly, a miserable ache in the pit of his stomach. "Of course, Ma, whatever you want." He stroked her hand. "Just take it easy, now, okay?"

"I don't want to take it easy. I feel like an old relic, locked up behind glass and useless. I hate what my life's become."

Rafaela studied Ma a moment, her gold eyes unblinking. "What is it that you want most of all in the world?"

Ma smiled. "Most in the world?"

"Yes, your heart's desire."

"I'd like to see my son and granddaughter happy." She took Barry's hand. "And—I want to see Ireland again."

"Go to Ireland, my friend, as soon as you can." Rafaela helped Ma from the table into a chair. "This is the time to go, now."

Ma's eyes widened. "Am I going to die soon?"

"The future is a dream, *amiga*. It is what we are doing now that matters. You have time—use it to do what you want most to do."

"The doctor says I should wait a month or two before I go anywhere."

"You have his advice." Rafaela took Ma's hands in hers. "What is it you wish, Catalina?"

"Catalina? Is that Spanish for Kathleen?"

"Yes, Catalina, it is. Tell me your wish—now, please? I want to pray for you."

"Funny you should ask. I've been thinking it over. If I wait too long, it will be winter. I want to see the late summer when the hay is yellow. I love the haying time." She laughed, putting her hand over her moist eyes. "I'd love for Barry to come, to bring Cecilia, but he's so busy."

"Young people!" Pilar clicked her tongue. "Always busy, but with what? *The young sell their flesh to the Devil, but the old give their bones to God*; that's what my mother always said."

"That old *dicho*—we remember it because there's truth in it!" Rafaela sighed. "Sometimes it's the other way around. God has taken many young bones, too. We never know what the future holds for us." She squeezed Barry's arm. "Take your mother to Ireland!"

"You're ganging up on me!" Barry jingled his keys in his pocket. "Before we think of Ireland, let's get Ma back in commission. You've had plenty of excitement, Ma. When I get you home, you'd better call the doctor."

"I just get tired sometimes."

"What do you expect, when you're gallivanting around like some hoyden lass? Taking the streetcar, I ask you!" He kissed Ma's forehead and helped her stand.

She leaned more heavily on him than he expected, her beautiful eyes shining up at him. "I do love you so, boyo."

Rafaela escorted them to the car. "It has been a great pleasure to meet you, Katy Sullivan."

"Oh, please, call me Catalina. Your language makes my name so pretty. Thanks for all you're doing, darling Raffy-ella. I'll not forget what you said." She wiped her eyes. "I will go to Ireland; I will take Barry and Cecilia to their roots."

"Yes, Catalina, help them put down roots—for this I will pray."

☆　☆　☆　☆

Barry took care of Ma all morning, heating a can of Campbell's Beef and Barley Soup for her lunch, and reading aloud to her from the *Maryknoll Missions News*.

Late that afternoon, when he returned to Rafaela's, he found Carmen napping in the living room, still in her uniform, her legs propped up on the sofa's arms. A breeze from the garden-side window wafted in the scent of roses. He enjoyed a moment, breathing it in, hoping the house's calm would permeate his worry.

A cement truck rumbled by, and Carmen murmured in her sleep and turned toward the back of the sofa. The wall above her was a gallery of saints. He recognized most of them: Mary of the Sacred Heart, Saint Joseph, Saint Francis of Assisi. The others he studied closely, trying to identify them by their clothing or the symbolism of their earthly accessories. Some of the older ones were framed in elaborate gilded frames. The reverence people like Ma and Rafaela paid for images made about as much sense to Barry as kissing a rabbit's foot for luck.

Slouched in the window seat, he gazed at the postman shoving mail into a box across the street. A small dog, a Chihuahua, nosed along the sidewalk all by itself and stopped to roll in the patch of lawn in front of Rafaela's house. The creature's simple joyousness wetted his eyes. He suppressed a sob, biting his palm. A dog! How he would have liked to give Ceci one! He had missed so many opportunities to make her life good. He leaned against the wall, eyes closing, too exhausted to entertain his regret. The front door opened, and rustling packages preceded Rafaela.

"Hello, Barry," she whispered. "Your mother? Is she better?" She set her bags on the floor.

"Must be better—she was ordering me around like a butler."

"She's not been waited on much in her life."

"Nevertheless, she takes to queendom like a duck to water." Barry's smile turned into a yawn. "I was thinking about taking a nap, like Carmen."

Following his eyes, Rafaela's face saddened. "A bad day at the hospital—a death. She needed to sleep off the sadness." She stroked Carmen's forehead with her fingertips. "Wake up, *m'ija*. You told me five o'clock."

"Ugh!" Carmen wriggled away from her mother like a grumpy child, rubbing her eyes with her fists. "Five already? I have to go!"

"It's five-thirty, *m'ija*. I didn't have the heart to wake you, so I ran to the store. Why don't you stay for dinner? Pilar has made enough food for an army."

"I promised Tito I'd take him to watch the big kids play baseball."

"Tito is playing with Cecilita; he probably forgot all about it. Adelita already did her homework. She—"

"The math, too? You're sure? She's been fudging lately."

"Oh yes, I saw the work, very neat: nice little rows of numbers."

"Little rows? They're equations. I'd better go check—"

"Forget the math and relax, Carmencita. Maybe Barry will play you some music."

He shrugged. "I should practice first. You don't want to hear that. It's tedious. Same thing over and over."

"Ah!" The *curandera* thought a moment, tapping her forehead with a crooked finger. "Practice downstairs in the cellar, then. After dinner you will give us a concert. Today we all have need of some music medicine."

"By order of Her Majesty, Doña Rafaela!" Carmen grinned. "Command performance."

"Of course, Madame." Barry bowed. "I'll go get my clarinet."

When Barry returned from upstairs, Carmen had moved to the window seat and was staring across the street, massaging the back of her neck. "A penny for your thoughts, Carmen."

A tear slid down her coppery cheek, and Barry offered his rumpled handkerchief. Carmen took it, but held it crumpled in her fist, the tear still coursing her cheek. She shook her head. "I don't know, Barry. It's not so easy to tell, or to hear, I think."

He sat down beside her, his back against the window. "Try me."

Carmen stared at her hands, silent. Barry's attention gravitated to her fingers: no nail polish, the nails round and short, the moons paper white, a nurse's capable hands, the left wrist circled by a white-banded Timex. Nothing about those hands to attract attention, except the kindnesses they performed.

"A patient died today. Needless death." Carmen hid her eyes behind the handkerchief. "Broke my heart."

Barry felt inadequate to comfort her; the only sorrow he knew was over his own tragedies. Her sorrows were an echelon above his. A patient died! How would it feel to every day save lives, to do such good while earning a living? Desire to succeed as a musician had driven his every decision, every day. He'd never shed a tear for anyone, except family. Red with shame, he shook his head. "Man! I'm a goddamn selfish bastard."

"You?" Carmen looked up at him, the tears still streaming. She laughed and blew her nose. "That's what I thought when I met you—what I told Mamita. Of course, I didn't use those words." She touched his arm, just a slight, quick touch, and folded her hands in her lap, clasping the handkerchief. "Now, I'm not so sure. You might not be so terrible. You're not altogether a bastard."

"Gee, thanks." Barry grimaced. "Don't fall all over yourself giving me compliments."

"I've seen you with Ceci and with your mother. You do care. You just have to learn how to show it by actions."

"I bet you're an expert at that. I mean that—sincerely."

"No!" She blushed. "No, not an expert. I don't think anyone is. It's so damned hard. So often I trip over my own good intentions."

He let that sink in. For years he thought women were much better at caring; could it be kindness was just as hard for everyone? Before he met Dora, he'd thought women's soft bodies made for soft hearts. His first impression of Carmen was so wrong; he'd expected neither kindness nor empathy—just disapproval and self-righteousness. "Tell me, what happened today? What broke your heart so?"

She closed her eyes, heaving a sigh. "You really want to know?"

"Rafaela told me someone died. Doesn't that happen a lot?"

"Obstetrics is mostly about new life, but there's tragedy. More than you'd think." She gazed out at the street and blew her nose, crumpling the handkerchief into a wad afterwards. "A young woman, a Chicana, the wife of a farmworker. They called me to the E.R. to translate."

"You translate?"

"Oh, God, yes—it's like my second job. My Spanish—once I even translated for a Brazilian who came in with a fishhook in his eye, screaming bloody murder."

"Brazilian? Don't they speak Portuguese?"

"Nobody there knew Portuguese. So I spoke to him in Spanish, and he spoke back in Portuguese. Some words are the same—near enough. We made it work. Just hearing something even close to his language calmed him down."

"You're a very valuable person. You can bridge the gap. You save lives, too."

"No—not today." Carmen's eyes welled again. "This girl—the one they called me for—barely conscious, she'd lost so much blood—childbirth complications. The midwife, an old neighbor woman, couldn't staunch the bleeding. They'd driven from hospital to hospital, the poor little mother in the back of a pickup truck, the father trying to get someone to help. No money, no insurance—so hard for them—"

She sobbed into her hands. Barry touched her shoulder, so lightly he felt the starched cotton of her uniform. "You don't have to tell more—not if you don't want to."

"No!" Carmen gulped a breath and wiped her eyes. "I want to. Someone should know about her—her story." She blew her nose. "Poor thing couldn't have been sixteen, sweet face like the Virgin, even in shock. After she died—she didn't—we couldn't—"

"There, there, Carmen. Leave it be—"

"Her story must be told!" Carmen pulled from his embrace. "Even after the little mother died, she didn't let go; she held onto her baby. He was rooting to nurse, even. The doctor pried her arms open, and I gave the hungry infant a bottle. Then we cleaned and swaddled him and brought him out to the poor father. My job—to tell him we couldn't save his wife—only his son." She looked down at her hands again. *"Pobrecitos—* poor baby—and the father—only a boy, really—"

Barry felt his own tears welling. The poor dying mother did not let go, yet Dora couldn't hold on—or wouldn't.

His eyes rose to Rafaela's altar, gazing at the crucifix hanging over it. He wanted to break that figure of the Suffering Christ over his knee. "It makes you wonder, doesn't it? What kind of God is He, if things like that can happen to good women? And yet, there's all these bad ones who—"

"It's not for us to decide who's good and who's bad."

"Still, that woman, she tried to hold on for her child. She's a heroine, isn't she?"

"Every day I meet heroes and heroines. Some are surprising."

Barry turned away from the altar. "What do you mean?"

"This Mexican man—he'd saved the life of a neighbor, an old man who fell asleep smoking in bed. Terrible fire—real hero—ran into a burning building. A beam fell down on him, burning three-quarters of his body, but he got the old man out."

"Yeah?"

"Emergency called me to translate. Later I had to talk to the cops. Turned out our hero had committed a terrible rape in Mexico. Here illegally, to escape conviction. Yet he gave his life selflessly for another. Death saved him from jail."

"Shit! So complicated—"

"Yes, complicated. The mother today—if the hospital had interpreters, she wouldn't have died. If only someone had understood the father when he ran in to E.R. begging for help to carry her from the truck—they'd have admitted her immediately. Valuable time was lost."

"Maybe. Or maybe they're just bastards and would turn them away, afraid they couldn't pay the bill."

"Yeah, you're right—they might have. Hospitals have often done that—even L.A. General," Carmen nodded. "I keep hoping it's just Anglo ignorance and not prejudice, that someday people will understand that *braceros*—the farmworkers—are human beings, not workhorses to abuse until they're fit for the glue factory." She folded her arms across her chest. "That's why I went to night school, why I left Adelita and Tito for Mamita to look after. I wanted to change things. Today, I don't know."

Eyes now dry, she looked sadder than ever, like one of those women Modigliani painted, sad and starkly beautiful. He thought about taking her in his arms and holding her, but hesitated—uncertain if it was just his own agony responding to Carmen's pain. Maybe he just wanted to prove his body still had the power to comfort someone.

More than that—maybe he desired the sweet consolation of a woman's softness. Did he really need a woman? No, he didn't, he told himself—no, he didn't. Carmen was not like other women he'd caressed on such a whim, to get over some hurt Dora had dished out. If he gave this passing weakness, she'd not mistake it for flattery. She'd probably deck him.

"Well!" Carmen rubbed her shoulders and stretched her neck. "I need a shower." She nodded at the clarinet. "You'd better get to practicing. I'm looking forward to the concert."

As she climbed the stairs, Barry picked up his clarinet and stroked its silver levers. Who would've ever thought the prospect of a little home music recital would make him so nervous?

After dinner, Rafaela drew the curtains as everyone gathered in the front room. The *curandera* clapped her hands. "Now our friend Barry will play for us!" She announced this with a bow. "Señor Barry Sullivan on the *clarinete!*"

Pilar, Carmen, and the children clapped politely until Rafaela signaled them to stop, taking her place on her favorite chair. As was his habit before playing, Barry stood before them, eyes closed, listening to the air. He lifted his clarinet, blew a few jazz riffs: sound haikus, he called them. Everyone sat attentive, like people in church waiting for a sermon. Barry began to perspire, unable to think of a song for this rare audience.

Rafaela tapped her thigh. Carmen's eyelids drooped. Tito crawled under the altar, peeking out every now and then from behind the lacy tablecloth. Barry let a grace note fade into the walls and paused.

"Please, Barry," Rafaela nodded. "Keep playing; it's a beautiful instrument."

There was a certain song that Ma had always sung too slowly, her alto tentative but haunting, Barry recalled. That's what the women would like—a Celtic melody, sweet and simple. Embellished with trills and jazz phrases, it could spellbind.

> *The water's deep and the water's wide*
> *I can't cross over, neither can I bide.*
> *Give me a boat that will carry two*
> *And both shall row, my love and I.*

Ceci began to sing along, at first tentative, then with confidence. She didn't cough once. At the end, Barry kissed the top of her head. "Baby girl, you remembered our song. Pitch perfect. I should play for you more often."

"Yes, music is good medicine." Leaning forward, Rafaela clapped her hands. "Let's have more! Do you know *Cielito Lindo?*"

Barry nodded. "The one that goes '*Ay, ay, ay, ay?*'"

"Yes! If you play, we will all sing, even the children."

He began with the chorus, and everyone sang:

¡Ay, ay, ay, ay! canta y no llores,
Porque cantando se alegran
Cielito lindo los corazones.

When they had sung through all the verses, Barry stopped and swabbed his clarinet. "Will someone tell me? I've played that one don't know how many times, but I don't know what the words mean."

"It's about not crying over love—about being happy." Pilar spoke while trying to smooth down Ceci's unruly curls with the palm of her hand.

"Here you go." Rafaela rose, opening her arms like an orator.

Ay, ay, ay, ay, sing but don't cry
Because singing will open your heart
To the joyful, evening sky!"

She gave a little curtsy. Ceci and Barry clapped, but Pilar shook her head. "It doesn't say anything about opening a heart, Rafaela. It says that singing makes your heart happy."

"*Cielito lindo los corazones*—the beautiful sky—"

"Rafaela!" Pilar wagged her finger. "It says nothing about an open heart."

"Come on, Pilar!" Carmen rose from her languor. "It's the feeling of the song!"

Eyes bright with mischief, Rafaela leaned back in her chair. "Let Barry decide; he's the musician."

"Well—er—I don't know." Barry peered into the bell of his clarinet, as if searching for a lost note. "Rafaela's words fit the melody nicely, and they rhyme. Further than that, I couldn't give an educated opinion."

"Such tact!" Carmen burst out laughing. "Learn Spanish, Barry! Until you're ready to give an opinion, Mamita and Pilar will have to call a truce."

"So—want another Mexican song, Rafaela? I know *Besame Mucho.*"

"No, please!" Rafaela waved her hand. "No more Spanish, and I give up the job of translator. Too political."

"Play another song!" Tito jumped up. "Play another!"

"Yes, play, Daddy!"

"Isn't it getting kind of late for little girls and boys?"

"Please, just one more song?"

Barry lifted an eyebrow, "Well, Rafaela, what do you think?"

"We have time. The *limpia* is short enough."

"I know—play something sweet and slow." Carmen yawned. "We can all just close our eyes and dream."

"Sweet and slow?" Barry wondered if anyone would recognize the theme song from the *Peter Gunn* on TV—*Dreamsville.* He loved it. Inhaling deeply, he lifted the clarinet and began to play the lazy, stretched first note.

The remaining tension on Carmen's face relaxed as the silky notes curled from his clarinet. Her head swayed slowly to the music, a smile lifting her cheeks. Heat shot up Barry's neck. For smiles like that he had become a musician. When he finished the song, he bowed to Rafaela. "Your majesty, the concert's over!"

"That was good!" Tito shouted. "Come on, clap!" He stood like a conductor before his family and everyone joined in, clapping and whistling.

"*¡Olé, olé, olé!*" Rafaela stomped her heels. "I am honored you're my guest, *amigo!*"

From her seat on Pilar's lap, Ceci glowed with pride. "Yay, Daddy!"

"Thanks!" Barry blushed. "Thank you, everyone. You're most kind. Should we get my girl ready for her—uh—thing?"

"In a few minutes," Rafaela nodded. "I'd like to give her a quick bath first."

"No bath!" Ceci squirmed out of Pilar's lap, but Rafaela caught her hand.

"Don't worry, just a sponge bath. I will soak lavender flowers in a bowl of warm water. *Lavanda* from my garden has blue flowers that the bees love. Now, bees know something about sleep; they get tired from buzzing around like they do. They love the *lavanda*—the lavender; it calms them down. Then early in the evening they can curl up to sleep in the honeycomb and wake up early to drink from more flowers."

"Well, maybe." The charm of the words seemed to have calmed Ceci already.

"Let's give you a bee bath, Ceci!" Barry carried his daughter upstairs to the bathroom. "Rafaela knows just how to do it so you'll like it."

There Rafaela sat Ceci down on the lid of the hamper, helping her off with her shirt. "It's true about the bees in the garden. *Lavanda* calms—so Cecilita will sleep like a little bee after the *limpia* and dream sweet dreams."

"I want to dream about Mama. I wish she could smell this."

Waves of the grassy sweetness of lavender rose from the enamel bowl as Rafaela stirred in the herbs, but Barry was aware only of the pang at hearing Ceci's longing.

Dipping a sponge into the fragrant basin, Rafaela lifted it to Ceci's nose. *"Lavanda!"*

"That's the smell, the one I smell when I see—when I see the dreams."

"Ah, yes, *lavanda*—the flower of visions and dreams!" The old woman stroked the brush gently through Ceci's shorn hair. "Your hair is the most beautiful color. It is like—oh, you will laugh at me. Will you, now?"

"I won't!" Ceci grabbed Rafaela's hand. "Tell me, please!"

"Zaino! On the hacienda they had big, handsome horses with red-brown coats. We call them *zaino,* but they look like *castaños,* chestnuts. I bet when your hair is longer it's even redder." She lifted up a strand between her index and middle fingers. "Like copper?"

"Yes, like a copper penny—and curly." Barry sighed. "Absolutely beautiful."

"Now, Cecilita, you must be brave. We have to wash your beautiful head." Rafaela stood Ceci on a thick pile of towels. "I will wash you gently, like I used to wash the big mother pig before she gave birth to her babies. Can you be brave for me, like a mother pig?" She held the soaked sponge over Ceci's belly and squeezed. The child shook, clinging to Rafaela's arm.

"Some Indians said that to me—be brave."

Rafaela dropped the sponge into the basin. "Who said that?"

"At the mission they said it. The Indians said to be brave."

"Oh yeah, those Indians!" Barry crouched on his haunches looking into Ceci's face. "You were quite adamant about them." He chuckled. "Indians!"

Rafaela smoothed a towel on her knees and lifted Ceci onto her lap. "Which Indians?"

"At the mission! They talked in Spanish, but I could understand them, and one of them gave me a white rock."

"Ceci, I don't want you lying to Rafaela, now." Barry picked the sponge out of the washbasin. "How 'bout we finish your bath?"

"I'm not lying!" Ceci squirmed and buried her face in Rafaela's chest.

"She tells the truth, this child. She has no lying in her." Rafaela began to towel Ceci's toes and legs. "Did the Indians tell you anything else, *chiquita*?"

Ceci's eyes misted. "Can't remember. Everything is mixed up—a whole bunch of things! There was the lady under the water, too. She looks like the lady on your door, and she talked to me, too. I can't remember what she said."

"*Cálmate, chiquita!*" Rafaela set her chin on top of Ceci's head. "Calm yourself. We will untangle it for you, little by little, starting with the *limpia* tonight. Don't worry, you will hardly notice anything I do, but afterwards you'll feel better. Every day you will heal a little bit more, until you are stronger than before." She handed the towel to Barry. "I must go down and prepare for the *limpia*. Adelita brought Ceci one of her outgrown nightgowns." She slid open a drawer. "It's in here with a toothbrush. Make sure she brushes her teeth. After the *limpia*, she'll want to sleep like never before."

"Here you go." Barry helped Ceci into the nightgown. "You aren't afraid of the *limpia*, Ceci?" He brushed Ceci's hair. "Are you worried about what it might feel like?"

"I guess not. Rafaela says it won't hurt."

As Barry carried Ceci downstairs, his thoughts raced—her recent traumas, Ma back in bed under doctor's orders, Carmen's tragedy at work, the goddamned *brujo* last night—and Dora leaving. It wasn't only Ceci needing healing; the whole world had slipped off its axis. If he broadened his focus to what was going on outside of his own little enclave, it was even worse—the Cold War, the A-bomb, segregation, crazy election uproar—and just about every one of his jazz friends hooked on one thing or another. The whole world needed a *limpia*, he decided.

They should line up all the *curanderas* in all the barrios and put them to work. What a frontline that would be: a battalion of elder Mexican women with their herbs, candles, lavender, and old lace—brewing teas, making poultices, and praying as they faced off the world's evil. He chuckled at how the world would respond to such an unlikely army.

Ceci looked up at him with those sea green eyes, so sleepy now from her bath. "What're you laughing at, Daddy?"

"Nothing! No, everything, baby—I'm laughing at everything!"

The *limpia* was not as he imagined it. Barry observed the ritual from the loveseat. Its reverent strangeness sat well with him, like John Coltrane's improvisations: uncanny but palpably real. It wasn't any weirder than Mass, really—Rafaela's herbs and incantations replacing bread and wine. Too bad stuffed shirts like Dr. Jensen never got to know someone like Rafaela; they'd show them more respect.

In a daze of appreciation, he followed the women upstairs to Ceci's room. Carmen lit the votive before the statue of the Virgin in the little wall niche. The room's old-world aura enhanced by candlelight and the moonlight through the deep-silled arched window belied that they were in downtown Los Angeles. Carmen transferred drowsy Ceci into his arms and drew back the covers, this moment as sacred as the *limpia*.

"She's already asleep," he whispered to Carmen as he smoothed the blankets up around his daughter's shoulders.

"She's been waiting to feel safe. Now that she is sure you'll stay with her, she can sleep deeply. It's your watch."

As if on vigil, Barry sat in the wicker chair under the window, matching his breathing with the rise and fall of Ceci's chest. He pondered Rafaela's matter-of-fact competency when she chanted the prayers and songs. The words in Spanish he didn't understand, but Carmen had translated one thing at the very end: the Twelve Truths of the World, a kind of Catholic "House that Jack Built," beginning with the Holy House of Jerusalem, then the Tablets of Moses and the birth, death, and resurrection of Christ, and ending with all the evil things of the world banished to their own hells.

At the end, his beloved daughter, Miss Cecilia Kathleen Sullivan, had arisen from her pallet in the center of the floor—a new child. Immediately Barry recognized something restored—the light in her eyes and the sheen of her skin, and her words.

"I'm hungry."

"Thank God! What do you want, Bean?"

"Hot cocoa!"

So Rafaela had whipped up delicious Mexican hot chocolate for everyone. Only few sips, and Ceci had already begun to doze over her mug.

Now, sitting at her side, his belly warm from the cocoa, Barry watched the candlelight jump and dance on the walls. Quite against his will, he fell asleep.

He awoke stiff and dizzy. He checked his watch by the light of the stub of candle: three A.M. Exhausted, he dragged himself to the attic room that Rafaela had prepared for him. Standing up from untying his shoes, he bumped his head on the sloped ceiling and dove into bed. He was still fully dressed and—for the first time in weeks—fully sober.

When he opened his eyes again, it was morning. He was surprised to remember a dream, one about Dora. He never could recall his dreams, not since childhood. It had played like a movie; even with his eyes open he could see his wife standing as she stood in the dream.

Dora standing over the ironing board, ironing sheet music—she calls out to him, "Play this song!" She is wearing a wedding gown, which is strange;

when they eloped, she wore a skirt and cashmere sweater. "I want this song for my wedding."

Muttering to himself in the dream, "Our wedding—it should be our wedding."

He walks out of the room into a hallway that's actually a desert. There is Ceci, silhouetted, darker magenta in the pink light of sunset—or is it dawn? Ceci grows taller and taller as she walks away from him. He is somehow paralyzed—unable to follow. Ceci turns just once, to wave, full-grown, beautiful.

He longs to run to her, to call out for her to stop before she walks into that big red sun, but he can make no sound; his legs are rooted in the sand. Then he realizes he is not only rooted, but sinking.

Remembering this dream, he felt an urgency, a need to get started, as if a war were going on outside the house, and he was the general with all the orders to deliver. Without washing up he jogged down the stairs, looping his tie. The telephone was ringing and ringing. He jogged faster, calling out. "Someone going to get that?"

When he reached the hall it was still ringing, unanswered. Almost breathless, Barry picked up the receiver. "Hello?"

"Barry?" Her breathy voice, the little whine of a question quivering— there was no mistaking it—Dora! He slammed down the receiver, blood beating a rhythm behind his eyes. A few moments passed in silence.

Barry glared at the phone as it rang again. If he answered, he felt he might collapse from the weight of his dread. Finally, shaking, he picked up the receiver.

"Hello, Barry?"

"What?" He formed that one word and slid down the wall to the floor.

"Is that you, Barry?"

He allowed himself to inhale and then growled, "How did you find me?"

Dora cleared her throat. "Actually, I wasn't calling to talk—not to you. I'm trying to find Pilar. Her neighbor gave me this number."

"Yeah?'

"Yes. I wanted to ask—how's Ceci?"

"Oh, really? How very kind of you. How goddamn motherly, all of a sudden!"

He wondered if the wood floor might catch fire under him.

"Now, wait just a minute!" Her voice was shrill, the breathiness gone. "I—"

"No, *you* wait!" He stopped for a breath. "You goddamn coward—do you know what you've put everyone through? If I could get my hands on you, I don't know what I'd do. What kind of mother leaves her daughter—in the hospital, for Chrissake? What mother goes gallivanting off to Mexico—leaving a sick child?"

"Mexico! How do you know where I am?"

"Rafaela told me. She knows everything." He laughed bitterly. "And—do you know what else? She said your leaving is the best damned thing that could ever happen. She told me many things. She's a goddamn wise woman, I tell you!"

He could hear Dora's angered breathing, just barely, but he knew the sound so well—those little puffs, as she collected her venom into words. He could see that gorgeous chest of hers heaving and her perfect, black eyebrows knitting over those incredible eyes—those bewitching eyes! Finally, the line grew quiet—not even her breathing audible.

"So, what are you going to do, Dora?"

"Just—well—I want a divorce."

"Yeah, Rafaela told me that, too."

"Why do you keep talking about this—Rafaela?"

"Don't you know her? She's your family *curandera*. She's helping your poor little daughter get over nearly dying while you—"

"Oh! *Doña Rafaela*, the *bruja?*"

"I don't know *what* the hell she is, but she's on my side."

"Oh, Barry, let's not take sides," she sighed. "I'd hoped—"

"Are you really in Mexico? That far away? I don't expect you can throw anything that far!" The cheer in his voice surprised him.

She sighed. "Grow up, Barry!"

"But are you—in Mexico?"

"Yes, I am. I'm in Acapulco. With Javier."

"Javier? What about that guy Carlos, what happened to him? Pilar told me—"

"Oh, so you're all in it together? You—Pilar—and the *bruja*—talking about me and plotting your revenge, I suppose. I've had it with all of you. None of you ever loved me. All you wanted was—"

Weary of her shrillness, Barry laid the phone beside him on the floor. He stared at the clusters of little holes in each end of the receiver: Dora's words buzzed out of the mouthpiece like insects. He smiled as Rafaela stepped into the hall from the kitchen, wiped her hands on her checkered apron, and squatted to pick up the receiver.

"*Rafaela de Aguilar, a su servicio. Doralinda? Ah, sí. No, no.* She's better, yes. Who are you with now? Really? Javier who owns all those canneries? Ah, he's a very good catch—yes. No, I only knew him by sight. The Quinteros were way too important for me. Oh? I wouldn't say that. I don't know. You'll have to talk to him. *Hasta luego, Doralinda.* I have to make your Barry some breakfast." Rafaela handed the phone to Barry and shuffled her bedroom slippers back to the kitchen.

"What was all that?" Dora's voice sounded even smaller and farther away.

"That was Rafaela," Barry laughed, "the *curandera*."

"I know her, all right!" Dora's voice turned sullen. "Too well. Pilar swears by her."

"She's the one, isn't she? The one who made your mother the amulets? The ones you were embarrassed about in high school?" Barry's voice lilted giddily. "But she's not a *bruja*—she's—"

"That was another one, in Santa Barbara."

"God, *curanderas* everywhere!" Yes, he was feeling great now. "Rolling eggs over all the crowned heads of Europe, hobnobbing with celebrities. Crazy old women, barging in where angels fear to tread!"

"Are you drunk, Barry?"

"No. Are you?"

"Of course not! Now, stop goofing around! We have to discuss the details."

"What's there to discuss? Tell me, what's next? After your Mexican divorce, will we just part ways, like two ships in the night?" He hammed a woeful sigh. "So poetic. Will we be rid of you forever? Pray God, yes!"

"There's no need to be cruel, Barry!" She coughed. "Javier has hired me an attorney. There are legal matters. I—I need you to send down—my things—and I will have to see Ceci sometimes."

"Ah, yes, it's your duty to see her—that would be the proper thing, wouldn't it? Guess what? She's doing just great—except for the matter of the drowning. She'll get well faster without your telling her how bad she is all the time. I'm fine, too, even though you didn't think to ask. I'm just ducky. I'm elated to know you aren't lying in a pool of blood somewhere. What the hell were you thinking, deserting us like that! Not even a note. I love you, damn it! Or at least, I used to."

"I meant to call, but I—I couldn't. I thought it would be better just to make a clean cut. Give you time to cool off. You understand, don't you? I mean—"

"A clean cut for you—a messy pile of carnage for me! Want your goddamn stuff? Send a postcard, care of Pilar, with your shipping address."

Barry dropped the receiver onto the cradle with an exhalation of finality.

"*Amigo?* Breakfast!" Rafaela called cheerfully from the kitchen. She had laid out a place for him and handed him a steaming cup of coffee. Barry sat down at the table with inexpressible gratitude for her nonchalance.

A blessed silence surrounded them, the sun warming his shoulders, the coffee clearing his fog. Rafaela poured herself a cup and sat across from him, studying him without smiling. Two minutes ticked away on the wall over the stove, and still Rafaela didn't remove her inscrutable gaze. Barry traced the handle of his spoon with his finger.

Finally, she cleared her throat. "I have been wanting to ask you something. What do you think of my daughter?"

"Carmen's a very good person, a good mother. I like her."

"You wonder why Carmen has two children, and no husband?" Rafaela slid an omelet studded with potatoes and chilies onto his plate. "How she can have a daughter who is ready to celebrate her *quinceañera*? You think she's old."

His fork slipped and clattered on his plate. "It's none of my business."

"That is the truth." The flecks of gold in Rafaela's irises glittered. "More tortillas, Barry?"

"No, thanks. Look, Rafaela, I know you have stuff to do. Don't get me wrong, I appreciate all this attention—but please, there's no need to fuss over me."

"Ah, *sí*."

Rafaela set to work filling cellophane packets, he supposed with some of her herbal remedies, stapling a paper label to the top of each bag. She whistled to herself softly, from time to time glancing at him over her shoulder. Barry sensed she was only passing the time until he showed his interest.

"Okay, all right, then, yes! I'm curious. How old is she?"

Rafaela shook some powder through a sieve and scraped it into a wax paper bag. "Carmen married very young—a rebellion against her *papá*. To me, years are nothing; it is the soul I study. My daughter came into this world old, and she has accepted her destiny. Hard work is her lot, and serving others. In this way, *amigo*, she is much, much older than you, *a viejecita*, a little old lady." Rafaela surveyed him, nodding slowly. "My friend, you are still a young buck, full of fight. I intend to help you, but I cannot force you; you would gore me with your horns."

"What am I—a bull or a buck?" Barry laughed and stared into his cup. Her good-natured delivery did not lesson the sting. How dare she presume to help him? He had not given permission.

Rafaela leaned toward him. "Ah, but you have—"

Barry froze, the mug at his lip.

"You have—a little piece of egg—right here." She pointed to her cheek.

Barry exhaled relief and wiped his cheek. "I thought you were going to tell me I've already given you permission!" he laughed, "You know, permission to heal me."

"With someone like you, I don't wait forever—not for permission. Do what you will. You decide whether or not to get well." She stood, hands on her hips. "Now, here is another matter to test your patience." She laid a roll of dollar bills onto the table. "This is a gift from Pilar and me, not for you, but for the child. She needs clothes—new ones, without the bad memories. Carmen will take you downtown to help you shop." She leveled her gaze, pushing the roll of bills closer to him. "Please, understand—I must repay my debt to Cecilia Montenegro. It's nothing to do with you."

"There's one other thing you can do." She climbed the stepladder to reach for a cookie tin on the top shelf and fished out a twenty-dollar bill. "Will you make sure Carmen has a good dinner, somewhere outside the barrio? Even though you don't always see eye to eye, she deserves that much for helping you today."

"All right, but—" Barry pushed back the twenty. "Dinner is on me."

"*Bien.*" Rafaela stuffed the twenty back into her pocket. "But you will accept the gift for Cecilita?"

"How can I?"

A clatter out on the front porch caused them both to turn.

"Someone to see me." She patted his hand as she left. "Be happy this morning, *amigo.* Time races."

He sipped at his coffee as she left. Why did Rafaela think he disliked Carmen? In fact, she was growing on him. He picked up the newspaper; Kennedy won another primary. Ma would be thrilled that her man now had a chance.

"Morning, Daddy!"

"Morning?" He looked up from the newspaper. "It's almost afternoon, but I'm glad you're catching up on your sleep."

"I'm hungry."

"At last, Bean!" Barry swept her into a hug. "Whatever you want—it's yours."

She laid her head on his shoulder. "Cereal—"

Frenziedly opening cabinets, Barry faced mysterious cartons—all Mexican brands. He peered into a box that looked promising. It contained soap flakes.

"Hey, Barry." Carmen stood at the back door.

"I didn't know you were here already."

"Tito and I checked the tortoise eggs. Are you going to do some washing up?"

"I'm looking for cereal."

"You won't find it under the sink." She reached into an overhead cupboard. "Here—will Rice Krispies do? What else?" Carmen opened the fridge. "How about some orange juice?"

Ceci nodded happily.

"And a banana?"

"Please."

Barry sipped his coffee. "Are you missing work just to take us shopping?"

"Not just." Carmen sliced the banana over the bowl. "I needed a day off."

"You could have done something for yourself."

"Please get dressed, Ceci." Carmen dabbed at Ceci's milk moustache, seemingly ignoring Barry. "Tito is outside. You two can play while we go buy you some clothes. Tell me, what colors do you like?"

A smile widened Ceci's hollowed cheeks. "Two colors—green and red."

"Ah, a little *chuparrosa,* eh? Hummingbird colors!"

"They're the ones with the long beaks?"

"The very tiny ones, yes. When you go outside, look up under the arbor where Mamita put three bottles of red juice to feed the *chuparrosas.* If you see one, it's lucky."

Barry poured Ceci a half-glass of milk. "Lucky for what?'

"*Chuparrosas* bring joy—and luck in love."

"That's why I never see them, then!" Barry rinsed out Ceci's empty bowl. "Hey, what's Tito doing out there?"

"He's watching something intently. Oh, Barry, look at that—a hummingbird! Even as we speak."

Ceci ran to the sink. "I want to see!"

Barry lifted Ceci to the window. Another hummer dove from the sky right over Tito's head, then another and another.

"Hey, they're divebombing Tito! Never seen so many of them!"

"Mamita's garden is a bird oasis." Carmen glanced at her watch. "We'd better get going, Barry; I only have a couple of hours. I have to pick Adelita up this afternoon."

"I wanted to take you out to dinner afterwards. I took your day off; it's the least I can do. Please?"

"Well—I—I could call Dolores and ask if she'd bring Adelita here—"

"I promise not to keep you out late, if that's what is worrying you."

"I'm not—" but she did look worried, the way she studied him, her eyes sidelong, her lips slightly pursed, "I just wasn't—"

"It's just to thank you for your trouble—not a date or anything."

"All right, Barry." She squeezed Ceci's hand, "Red and green, that's what we'll find for you—like Christmas. Now, I'd better call Dolores."

Barry and Ceci smiled at each other.

"Daddy, I like Carmen."

He surveyed her, feigning suspicion. "But you like everyone, right?"

"No, I don't."

"Who don't you like, Ceci Bean?"

"I don't like Val—or Kyle. I really don't like them."

"Do you want to tell me why?"

Without meeting his eyes, she stood, pushed her chair in, and wiped up a little drip of milk with her napkin. "May I be excused?" She didn't wait for his answer.

He followed her upstairs. "Ceci Bean, you can't keep secrets from your old daddy. I need to know everything. What did Val and Kyle do to you?"

Ceci sighed and stepped into the same pink shorts she had worn for days. "Daddy, I want a green dress, okay?"

As she pulled on a too-big tee shirt from Adelita, Barry gazed at her gauntness, heartbroken. "Can I have a green dress? A green party dress with stars."

"Sweetheart, I don't know if they have dresses with stars. I'll try."

"That's what I want—a green dress with stars."

☆   ☆   ☆   ☆

"I think something else happened," Barry told Carmen as they boarded the streetcar. "Something else happened to Ceci—besides the stuff about Dora and me, and the drowning. I think there's more."

"She'll have to recover, Barry, before she can tell everything." Carmen's eyes pitied him, her voice gentle. "Leave the healing to Mamita. Our job is to find new clothes. That will lift her spirits more than you'll believe."

Barry winced back tears. "She wants a green dress—with stars. How will we ever find such a thing?"

"Remember the scarlet ribbons? You must have heard the song. Oh, who is it? Dinah Shore? You know: *'If I live to be a hundred, I will never know from where, came those lovely scarlet ribbons, scarlet ribbons for her hair.'*"

"Oh yeah, that one! The little girl prays for them. The father can't buy them. Presto, change-o, ribbons appear—sentimental drivel."

"Maybe so, Barry, but if ever a little girl deserved a green dress with stars, it's your Ceci. I believe we'll find one."

Barry sighed, "You and your mother must have cast a spell on me."

"How do you mean?"

"Normally, I would've wiggled out of this shopping trip. The two of you are like a tag team."

"Mother would laugh at that! I'm a constant trial to her."

"Nonsense! You believe in your mother's strength. You champion her work. You're a nurse; you've a science background. If you think miracles can happen, who am I to argue? I'm just a numbskull musician."

"Ha! You argue plenty, *señor*." Carmen pulled the stop cord. "Here's our stop."

"Bullocks Wilshire?" Barry looked at the glamorous display windows, uneasy. "How will we afford that?"

"They're having their big sale. Mamita and Pilar stressed that the clothes better be top-notch and fashionable. Cecilita should look like a princess when you take her to Ireland."

"I haven't decided about Ireland." He pushed open the glass door for Carmen. "Not yet, anyway."

She knit her brows. "Oh, I see."

"I don't know if you do. I've given in to everything, so far—but I do have limits, Ireland being the outermost."

"Okay!" Carmen studied the store directory sign. "Ah, second floor—Children's Department." She took his arm. "First thing: some new clean underwear."

"I mean it; I'm not interested in Ireland."

"Okay!" she laughed. "I believe you. Do you want to take the escalator?"

Barry studied her—not a glimmer of anything but interest in the bright merchandise all around them.

"Ireland is a dreary place, Carmen."

"Have you been there?" her eyes met his, teasing. "Bet you haven't."

"I was born there." He folded his arms over his chest.

"Oh, and you came here at what age?"

He looked away, mumbling. "Two—and a half."

"What?"

"Two and a half!"

"Ah, yes!" With a little flounce, she stepped off the escalator. "Makes a big difference, the half year. You had the full span of the seasons."

"I can remember this—it rained nonstop. Day we arrived in the Big Apple was the first sun I'd seen in my entire life."

Hands on her hips, she nodded sagely. "Sorry to change the subject, but Ceci needs some underwear, socks, and pajamas. Then we'll have to look for the green dress with stars."

"I shouldn't have gotten Ceci's hopes up."

"Good, let her hope. I'm going to hope, too."

"I don't hope very well, Carmen."

"Here we are—little girls' underpants. She'll need one pair for each day of the week, at least."

"What size?"

"You don't know? She's your daughter, for Pete's sake!"

"Dora did all the clothes shopping."

"What kind of shopping did you do?"

"Whiskey—and sheet music."

"Men!"

Staring at sheaves of cellophane-wrapped packages, Barry made a choice and held up some underpants for Carmen's approval.

She studied them, he thought, entirely too long. "Better still, how about the ones with the pink flowers? The other ones, no—the wrong size. Those are for a two-year-old!"

Barry jammed the package into the rack. "Ouch, I bent back my nail!" He plunged his smarting forefinger into his mouth.

"Oh, Barry, stop acting like you're getting a root canal!"

"I'm not." He shook his finger, still wincing over the bent fingernail.

"You are! Try to imagine how happy Ceci will be to have some pretty things. That should make it more interesting."

"I'm interested, Carmen, really—"

"I'd hate to see you when you're bored. Here, look at these blouses. Which one would you choose?"

"The blue one's cheaper."

Her lower lip pushed out sightly. "Imagine Ceci's little face. Oh, Barry, she's so cute. Imagine which blouse would set off her face."

"Set off? You mean like a firecracker?"

She pressed her lips together. "You know what I mean—those soft green eyes, that tawny skin. Which would flatter her more?"

He thought a moment. "The blue one."

"Why?"

"Because—it's softer, and she's soft, and a little shy. If I bought her red, it would have to be—a gentler red."

"Atta boy!" She squeezed his arm, and warmth shot through him.

"How about that light green blouse, Carmen? It'd match her eyes."

"See, Barry? You're a natural at this fashion stuff."

"No, I'm not. Look at my clothes—awful."

Carmen surveyed him. "You could use a new shirt."

"I've got shirts. I just need to get my stuff out of the house. Pretty soon the landlord will throw everything into the street. Haven't paid the rent this month."

"Stop worrying, Barry! We'd better look at dresses. We'll get socks to match whatever we pick out."

"I seem to remember Dora always got the plain white."

"Well, now you get to decide. See any green dresses with stars? Let's make it interesting; I find the dress—you buy me dinner. If you find it, I'll buy."

They perused the sale rack. The dresses were pressed so close together that it was almost impossible to pull out a hanger to look at one.

Barry sighed, "No stars in this mess."

"Try to find a green dress. Then we'll worry about stars."

"She's not going to settle just for green. Ceci's not the kind to settle."

"Wait—oh, look!" Carmen held up a green voile dress with a white lace collar.

"It doesn't have stars."

"It does!" Carmen's eyes glistened. "Better than stars—"

"Where?"

"You tell me; just look, Barry!"

Then he saw them, the row of rhinestone buttons. "Stars! Carmen, you're a genius!" He sang out, "Seven little stars!" He grabbed Carmen's waist and danced her around the floor. "I'm going to buy you the best dinner you've ever had. How about the Brown Derby? How about it?"

"If you ask me, Daddy Warbucks, I'd settle for some good Chinese food."

"You're too good, Carmen, just too damned good."

Carmen's eyes clouded; she turned away.

"What's the matter? Did I say something wrong?"

"I can't believe how it still hits me." She covered her eyes.

"What?"

"Juan used to say that. Always said I was too good, that I made him feel worthless." She forced a stiff little smile. "I've always been a goodie-two-shoes. Trying to make up for nearly killing Papá, I guess."

Barry's jaw dropped.

"Oh, I didn't try to murder him. The night I announced my engagement, Papá had his first heart attack. Papá never liked Juan, said he was a *malvado*. I swear, even the milkman told me Juan was a bad egg. *El amor es ciego, pero los vecinos no*—Love is blind, but the neighbors aren't. Juan had been cheating on me from day one. After we were married, it got worse, and my father never got his health back. Papá died a couple of years later."

"I'm so sorry, Carmen. That's a lot to bear. So where is this Juan jerk now?"

"In Mexico."

"One thing we do have in common: spouses in Mexico."

"The only thing?"

"Also our impeccable taste in clothes." Barry held up the green dress. He noted the sadness behind her wry smile. "Seriously, Juan is a goddamn fool—"

"It's all right, Barry." She patted his shoulder. "I'm mostly over it—just a twinge now and then. Your wounds are still fresh."

"I know what you mean. I'm beginning to see that Dora and I—that we might be better off apart. At least, in my head I do. My heart is all torn up, and I keep asking myself what-if questions. You know what I mean? What if I'd done this or said that. It keeps me up at night and follows me around all day. I wonder, will I ever heal?"

"You will, but it takes a long time. You develop a little scab, it falls off, and you bleed again. You just have get used to it—to hurting."

"Ma used to tell me, 'You blistered your bum; now you've got to sit down on it.'"

"She's right, I guess. Back to practical matters—shall we buy these, then?"

"What about shoes?"

"I think she'll be okay till school starts, but let's pick out some socks."

Carmen was all business, her cheer diminished. Longing for the breezy camaraderie they had had before Dora and Juan invaded their thoughts, Barry lifted a pair of socks, dancing them across Carmen's arm.

"How about these? Cute little socks, eh?"

She smiled wanly. "They're baby socks."

"Ah! Instead of baby socks, we have to find some bobby socks." He spun the rotating display rack. "Round and round and round she goes, where she stops, nobody knows. There!" He grabbed a pair of brown knee socks from the hook.

Carmen giggled behind her hand. "Huge!"

"She'll grow into them, right?"

"Her freshman year of college, maybe!"

Barry's eyes shifted. "Isn't this the Children's Department?"

"Put them back, silly!" Her smile was wide and easy again. "If we get these plain ones, we'll have barely enough left to get the green dress. We might each have to chip in a little extra. Let's get these rung up before we change our minds."

By the end of the afternoon, Barry was dragging, and Carmen was still fresh as a daisy. How did women go shopping, season after season, and still want to shop for recreation? If he'd been shopping with Dora, listening to her rationales for buying things too expensive on credit, he would have tired even faster than he did today. He had always followed Dora to the cash register with a knot in his stomach, wondering if her extravagant purchases had left any cash for paying the bills.

Carmen was a more tentative shopper. Even though she had advocated for the green dress, she still advised him to cut back on what he spent on everything else, including dinner, so Ceci could have her heart's desire.

As they boarded the streetcar, he decided would make it up to Carmen with some treat. Soon she was dozing next to him, her head falling forward until they jerked to a stop. He knew a Chinese place, cheap, but a favorite haunt for jazz musicians. It would be fun for her; sometimes Michael Chan even let some up-and-coming guy play in the lounge for tips. A clarinet aficionado, Chan had helped Barry get his start in L.A. and was always glad to see him.

"Carmen, kiddo, wake up. This is where we get off—Chan's Chinese Garden."

When he first arrived in California, Barry had befriended the Chans, the restaurant a kind of second home until he'd moved to San Pedro. As he got to know Barry, Michael had told the story of how they'd immigrated to Los Angeles after World War II, financing their restaurant with jewels Junlan had sewn into the lining of her traveling coat. Always good for an extra bowl of rice or a fortune cookie for Ceci, Junlan and Michael had helped Barry through many a hungry time.

"They serve great food, Carmen, even though the décor is wacky. Junlan gets all those old movie posters at the flea market. She's crazy about Hollywood. If I told her you were Dolores del Rio's cousin, you'd get free dinners for life."

"Alphabetical order." Carmen tilted her head. "The posters—Gone with the Wind, and then Gunga Din."

"Oh, yeah, I guess we're at the 'G' table. 'G' for 'go' or General Tso's chicken." God, what a stupid thing to say, he thought, but Carmen just smiled and shook her napkin onto her lap.

Michael Chan brought them menus. "My friend, Barry!" He did a double take. "And a new lady friend—"

"Michael Chan, this is my friend, Carmen. Gosh, Carmen, I don't even know your last name."

"Arroyos." Carmen shook Michael's hand. "Carmen Arroyos."

"Look like Dora." Chan grinned. "You her sister?"

"No, Carmen's an old friend of the family. Still serve drinks, Mike?"

"Wine," Chan nodded. "And beer."

"We'll have the Dinner Special for two, and you want something to drink, Carmen? I'll have the red wine."

"I'm fine with tea."

As Chan left, Carmen scanned the room. "Oh, no! Don't turn around."

"What's the matter?"

"It's Jiménez and his cousin," her voice was barely a whisper. "No, don't look!" She pulled his hand. "Please! They're watching us."

"Who?"

"The *brujo*. He's got his cousin with him. No, don't turn around."

"Oh, come on! Why?" Barry made to turn.

"No!" Carmen whispered harshly. "I'm serious, don't turn—"

Barry swung around.

"Oh, Barry, why did you have to do that? I told you."

"He looks harmless enough. I don't understand the intrigue with the *brujo*."

Her eyes shifted downwards. "I wish you hadn't turned. Oh well, he's gone into the lounge." She exhaled. "God, he makes me nervous. I hate being followed."

"Sure, but what does it matter? What's he going to do to you?"

"He wasn't looking at me, Barry. He has another target."

"Well, then, what's the big deal?"

"He was looking at you."

"Me?" Barry laughed. "Why would he aim his sights at me?"

"I don't understand Jiménez's motives. Why doesn't he just improve his medicine? Why does he resort to this—crap?"

"I've never seen you so het up."

"Well, he makes me mad. Mamita has worked so hard all her life. She has earned respect. Evil people, they ruin everything."

"Have a drink. It will relax you."

"No, thanks." She glanced over his shoulder again. "Jiménez has cousins all over the barrio. There's another one, at the cigarette machine. No, don't turn." She gripped his hand, and for a brief second, Barry felt a surge of gratitude for the *brujo's* cousin.

"They'd mess with me, eh?" He flexed his muscles. "Clarinet players are quite a threat to these mobster types! I'll just blow them down."

"It's no joke. He's already threatened to harm Mamita. He doesn't like her helping you."

"But why? I'm just a skinny, unemployed musician with no prospects. The only thing going for me is the distinct pleasure of taking the belle of the barrio to dinner. No wonder he's out to get me. He probably wants you all to himself."

To Barry's surprise, Carmen blushed a deep crimson.

"Just look at you, blushing like a—wait a minute!" He sat up straighter in his chair, goosing his neck to see over her head. "Whoa! Will you look at who just walked in? Behind *you,* this time—must be old home week for jackasses."

"Who is it?"

"Mitch Comaneci, a jazz impresario—lives in Santa Barbara. Go ahead, check him out; he doesn't have any whammy, just money. He's a big honcho, though."

Carmen swiveled to check. "That guy in the expensive suit?"

"That's him. Glory be, he's going to grace us with a personal appearance."

Mitch swaggered to their table. "Saint Sullivan!"

"Well, well!" Barry stood to shake his hand. "Mitch. What are you doing in Chinatown? Slumming it?"

"You know I'm always looking for new venues. Chan called me."

"No kidding—Chan? It certainly is a small world."

"Who's the lovely lady, Barry?"

"Mitch Comaneci, I'd like you to meet a friend of mine, Carmen Arroyos."

"Pleased to meet you. Carmen, is it?"

"Yes."

"You a singer? We're looking for a girl. A Cuban group I'm booking—"

"You've got to be kidding, Mr. Comaneci! I can't carry a tune in a bucket."

"Maybe you dance?"

She laughed. "No, I'm completely hopeless as an entertainer."

"Pity, that." The spark in his eyes fading, Mitch dropped her hand. He turned to Barry. "Listen, Sullivan; Schwann is still looking for another lead clarinet. They extended their tour; they're heading to Seattle and Vancouver."

"He said he knew this guy in Seattle."

"Randall? He's in some trouble or other. George said he'd hire you back in a heartbeat. All you have to do is drive back up to Frisco tomorrow morning and catch them before they hit the road. They're still at the Mark Hopkins."

"That's great news, Mitch!" Barry glanced at Carmen, her smile frozen in a stiff line, her eyes wary. "I might make it, if I start at the crack of dawn."

"So you'll agree to go?" Carmen coughed. "What about Ceci?"

"Oh, Pilar or somebody can take care of her."

"Excuse me!" Carmen slid out of the booth. "I have to powder my nose."

Without acknowledging her, Mitch moved in closer to Barry.

"So, the gig's settled? You'll be there by tomorrow?"

"Sure thing," Barry nodded. "I'll be there."

"Good; I've got to talk to Chan now. Ciao, man!"

When Carmen returned, Barry lifted his glass to her. "What took you so long? I could've gotten you a gig with the Cubanos. I'm on Mitch's good side tonight."

"Isn't that nice for you?"

The chill of realization flooded Barry's pleasure. "You're mad at me."

"Of course I am!" Carmen's gaze flew from the red paper lantern hanging over their booth to her hands, clasped together almost prayerfully. Barry wondered if she would cry, or yell at him.

"Come on, Carmen; what's eating you?"

"You're an idiot."

"I am!" Barry leaned forward and patted her hand. "I know. I know!"

"No you don't!" She slid her hand away. "You don't know. You have no idea."

"Look, Carmen, I'm sorry I interrupted our dinner to deal with Mitch."

"It's not the interruption! It's that you're considering leaving now, when—"

"Oh," Barry smiled. "We'll have plenty of time to get to know each other later."

"God!" She slapped both hands on the table. "You're more of an idiot than I thought!"

"Try to understand. It's early days yet to get serious about a new woman."

"New woman!" Carmen's hands flew to her cheeks. "Oh my God, you think—I want you to stay for *me*?"

Barry inhaled, anticipating a scene. She didn't speak, staring at his face, the anger seeping out her eyes as she did so. He watched her helplessly, and then she threw back her head and laughed till her eyes watered.

He knew what was coming: disillusionment, disappointment, and loss. He was going to lose her, because he had dared hope she might be falling love with him.

"You big dope. You haven't a clue." Wiping her eyes, she leaned forward and took his hands. "I'm disappointed! I can't believe you would agree to leave your daughter—not when she's so fragile." Shaking her head, she let go of his hands. "I don't care one whit about you—leaving. It's Ceci you ought to think about. She needs you."

"Sure she does. She needs me to make a living."

"That's no excuse for abandoning her. You could find a job here, or take her with you."

"Take Ceci on the road? With a jazz band—a bunch of dope fiends, crumbs, and hop heads?"

"All right," Carmen sighed. "Don't take her with you, then. Why not stay here? Make her a home. You said this band of Schwann was—how did you put it—schmaltzy? Is it really worth jeopardizing your daughter's health for this job?"

"It's a paying gig. There's nothing left for me here. I've got to go, Carmen. Pilar can take care of Ceci a damned sight better than I would."

"What about your mother? Is Pilar going to take care of her, too? You realize Pilar is seventy and in poor health? She can't pick up every responsibility you drop in your wake."

"Pilar has more energy than you and me put together. She'll be fine."

"She has hypertension and an ulcer. It's duty that drives her. You could take a page from her book, you know. You could put family first."

"I am; it's my duty to make a living, even if it requires me to travel."

Junlan brought the big round tray with their dinner. "People hungry now?"

"No, I'm not hungry anymore." Carmen shook her head. "Sorry, Junlan, I'm afraid I'm going to have to go. It was so nice to meet you."

"You stay and talk. He need good woman. Settle down."

"Yes, I'm sure he does. But he'll have to look elsewhere. I've got to go."

Barry reached for Carmen's hand. "Please, I didn't mean—"

"Don't flatter yourself. You haven't upset me. You blistered your own bum, buster. Now sit on it!" She fished up the Bullocks bag from under the table, brushed a strand of hair from her eyes, and made for the door.

Barry rose to follow Carmen. Junlan tugged him by the shirt back to the booth. "Let her blow steam off. Her head is hot."

"She isn't a hothead, Junlan."

"All the Mexicans that way, Barry, very hot head. Like the girl you married. Mexicans always mad."

"Dora? Now, *she* was a hothead. Not this one, she's different."

"Ah." Junlan's brow furrowed. "You like this new one?"

Barry could only nod.

"Kind of old."

"A couple of years older than me—"

"Old!" Junlan pushed the plate toward him. "You eat; you feel better. Don't worry; you find new girl. Young one."

"Another glass of wine, okay, sweetheart? Chianti this time." Barry pressed his heart with both hands. "To ease my pain."

"You drink too much, you lose girl for sure." Junlan hobbled away on her Hollywood high heels.

Staring at his food with indifference, Barry sipped his sour red wine, thinking Chan should offer a better vintage if he wanted to attract an elite clientele. Finally, a meek young waiter brought him the Chianti. Before he downed it, he peered under the table at something against his feet. Carmen had left one of the bags. He looked inside to find the dress with the diamond buttons.

He stuffed the dress into his coat pocket and crumpled the bag into a ball, remembering how finding the dress had pleased Carmen. He had thought she liked him—was attracted. He felt an attraction. Was it all his? He was thinking like a teenaged girl, he told himself—like a girl picking petals off a daisy to guess at how someone felt. He didn't want to get entangled. He was still half crazy from Dora's betrayal—that had to be it. It couldn't have been love, but he was sure there'd been *something* between them today, a sparkle.

Wishful thinking! Barry toyed with the Chow Mein noodles and then pushed his plate away. The truth was she wanted him to give up the gig with Schwann. Any musician in his right mind knew that during a dry spell, you didn't refuse any paying gig. The hell with women, he told himself; they understood nothing about the real world. If Carmen disapproved, that was too damned bad.

As he settled the check, he glimpsed Carmen through the window. She was getting onto the streetcar. To avoid her, he decided to hoof it. He was halfway down the block when he heard Chan running up behind him.

"Barry!" Chan waved a ten-dollar bill. "You paid too much."

"Consider it a big tip."

"You crazy guy!" Chan handed Barry a fortune cookie. "Take this for little girl."

"Thanks." He thrust the cookie into his pocket, where it crunched into the wadded dress.

"Now take your money. Ten dollars tip is too big. I do a good business, don't need to overcharge."

"All right," Barry took the tenner from Chan. "You drive a hard bargain."

"You all right? You don't look too good."

"I'm fine. Just woman trouble."

"Ah, I know this woman trouble. I've got big trouble at my house, too."

"Junlan?"

"Yeah, Jun, she wants big nightclub like Hollywood movie. No more little restaurant."

"Well, maybe she's onto something. You have the best ear in town for jazz, Chan. I wish you luck, friend."

"You, too!" Chan waved and jogged back to the restaurant.

The evening was oddly cool for summer. As he headed down North Broadway, toward Brooklyn Avenue and the barrio, the difference in the sky struck him. There were ribbons of orangey clouds, and evening was darkening around the insistent hum of traffic.

Streetlights blinked on overhead, a police car passed, and a city bus hissed to a stop up ahead of him. A handful of people got out with their shopping bags, lunch boxes, and briefcases, bidding each other goodbye in that familiar way of regulars. Everyone seemed to have somewhere to go and someone to go with—everyone but him.

Hands stuffed into his jacket pockets, he felt the fortune cookie. He pulled the crumbs from his pocket, tossing them into the gutter, at the last minute deciding not to throw away the fortune. It read: *There is yet time to choose another path.*

The words echoed in his head. Another path! What other path? There seemed to be no path except the path straight to one hell or another. Just when he thought he'd found a friend, someone who he could trust, he'd gone and blown it straight to hell. God, he needed a drink! He had to find a real bar: a place where he could settle in, marinate his misery.

Nothing around but closed-up dress shops and offices, marble facades and glass, so he crossed the street and made his way up a narrow side street toward Olvera. He thought he'd seen a tavern around there. He'd just have one drink, stall a little to give Carmen time to pick up her kids and go before he arrived at Rafaela's. Whiskey always gave him perspective, setting the agony at a bearable distance.

Everything had become claustrophobic, the stressors closing in so fast. Cooped up with bossy women for days on end, he longed to lift a drink surrounded by whiskered faces, smoke, and indifference.

He knew he was entering the barrio. English had almost disappeared. Dimly lit storefronts meant nothing to him beyond the faded paint, the plastered layers of peeling handbills—all indecipherable, all in Spanish. Now that Dora was gone for good, what had he to do with Mexicans anymore? Chan was right—crazy people, Mexicans, always up in arms about something.

An aroma of tortillas wafted past Barry's nose: maybe a tortilla factory, or just some industrious homemaker preparing for the morrow. He shook his head. The barrio was like a foreign country. A gringo couldn't even find a bar without a guide.

Slouched on the bench at the bus stop, a plump young woman folded her magazine and slipped it into her basket. Barry stepped into the circle of light under the street lamp. "Good, evening, Miss. Can you direct me to a bar?"

Her basket clutched to her chest, she shook her dark head adamantly and shrank away. *"¡No hablo inglés!"*

"Please, Miss, I just want to know where I can get a beer—*cerveza?*"

Before the bus completed its stop she was banging the door, seemingly terrified that Barry might accost her. The door opened, and she leapt up the steps. Barry started after her, his arms at his side, his palms open. "Please, Miss, I'm sorry. I just—"

"You getting on board, Romeo?" The driver asked. "Or looking for trouble?"

"What's with you people?" Barry yelled after the bus, shaking his fist. Then, embarrassed, he backed up from the curb, something yielding under his right foot—a white baby shoe. He picked it up. Its pink laces still tied neatly, its white so clean and hopeful. Something tightened in his chest. "Ceci!" he whispered, tenderly smoothing the laces. "Ceci."

His daughter belonged to this barrio, almost as much as Ma did to Connemara. It was as if a line had been drawn through his daughter, dividing her between two worlds. What of Ireland? Did she belong there, too? Ceci—the half and half—because of her parents, was she doomed to two disparate worlds? He turned the baby shoe in his fingers, a little bell someone had attached to the lacing jingling. Someone would probably come back for this treasure, he told himself, and set the shoe on the bus bench.

"Quit bothering our women!" a voice fired out of the shadows, and a young man, his posture taut, emerged. He jabbed a cigarette into his sneer, puffed unhurriedly, and exhaled a smoke ring.

"Hey!" Barry shuddered involuntarily, then steeled himself. "You're that *brujo's* cousin, aren't you?" he snarled, he hoped menacingly. "Yeah, you're the one! You followed us today."

"What if I did?" The young man took another drag on his cigarette. "You don't belong here. Why don't you go back to the suburbs? Leave us be!"

A tremor climbed Barry's back; he feared the kid saw it. It was like that tiny rip they put at the top of a bag of peanuts: the place to tear it all open. Any minute, the kid would pounce. Barry stared back into those hating eyes, his fists clenched at the ready.

Behind a cloud of exhaled smoke, the tough smirked, curling his fists so that his muscles rippled up his arm. "You want to hit me, *pendejo?*" Studying Barry intently, he dropped his cigarette, crushed it with the toe of his cowboy boot, and disappeared into the shadows between the shuttered storefronts.

For a moment Barry considered going straight to Rafaela's without stopping for a drink, but the unreleased anger burnt at his throat, the kind of burn that thirsted for whiskey. He wondered if Dora had sent that hood after him, if this whole scenario weren't some Latin conspiracy to bring down the Irish. He laughed, a cold, humorless laugh, and shook his fist at where the kid had disappeared. "You don't own this town! I've a right to talk to anyone I please! I'll do whatever the hell I want, I tell you, whatever I damned well please!"

Then he saw the bar. It glistened like a jewel among the unlit buildings. *Taberna El Serafino,* the neon-cursive sign blinked over a dingy window placard of a cherub brandishing a tequila bottle. Drinking man's instinct told Barry all he needed to know. He expected a pleasant shabbiness bound to discourage the confusing presence of womankind. He hoped they'd have a bottle of Old Bushmills to soothe the anxiety that snaked in after his thirst.

As he walked through the door, reassuring swirls of cigar smoke greeted Barry's nose. Clinking glasses, beer taps swooshing, and jovial male voices—all balm to his ears, but not a white face in the room. With a shrug, he hung his jacket on the coat tree and took a stool at the bar. Tonight he'd have to go native. At least it was a man's bar.

Such a macho décor! Walls dark and enclosing. A huge calendar of a cone-breasted Aztec princess swooning over the lap of a hawk-nosed warrior, both in feathered headdress. Some reprobate had hastily taped some girlie photos around the cash register— Marilyn Monroe, Bettie Page, and Jayne Mansfield—the only other whites in the bar. Over the bar, in the center of all this fleshy prurience, an ornate golden frame encased a huge portrait of a doe-eyed Madonna.

For a long while Barry stared at the incongruity of her chaste pose, somehow more alluring than the others—a real woman one could love, not a wet dream. Yet did such perfect women exist? Were there angels to save men from their coarser desires? He shrugged away this insight. Better a feathered floozy than those tender eyes so judging.

The barkeep polished the same small circle of the bar, listening to an old man in a straw cowboy hat, for quite some time. He ignored Barry, giving him sidelong glances, until finally, pressing his lips into a smirk, he sidled over. He tucked his bar towel into his apron and nodded at Barry. "What'll it be?"

"You've got any good whiskey? Irish?"

"Jack Daniels." The bartender waited, his eyes daring Barry to disagree. "Good whiskey."

Barry scanned the wall of gleaming bottles behind the bar. "No Irish?"

"Jack Daniels is all."

"Well, when in Rome—" Barry winced. "You have tequila?"

"Is the pope Catholic? Which tequila you want?"

"Just give me something that won't rot my gut."

Shrugging, the bartender took a bottle from the shelf, poured a shot into a glass, and plunked it down before Barry. "*Salúd, gringo.*"

Barry stared. "What the hell does that mean?"

"You ain't heard Spanish before? You, a man of the world, coming all the way into the barrio to drink tequila?"

"Don't shit with me! I'll drink wherever the hell I want!"

"Okay, Okay! Simmer down, mister." The bartender wiped his hands on the side of his apron. "You don't look like that kind."

"What do you mean? What kind?"

"The kind that throws his weight around."

"Well, I've had a goddamn shit of a day." He threw back the tequila, coughing it down. "Goddamn shit is right!"

The barkeep poured more tequila into the glass. Barry let it flow down his throat without tasting, wishing to hurry on the numbness. "How 'bout the good stuff this time?"

"Okay." He lifted another bottle for Barry to inspect. "Hundred percent agave."

"Yup, that's better. Pour me a shot." Barry took a gulp, sputtering.

"You have to let it roll down your tongue, mister. Maybe you never drank tequila before. Want a beer for a chaser?"

"No beer, man," Barry grimaced. "My wife is Mexican. Her father gave me tequila, good stuff."

"She from this barrio, your wife?"

"From Santa Barbara."

"*Santa Bárbara? ¡Ay Chihuahua!* You married rich?"

"Shit, no! Her family lost everything long time ago. Her father had a thing for horses, fast women, and—tequila!" He lifted his glass.

"The thing what men have for liquor, that's the thing what keeps me in business." The bartender refilled Barry's glass and moved on to the elderly man at the end of the bar.

A good, stiff drink could cover a lot of sins. Even the lousy tequila felt like the oil of divine unction. One drink relaxed him, and two transformed the Mexican strangers into brothers sharing the ritual of escape. He gazed with new affection at their brown faces. After all, his daughter was half Mexican. One of these guys could become his friend. And what if one—?

What if Ceci returned home from college with a Mexican sweetheart? Could he accept him as sweetly as Ma had Dora? So much ahead of him! Ceci would be grown and gone before he knew it. He clutched the edge of the bar. There is still a long time, he told himself. Don't be silly—a long time before she grows up.

The fortune cookie Chan had thrust at him: *There is yet time to choose another path*—those words came back to haunt him.

Sage advice: it sounded like Rafaela. That's what the infernal woman sounded like—a damned fortune cookie! Phony magic based on psychology and mumbo jumbo—Rafaela and Carmen's advisos no more relevant than a damned fortune cookie! Fortune cookies made in factories rolled right down the assembly line just like Fords, just like memories rolled along the brain's conveyor belt. You couldn't stop them. A hundred shots of tequila wouldn't block the images that converged.

The whole day marched before him—and all the other damned days leading up to it, all reflected in the eyes of the females who haunted him. The hardest to take were Ceci's sad eyes, but no less disturbing were Carmen's cognac eyes pleading with him over the table, Rafaela's gold-flecked twinkle, or Dora's ebony eyes, condemning.

Once, Dora's eyes had shone only love. When had that been? Was it so long ago they were making a start in Los Angeles together? He remembered how it felt to be in the warmth of Dora's loving gaze, like heaven on a silver plate. Especially the night he learned he'd be a father. They sat in a red leatherette booth at Chan's under a pink paper lantern. She looked like a million dollars in that tight black sweater and that little string of fake pearls he'd bought her for an engagement present.

She'd just broken open her fortune cookie. There were two fortunes, folded together like the pages of a love letter. She'd read them aloud, cheeks glowing, eyes soft. What exactly had they said? He couldn't remember, but all through the meal, every time he had looked at her, his heart had jumped as if he'd been running without breathing.

"Barry, I usually don't pay these things any mind, but this is a sign."

"What, doll?"

"Getting two fortunes in one cookie." Her eyes like onyx cabochons reflected the lantern light. "Two fortunes, Barry, for two! I wasn't sure whether to tell you yet. Now I know. I'm having a baby—five months along. Are you glad? Say you're glad, please, because I'm so scared. We only just got married. People might do the arithmetic."

The hell with arithmetic! Glad? He was elated, crazy with happiness, the whole night long. Almost giddy with joy, they'd sat together at the double-bill (he forgot which movies) and sipped coffee afterwards. Honeyed, and exhausted from love-making—even deeper joy in their squeaky bed—in that hole of an apartment, the yellow neon light from the hotel across the street flooding Dora's pillow, a halo around her beautiful face. He'd never forget that night. But now—

There is yet time to choose another path.

Dora had chosen another path, all the way to Mexico. Was she the only one able to to start over? Why was he left holding the bag? What a thing to call Ceci—a bag! Why not call her an angel—a beautiful, loveable, perfect angel of retribution for her parents' mistakes, a wingless angel Barry would have to carry alone.

No matter what Carmen or Rafaela said, no matter how Pilar clicked her tongue and looked down her nose, Ceci was his—and his responsibility. His decision was final. It was his role to decide his and Ceci's fate. He saw no way forward but to go back—to Schwann—let the chips fall wherever they may. He had to have money to take care of Ceci. He had to work.

The bartender swept by with the bottle of tequila, refilling Barry's glass. Replete with warmth toward him, Barry clasped his forearm. "Pancho, can I ask you something?"

"The name's Enrique."

"Well, you look more like a Pancho, if you ask me."

"You're drunk, mister."

"Okay, okay, so I've had a bit to drink. Just tell me this one thing. If I don't work, 'Rique, who the hell's paying for dresses with diamond buttons?"

Enrique looked at Barry as if he had sprouted horns; his jaw dropped, his mouth closing into a smile. "Doña Rafaela! You've never come here!"

"*Hola, Enrique.*" She climbed onto a stool beside Barry. "*Un vino, por favor.*"

Barry leaned away from her. "What're you doing here?"

Ignoring Barry, Enrique leant over the bar, his voice confidential. "Doña Rafaela, I've been meaning to ask something. My Rosa—I wonder—"

"Rosa will be fine. She came in this morning. Could I have a glass of wine, please, a nice red one?"

"We're all out of vino, Doña Rafaela."

"Just bring something you think I'd like, then. My friend and I will go to one of the booths." She led an astounded Barry by the hand to a booth toward the back of the tavern, her big purse bouncing against her hip. "I should come here more often."

She gazed about the room appreciatively, waving and nodding to several men who were craning their necks to get a better look at the *curandera* and the gringo. She slid onto the leatherette bench. "I need to talk with you. It's a serious matter, *amigo*."

The barkeep brought Rafaela a tall pink drink, replete with toothpicked fruit and a paper umbrella. "On the house, *Señora*."

"No, Enrique!" Rafaela pulled a twenty from her purse. "You must let me pay." She flattened the bill onto the table. "It should cover my friend's drinks, too."

Enrique stared down at the twenty. "Yes, of course. I'll get change."

"You are forgetting the tip, *amigo*. Go buy some flowers for Socorro; maybe she'll forgive you for the—er—little matter of your forgetfulness."

The bartender scurried away with the twenty.

"What forgetfulness?" Barry scooted forward on the bench, intrigued.

"A confidence, *amigo*. I cannot repeat it."

"You are always so mysterious."

"Not mysterious—ethical. I have a question for you, and *you* are not allowed to be mysterious." She clasped his hand in hers. "What have you done to my daughter?"

"What's the—did she get home all right?" The hair stood up on Barry's neck. "The *brujo's* nephew was sniffing around at the restaurant."

"Yes, she made it home. She's not happy, though." She waited, an eyebrow raised, for him to talk. He tried to match her stare, but her gold gaze unnerved him.

Barry looked into his empty glass. "We had a quarrel."

"I know. She told me."

Irritation tensed Barry's throat. "Then why ask me?"

"She is not telling me everything." Rafaela examined him like a coyote scoping a field for rabbits. "You're drunk, but I bet you're able to tell me your side of the story."

"Darn tootin', I can. I've suddenly got work—in a band. Told Mitch I'd meet Schwann back in Frisco tomorrow morning. For some reason, this bent Carmen out of shape. I really made her mad when I said she'd miss my sorry face. She let me know—in no uncertain terms—that she has no interest in me, at least not as anything more than Ceci's caretaker."

"Ah!" Rafaela chuckled. "Carmen is conservative."

"What the hell does that mean?"

"She's an old-fashioned mother—everything for her children. Ever since her man left, she has done nothing else but give, give, give. She's looking for the man who stays. How can she understand a man like you, an artist, who must give up his daughter for the *clarinete?*"

"Wait a damned minute, here!" Barry slammed his fist on the table. "I'm not giving up my daughter!"

"Shh!" Rafaela leaned toward him, "Careful, *hombre,* I'm afraid this crowd is—"

"Is this man bothering you, Doña Rafaela?"

"Oh, no. He's just a little *borracho*—the tequila, you know."

A big lout in overalls loomed over them, arms crossed over his barrel chest. "Sure, now?"

"Yes, Luis. Just give us a moment of privacy, and then you can escort me home, if you please. I would appreciate your company."

"It would be my pleasure, Doña Rafaela." He bowed and made for the bar.

"Well, if that don't beat all." Barry took a swig of his drink. "You're quite the woman about town, a femme fatale. These guys are falling over themselves."

"Me? I'm an old—what do you say? A hag!" Rafaela took an exploratory sip of the pink drink. "Terrible stuff!" She pushed it aside. "As I was saying about Carmen, she's disappointed that you are not ready to sacrifice everything for your kid's sake. That's what she would do, in your place. She must be very boring, after Doralinda."

"No, she's not boring, just different. Just tell me this, would she sacrifice her career, I mean as a nurse, for her kids?"

"She has to work, *amigo.*"

"So do I. And I'm a musician."

"Yes," Rafaela nodded, "but not a happy one."

"Who the hell is happy? Is Carmen happy? Not bloody likely, with everything that's on her plate. She hasn't—"

"Enough about Carmen! Let's talk about you for a minute. What I see is this: you don't see how you can take care of Cecilita and be a working musician."

"Don't put words in my mouth, Rafaela."

"Yes." She closed her eyes and folded her hands, as if praying. "You are right. I will tell you what I see, not what you think."

Again the closed eyes, and a silence. Finally she nodded, as if she had been having an inaudible conversation with herself. "Yes, this is the thing. You will never be great unless you learn to love. Until you can learn to take care of Cecilita like a father—"

Barry made to protest, but Rafaela patted his hand. "Let me finish, *hombre.* Cecilitia is a gift from God, just like your talent." She waited another minute, her eyes searching his. "Do you know this?"

"Of course I do!"

"Then you must also know this, *amigo.* Only when you learn to love what is given to you—love without thinking of yourself—can you really be the artist you're intended to be."

He stared at his drink, sloshing the amber liquid from side to side, unable to reply.

"You are supposed to be Saint Sullivan, right?"

His neck prickled—how did she know all these things?

"Saint Sullivan, that's you, yes? You're a saint, called to play music from the heart, Barry—not from the head." Rafaela lifted her purse on her lap, clicked it open, and rummaged inside. A slight fragrance of flowers emanated from the saint card she placed on the table.

Barry picked up the card, a faint smile of recognition lifting the corners of his mouth. "Saint Cecilia herself! Schmaltzing it up on the pipe organ, cherubs her back-up singers. Just happens to be the patron saint of music."

"Remember Saint Cecilia's story?"

"Oh God, somebody cut off her head or something!"

"The music at her wedding—"

"She's a saint!" Barry shook his head. "What wedding?"

"Saint Cecilia's! Read the back of the card." Rafaela took the card and pointed to a line before the prayer. "Here," she tapped it with her fingernail. "Saint Cecilia sang out from her heart to God."

"Excuse me, Rafaela, but I live in the twentieth century. Care to join me? I'm done with saints, with martyrs—all that crap. Done!"

"You might be done with the saints, but they aren't done with you. They yearn for you to wake up to your responsibility. You wait on a bridge between heaven and everything else—spanning dangerous waters. Like the guardian angel."

The room chilled around Barry, as he remembered the picture Ma gave Ceci.

"From the moment of conception, Barry, our purpose is to guard our children from harm. Every parent is to be a bridge between heaven and earth. A child only knows heaven. Crossing into the world with all its trouble, the child is in peril. The parent is like that guardian angel, offering a hand to guide the child over the broken places. Our love makes it up to them for having to leave heaven."

"How—how can a lousy, no-good man do the work of an angel?"

"Full intention, Barry, that's what it takes. You can't be a parent part-time."

"That's the same axe Carmen grinds. Listen, I *have* to work, Rafaela!"

"Everyone works, but not so far from their children. Until Cecilita is stronger she needs you close by." She tapped her heart. "Right here! Later, she will be strong enough for you to go sometimes. Please stay with her now, *amigo*. Care for your daughter. Help her heal—not from a distance, but close up!"

"You don't understand! If I let Mitch down this time, I'll probably never work in California again. Hell, I might not work anywhere. I'm lucky to get another chance after leaving Schwann in a lurch in Frisco. Where's that barkeep? I need another drink."

"You drink too much, *amigo.*"

"Is that so? Well then, maybe I'm not the one to care for Ceci. Maybe—"

"You don't drink like your father did, Barry. You can stop. The traveling makes you drink so much. You can't ground yourself. You become fearful."

"Fearful?" Barry laughed. "Come on!"

"Every time you're alone, a fearful pain rattles you. You drink to dull it, but a little of your soul loosens from your body. Pieces of your soul chase you from town to town but don't catch up. If you were to make a home—a happy one—you would not need to drink."

A derisive laugh froze in Barry's throat; he couldn't bring himself to hurt her, so mesmerized was he by the compassion in her gaze.

"Barry, are you afraid to be happy? Your soul longs—"

He attempted a chuckle, which came out a wheeze. "You reckon I have a soul?"

"Oh yes, a fine one. If I could do a *limpia* for you—"

"Oh, so that's what all this is about! You're trying to drum up business!"

Rafaela laughed. "You are drunk, *hombre,* or you would know better than to say such a thing to a *curandera.* Now, I must go. Promise me you'll be careful."

He raised an eyebrow. "Why?"

"The *brujo's* cousin might find you here. I hear he's been following you."

"Aw, I already scared that punk away."

"Ah," she nodded somberly. "*Adios,* then."

"Yeah, well, thanks for the drink."

He watched her leave. Waving back at those who greeted her, she strode through the smoky bar with her palm on that lout Luis's ham of an arm, no bigger than a child, her purse bouncing against her hip like a school bag. Though she was older even than his ma, Rafaela was still a vital part of the barrio community. Barry expected Carmen would be the same, taking care of others till she died, never tiring of sacrifice or devotion to the cause of healing. Eager to dull the ache of longing—for what, he didn't know—Barry signaled the bartender. "Another tequila!"

Enrique's eyes were warm with a new respect. "So, what business do you have with our *curandera*?"

The room tilted, Barry's stomach jolted—a metallic taste rose in his throat.

"Shit."

"All right, *señor*?" The barkeep grasped Barry's shoulder. "Maybe it's time—"

"Gotta go to the can." He clung to the table as he stood, his legs rubber.

"Better take it slow, gringo. Behind that door, straight down the hall, right next to the pay phone. I'll show you."

Shrugging from Enrique's outreached hand, Barry lurched through the crowd to the dingy restroom. He steadied himself in front of the tarnished mirror, loosening his tie. The slackness of his reflected face surprised him—blurriness around the jaw that might sag into jowls like his da's. He prodded the puffiness around his eyes, asking his body: Why can't you just vomit and get it over with? Then—half of another, darker face appeared in the mirror, and Barry's shirt collar tightened like a noose from behind. The attacker took hold of Barry's hair.

"Leave our women alone, *pendejo*! Go back where you come from!"

Another voice, and then another—at least three men moved in to surround him. Barry staggered forward, but the attacker didn't lose his grip. "Even the old woman, that *bruja,* stay away from her."

The first attacker arched Barry's head backward by his hair, so that Barry stared up at the stubble on the punk's neck. Grunting, the thug released his grip, and Barry's nose met the edge of the sink, blood gushing into his mouth.

Numb from the tequila, he could neither fight them off nor fully sense the force of the blows coming at him from every direction. Eyelids swelling, he could just make out hanks of his own coppery hair clenched in the fist that flew toward him, the silver pointed tips of cowboy boots, and blood. Blood—streaming the slope of the cement floors to the silver circle of the drain—blood on his hands as he tried to stand.

"That's right; crawl, *chingado!*"

Despite the boots jabbing at his ribs, Barry struggled onto all fours. A surge of hot vomit stopped him groping for the door. Tequila and Chinese rice roiled up his gullet. He collapsed onto his side, the eddy of brown faces circling him.

"*¡Está muriendo!*"

"No, he's not dying—just dead drunk!"

"Ceci!" Barry moaned—and passed out.

Dawn's cool light filtered down the rooftops into the alley behind the bar. Every muscle wracking with agony, Barry came to consciousness and a pain so sharp, shards of glass might have been driven into his brain. Wedged behind garbage cans and stacks of cardboard, he freed himself enough to touch his smarting face.

His nails were jagged, broken below the quick and sticky with blood. The stink of vomit and piss assaulted his nose—his or some other drunk's, he didn't know. Spasms stabbed his back, and a new trickle of blood forced through his throbbing lower lip.

His hand a numb paddle, he slapped at his back pocket—wallet gone. Barry groped the rotting debris until he found his sports jacket, foraging its pockets for something to clean his face, pulling out a large cloth, barely recognizable except for the diamond buttons twinkling like morning stars. The green dress he and Carmen had bought together. Hhe clutched it to his cheek and wailed at the chink of steely sky.

"Ceci!" How long had he lain here, he wondered—leaving Ceci an orphan to his drinking? Hours? Days? Weeks? What would he tell her when he saw her again? How could he make up for this?

If he made it back to her, he told himself, the words would come. He thrust the dress back into his pocket, without using it to wipe his face. He must take the dress to her; he must go to her now and let her know she still had a father who would never, ever leave her alone again!

He had to concentrate on standing, on taking one step at a time back to Ceci. Grabbing hold of a garbage can, he sweated from the exertion of standing, reeled from the lightning intensity of the pain everywhere in his body. Stumbling over at first, he righted himself and took careful steps along the wall, gripping at chinks in the brickwork. With each excruciating step, Barry inched toward his goal, a column of light at the end of the alley—toward the brightening dawn.

Part Four
The Convergence of the Saints
End of July, 1960

Saint Raphael: Archangel and Healer

In the Los Angeles barrio, the morning birds sang even louder than the birds of the mountains. They had to shout their songs to be heard over the rousing groans of the city. Maybe it was this raucous singing that always woke Rafaela so early. Or, she thought, it might be her guardian angel, reminding her that she needed to breathe the fresher morning air. Fresh air was like food to her—fresh air, the bird song, and the dewy air vitamins for her soul.

She loved each new day, as sweet as baby's breath. *La madrugada*, the dawn, the mother of morning—a time for prayer, a time for gathering the *hierbas*, a time for communicating with the spirit in all things.

At dawn, Rafaela's shadow still remembered dreamtime, putting it aside slowly as she looked at this world's work. Every morning she centered herself, her soul's light streaming down into the earth's core, with every prayer sending her love to earth. The earth sent back its strength to her; she could open her palms and feel the life in the air.

Each morning, as she prayed her rosary, she could feel God listening. She could sense the warmth of God's breath, so near to her that she could barely form the *Nuestro Padres* and the *Salve Marías* without tears of wonder. How she loved to pray!

The oldest prayers she knew were dearest to her: not the Catholic ones, but the ancient Huasteca prayers her great-grandmother had taught her. Prayers so much a part of her thinking and the way she saw the world—petroglyphs etched by daily repetition on the rock of her soul. Earth and everything here, heaven and earth converging, she would wait silent and open as the sky for grace to enter her.

Sometimes a crow would caw, or she would feel a change in the texture of the air, like the difference between silk and wool—and then she would open her eyes to see the sun arisen and the day beginning. Sometimes, before she opened her eyes, a picture would come, or a thought, or a whisper to guide her way. Then the day's agenda rolled out like a scroll before her, and she began her work.

This morning, after a sleepless night when Barry did not return, Rafaela received all three: a glimpse of a wounded face, a stabbing sense of danger, and a whisper: *Go to the alley!* As she almost always did, Rafaela followed these leadings. She went to the alley to see what God wanted her to do.

She found Barry unconscious just outside her garden gate, a mess of filth and blood. It was a miracle that he made it back to her in such a condition. Rafaela knelt beside him and laid her head against his chest. His heartbeat and lungs sounded all right, but his hands were icy and his pulse erratic. Yanking off her sweater, she laid it over his torso and went to ask Carmen's help. Using an old screen door for a stretcher, they carried Barry inside. They laid him on a makeshift mattress Carmen devised: some piled-up blankets on the kitchen table.

As they ministered to his wounds, Rafaela's first prayer was that he would remember everything that had happened to him—however bad it had been. With such knots on his head, she doubted he would. Yet if he did, by the grace of God there was hope for the Sullivans.

Rafaela respected God's economy. For Barry to remember would be a miracle, but if the saints would grant just this one, she might heal Barry and Cecilita. So prayed the *curandera*, and when Pilar came upon the two of them ministering to Barry, Rafaela took her aside. "You must remain calm, *mi amiga*. There's no room for the *miedo*, Pilar. Send your fear into the West. Blow it into bits and send it away."

"But Rafaela, how can I? My family is in the devil's claw!"

"Never mind the devil, *querida*. Imagine a rose behind your closed eyes. Make it your fear. Grow it bigger and bigger, and then when it fills the inside of your eyelids, blow it to bits! Send all the fear to Our Mother in the West. She knows what to do with it. No room for fear here, only love."

No room for fear. Through years of hardship, Rafaela had fought fear tooth and claw. In her old age it had finally retreated, because the *curandera* no longer had time for it. Love was so time-consuming. Less than a dozen more years she reckoned remained her, and there was so much left to accomplish. Rafaela could not allow fear to do more than surface. She'd have to transform her own fear and doubt into roses and explode them over the Pacific Ocean like so many fireworks.

Reminding herself of this truth, Rafaela attacked her dread of the *brujo*—of his weakening her medicine—and of the reality of old age. Instead, she focused on her heartfelt desire to relieve Barry's suffering, a task she must set about completing before Cecilita awoke and came downstairs, hungry for breakfast.

With a shiver and a last longing look into her garden, the *curandera* understood one more thing. This would be her final great healing. There would be rashes and bellyaches, but no more feats of *curanderísmo* equal to this occasion. No room for fear; no room for failure, either.

"Look, *m'ija!*" At the window, the first morning hummingbird hovered to drink from the feeder. "A good sign. Will you sew his stitches, daughter?"

As Carmen swabbed Barry's head with alcohol, Rafaela began to make a salve for his wounds, grinding *árnica* flowers with her mortar and pestle. While Carmen stitched, the old woman knelt at her living room altar and lit four candles—Saint Jude of Tadeo, Saint Joseph, Guadalupe, and San Martin de Porres—and prayed a decade of the rosary. Then she returned to the kitchen to finish the salve.

With deft fingers, Carmen drew a stitch through the skin of Barry's forehead, pulling the wound together in a neat seam. His eyelids fluttered, as if he might wake. Rafaela held her hand over his eyes, not quite touching his face, until he stilled into sleep. "Don't wake, *amigo;* we must sew you together, body and soul."

Carmen surveyed the seam in Barry's forehead. "That came out better than I thought—might not leave much of a scar."

The *curandera* nodded her approval. "Good work, *m'ija.* Do you think we can carry him upstairs? The children must not see him like this. Lucky for us, he's still too drunk to wake." They eased him onto the screen door, lugged him upstairs, and settled him on Rafaela's bed.

"He can sleep it off for now. Tomorrow you will bring that fellow, the communist—"

"Jorge?"

"That one, the doctor—the Cuban. That should satisfy Barry, that a real doctor checked him out. Wouldn't want him to think I healed him with mumbo jumbo only."

"Mamita!"

"It's all right. Just bring Jorge. Promise him tamales. I think I have some in the freezer. He will tell us Barry is going to be all right."

"Mamita, I wonder." Carmen studied her mother. "Are you sure it won't be too much to watch Tito tonight? Dolores could watch him. You look a little shaky, Mami."

"You think so?"

"Mamita, you just can't keep up this pace. It will take its toll on you. You should be relaxing at your age—pursuing hobbies—"

"My age!" The *curandera* wanted to explain that her life did not belong to herself, but Carmen would not understand. "I am not so old as a tree."

"Mamita, I am serious. You need to rest." Carmen stared back, unblinking. Pilar pretended to be absorbed in smoothing Barry's blankets.

"Rest? How can I rest when all the medicine has been turned upside down? All we set out to do—I can't rest until I repair the damage that *brujo* has done."

"You can at least take an evening off, Mamita. Do something relaxing. Please."

Rafaela scanned her wits for a tart answer, too soon realizing her wits were failing; she did need an evening off. "You know what, my daughter? You are right. Tell Adelita to come on over after school to babysit for Tito and Cecilita. Pilar and I are going to play Bingo."

"Bingo?" Carmen rolled her eyes. "That isn't what I meant by rest!"

"Every Friday night, at the church, I lose at Bingo. This could be my big chance, with my *amiga* to give me some fresh luck." Rafaela smiled at her friend. "What do you think, Pilar? You want to go to Bingo?"

Pilar turned from the stove, where she'd been making coffee. "I love Bingo!"

"I was thinking of you taking a nap, or resting in the garden." Carmen glanced at the bed where Barry lay sleeping. "If you go, is Adelita able to care for your patient?"

"He won't be needing anything but sleep. Pilar needs to have some fun in the big city before she goes home."

"Me?" Pilar startled, "I'm going home? Really?"

"Yes, in a few days you will go home. Our work is almost done."

Pilar wrung her hands. "But what about Barry?"

"We'll see about Barry," Rafaela clicked her tongue. "Carmen, please find that trunk in the attic, and bring us one of your papi's nightshirts, will you? We'll have to clean him up a little."

"It will take a while to find it in all that junk up there, Mamita."

"Fine. Pilar, will you help me get these things off him? We have to sponge him. I will wash, and you can mend his shirt. Tonight we will relax and play Bingo."

So that is how Barry happened to be tucked up in Rafaela's bed, in her dear, departed husband's fancy embroidered nightshirt. Ceci and Tito played downstairs, Pilar mended, and Barry lay sleeping, while every hour on the hour Rafaela dabbed her secret salve on his wounds, praying to the saints and singing the sacred songs of the Old Ones.

Saint Cecilia: Patron of Musicians and Poets

Three times old Rafaela had given Ceci *limpias*, rolled the egg over her joints, and made her drink medicine to take away *susto y tristeza*: the fear and sadness. Growing stronger and stronger—and so hungry—Ceci held up her cup for Pilar to pour it full of cream for breakfast. It was so delicious and sweet; Ceci felt it was medicine, too. Yet, when she tried to smile, it didn't match her insides.

She couldn't tell Daddy how she wished she could play with Mickey, how she missed the seagulls that circled over the beaches and landed in her San Pedro backyard. There was this little hurt behind her eyes and in her throat, like something pulling from her stomach. She missed the sea.

And she wished she could miss Mama—even be sad—without remembering how Mama's beautiful red mouth turned ugly. Mean words hurting more than Fire and Ice, even more than all those spankings with hairbrushes, yardsticks, pancake turners, clothes hangers—anything in reach. She couldn't tell about what Mama did when Daddy wasn't there; it wasn't Mama's fault that Ceci couldn't be good. If Daddy knew, he might want to go away, too.

She fanned her face. It was so hot, and the flies stuck to Ceci's sweaty skin. Closer to the sea, the air was cleaner, and there were no bugs or smog. Here the stink of the chicken pen drew flies, and bees buzzed around her head on their way to the herb flowers. The noise of cars passing, and the freeway in the distance, competed with the worried clucks and squawks of the chickens.

Grandma telephoned, and Ceci whispered to her about missing people and things, about the hole in her tummy that breakfast cream would not coat.

"I know that hunger, macushla—like mine for Connemara. Soon we'll go there, if your da will take us. You wait and see how lovely it will be! Sure, it will fill the emptiness—Connemara is just that sort of place."

Ceci didn't know if she wanted to go to Connemara—another thing she had to keep to herself. Daddy said it rained all the time, that the wind sang ghost songs at night, and the poor felt lucky even to have potatoes for their dinner. She wanted her home—but where was home, now that everything had changed?

"Get some air, Cecilita!" Pilar said, waving her outdoors with her apron, like one of the chickens. Ceci ran to the back of Rafaela's garden. She watched the hens pecking around her feet at bits of corn, and her sadness began to melt like a pat of butter on a warm tortilla—softening at the edges and still cold in the center.

Then Tito stood in Lupe the tortoise's pen and whistled with his fingers in his teeth for Ceci to come. He lifted a handful of golden straw and showed her Lupe's seven eggs about to hatch. Ceci felt the last bit of sadness disappear, looking into the tortoise's nest with Tito.

The eggs were miracles waiting to happen. Tito was right, they did look like ping pong balls, and she was sure she saw something move inside—baby turtles growing and moving, and getting ready to hatch.

"Will they hatch before I have to go, Tito?"

"You're not going to go, not yet. You just started to get fun."

"Fun?"

He toed the ground. "Funner than Adelita, anyway. She only thinks about boys."

"Why is she so quiet?" Ceci knelt close to the tortoise. "What's she doing?"

"Who? Adelita?"

"No, Lupe."

"Oh, her? Nothing!" He squatted beside Ceci. "Lupe's just lazy. She always lies around, except when she's eating. I'd rather have my horse any day."

"You have a horse?"

"My dad does, in Mexico." Tito puffed a little, his arms crossed like a genie. "I can ride it any time I want—any time I'm in Mexico visiting."

"Mexico, isn't that far?"

"Kind of, but sometimes I go see him." Tito frowned. "Sometimes—when papa remembers." He stuck a hand in his pocket. "You know what? I have a whole quarter. Adelita gave it to me." He fished the quarter out of his pocket. "See? I'm gonna spend it, too. Come on, I'll show you. Come on!" He took her hand. "See, across the street. That's the *tienda.*"

"What's that?"

"A store! They got everything!"

"Puppies?"

"Everything!"

The two of them stood together on the gate to get a better look at the *tienda's* red, white, and green front. Ceci loved it: the colors of a Christmas package!

"I bet I can beat you 'cross the street!" He climbed over the gate and did a cartwheel on the front lawn. Tito stuck his head over the gate. Under the straight black line of his brows, his eyes danced. "Scaredy!"

"Rafaela said not to—"

"You chicken? Chickens are so stupid. They never fly or nothing."

"They can too fly."

"No, they can't."

"Yeah, they do." Ceci leaned over the gate, sticking out her tongue at him. "Rafaela told me she has to clip their feathers or they'd fly out of the yard."

"Well, you're a chicken with no wings—scared to come over the fence."

"Am not scared."

"Prove it." Tito put his hands on his hips. "Climb over."

Scraping over the gate on her stomach, splinters stuck into Ceci's shirt, but she made it. She landed on the other side, barely catching her balance.

"You climb just like a stupid chicken."

"I'm not a chicken." Ceci didn't like the look of that street—too wide.

Two cars whizzed by, then three more. "You're allowed to cross this street?"

"Yeah, we cross all the time." Tito's tongue circled his cheeks. "You have to look both ways. When the cars don't come, you run across. It's easy."

He offered his hand, and Ceci looked back at the gate. "I better not, Tito."

"Well, I'm going!" Tito dropped her hand and hooted across the street, patting his mouth like an Indian. He waved to Ceci. "Come on, chicken!"

"I'll show you!" She crossed at a run, the breath in her throat sharp as scissors. Tito pulled her into the store. *"Hola, Señor Mañuel,"* he called out.

A fat man with a big moustache like the wings of some gray bird was filling the gumball machine by the door. *"Hola, Tito.* Hello, little girl."

Ceci turned slowly, taking it all in. The store smelled of bags and cardboard—and other things she could not make out. Strings of red and green lights blinked in the window, naked chickens hung over the butcher's counter, and in the glass case: yellowy pigs' feet and squinty-eyed pig heads, pink as party dresses. Some snow skis leaned against the wall, spider webs dangling off the curled-up ends. Tito was right; it seemed this store had everything.

Everything! Purple velvet sombreros, leather cowboy hats, tall boots with high heels, and white baby shoes marching in rows—barrels of pinto beans and flowered-cotton sacks towered from floor to ceiling. Dried red peppers hung in long ropes, almost low enough for Ceci to touch. Baskets of fresh green peppers, garlic, and vegetables piled every bin.

Tito pressed his nose against the glass candy case, staring at blocks of red and green candy. Ceci guessed the store man might slice this candy like fudge, if you knew how to ask for some. Mañuel lifted Tito away from the glass by the back of his belt.

"Get your snotty little nose off my clean glass!" Mañuel let go of him and Tito stared up, mouth open. "So, are you here to do business with me today, Tito?"

Tito held up his quarter.

"Ah, you brought money this time. Okay, Mister Millionaire, what'll it be?"

Several times Tito opened his mouth and closed it again.

"Come on, Tito! Tell me what you want. Or do you want I should call your *abuela* and ask her?"

"These!" Tito pointed, his voice almost a whisper. *"Esas, por favor."*

"Ah, *limón*," Mañuel picked up a big metal scoop. "How much you want?"

"How many lemon drops can I get for this money?"

"Hmmm—let's see." Mañuel held Tito's quarter up to the light. "Are you sure it's real? Lot of money for a little squirt like you."

"It's real. Adelita gave it to me, just for shutting up."

"Just for that? You're kidding me. No, that is not what happened. You must have stolen it." He grinned at Ceci. "Tito the Bandito."

"No! She gave it!" Tito made two fists. "I saw Adelita walking home from school with a big boy, and she gave me a quarter not to tell our mother." Tito stood silent a second, and then covered his mouth.

"Spilled the beans, eh?" Mañuel held onto his belly; his laugh began there silently, until it climbed up his round front and flew out of his mouth, like a cough. "Ha! Ha! It's a good thing you're spending that quarter before Adelita wants it back."

Tito poked out his lower lip until it looked like a fat pink eraser. "You ain't gonna tell her I said that?"

"*Ay, hombre,* cheer up! I won't tell a soul." He pushed a little white bag over the counter. "Here, twenty-five cents worth—half a pound. Now, can I help you, little girl? What are you looking for, little beauty?"

"Yes, please, sir! Where are the puppies?"

"Sorry, no puppies." Mañuel took a little yellow box from his pocket. "Ever seen one of these?" He held the box out to her: an oval—she'd learned that at school—decorated with green and red dots of paint. He turned over her hand and laid it on her palm. "Go ahead, open it. There's magic inside."

She opened it carefully. Inside were six dolls, barely more than matchsticks, each one dressed in a tiny bit of cloth, their hair and faces just flyspecks of paint. "Magic?"

"Yes! Take them home and ask the *curandera*. She knows how they work."

"I can't." Ceci set them back on the counter.

Mañuel frowned. "Why not?"

"Don't have any money."

"For Tito's girlfriend—no charge."

"She's not my girlfriend!" Tito shook his head. "She's not!"

"Are you sure, Tito? She's a cute one! Some other lucky guy would jump at the chance of having a girl like her. My Felipe needs a girlfriend."

Tito grabbed Ceci's arm. "No, he can't—she's—she's my Cecilita!"

"Your Cecilita?" Mañuel mussed Tito's hair. "She's far too cute for a *sapo* like you. Why, she'll forget all about you, soon as she meets my Felipe."

"She won't!" Tito made a face and tugged Ceci's sleeve. "Let's go! Come on!"

"Not yet!" She squirmed from Tito's hand and asked Mañuel. "What's a *sapo*?"

"You don't know? Well, my little one, a *sapo* is a toad!"

Tito took off at a run, yanking Ceci after him, out the door into the street. Someone screaming—the red car—the screech of brakes—Mañuel and Pilar yelling— all those hands grabbing and lifting—then two fat, soft arms wrapping around her, Tito right there crying into Ceci's ear. The driver shook his fist, yelling at them in Spanish: words so angry, they made Ceci cry, too, even though she did not know what he said.

Held so close, Ceci heard the drum of Pilar's heart bumping and the juices of the old woman's stomach bubbling. "¡Ay, dios mio! Such bad children!" she scolded, covering Ceci and Tito's faces with kisses.

"They just ran out—of nowhere." The young driver shook his head. "Right in front of me. Barely missed them! My God, I could have killed them! Somehow, I stopped."

"Thank God." Pilar wiped her brow with her handkerchief. "Thank God."

"Somebody better keep an eye on those kids, old lady."

"What happened? ¡Ay, Dios!" Rafaela stepped onto the front porch, a dishtowel still in her hand.

"These rascals—Ceci and Tito," Pilar guided the children up the steps, "they ran right out into street—almost got themselves killed!"

"You're Doña Rafaela!" the driver said, extending a hand.

"Yes," She put both her hands around his. "The little boy is my grandson."

"Well, sure glad I didn't hit 'em."

"Thank God! Yes, and thank you. You want to come in for some coffee?"

"No thanks, Señora—on my way to work." He nodded to Pilar. "You better watch them kids." The man shrugged his shoulders as he got into his car. "Maybe they need a good whipping, those two."

Pilar sighed. "He's right, you know, Rafaela. I'm going to spank the—"

"Please, *amiga*!" Rafaela slipped her arm around her friend's shoulders. "Leave the children to me."

"A good spanking, that's what they deserve. You will spank them?"

"As good as." Rafaela patted Tía Pilar's back. "Make us a nice cold pitcher of *leche chocolate*, will you, please, and a little plate of cookies?"

Pilar shuffled into the kitchen. "Chocolate milk! Cookies! For devils—"

"Come with me, children!" Rafaela marched them all to the front room, and fell into the loveseat, pulling them close to her knees. "What am I to do with you children?" She waited, as if she hoped Ceci or Tito might tell her just what to do. "Whose idea was this adventure? Yours, Tito?"

"No!" Tito stuck out his chin. "No! You're a stupid head!" He spun on his heels and scampered away. Rafaela caught Ceci before she could run after him.

"Stay here, Cecilita. Sit down right there. Tito? Tito—o—o!" The *curandera* called in a louder voice. "Oh, where has that foolish boy gone? I think he will run away to New York. Or Texas, maybe?"

Ceci heard Tito creep down the hall, and the creak of the coat closet opening.

"Ceci, we will play a little game, you and me." Rafaela whispered. "Tito's hiding from us; he's in the closet. Let's have some fun with him." Then she spoke very loudly. "My heart almost stopped! And poor Pilar, she screamed like—like I don't know what. Oh, Cecilita, what a bad idea, to go out without asking! If that car had hit you, my God! We would have died of sadness—everyone, your *papá*, your *abuela*, Carmen, Adelita, even me—we would just die if anything happened to you!"

Not able to see the game in this, Ceci fell into the old woman's arms, crying.

"There, there, you have learned something important today." She patted Ceci's hair. "It's not the end of the world, child. Here's a hankie." It smelled of *lavanda,* and Ceci snuffled into it until she stopped crying.

"Okay! Ready for the game?"

Ceci nodded, wiping at her eyes. They tiptoed hand in hand down the hall to the coat closet. There Rafaela waited a moment, then smiled and winked at Ceci.

"Listen, closet, I want to speak to you!" Rafaela pointed her finger at the door. "I don't know what to do. Cecilita's heart is breaking, while my *picaro,* my rascal of a grandson, ran away and left her to take all the blame. Well, she said she is sorry, the poor little one. It's time for Tito to do the same. This game of hide and seek has to end. If he's in there, you better send him out, closet. That's an order!"

She listened at the door a moment. "You say no? Isn't he in there? Well, I'm just going to check! Excuse me, closet." Rafaela opened the door; Ceci saw Tito's blue sneakers poking out underneath the long coats.

"No Tito!" Rafaela winked at Ceci. "I guess he's run away. We'll have to eat the cookies all by ourselves." Rafaela shut the door, pressing her cheek against it. "What's that you say, closet? Tito's gone to Texas?" Rafaela tilted her head, as if she were thinking. "Yes, that is possible. He is a very fast runner. Just today he was running out in the street, like a rabbit on hot sand. Why, he talked to me just like a *pachuco,* rude as can be! He'll probably join up with some outlaws down there in Texas. Poor Carmen and Adelita, how they will cry!"

The doorknob jiggled just a bit, and Rafaela grabbed it with both hands, leaning her shoulder against the door. She sighed a weird little note, like an untied balloon. "You know, closet, I think I'll miss Tito just a little! He made me laugh—sometimes." She let this sink in, and sighed even louder. "Ah, well, more cookies for us."

From the closet a squeal, a puppy whine—the door shook against Rafaela's shoulder. "Wait a minute! Do I hear a little *diablito* in there?

Quick, I will have to get my smudge stick and smoke him out!" She let go of the knob.

The door flew open, and Tito jumped out, his cheeks red. "No, Abuelita! No smudge stick! Please! It makes me cough!"

"Really?" Rafaela pinched her chin, staring down at him as if he were a puzzle to put back together. "But that's what I always do—with *diablitos,* that is. I smudge them."

"It's not a devil; it's me, Tito!"

"No?" Rafaela looked him up and down. "Are you sure?"

Tito puffed out his chest and pointed to his heart. "I'm me! Tito!"

"No, you can't be Tito—your face is too red. Tito is a nice light brown, like me. You must be a *diablito.* Why, Tito is probably in Texas by now."

"I'm Tito!" Fat tears waited, ready to drop from his eyes. "Abuelita, it's me!"

"Well, you do sound kind of like him. I'd better check your eyes. Hmm—" Rafaela stuck her nose against his. "Maybe you're just a tricky devil who wants all our cookies. Your eyes are kind of red, like a devil's."

"But I'm not a devil!" Tito cried, "I'm Tito, *tu nieto!*"

"Couldn't be—my grandson has gone to Texas, *diablito.* Tito ran away."

"I didn't run away! I'm Tito! I hid in the closet because you're gonna spank me!"

"Spank you?" Rafaela's eyes flashed. "Spank you, *diablito,* why would I do that? Have you been naughty?"

"Yes—cause I went 'cross the street to the *tienda* without telling you. Ceci didn't want to." He rubbed his eyes. "I made her, and—I got mad at Señor M-m-mañuel, and ran 'cross the street, and then the car almost ran us over. Now you're gonna spank me, 'cause I was bad, and Ceci—even though she didn't do nothing—"

"Whoa, little red devil, you talk too fast! I can barely understand. Are you telling me you're really my *nieto,* Tito, who ran away to *Nueva York*—or was it Texas? Are you Tito, the little boy I loved since the day he was born? Tito, whom I will never stop loving? My own Tito?"

"Yeah!" Tito nodded, wiping his nose with his sleeve. "That's me."

"You are my Tito, then, and you are saying—you're sorry?" Rafaela's face grew so serious that Ceci felt a shiver climb her back. The tears were welling in Tito's eyes again. "You're saying you told a lie to Cecilita, so she'd join in your mischief, without knowing she'd get into trouble? You fooled her into it?"

"Well, I—kind of did—on accident." Tito tried to look at his feet, but Rafaela lifted his chin. "I'm sorry, Grandma."

"Are you sorry for scaring Pilar so that her heart nearly stopped? Are you sorry for calling me stupid, and for running away? Is that what you want to say, *diablito?*"

A tear splashed his cheek, and he wiped it away. "Yes, I'm sorry. I won't never do it again. Not ever!"

Rafaela's face lit with joy. She kissed the top of his head. *"¡Grácias a Díos!* Then you must be my Tito come back! Welcome home." Rafaela led the children by the hand to the kitchen. "So, are you hungry?"

"You can pour your own *chocolate!*" Pilar set a plate of cookies in the center of the table with a thud. Bowing to Rafaela, she untied her apron, threw it onto a chair, and marched out, grumbling under her breath.

"You'll have to apologize to Pilar, *mi nieto.*" Rafaela bit into a cookie and brushed the crumbs off her front. "We'll have no peace around here until you do."

"I can't!" Tito stared at the apron on the chair as if it were Pilar's ghost. "She wants to spank me."

"That being so, you will still have to tell her you're sorry."

"Abuelita, you don't love me anymore, or you wouldn't make me."

"I will make you—and prove that I love you enough to make sure you do right. If I stopped loving you every time you were naughty—" Rafaela passed the plate of cookies to him. "I'd have to stop so often, there'd be no time left to love you."

"Un-uh!" Tito eyed the cookies but didn't take one, crossing his arms in front of his chest. "You wouldn't have to—"

"Es todo—that's all. You must be brave, and tell her you're sorry. *Sí, nieto,* you must. I'm only doing my job, to teach you what's right. Even if I gave you a spanking, I'd still be loving you just as much." She stood and

kissed the top of his head. "Love doesn't run away when it gets angry—love stays forever."

"No, it doesn't." Ceci set her glass on the table with a clink. "My mama didn't stay. She ran away to Mexico."

"Yes, Dora is an exception," Rafaela sighed. "She has made a big mistake in running away. Grownups make much worse mistakes than children. Better a spanking or scolding when you are little, than great big heartbreak when you are all grown up. I'm certain you won't make the same mistakes your mama is making." Rafaela folded her hands and sighed. "Speaking of mistakes, your *papá* came home sick last night. He's sleeping—that's why I told you both to be quiet and go outside. I'm sorry that being quiet has led to so much trouble."

"Has he got a funny head? He gets that sometimes."

"Something like that, yes. Carmen will bring a doctor to check him."

"Why does he need a doctor?" Tito grabbed a cookie from the plate. "Can't you fix him, Abuelita? You and Mamita?"

"Oh, I can fix him. I just think it will be good to get—what do they call it—a second opinion! Cecilita's papa likes real doctors, and I am feeling very old and tired."

Ceci hugged Rafaela. "You aren't old—you're just—like Lupe. I mean—"

"*¿La Tortuga?* Like her?" Rafaela grinned. "I know, I know—my face looks like a dry river bed. And my neck—"

"Silly!" Cookie crumbs fell from Tito's mouth. "Grandma's not a *tortuga.*"

"Cecilita's right!" Retying her apron, Pilar swished back into the kitchen. "You are a tortoise, Rafaela. You move without hurrying, but you get everything done."

"You have something to say to Pilar, Tito?"

"Yes, I do!" Tito slammed his fist on the table. "My *abuelita* is not a turtle!"

"I'm sorry, Pilar. He will say he is sorry when he cools down a little. He's not so bad as he appears."

"I know, *amiga*. I raised a son." Her face crumpled. "How I miss—"
She began to cry into her apron.

"A fine son, Eduardo—you can be proud." Rafaela held her friend.
Over Pilar's shoulder the *curandera* gave the children a little nod. Ceci took
Tito's hand, and they made their way back to the garden.

Saint Luke: Patron of Doctors and Nurses

Jorge patted his stomach. "Best tamales I've tasted in a long, long
time—a fitting payment for a house call!"

"No, señor, a few little tamales are not enough payment for coming
out here on your lunch hour." Rafaela poured him another cup of coffee.
"There always must be a fair exchange for our labors."

"Ah, the rate of exchange in the barrio—I can never figure it out! Maybe
that's the reason my Mexican patients prefer go to the *curandera*."

Carmen laughed. "Because of tamales?"

"At our capitalist hospital they must pay cash—whereas your mother
will work for almost nothing. A bag of walnuts, an old hen for the soup
pot—amazing!"

"Listen, *ese*!" Rafaela crossed her arms over her chest. "I did not pay
for my children's educations with chickens and walnuts. I'm a widow who
must make a living—and I'm a capitalist."

"*Perdona, señora,* but you're a communist! You charge according to
their ability to pay, right? That's communism. You give treatment for
whatever they can pay."

"*¡Ay, no!*" A slow smile spread across Rafaela's face. "You can't really call
what I do a treatment. I'm just an *abuela*, helping like the grandmothers
before me: herbs and potions, that's all."

"Simple, ha! I've never seen a bad gash like that heal so fast." Jorge
spooned himself some more rice. "You sure it's only been twenty-four hours
since the laceration?"

"Yes, the *bizma* Mamita makes, it's so—"

"It's not just the salve!" Rafaela cleared her throat. "What about your fine stitches, daughter? Pass Señor Jorge the grapes, Tito."

Tito walked around the table with the fruit bowl, his round eyes on his mother, who, everyone could see, was about to lose her temper. He looked longingly at the backyard.

"No need for modesty, *Señora.*" Jorge winked at Rafaela. "If we had something like your *bizma* at the hospital—what did you put in it, a magic recipe?"

"No magic—I throw in whatever is in the kitchen and mix it up with a little *manteca.*"

"Stop playing, Mamá!" Uneasy quiet fell over the room. Carmen sat stiffly, watching her mother clear the table, and Jorge kept shoveling in the tamales. "Tell him the recipe!"

Rafaela and Carmen stared at each other without blinking.

"May I be excused?" Tito cried as he ran out the back door.

"Very well!" Rafaela climbed the stepladder, pulling some large, battered tins from the shelf. "You see? A little lard—and whatever herbs I can scratch up."

"Don't be fooled, Jorge. Mamá studied for years to learn what she knows. She has hundreds of effective remedies—all of them ancient and proven."

Jorge's eyes widened. "Hundreds?"

"Not near so many. Carmen exaggerates. I'm just an amateur—but it is a good living. I can't complain, can I?"

"You're doing something right, Doña Rafaela. I've never seen wounds heal so quickly." He folded his napkin and laid it on the table. "I've a meeting with the surgeons at two-thirty. You need a ride back, Carmen?"

"No, you go on. I'll take the streetcar. I want to talk with Mamita—right now!"

After Jorge said goodbye, Carmen cornered her mother in the kitchen. Her eyes were black, just like Mama's got when she fought with Daddy. Ceci worried, would they throw things and yell?

"I can't believe you! Just what were you trying to do?"

"What?" Rafaela smiled sweetly. "What can't you believe, *m'ija?*"

"Don't you pull that innocent face!" Carmen stamped her foot. "First you tell him that *curanderísmo* put us kids through school, and then you act like you're nothing but a grandmother whipping up home remedies! What's he supposed to think?"

"Eh! I don't care what he thinks." Rafaela tightened her apron sash, turning to the kitchen sink. "He's too nosy about my *bizmas*. I just don't want to tell him."

Carmen let out a big sigh. "You don't like him, do you?"

"Just a minute, *querida*—" Rafaela squatted at the refrigerator, took the lid off a dish, and made a face. "*¡Ay!* Better throw this out."

"Mamita, listen! Why don't you like Jorge?"

"Why do you care so much what I think about him? Are you dating?"

"No—well, he's asked me out before—yes—but Mamita, that's not the point! Why do you pretend to know nothing? He is trying to learn about Mexican culture, to help us! He is on the side of the poor."

"He may be. I don't tell everyone what I know, *m'ija*. Jorge doesn't understand my medicine, and even if he did—he's a *comunista. ¡Gracias a Dios!* You know what they did to Mexico!"

"So what? What does Jorge's politics have to do with sharing the ingredients of your poultice? Mamita, tell me, or I swear I'll go out on a date with Jorge just to spite you! He's not bad looking, and—"

"Good!" Arranging a bouquet of spoons in the dish drainer, Rafaela laughed. "God be praised! Go out with someone—even a communist—and I'll say a novena!"

"Don't change the subject, Mamita. What's wrong with Jorge? I work with him. If there's something wrong with his medicine—something's wrong with mine!"

"Oh daughter, it has nothing to do with Jorge's medicine. It's his religion."

"He has no religion!"

"Yes, that's exactly why I can't share what I know with him. If he used *curanderísmo* without God, he'd be no more than a *brujo*. If it's not about God, it's about power—and there's sin in that. The medicine would not work in his hands. It would be like giving my secrets to the devil. He is an atheist—a man who'd—"

"He's not a devil!" Carmen threw back her head. "Mamita listen! He's—"

"No, you listen to me, *m'ija*. A *curandera* cannot heal without giving credit to Creator. Even though you work in the hospital with doctors like Jorge, you know this in your heart. You are often angry with God—but when you see a miracle, you know it. You believe. That is how you are different from Jorge. He is not ready for *curanderísmo*. You are. If only you'd—"

"We're talking about Jorge, now, Mamita. He doesn't need to become a *curandero* to understand when Mexican patients come in—how to talk to them about their illness. He doesn't have to believe in God to be compassionate! He's the only person at the hospital, besides me, who speaks Spanish! Can't you see how necessary it is for at least one doctor to understand *curanderísmo*, if I'm to be the bridge you want me to be? I can't do this all by myself!"

"I can't dishonor my medicine," Rafaela shrugged. "You can go ahead and tell what you know, if that's what you want. Just don't ask me to teach him. I'm set in my ways. You must take me as I am. *Si quieres el perro, acepta las pulgas.*"

Ceci tugged Carmen's sleeve. "Please? What will you do about the dog?"

"What are you talking about, what dog?"

"Rafaela said you have to love the dog—"

"*Si quieres el perro, accepta las pulgas?*"

"Yeah!" Ceci nodded, "That dog. Can't you use some flea powder?"

"Flea powder!" Mother and daughter fell into each other's arms, laughing. Ceci joined their hug, squeezing in between them.

"What is it in English, Rafaela?"

"It's just a saying—if you love the dog, get used to his fleas! Understand?"

Ceci nodded. "Are you going to stop fighting now, please?"

"For you, little one—anything!" Carmen hugged Ceci to her side. "We weren't really fighting, sweetheart, just disagreeing. You see, I want to see things change, and—"

"Never mind!" Rafaela held up a hand. "I'm not going to share my *bizma*! But I'll be glad to sprinkle some flea powder on Doctor Jorge any time you want."

Jude of Tadeo: Patron Saint of Impossible Causes

When Barry regained consciousness, he asked for something to read. Rafaela dug up a two-year-old copy of *Reader's Digest* and an even older copy of *Time,* which Barry gladly accepted. As he leafed through the magazines, Pilar mended his shirt, stealing glances at his wounds. Carmen's neat sutures and a few purple bruises remained, but he looked so much more himself. "You know what, Barry?"

He lowered his magazine with an irritated sigh. "I'm trying to read."

"Never mind!" she shrugged, suddenly busy with her sewing. "It's not so important."

"Really?" Barry waited, and when she didn't speak, picked up the magazine with an irritated flourish. "Then I'll get back to the Eisenhower—"

Pilar cleared her throat. "Barry? You do know. I mean—"

He slapped the magazine onto his lap.

"You do know what has happened, don't you?"

He raised an eyebrow, and winced. "To Eisenhower? He's a lame duck now."

"No, *tonto*, I'm talking about you. You've made a miraculous recovery. Even the doctor says so. It's Rafaela and Carmen's doing, you know. You could've—"

"Excuse me, Pilar, but I don't feel like a miracle—not quite yet."

She cleared her throat again. "Your mother called, you know." Settling in her chair, Pilar let the words sink in.

"My mother!" He tossed the magazine to the foot of the bed. "She did?"

"Yes! Rafaela spoke to her. Your *mamá* is coming tomorrow."

"Oh, God!" He held his head in his hands. "What next?"

"Rafaela wants to give you a *limpia*, before you go—"

"Before I go to Frisco?"

"Frisco?" The shirt fell from Pilar's hands. "You've got to be kidding! You're still thinking of going back there?"

"Well, I had been, before the—"

"Before that *pachuco* beat the hell out of you, you mean?"

"Pilar! Such language! I never expected it of you."

"Sometimes strong words are appropriate." She picked a stray thread from her lap, winding it around her finger.

"Schwann's probably found someone else by now. Even if he hasn't—I have to recover before I go."

"Go?" Pilar peered at him through her magnifying lenses; maybe he was suffering from a concussion. "What do you mean?"

"I can't be any plainer, can I? I feel like death warmed over."

"Oh. *That!*" She picked up her sewing and held it very close to her face, biting off the thread with her teeth. "I don't think Rafaela was thinking of San Francisco, anyway, when she said, 'before he goes.'"

"Well, she shouldn't. I'm not going anywhere—not while my brains are falling out." He rolled onto his side, gasping. "Jesus Christ, I need peace and quiet!" He pointed a shaky finger. "Tell Rafaela—mind her own business. And—leave me be, God damn it! Get out of here!"

Pilar hurried out to the garden. "Rafaela! Rafaela! He's swearing like crazy—thinks his brain is falling out. Is it time for his *limpia*? I think he's feeling better. I think he's ready. I've never seen him so mean."

"Not yet!" Rafaela placed a sheaf of lavender in her basket. She patted her old friend's arm. "Let him stew a little bit. I've got a lot of work to do. Saint Jude, and little Katy Sullivan—they will help us."

La Llorona: the Weeping Woman

Pilar's list of favorite Santa Barbara pastimes featured Bingo in the smoky fellowship room at Our Lady of Sorrows. Once Pilar took Ceci with her to help hunt the Bingo card for B-1, I-5, and N-3. Then, BINGO!

Someone else won the hula girl lamp with a real grass skirt. Nothing good left—just a clock radio, a set of pancake turners, and a bus ticket to Reno. Still, Tía Pilar had kept on playing, until Ceci had fallen asleep with her head on the table. They'd walked home through the dark streets, Pilar grumbling about having lost again—but for a good cause, she'd made sure to say, crossing herself just in case the saints were listening. A very long, boring night, Ceci thought.

So when Rafaela and Pilar put on their hats to go to Bingo at Our Lady of the Angels, Ceci was glad to stay behind with Tito and Adelita. Carmen would come to check on Daddy's sore head on her dinner break. There was nothing to worry about but behaving, and Ceci had a plan for that. If Tito called her chicken, she would plug her ears and hum until he let her be. It was not easy.

When Tito dared her to taste some of the medicine on the top shelf next to Rafaela's altar, she plugged her ears and hummed *Twinkle, Twinkle, Little Star*. He made a face but got out the checkerboard. "First on red!"

"What's that mean?"

"You can't play checkers? Boy, Ceci, you are stupid!"

"I am not!"

"Everybody can play checkers, 'cept you." Tito craned his neck. "Adelita!"

A white dishtowel tied around her skinny hips for an apron, Adelita came to scold. "Tito, I'm trying to make dinner!"

"Ceci can't play anything. She's just dumb."

"Tito!" Adelita took him by the ear. "You're being mean. You stand in the corner and think of what you did."

"Stand in the corner?" He shook his head. "Mami never makes me do that."

"Well, I'm in charge, and I say you're standing in the corner." Adelita tugged him by the ear to the corner. "Stay there, and just think about how mean you are. You're lucky Ceci didn't hit you!"

Adelita picked up the checker game. "Do you want to play, Cecilita?"

Ceci slid one toe of her sneaker over the other. "Yeah."

"Let's go to the kitchen and play, so I can keep my eye on dinner. Don't worry, Ceci. Tito doesn't mean anything by what he says. He's just spoiled. He likes you."

"He does?"

"Yeah, a lot! He says he's going to marry you when he grows up."

"I don't want to get married. If I have to, I'm marrying Mickey, though."

"Who's Mickey, your boyfriend?"

"He's my neighbor in San Pedro."

"Well, he's going to have some competition." Adelita unfolded the board on the kitchen table. "You can have the red checkers. Put them on the black squares. Like this: two rows."

The floorboards creaked. Ceci turned in her chair. Tito was sneaking up the hall. Adelita winked, whispering. "When he comes in, act like you can't see or hear him."

Ceci nodded. This might be a game like the one Rafaela had played.

"Here's how you can move your pieces. See? If you get here, you can jump over me and take the checker."

Ceci pretended she didn't see Tito sneak up behind Adelita.

"I learned my lesson, Sis."

Adelita winked at Ceci. "My move."

"Hey, I'm good now, Adelita."

"See how I did that?" Adelita pushed her checker into the center square. "Your turn, Cecilita."

"I'm good now! I won't be bad any more."

Ceci moved a checker one space. "Like this?"

"It would be better if you did this, so you maybe could jump this guy."

"HEY! I want to play." Tito was right behind Ceci; she could feel his breath on her neck. Adelita raised her eyes to meet Ceci's.

"You looked at me!" Tito jumped over to Adelita. "I saw that! You winked!"

"Aren't you going to take your turn, Ceci?"

"Stop it!" Tito swept his hand across the checkerboard. "You're being meanest!"

"Tito!" Adelita grabbed his hand. "You messed up our game!"

"I don't like it when you pretend I'm visible."

"That's *in*visible, *tonto*! "Now clean up these checkers."

"No! You're just mean!"

Adelita grabbed him by the arms. "Look, you were mean to Ceci."

Tito laughed. "You don't scare me!"

Adelita rolled her eyes. "You have to say you're sorry."

Tito shook his head and kicked at Adelita's belly. She swept him off the floor.

"That's it! Now you're going outside! She swung open the squeaky screen back door and stood in the doorway between the kitchen and the porch. "I'll leave you out here for *La Llorona*."

"No!" Tito squimed, trying to get out of her arms, but Adelita held tight. "I'll hide somewhere she'll never, ever find me!"

"She'll find you, all right. Bad little boys have a smell all their own." Adelita set him down with a grunt. "Especially chubby little ones like you."

Ceci tugged Adelita's sleeve. "Who's *La Llorona*?"

"Don't tell her, Adelita; Ceci's a scaredy cat."

"Ha! You're the one scared. You're so scared you've never heard the whole story without covering your ears."

"Yes, I have! *La Llorona* is a ghost. I know all about her. Ceci doesn't."

"Well, then you know everything." Adelita stared out into the garden, her voice low and mysterious. "How *La Llorona* hides down by the river, out by the railroad tracks—how it's bad kids like you, Tito, that she wants."

Tito slapped Adelita's arm. Rubbing the spot he hit, Adelita made to go back to the kitchen. "I guess you don't want to hear the story."

"I do!" Ceci felt she had gotten on a ride she couldn't stop, but she didn't care. She had to hear that story. "Please, Adelita!"

Adelita cocked her head. "Sure?"

Ceci nodded.

"All right." Adelita pulled an empty crate over from the corner to sit on. She closed her eyes, head cocked. "Okay, then. If you don't like it, don't blame me. I didn't make it up. It's a true story—

A long, long time ago, there was this one Indian girl, María, who was so beautiful that she thought she was better than the others. All the boys were in love with her, but they were poor and she'd have nothing to do with them.

One day this handsome guy came to town. He was Don Navarro, and he played the guitar and sang just like an angel; everyone said so. They said he was the son of a rich man, and one day would have much land.

Even so, María turned up her nose when Don Navarro came to ask her out. She stood in her door and turned her back on him. When she did this, Don Navarro saw his reflection in the shine of her long black hair, just like a mirror.

He fell in love that minute, but María would have nothing to do with him. Don Navarro was so in love, he decided he would have to have her, no matter what it took."

"This isn't the story!" Tito stood up and crossed his arms. "Tell *La Llorona!*"

"Yes, it is," Adelita sighed. "This is *La Llorona.*"

"What's all this love stuff got to do with it?"

"Wait and see, baby brother. Love and ghosts go together." Adelita pulled him by his belt loop and lifted him onto her lap. "This how Mamita told it to me and how Abuelita told it to her. Now, where was I?"

"The guy with the guitar." Ceci leaned against Adelita. "He was in love with María."

"Oh yes," Adelita pushed her braid over her shoulder, "Don Navarro—

He came riding his father's coach, four white horses pulling it, and he wore a fancy jacket with gold buttons. He was a soldier, you see. He sang a song under her window, a song so pretty, María said, 'Yes, come up,' just to hear him play the guitarra *and sing one more time.*

For a while, the two were happy. They had three boys, one right after another. Beautiful boys—how could they not be, with such a father? The sons looked so much like Don Navarro that he no longer looked in the mirror of María's beautiful hair, but into the faces of his sons, to see himself. It was then that the trouble started.

After a while, Don Navarro's father died and left him the hacienda in the hills. Don Navarro would go there and enjoy the pretty Spanish ladies, leaving María all alone with her children, only visiting to play with his boys. He never sang to María any more.

She got jealous; she grew so green with envidia—*so ugly with her jealousy— that Don Navarro spent more time away. María cried so much her eyes turned red, but Don Navarro would not come home to stop her crying. He didn't even care for his little sons anymore. Her heart broke, and she couldn't stop crying, no matter how hard she tried. The pueblo began to call her* La Llorona, *the crying woman."*

Adelita stopped, her eyes closed. The wild summer wind that had wilted Rafaela's flowers and lifted swirls of dust all day seemed to blow cold. Ceci's heart fluttered in her chest, like a butterfly caught in a net.

"Yes, she was becoming La Llorona! *One day, María took her little sons down to the river and THREW THEM IN!"*

At these words, Ceci's heart jumped into her throat; she dug her fingers into her knees to hang on, remembering the waves and going down, down into that darkness. She wanted to yell "Stop!" but she could not speak.

"That springtime, the Los Angeles River was flowing high and fast, through the canals toward Long Beach. Sorry for what she'd done, María tried and tried to fish her sons out. It was no use; the water took them away."

The ocean that had taken Ceci rushed in again to choke her breath. She began to gag and cough, as she fought for air.

"Ceci! What's the matter?" Adelita took Ceci into her arms.

The porch door screeched open, and Carmen rushed in, still in her white nurse's dress. "Adelita, what's—why is Ceci gagging?" She lifted Ceci into her arms and carried her to the kitchen.

Tito followed his mother. "Sister was telling *La Llorona*, Mami."

Carmen rubbed Ceci's back in warm circles to calm her breathing. "Adelita, have you lost your senses? *La Llorona* is no story for Cecilita!"

"I—made—her—tell," Ceci coughed.

"Is that so, Adelita? Did the *pobrecita* force you to tell her?"

"No, she didn't." Adelita's eyes swam. "Ceci is just trying to help me."

"What got into you? Explain to me why you made such a bad choice."

"I was mad—at Tito. He was really bad tonight. I just wanted to scare him. I didn't think Ceci would get sick from it!"

"Not sick!" Ceci coughed. "Am I, Carmen? Not again?"

"No, darling!" Carmen set Ceci onto a chair. "I'm going to make you tea to help you breathe—and relax you a little. "How much of the story did you tell, Adelita?"

Adelita whispered in Carmen's ear.

"Oh, my daughter, what am I to do with you? Just when I think you're all grown up and responsible—"

"I won't do it again." Adelita looked from her mother to Ceci, tears rolling down her cheeks. "I'm so sorry, Cecilita. I didn't mean to scare you to death!"

Carmen sighed, "Ah, here's your *abuela*, home already. What will we tell her?"

They all heard the old women's heels clicking down the hall.

"You're just mad you didn't win as much as I did," Pilar laughed.

Then Rafaela, "Nobody wins as much as you do, *amiga*. You must be a *bruja*!"

Tía Pilar stuck her head into the kitchen, cheeks rosy with laughter, until she saw the tearful faces. "What's going on?"

Tito ran to Rafaela, burying his face in her skirt. "*La Llorona!*"

The *curandera* set her big purse on the kitchen table. "*La Llorona?*"

"Adelita told us *La Llorona*, and then Mami came home—now Cecilita's scared, and she's coughing. You'll have to do all the *limpias* all over, and Ceci is going to have to stay forever! And she's—she can't breathe!"

"Whoa, Tito! I can barely make out your words!" Rafaela tousled his hair. "What's going on?"

Tito gulped air. "Ceci's scared because Adelita told *La Llorona*."

"I don't suppose you are scared, are you, Tito?"

"No! Well, just a little."

"Good!" Pilar nodded. "He could use a little scaring, if you ask me."

"Adelita should know better than to tell such a story." Carmen looked at her daughter with sad eyes. "She usually has more sense."

"But, Mama, you're the one who told me *La Llorona*."

"I did not."

"Ah!" Rafaela laughed, "Ah yes, you did, Carmen. I remember!"

"I did? When?"

"When Adelita lied to you about meeting that boy at the movie theater."

"Well, Adelita is older. Everyone knows *La Llorona* is too scary for little ones." Carmen poured Ceci a cup of camomile tea. "Drink this *manzanilla;* it should calm you. Sip it—it's hot." She poured a second cup and gave it to Tito. "You, too."

"La Llorona!" Rafaela sighed. "Sooner or later, we all tell that one. We mothers grab whatever we can find. You told the story so Adelita would understand the dangers of sneaking off at night. Adelita told Tito *La Llorona* so he'd be kinder to Cecilita. It's natural."

"But the story didn't help Ceci any. She's beside herself. And she'll probably be up all night, afraid to sleep." Carmen smoothed Ceci's hair. *"Pobrecita—"*

"Yes," Rafaela nodded. *"La Llorona* might keep Tito in hand, at least for the moment, but then what? Adelita, you must save *La Llorona* for the big things, otherwise she will tire of helping us. We should invite her only when we really need her." Rafaela touched Adelita's chin. "If you are to be a storyteller, a *cantadora,* remember, there is no such thing ever as "just" a story. Stories are strong medicine. Now, shall I give us one more story, to undo Ceci's fright? Come, sit, Carmen, and Pilar can hear it, too, so even our dreams will be undisturbed."

Moíses: el Curandero

Before she began telling, just as Adelita had done, Rafaela closed her eyes and listened to the wind. Then she took a great breath, her hands on her belly. Ceci thought that the stories must be swirling around the house like invisible smoke, and a storyteller had to breathe them in before she could tell them. "It is a very old, old *cuento,* from the Holy Bible. Do you know about the Bible?"

Ceci shook her head.

"It is a book of power and magic. You will in your life hear its stories told to heal and, sometimes, to hurt. It is up to you to know the difference, to choose what you take to heart. And Adelita, when you tell the stories, it's your responsibility to know which ears are ready. Story medicine is like that, very powerful. Like *La Llorona*. This is the story of a *curandero*: a healer like me, but much greater.

Everywhere and always, my dears, there have been curanderos—*men and women who heal with God's help. This was even true for the Hebrews in Egypt. Like so many of our people, they had come far from their homeland and were forced to work hard for cruel bosses. If it weren't for the* curanderos, *the hard work and poverty would have killed them. Even now this is so.*

Moíses's mother and father were Hebrew curanderos. *They treated the sick and gave them medicine made from the plants of the Nile. Instead of dying from slavery and sickness, the Hebrews grew very strong, had many children—strong, straight, and beautiful as the cedar trees left behind in their homeland. The Hebrews were growing to be so many that the Egyptians became afraid.*

'Too many foreigners!' the people told their Pharaoh, 'They will outnumber us and take over our country.'

He was a lazy king, who liked having these strong slaves to do the work. Someday you will hear of the great pyramids these slaves built, each brick weighing more than a horse. The Hebrews carried these bricks on their backs; that's how strong they were, as strong as the Mexicans who toil in the farms and ranches. Watching them grow so strong, even Pharaoh got nervous.

Finally, Pharoah called all the Hebrew parteras—*the women who brought babies into the world. He told them, 'There are too many of your people. You must kill the baby boys. Only let the little girls grow up.' But the* parteras *listened to God before Pharaoh. They let the baby boys live. This pleased God, but Pharaoh was angry.*

'Why do you disobey me? Each night the Hebrews rock newborn sons to sleep, and each day more sons are born.'

To answer this, the parteras *looked to their eldest, a wise woman who had outlived her fears. She looked him in the eye and spoke plainly, 'Pharaoh, we cannot help you. Much work has made the Hebrew women strong, like wild mares. They give birth without help in the night. They hide their sons from us that way.'*

Pharaoh then ordered the parteras *to find these hidden sons. If and when they found them, he ordered that they should kill them. Now, it is not in the heart of any* partera *to kill a baby. So, they disobeyed. Again, God was pleased. Even more children were born, and the* curanderas *helped them to grow up healthy.*

You can imagine old Pharaoh's anger. No slave could be allowed to disobey. He ordered the Hebrews to kill all their newborn sons, to throw them in the river. People feared Pharaoh would send his soldiers to kill everyone if they did not obey. Life became even more terrible for the Hebrews. They spent their days looking over their shoulders and their nights without sleeping, clinging to their boy children with all their strength.

During this time, the curandera *mother gave birth to a fine son, the most beautiful child anyone had ever seen. There was a glow about him—for he had* el don, *the gift of healing. How could the* curandera *drown such a son?"*

"Cecilita—listen." Rafaela reached across the table to take her hand. "No mother in her right mind would choose to hurt her child. *La Llorona* even weeps for her own babies. Every mother has a sin she regrets, but the *curandera* had great wisdom. She found a way to obey and disobey Pharaoh at the same time. It would require great sacrifice—and great love. She wanted her son to live."

"She didn't throw him in the river?"

"*Oh no. Instead, she gathered the leaves of the tall plants growing by the river, the* enea, *to weave a fine basket the shape of a cradle. When she finished weaving it, she put the sticky sap of a tree all over the basket to keep out water. Yes, she was making a little basket boat for her son. With the finest linen from her homeland, she swaddled her baby and laid him in the basket for a siesta. She put this basket in the river, among the tall reeds, so he would not float away. Then, she sent his big sister to watch over him from a hiding place, to make sure he was safe.*

Pharaoh's daughter came down to the river for her bath. It was her habit to send her lady maids to walk along the riverside to make sure no man was watching. As they walked by the tall reeds, they found the beautiful basket and the dear little baby. A lady maid called out to Pharaoh's daughter, 'Look at what a sweet thing we've found!'

The baby boy opened his eyes and began to cry. 'Poor niñito,' *Pharoah's daughter sighed, 'his mother has put him into the river, as my father commanded. He is such a beautiful baby. I will keep him to amuse me.'*

One of the lady maids spoke up. 'I know the mother; I will bring the woman to you so she can give the baby milk.' So that is how the wise curandera *nursed and cared for her son without fear of Pharaoh's soldiers. The baby grew strong, and when it was time for him to be weaned, his mother brought him to Pharaoh's daughter and gave him to her."*

"Why? Didn't his mama want him anymore?"

"Oh yes, Cecilita, his *mamá* wanted him. But even more than she wanted him with her, she wanted him to use his *don*—to use his gift—and help their people. She knew they must both make a sacrifice."

"How did his mama know?"

"She knew this from the dreaming. Thus the *curandera* learned that her son would do great things. It was not easy to give him up, but that is the way of life for many a *curandera. Caminaba para su destino.* She walked toward her destiny."

Ceci laid her head on her arms, a little sleepy now, watching how the words traveled up Rafaela's tortoise neck to her mouth, the skin wiggling just a little bit.

"Each one who follows *destino* will face a sacrifice. That is what love is about. But back to our story—this part you must hear, Cecilita. It is like your own story.

Pharaoh's daughter gave the baby an excellent name, Moisés, which means 'saved from the water.' He might have drowned, but he was saved just like you, chiquita. *He grew up to be a great* curandero, *a leader and healer.*

God spoke to Moisés from a bush that burned but never turned to ash, and God gave him a magnificent staff that could turn into a snake. With this staff Moisés made a path through the sea and led his people away from Pharaoh's soldiers. The Hebrews never forgot him. And the Christians remember him, too.

Even in the barrio we remember Moisés when we feel lonely, far away from our own homelands. Many remember him when in secret they must cross the Rio Grande to America and work the fields. So many in this country have come from far away.

The Africans long for the lions and elephants, for their old religion, for their dances and drums, and Chicanos miss beautiful Mexico—the sunshine and flowers. For me, it is for the dry mesa of the Southwest, where I walked with my abuelita—the wild places where we gathered our herbs. Katy Sullivan longs for Connemara, land of green and mist. And Cecilita, you want to return to the days when your mamá and papá were happy.

Remember, you are like Moisés, taken out of the water for a great destiny. God has a great purpose for you."

"That's my story, dear ones, such as I heard it from my mother's knee." Rafaela yawned, "Oh, Pilar, *mi querida amiga*, you have worn me out with all your crazy Bingo."

Pilar pulled a stuffed Bugs Bunny from her purse. "Bingo was good to me. Here, Cecilita, since you don't have your Loli Bear."

"A very expensive replacement! Pilar played seven cards at once, all evening long. But it paid off!"

Ceci petted the rabbit's ears—he wasn't a bit like Loli, who had lived with her forever, and was worn to a softness that fit her. "Thank you!"

Carmen stood and stretched. "It's time to go home. You ought to turn in early, Mami. Barry's much improved; he should be up and about tomorrow."

"Carry me, Mamita," Tito lifted his arms. "I'm too tired to walk."

"I'll carry you, brother." Adelita scooped him into her arms.

At bedtime, Rafaela opened the yellow box Ceci had gotten at the *tienda* and held the tiny dolls in the palm of her hand. "A *curandero* from Guatemala told me about these. They will take away your nightmares. Every night, tell your worry to a doll and put it under your pillow. By the time you've put seven dolls under your pillow, they will have carried all your worries away and left beautiful dreams in their place."

"How do they do it?" Ceci yawned.

"That's just their magic." She set one doll into Ceci's palm, touching a finger to her lips. "Don't tell anyone what you ask them to take, until it is gone—all gone."

Ceci folded the tiny doll into her hand, kissed it, and whispered her worry. The blanket of the Moisés story surrounded her as she closed her eyes to sleep.

Simon Peter: Patron Saint of Indecision

Basking in the kitchen quiet, Rafaela savored her solitude. Pilar had left with Carmen to fetch Katy Sullivan. Barry and Ceci were still asleep. The *curandera* had risen before dawn to prepare for Barry's *limpia*. Not so young today as yesterday, she pondered the work to come. She poured herself a second cup of coffee to banish the desire to sneak in a *siesta* before lunchtime.

Shortly after sunrise, she and Pilar had breakfasted and set about cleaning house, scrubbing floors and dusting every surface to purify the energy for the *limpia*. How Pilar grumbled, striking the old rugs with the rattan tool Rafaela kept for the job. "Too much work, this! Why don't you have a vacuum cleaner like a civilized person?"

Rafaela had always sworn by the benefit of deep cleaning for the soul as well as the constitution. She hid her amusement as her friend gradually began to enjoy the exercise and whacked at the rugs with new vigor. Finally, Pilar swung the clean rug over the fence to air and found another to beat.

"Ah, now I see why you don't buy a Hoover! Just like this—whack— with this thing I could smack that Dora's behind! Saints forgive me. I might even lose my *panza*—now that I've got the hang of it."

"You've found my secret!" Rafaela laughed, patting her flat stomach. Even in this city of fast cars and movie stars, she clung to the old-fashioned things that reminded her of her grandmother and the sage-scented mesa where she had learned to be a *curandera*.

No desire to drive, she didn't own a car—or a television. Her own medicine had served her so well for decades, she'd brushed off Carmen's urgings to go in for an exam at the clinic for many months. She was feeling the years today, even as she rinsed out her coffee cup—her knuckles complaining she'd done enough. "Quiet!" she scolded her hands, "there's still much to do!" For instance, hanging the clothes to dry—

How her knees creaked as she scooped Ceci's new green dress from the basket! The bloodstains had washed out, thanks to a good douse of vinegar. She held it up to the sun, and the rhinestone buttons sparkled—not a hint of the carnage Barry had bled onto them.

So much trouble, that man! If he continued to resist her help, she was of a mind to send him on his way. Reaching for a clothespin, Rafaela felt a familiar twinge in her shoulder. Her body was reminding her of the countless times she had repeated these tasks. Now it was wearing out like an old jalopy, and simple things became difficulties. She shuffled back to the kitchen to prepare herself some medicine.

Perhaps she was growing too old for fighting off *brujos* and all the spirits they shook loose, wraiths hungering for the light she carried. On a lower shelf she found her jar of *árnica* salve, massaging it onto her aches, wondering how many healings were left in her. Should she do this *limpia*?

It was always her choice, to do the work of *curanderísmo* or to retire and spend the rest of her days in her rocking chair, knitting *rebozos*. She snorted, imagining herself knitting shawls; she didn't even own such a chair. She should get back to work. Cecilia had need of a real father, and the only way she was going to get one was if he shook off his demons.

When she decided to do the work of healing, it was always the same: she found a new strength—not her strength, but God's. *Jesús Cristo* would be her guide through this. She envisioned his sinewy carpenter's hand taking hers, passing on his courage. Within her the Spirit stirred, alive as molten gold, with God's light.

She lowered herself into a chair, kicking off her house slippers, pressing her feet into the cool linoleum. Imagining a taproot emerging from her heels, forcing through the floor and into the earth, she allowed the strength of earth to surge up into her.

Rafaela prayed down light, mixing the energy of sky and earth until she felt perfectly anchored and present, ready for the work ahead. She sprung from the chair and set about gathering the herbs she'd need, unfastening a sprig of dried *gobernadora* leaf her cousin had sent from Texas. After measuring out some of these precious leaves into a cup, her worry returned with the teakettle's whistle.

She pondered, allowing the teakettle to boil longer. Would she have the power to undo the damage of Barry's drinking, to heal Dora's desertion and the *brujo's* blows? Could she find the force to do yet another *limpia* so soon after the others? The whistle had become so shrill, insisting she remove the pot.

Ignoring it, she scolded herself. "Fool, do you think God needs help from you? What does it matter how you feel? God is strong enough! Now, take off the kettle!"

She laughed aloud, pouring the boiling water over the *gobernadora* leaves.

Barry coughed behind her.

She swung around, her hands to her cheeks.

"Good morning, Rafaela!" He yawned and pulled out a chair. "Having a little chat with yourself?"

She flushed. "No, not with myself. Er—praying."

"You laugh when you pray?"

"Yes! God tells such good jokes; it would be impossible not to laugh."

"God pulled some jokes at my expense, but I failed to see the humor." Barry eyed Rafaela's mug. "Don't suppose you have any coffee?"

"Of course!" She studied him carefully. The sutures had healed; his eyes looked clearer. "I was planning to make you some breakfast, too. Some *chorizo*?"

"Just coffee is fine. You'll make me as fat as Pilar."

She smiled, patting her belly. "You've noticed her *panza*."

"How could I miss it?"

"She tries to hide it with a girdle. You know, she was so beautiful as a girl."

"Pilar?"

"Oh, yes, beautiful! *Tan ardiente,* full of fire she was—"

Barry took the steaming mug Rafaela held out to him. "We're talking about the same Pilar whose idea of a thrill is Bingo night at the Parish Hall?"

"Huh! You think Dora is something? She doesn't have half the fire Pilar had before age mellowed her. Pilar was like a shooting star; she made people sigh."

"Ah!" He looked into his coffee cup. "Maybe someday Dora's fire will mellow."

"Amigo," Rafaela pulled out a chair and fell into it. "Dora's fire is different. It's not refining her. In time, it will destroy her, I fear."

"When will that happen?" Barry's eyes were a sea of pain. "So far, Dora seems untouched by the hurt she's given me. The consequences seem to bounce off of her, onto—the rest of us."

"For now, yes. One day her magic will run out; there will be no more men to use it on. She will be old and alone. Then her fire will use her for fuel. I fear it will be cancer that kills her—or something worse."

For a long time neither of them spoke, considering the demise of the beautiful Dora at the hand of some fearsome disease. It was beyond imagining. Barry wiped tears from his eyes, reached across the table, and gripped Rafaela's forearm. "No matter what harm she's done, I can't bear to think of her hurt. If she were to come back, I don't think I could turn her away. And yet, I know that I should—if not for my sake, then for Ceci's."

"Every time you think you're over Dora, and your heart might be moving elsewhere, you'll feel the old scar reopen. She is dangerous to you, *amigo.* In her own way she knows it; that's why she left you—and Cecilita. You need protection."

"What can I do?" Barry sighed. "Protection? Easier said than done. Dora will want to see Ceci again. How will I stand it?"

Slowly, sadly, Rafaela shook her head. "You will hate every minute, *amigo.*" She took another sip from her chipped mug, her eyes never leaving his face. "Torture!"

"What do you suggest I do, then?"

"Let me give you a *limpia*. I'll disconnect the cords she's fastened to you. It can be easier with Dora if she doesn't have her hooks into you. If you can only bring yourself to trust me, *amigo*—then I can help."

Barry was so quiet that Rafaela could hear her heart thumping in her chest. He took some sips of his coffee and looked up at her, his eyes still brimming.

"When could you do it? This *limpia*, I mean."

"Today."

"Don't you have customers—er—patients coming?"

"Your mother will come."

His face contorted. Rafaela wondered if his wounds were hurting him. "She's coming to help us. That is, if you'll let me perform the *limpia*. We have been praying that you will. If not—"

"You and Ma!" He slapped the table. "You crafty devils! You were planning this all along! Is that what you and God were laughing about?"

"What God and I say to each other is none of your business! But you came down to tell me something?"

"I don't know quite how to say this. I want to thank—I'm—a grateful man. I believe you've saved my life. Pilar told me a doctor even said as much. Of course, I was out cold. But I'm sure you're the reason I'm up and around."

"It was not only my doing." Rafaela clasped her hands at her waist. "God has a hand in all of this. You can go on your way—rejoin the corn cob band or whatever you want, now."

"No, Rafaela, I'm beginning to see my way clear, and it's not to San Francisco. You, Carmen, and those goddamned thugs have made me see. I—well, I could have lost everything! Ceci needs me, and what about Ma? Who will take care of her? Coming that close—I mean, I could have died in that alley! All that time I lay upstairs—Pilar watching me like a hawk." He placed both hands on the table, steadying himself. "I've come to a decision."

"A decision?" Rafaela raised her eyebrows. "You?"

"Saint Sullivan, the patron saint of indecision, has made up his mind! Do a *limpia*, or whatever it's called! You and Ma live it up! I owe you that—and more."

She covered her mouth to quiet her emerging giggles. He owed her? At the thought of it, Rafaela shrieked with laughter, holding on to the chair so she would not fly off and roll on the floor. Again and again she hooted, until at last she was able to stop for a breath. He gazed at her like a tuna on ice at the *pescadería*. Even the handsome look ridiculous when confused, Rafaela thought. She untied her apron and flung it at him. "You owe me something, Saint Sullivan?"

"Yes, Rafaela, I owe you—everything!"

"Then wash the dishes, *amigo*!" she said, and dashed out to her garden to tell Pilar, leaving Barry to think whatever he might.

Nuestra Señora de Pilar: Our Lady of the Pillar

"There is a nip in the air. You'd think it was fall already." Katy had dressed up in her best Donegal tweed skirt and jacket. "Mind if I lean on you a bit, Pilar?"

Poor Katy had let herself get so thin, the slightest draft probably sliced right through her, Pilar thought. "We old folks must support each other." She pretended she needed to rest, stopping to dab her handkerchief at nonexistent sweat, so that Katy would pace herself. Her sister, frail with cancer, had leaned on her just so. She heaved a sigh, remembering.

Katy tightened her grip on Pilar's arm. "Are you all right?"

"I was just remembering."

"Ah," Katy nodded. "Memory."

"I was thinking of my sister, Cecilia."

"The one you lost?"

"It was ever so long ago, dear. But still—"

Katy patted Pilar's arm. "Yes, I understand."

Each remembering their losses, the old women sat silently until the bus finally reached Olvera Street. Katy leaning on Pilar for support, they walked their tortoise way to Rafaela's adobe, admiring the blooming flower boxes and bougainvillea vines.

"It's such a fine house!"

"Yes," Pilar sighed. "I was raised in an adobe in Santa Barbara. Gringos bulldozed it."

"Crying shame, 'tis. There aren't many old buildings in this part of the world. Funny thing, most of the old things out West aren't American."

"Ah, they're American, *amiga*. Just not gringo."

"Fancy that!" A tinge of color returned to Katy's cheeks. "Those who think they're the original Americans are actually the new people, aren't they?"

"You're the first gringo I've ever met who understood that!" Pilar put the spare key Rafaela gave her into the lock. "They act like I'm the foreigner."

"I'm not a gringo! I'm an Irishwoman! The Irish know what it's like to—"

"Grandma—Tía!" Ceci threw her arms around her grandmother first, then her great-aunt. "Daddy's going to have a *limpia!*"

"That's grand!" Katy grinned. "Look at you—that green hair ribbon—beautiful!"

"Adelita gave it, and Daddy gave me this dress. It's got stars; see 'em?" She pointed to the rhinestone buttons marching down the front.

"Pretty fancy. Is there going to be a party?" Pilar wiped a crumb from Ceci's cheek with her forefinger.

"Just the *limpia*—I have a special part, and it's a secret!"

"Well, Grandma will just have to wait." Katy caught hold of Pilar's arm, and Pilar led her to the living room, where Rafaela had already begun to set up the *limpia*. With an interested glance at the altar, Katy lowered herself onto the red settee. Pilar's squeezed Katy's arm. "Barry has agreed to everything. Soon the family will be healed!"

Catherine of Alexandria: Patron Saint of Little Girls

Ceci fingered the pink beads that hung from Katy's fist. "You want to go to Ireland, Grandma."

Katy looked into her granddaughter's cool green eyes, so like her son's that her heart squeezed with the memories of so many failures with him—especially her inability to convey her faith. She had prayed to the Virgin to help her be different with Cecilia, to listen more and preach less. "Yes."

"Pray for that, Grandma."

"You think I should?"

Ceci nodded, everything about her sparkling with health. To see her granddaughter thriving, there was nothing more Katy could ask from God, except—

"Grandma, can I go with you to Ireland?"

"So you shall, macushla."

"What does that mean, that word? You always say it. Is it Spanish?"

"Not Spanish, darling. Macushla means 'most precious' in *Gaeilge*, the language I spoke in Connemara. In English they call it Irish. *Gaeilge.*"

"Will I learn Irish?"

"I hope you will learn Irish, Spanish—all the languages you want."

"I want to learn how to talk to animals, too."

"Well, now!" Katy laughed, "Just like Saint Francis!"

"And Rafaela! She talks to Lupe and the chickens."

"Like Bridie back home. Her hens laid twice the eggs of any in the neighborhood. That was her secret—the talking."

Pilar returned with a clean apron tied around her. "Rafaela wants to smudge us first. You should stand in the doorway."

"What's smudge?" Katy slowly rose from the settee.

"Like incense. Ceci, you and your grandma stand here. Rafaela will light the candles and then start the smudge sticks burning."

Resplendent in her purple flowered dress, Rafaela appeared with a large abalone shell in her hands. "Good morning, everyone! Here's how we will begin. First, I will set up candles for each direction, like the cross. Then, I will light this little bundle of sage, so I can see in the smoke what things need to be cleared."

The sage smoke reminded Katy of the scent of a bog fire. She remembered the hearth fire and the copper kettle her ma hung over it for tea. As clear as day—the memory almost swept her from where she stood.

"Please, Catalina, stand facing me. Turn clockwise. Yes, that's right." Swathed in a veil of smoke, all the while reciting prayers in syllables as soft and musical as Irish, the *curandera's* face had the look of a priest's about it. Katy took her rosary from her pocket and began to murmur her prayers.

As Barry entered the room, and Rafaela swirled the smoke around him, Katy's breath caught. She could have sworn, just for a moment, that she saw a thin rope coiled around his chest, its ends trailing in the air. She blinked. It must be the smoke, she told herself, and pressed her hands to her chest to stop her heart from pounding so hard.

Saint Raphael: Archangel Healer

As she swept the sage smoke around Barry with her feather fan, Rafaela took note of the cords that bound Barry to alcohol. She asked the spirits in charge of them to take them to the West, where everything we no longer need must go. She lit the candles: first *María de Guadalupe* to ground them in love, then *Santa Barbára* for courage and devotion, *Santa Marta* for impossible causes, and *San Cipriano* for magic and healing. In the window, she set a Jesus candle, which she lit with a special prayer.

This Jesus candle served to warn her of any change in the energy of the room. If the flame surged or flickered, she would pay extra attention to the aura of the room. If the *brujo* had somehow learned that this cleansing was occurring, there was a good chance he might interfere with the medicine.

As she began the Huasteca song her grandmother had taught her, a shiver of awe traveled her spine. She called in her ancestors to help with this work, to remind her of anything she might have forgotten, to keep watch over her medicine.

She knelt down on the sheet she placed in the center of the floor for Barry, rolling a whole egg over his joints in little crosses, beginning with his neck and chest, taking care not to break the shell. Thousands of times she'd done this same ritual. This was her destiny: to heal, her touch light and swift, her mind steady. While giving a *limpia*, she felt like an arrow shot out of God's heart.

Saint Sullivan: Himself

Barry closed his eyes. Nothing but darkness and Rafaela's chanting, then—*a wisp of a vision, moonlit, pearl white: Dora's dark face framed with pale flowers, the smell of orange blossoms drifting the atmosphere.* He tried to shake this image. There had been no such flowers at their elopement, no finery, no veil. Dora had worn a pink tweed suit. *Now she clasped another man's hand, walking away with a swoosh of pure white satin. Barry grasped at her veil, a receding tide of white lace. She glanced back, her eyes afire, her lips parted, her teeth glinting in a half-smile. Then she turned her back and laughed, disappearing into a shaft of moonlight. Her laughter glittery and cold, like sleet*—through this fading laughter, Barry could hear Rafaela whispering her prayers right into his ear. Dora's image faded. The smell of orange blossoms was overtaken by another smell: milk, soap, and sunshine. Warmth closed in on his side.

"Daddy, don't be afraid." Ceci whispered close to his ear, wrapped her arm around his chest, and buried her face in his neck. Somewhere, it seemed a million miles away, Rafaela was chanting and the rosary beads were clicking, but all he needed in that moment was this child. Ceci, the love of his life! All he needed to do was to make up these months of spiraling neglect. He had almost lost her to his selfishness. All he needed in life was to be a father. All he needed in life was right here.

In a flash of certainty, Barry knew several things: One, he must take Ma to Ireland. Two, he must make a home for Ceci. And three—he must let Dora go. If he could do these, he would be the man God intended him to be.

And if while doing these things he could make it with jazz, fine. If he had to slog through some less creative livelihood until Ceci was grown, he could swing it. He sat up, still holding his daughter close to him.

"I can swing it!" he proclaimed. "I can do it!"

Rafaela helped him up from the floor. He guessed she knew better than to ask what he had experienced. Whatever he learned was his alone.

She spoke softly, holding a bowl in her hand. "Let us take a look at the egg together, and you will see what there is to learn there."

Carmen: Not Yet a Saint

Before emerging from her car, Carmen flapped down the sun visor to check her lipstick. She had reapplied it twice, only to chew it off in her nervousness. What did one wear to a jazz club? She was hopeless about any clothes besides starched white uniforms and sensible lace-up shoes.

Beside her in the front seat, Adelita studied her, appraising. "Mamita, you look nice. Just go in!"

"I don't want to look nice. I want to look—"

"You're pretty!" Tito tapped her shoulder from the back seat. "I like that silver thing in your hair."

"What silver thing?" Carmen groped the back of her head. "Oh, for goodness sake, I left a clippie!" She pulled it out and combed the back of her hair with her fingers. "Oh, Addie, I wish I hadn't let you talk me into wearing it down."

"It's really stylish, Mamita."

"It might be windy." Carmen frowned into the mirror. "It'll all muss up."

Tito opened his door. "Come on!"

"Now, Mamita, try to act normal. I know you can!" Adelita squeezed her mother's hand. "You look good—for once!"

"Just what a girl wants to hear!" Carmen laughed, and rummaged in her purse for her lipstick. "Where's that—"

Adelita snatched Carmen's purse and snapped it shut. "C'mon, Mamita! Tito is already inside. They're going to wonder—"

"Addie—I don't know," Carmen sighed. "I don't want to go."

"Yes, you do! C'mon, get out of the car!"

Carmen wondered: How had she ever agreed to this date? Barry said it was to make up for their quarrel the other night, just a friendly outing, and no strings attached. That was just it—no strings—he was leaving town—probably never see him again. Feeling her curls for more clippies, she dropped her purse, then crouched to pick it up, grumbling. "Can I help it if I love people?"

"What?" Adelita stopped on the middle step, looking back at her. "What did you say, Mamita?"

"Oh, nothing. Let's just go in."

Carmen slid through the door right into Barry, who caught her by the arm.

"Wow, Carmen, you're dressed to the—you look, uh, great! They'll not know what to do with you at the Lighthouse Café."

She suddenly regretted wearing the little black dress Adelita claimed looked like a million dollars. "I knew it—overdressed! I wanted to wear slacks, but Adelita insisted."

"Oh, you're good. You're fine." He tugged on the sleeve of his rumpled sports jacket. "I'm kind of limited in my wardrobe, you see. Always casual."

"Never mind; I'll blend into the woodwork."

"Looking like that? You gotta be kidding, Carmen. All eyes will be on you! And they'll be happier for it, I kid you not!"

Before Carmen could sit in his car, Barry had to throw his coat, a duffel bag, and his clarinet into the back seat. "Kind of using the Merc for storage these days."

"Is everything out of your old place?"

"Most of it went to Goodwill, except for Ceci's toys. I crammed all my suits into one suitcase." He took another look at her. "Should I go in and change? I might have a black suit shoved in there."

"No, you're fine." Carmen straightened his tie. "Let's just go as we are."

"That's what I like about you, Carmen." Barry squeezed her arm. "You can roll with the punches."

Roll with the punches? For most of the drive to Hermosa Beach, Carmen ruminated: Whatever did he mean—roll with the punches? Had she donned her best dress to remind him of prizefighters? She didn't know whether to laugh or cry her embarrassment. Who takes fashion advice from a fifteen-year-old? An overworked mother who hasn't been on a date since said teenager was born, that's who! Ridiculous to let Adelita convince her this was a real date! A man who'd just lost a woman like Dora wasn't about to romance a plain old nurse from the barrio.

Stumbling out of the car, and sprinting to keep up with Barry's long strides, Carmen entered the Lighthouse Café and hoped he couldn't see her disappointment. This wasn't her idea of a nightclub. It should be a swanky place with silk-shaded candle lamps and white tablecloths. This dive was nothing like the clubs Carmen had seen in the movies—the only ones she'd seen.

The Lighthouse Café was more like a campus roadhouse: red brick walls and candles stuck into Chianti bottles. No enigmatic gamines lounged around with long cigarette holders. Not a Bing Crosby or Frank Sinatra to be seen—but no artsy unknowns with bongo drums, either. Not a beatnik in sight.

A few fresh-faced young women, probably from UCLA, leaned on the bar. They wore beach clothes—untucked shirts and Capri pants. More kids slouched over the tables affecting boredom, as if a night out were an entitlement rather than a rare indulgence.

Carmen tossed her hair to stave off these thoughts. Of course she wished she'd worn slacks, but here she was on her first night out in almost six years. She might as well make the most of it. She took Barry's arm, and he smiled back at her, his eyes lit with joy. The rumpled shirt and shapeless sports coat looked appropriate; he was in his element, sporting an easy elegance not unlike Frank Sinatra—or that handsome presidential hopeful, Kennedy. "Barry, I see why you love this place; it's just like you."

He glowed back at her, squeezing her arm. "Yeah, kind of run down— but the music, oh, you'll love it!" Posters of jazz greats hung behind the bar: Louis Armstrong, Billie Holiday, Charlie Parker—Barry was as gleeful as a kid in a candy store, pointing out each one and telling her about their sound. "You listen to much jazz, Carmen?"

"No. Jazz is not so big in the barrio, but—"

"Well, I'll be a monkey's uncle!" The bartender waved. "Saint Sullivan, what the hell have you been up to?"

Carmen shot Barry a quizzical frown. Saint Sullivan?

"Up to no good, Andy. Hey, I want to introduce my pal, Carmen."

Andy gave Carmen the once-over, whistling through his teeth.

"Where do I find a pal like you, Carmen? You really class up the joint."

She flushed, looking down at her dress. "Well, I—I didn't know what to wear. You see, I thought—"

"I see and I like! Say your name again for me, honey?"

"Carmen—Carmen Arroyos." She offered her hand.

The bartender took her hand, but didn't shake it. He held onto it with both of his. "Ah, a movie star name, Carmen—exotic."

Determined not to blush again, Carmen bit her lip. "There must be thousands of Carmens in the barrio."

"Not another like you, baby." Andy squeezed her hand.

"Hey, bud!" Barry gave Andy a playful punch, "If you'll just let go, I'll take Carmen to meet the guys before their set."

"Better hurry. I heard Miles might join them."

"No kidding?"

"Yeah, man, Miles Davis. The genius himself!"

"We lucked out, then!" Barry squeezed his lips together. "C'mon, Carmen. You're in for a treat!" He led her toward the rear wall and a low stage that supported a baby grand piano, a drum set, and a few stools and microphones. No curtains or footlights, only a few darkened fixtures directed toward the platform from the low, slatted ceiling. A sickly philodendron suffered in the dark, left of the stage, and a young man fiddled with an electrical tangle at the center.

"Smitty!" Barry stepped onto the stage to help.

"Hey, Saint Sullivan, long time no see. Is it really you?"

"Yeah, man, give me some skin." Barry thrust out his hand. "Good times back then."

"Yeah, we're cool, baby. Who's the fly chick you got there, man?" Smitty finally coiled the cord at the base of the microphone stand.

"This is my friend, Carmen. Still time to take her to meet the All-Stars?"

Smitty nodded. "They're out back. Preparing, if you catch my drift."

Carmen flushed. "If it's going to be an inconvenience—"

Smitty hopped off the stage. "Hell, no, a doll like you will fracture them."

"Translate, please? I don't speak whatever that is you're speaking."

"Hep talk, baby." Smitty put his arm around Carmen's shoulders. "Fly means, like, you've got it all together and know right where to put it. Fracture, well, fracture is cool. They'll like you, baby; you're a real gone chick, super murgatroid." Smitty waved toward the exit. "Better catch them outside before they go on. I gotta check the speakers." He kissed Carmen's cheek. "Stay beautiful, baby."

"Quite a character!" Carmen watched him sprint off. "Is he a musician?"

"Smitty? He's just a gofer for the band, but he's sure got the lingo down." Barry led her through a door under an exit sign. In the shadows of the back alley, five men gathered in a little circle passing a hand-rolled cigarette, taking long, sucking drags. Carmen knew the aroma from the barrio: marijuana. She dropped Barry's arm, swallowing a little gasp of disapproval.

What they were doing didn't seem to bother him one whit. "I'll see if they have time to talk. Wait here!"

Carmen glanced up and down the alley. What if the cops came? Stop worrying, she told herself, and leaned against the door, watching Barry saunter over to his friends. They greeted him with a clamor of banter and backslapping. "Hey, Saint Sullivan, where the hell have you been? Where's Dora been keeping you? Did she Shanghai you off to Mexico, or something?"

Barry gathered them into a huddle. One of the guys, a lean nervous-looking man, dropped the cigarette, crushing it under his shoe. One by one, each furtively looked her way. Barry was probably explaining about Dora. Carmen resisted an urge to flee.

Barry waved. "C'mon over, Carmen, I want you to meet my friends, the Lighthouse All-Stars."

Purse pressed against her chest, Carmen advanced to the little circle of men. She never felt so foreign in her life, so far away from where she belonged and mattered. She forced a smile. Barry pulled her to his side.

"Guys, this is my lovely friend, Carmen Arroyos."

The men stood at attention, grinning like schoolboys on the first day of summer.

"Miss Arroyos!" Almost in unison, like a song—

"Please, call me Carmen," she offered her hand. "I'm thrilled to meet you."

The tallest took her hand. "Rumsey's the name, and the thrill is all mine, baby."

"Rumsey here plays the bass. He's the main man, the leader."

"If you can call it that. Hey, Carmen," he put his arm around her and drew her aside. "I'm working up some Latin stuff that I'd like your opinion on. I spend so much time in Mexico, gathering inspiration. If you—"

"Gathering weed, more like." A dapper young man in a blue-grey suit that matched his eyes exactly took Carmen's hand. "Bob Cooper: I play tenor, tenor sax."

"I couldn't really help you, Rumsey. I don't know anything about jazz. I don't even know what a tenor sax is. How is it different from a real sax? Is it higher or something?"

"Higher? No." Bob Cooper laughed, "That's what lots of people think. Actually, the tenor sax is somewhat bigger. Lower. It's really mellow, has kind of a dark tone. If I play a C on the tenor sax, it's really a B-flat, an octave lower."

"I wouldn't know an octave if it bit me. Quite uncultured, really—"

"It isn't about culture, baby. It's about soul. Don't worry about that stuff. You hang out long enough with Saint Sullivan, you'll learn all you need to know."

There it was again—that nickname. "Why do you all call Barry Saint Sullivan?"

"Funny, that." Bob Cooper shook his head. "Far as I know, he's not been canonized yet. You know why, Rumsey?"

"I tell you, the Pope should get right on it!" Rumsey brushed some ash off his lapel. "Sullivan's a regular saint: doesn't do dope, shows up for practice, doesn't chase skirts. All he does is play that licorice stick like a goddamn angel. The patron saint of the clarinet, far as I'm concerned—fit for the angel choir."

"Lot of good that does me, man." Barry laughed. "Maybe the devil is in charge of jazz. Can't get a gig to save my life. I think I'm going to give it up."

"That's a goddamned sin, Sullivan! A sin! You've got the chops, man." Rumsey wagged his head. "Don't give up. Make the devil a deal. You're down by law."

Barry scuffed his foot along the uneven pavement. "Fat chance of that, even!"

Rumsey slapped his own cheek. "Wait a minute, Sullivan! Why don't you join us for a few numbers?" Rumsey scanned his fellow band members questioningly. They were all smiles and nods.

"Yeah, man!" Cooper slapped Barry's back. "Miles is in the house; he asked to jam with us. You ought to meet him, at least."

"I couldn't horn in on your big night."

"I insist!" Rumsey grinned. "You have to, man. We've got this number, "Dreamsville." You know it. I'll give you the change-ups. These opening blue notes: I'd imagined an oboe for the recording, but clarinet would be even sweeter."

"I can't ask Carmen to sit by herself. Miles can add the blue notes."

He wasn't going to give up this chance to join his friends because of her, was he? "Go ahead, Barry. I'll be fine." She squeezed his arm encouragingly. "Please!"

"But I brought you here to thank you."

"Thank her, eh?" Bob Cooper socked Barry's arm. "You lucky saint, you!"

Carmen suffered an uncontrollable blush. "You can thank me by playing, Barry."

"Listen to the lady! Come with us and meet Miles. We'll go over the changes."

"There's time?" Barry looked at his watch. "Before you go on? I do have my clarinet in the car—if you think I can—"

"You're always a quick study, Saint." Bob Cooper took Carmen's arm. "I'll show this fine chick back to a table."

"Let's find a good spot." Cooper scouted out a front table near center stage. "We'll look down at you for inspiration, baby."

"I thought that was what the marijuana was for."

"Sizz!" He shook his hand as if he'd touched a hot stove. "I like the way you say that word: mari-*juana*. Much more sexy than Rumsey says it."

"Sexy!" Carmen laughed. "It's just a weed in Mexico. Takes the gumption out of people, though, and—" she whispered, "illegal, last time I checked. The last thing Barry needs—"

"Don't worry, baby; the Saint's not going to get into mischief with us. Rumsey's right; Sullivan's clean as they come in this business. You have yourself a real good guy." He squeezed her hand. "Lucky guy, too."

Carmen sighed. Barry wasn't hers to have, good or not. "Thanks—and nice to meet you, Bob."

"Same here." He drank her in with his cool blue eyes. "You're a real barn burner, honey. Hope you dig the jazz."

"Oh, I will." Carmen watched as Bob strutted off. She knew he was just the kind of guy Adelita always liked. She herself preferred men who looked like men instead of boys—dark-haired and dark-eyed—Latinos all. Yet, maybe—no, she would not let herself think of Barry that way. Nothing more than friendship, and it would stay that way. The last thing he needed was another complication. She let herself take in the bar and the people who had filed in since she'd met the band.

Carmen untied the scarf from around her neck and stuffed it into her purse. Everyone looked like they'd walked in right off the beach. What was it about rich young Anglos? They loved to dress as if they didn't have two dimes to rub together. Not so in the barrio. Why, a Chicano would never step out looking so shabby.

Hermosa Beach might as well be a million miles away from Olvera Street. She slipped off her pointed-toe high heels. Her next date with an Anglo, she should wear sneakers. The thought made her giggle—sneakers!

Catching her eye with a nod, the man at the next table winked and blew her a kiss. Carmen dropped her gaze, cheeks hot. Why was she attracting so much attention? In the barrio, she was old—a mother—and as the daughter of the *curandera*, a caution. She made more money than most of the men in her neighborhood, was divorced—and there were her children. Since her husband had left her six years ago, she'd had flirtations, but not one date. She'd barely had time to notice she was a woman.

The tables were filling with a little older clientele than the slouchy college kids, and better dressed, but hers was still the only brown face. The descendants of the Mexicans who had named the beach Hermosa were nowhere to be seen. They'd probably been run out of town by some Anglos—but not by these jazz aficionados. They were either too cool, or too high, to run anywhere after anyone.

She grinned, thinking of these slouchy kids on the rampage. The man at the table waved again. Must be the candlelight, she sighed. If he could see me in daylight . . . .

Saint Sullivan's Heaven

Right in the middle of the Mancini tune, "Dreamsville," Miles struck a decisive diverging note—an opportunity for a train wreck. Barry was supposed to pick up on Miles's lead and slip into his heat—the solo riff he'd laid out at the beginning. He'd either lose his way, and everyone's riffs would crash in a fatal pileup, or his solo would lead them to a smooth convergence down the track. Barry breathed deep, the drumbeat tingling in his muscles, in his brain, in his blood, his whole body an ear. The air pulsed, electric.

Miles trumpeted that gorgeous note, as blue and shimmery as slow water. Bob, on tenor sax, took up the slight drop in pitch and lowered the melody an octave. Rumsey grounded the tune with a new, slower bass line, nodding for Barry to come in for the changeup. Barry closed his eyes and lifted his clarinet.

Blessed Carmen of the Barrio

Barry blew out that perfect note, and Miles threw back his head with pleasure. It might have been a lullaby; it might have been a sonata; whatever it was—perfect, luminous, and sweet. Lit honey poured out of that old clarinet, gilding the room. Delicious!

The crowd hushed. Carmen leaned forward to soak in Barry's light, sweet high notes. The drummer brushed the cymbals. Then, his shoulders rocking forward on the beat, Miles slipped the mute on his trumpet to play. What was that, a harmony? The clarinet and trumpet notes swelled together, as if Miles and Barry had been playing together for years.

She sighed her pleasure, her whole body relaxing with the slow dreamy flow of sound. Clarinet and trumpet sang one ecstatic song. When they broke apart and Miles again took up the melody, Barry dropped back. It was like the dissolution of a climax. Several in the audience gasped.

Her heart beating syncopation, her knees rubbery, Carmen gripped the table. So this was jazz! This music was more like sex than she could ever tell anyone. She rose with the entire audience; people were shouting and stomping, a shout of joy escaping from her before she could stop herself.

"¡Olé! ¡Olé!"

Barry stood back in deference to Miles, who gestured for him to come forward. "Ladies and gentlemen, I give you—Saint Sullivan on clarinet."

Almost shyly Barry bowed and made to step down from the stage.

The crowd roared. "More clarinet! More!"

Rumsey grabbed Barry's arm, while speaking into the mike. "We're not letting this guy sit down. He's burning 18 karat up here tonight. You gotta stay with us, Sullivan."

"Saint Sullivan!" Someone yelled from the back.

The crowd took up the chant. "Saint Sullivan! Saint Sullivan!"

Rumsey raised his hand for silence. It took a minute for the crowd to quiet. "Who'd-a thought a clarinet was just what that song needed? Stay up here, Saint Sullivan, and show us what else you can do."

"You're in your element, Barry," Carmen whispered to him during the break.

Barry took her hand. "I think you're lucky for me, Carmen."

He didn't let go of her hand the whole intermission. Several times Carmen thought she'd pull her hand away, but he only gripped it tighter, as if reading her mind.

Brushing off a feeling of proprietorship, Carmen watched him take the stage. Luscious song after song, Miles and Barry jammed as a duo. The Chianti bottle candles burned to waxy nubs. The club nearly dark except for the stage lights, not a one in the audience stirred.

After the All-Stars finally took their bows, glasses began to clink, the house lights turned up, and someone put on the hi-fi. The canned music was so shallow in comparison, like a fly buzzing on a windowsill. It put Carmen on edge.

She craned her neck, searching the club for a glimpse of Barry. He must have gone backstage with the band. What was taking him so long? She hoped he wasn't drinking; she was too sleepy to drive. Finally, she laid her head on her arms, exhausted.

"Carmen, Carmen, wake up!"

"What—what time is it?"

"Kind of late, honey."

"Oh, Barry, you're still recovering!"

"I'm okay! Wait till you hear what happened!"

"So, tell me." She rubbed her eyes. "What happened?"

Barry held back a moment, his arms folded on the table, his gaze clear, just glowing joy. She savored the happiness in his face as if it were Adelita's or Tito's.

"Miles asked me to come with him on tour—to Europe."

"You're not serious?"

"I am! He said it's time the clarinet had itself another heyday."

"Wow, Barry! Congratulations." Carmen wrung her hands. Oh God, this was a great, great thing at the worst possible time. Far be it from her to be the one to tell him. Far be it from her.

"You don't look so happy, Carmen."

"Of course, I'm happy. I just—"

"You just know better." His grin widened, his eyes all mischief.

Carmen stared. "What?

"I turned him down! I turned down Miles Davis! Aren't you going to congratulate me? I turned down Miles Davis!"

Before she could stop herself Carmen slapped him, hard as she could.

Barry rubbed his cheek. "What the hell was that for?"

"Oh, damn it!" Carmen threw her arms around him, weeping. "I'm sorry!"

"Eh! It didn't hurt that much." He hugged her. "For a strong woman, you sure have a wimpy left hook."

"No, no, not sorry for hitting—but, what if you regret it? This is your dream come true. You're a jazz musician. Miles Davis! What more could you want than to join him?"

"To take Ma to Ireland."

Carmen pulled from his arms. "Ireland?"

"She's already booked a flight for us from New York."

She wiped her tears with the back of her hand. "You agreed to go?"

"Yeah, it's about time Ma got something she wanted."

"And Ceci?"

"She's coming with us."

"What about your music, Barry? This big chance?"

"Maybe I'll catch up with Miles again—someday—maybe even in Ireland."

"Maybe not, though." Carmen took his hand. "Then how will it feel, when the glow of tonight has worn off?" She searched his eyes; they were a clear, calm sea of joy.

"I'll make it, now I know I can do it. I'm good enough. Even Rumsey is encouraging me to look him up. Right now, fame is the farthest thing from my mind. Because I'm looking at you, and realizing what really matters." He touched her chin, tilting her face toward his. "I'm looking at you and loving what I see."

Carmen bit her tongue, wanting to tell him something, anything, to deflect the discomfort, but she could not deprive herself of this moment. She was thirsty for the longing in those watery eyes of his.

"I like what I see in you, Carmen. I—you—you're—I just don't know what to say. I think I'm falling for you in a big way."

Like a surprise cloudburst, guilt dampened her joy. This could not be. Barry had too much to heal before he could love a woman again. Suffering the dear expectance of his gaze, she feigned a yawn. "Barry, I'm beat. I'd like to go home."

She struggled to her feet, fled the Lighthouse Café, and leaned against the brick wall outside the door. The foggy air soothed her burning cheeks.

"Hey, *señorita*, don't you need these?" Barry held her shoes out. "You'll tear your stockings."

"Too late." She wiggled the toe that poked through her hose. "And it's *señora*."

"Here you go, Señora Cinderella. Give me your pretty little foot."

"Idiot!" She let him help her on with her shoes. "I've got big, wide feet." She glanced away. "And I'm old, too."

His eyes searched her face. "Old?"

She couldn't bring herself to say thirty-five. "Older than you."

"Ninety, are you?"

"Past thirty, past hoping—for anything but seeing my kids grow up."

"You could be surprised, still. You might fall in love someday."

"Someday!" She shivered, her drop pearl earrings drumming her jawbone. Barry wrapped his sports jacket around her and offered his arm. She answered the gesture, as if it were a proposal. "No, Barry. It's too soon."

"Too soon for what?"

She studied him: his head was cocked; his eyes sparkled as innocently as Ceci's.

"You honestly don't know?"

"Well, I can guess. You don't dig me, and you're trying to find a way to let me down gently. You think I'm an immature idiot."

"Oh, you are! You're idiotically immature!" She smiled, "But that isn't it. I'm just too straitlaced for my own good, I guess. I want you—yes. I just want you—and Ceci—to heal, and bond, without me in the way."

"You won't be in the way. Not you." He unlocked her side of the car and held the door for her. "You're not that kind of woman."

"What kind of woman?" She couldn't resist the question leaping from her heart. "What kind of woman am I, then?"

"The best kind of woman! So good—so rare, and real—I'll never find anyone else like you."

Resting her palms on the Mercury's dilapidated upholstery, Carmen sought his eyes for a hint of the usual bravado—the merriment that tormented yet delighted her so. His gaze was so bereft, so vulnerable; she feared she would lose her resolve, throw herself into his arms, and declare her affection. She steeled herself. Her back teeth locked together; her arms folded across her chest. "You'll see—there are many like me."

"You're the one for me. You're the only one." He leaned toward her but didn't take her into his arms, his eyes pleading. "The only woman that I can love—"

"Ah, there you're mistaken." She turned away, staring out the side window at the Lighthouse Café. The neon sign flickered just once and turned off. "So you think. So you thought before, with Dora."

"I'm older and wiser now, Carmen. What will I do, if I can't have you?"

The two of them sat looking out the windshield at nothing but the occasional blurred light of a passing car. Carmen composed herself, trying to find the wisdom her mother might offer. If only she could be impetuous—if only she might respond without examining her intentions like specimens under a microscope. Not only a nurse, doomed to chart her observations, but her mother's daughter—she must view life like a *curandera*, with a nod to destiny, looking for the signs of God's blessing. It was not the right time for Barry to love her, with Dora's betrayal so fresh a scar.

"Give yourself time, Barry. That's what you can do without me clouding up the picture. See how you feel in six months. Then you can talk to me about love, if you still want to." With a shrug, she shot a glance at the café. "Look, they've turned off the sign; it must be very late. Can we go now?"

"Carmen!" His eyes locked with hers. "Say, you love me, too!"

She did not soften her resolve, but smiled back like a stern but kindly mother, hiding all the regret that surged up in her telling her to give in! Years of practiced self-discipline and sacrifice weighed down the impulse.

"It's too soon, Barry." She looked away and pressed her eyes. "Take me home, please! I have to get up early tomorrow."

"All right." He nodded sadly and turned the key. "Home it is."

She shut her tired eyes, hoping Barry would sense her need for silence. There was nothing more to say, and no way to take back what had already been said.

Part Five:
Saint Sullivan's Daughter
August 1960

"I had another dream last night."

"Yes, you will be dreaming again." Rafaela handed Ceci a ball of masa. "Can you pat this into a tortilla, like I showed you?"

With a nod of her head, Ceci began to pat the dough between her hands, switching it from palm to palm. "It was a bride dream. Mama got married in my dream."

Rafaela leaned back against the sink, brushed her hands off on her apron, and took a loose hair from Ceci's cheek. "Tell me more, *querida*."

"She got married—not to Daddy. Someone else. She talked about marrying Carlos once, and then she got mad at him. I guess Mama likes getting married, but I don't think she likes men very much." Ceci held up the blob of dough for Rafaela to inspect. The old woman pressed her lips together in a straight line, but her eyes sparkled with laughter.

"Is my tortilla bad, Rafaela?"

"No, *chiquita!* Something just struck me as funny. It's a lovely tortilla."

Standing on the step stool at the sink, Ceci could see out the kitchen window. Tito was jumping up and down by Lupe's pen. "What's he doing?"

"Let's go see."

Tito met them at the back door. "The turtles came out!"

"Rats!" Ceci ran to Lupe's pen. "I wanted to see them hatch."

Rafaela lifted the straw from the tortoise's nest. "Tito, go get a head of that lettuce from the icebox. "Look, there are still two more to come!"

Slowly tearing open the skin of the egg, another baby tortoise pushed out, while his mother napped in the sun as lazily as ever. Ceci frowned. "Lupe doesn't even care her babies are coming! She doesn't even help them."

"How could she help, Cecilita?"

"She could get them food."

"They already know how to find food. She gave them that knowledge in the water of her egg. Before they were born, they ate all they needed to know. In the desert the babies would crawl off and find their own way. Lupe can do no more for them."

"But, she's not—Lupe doesn't love them."

"We do not know what Lupe feels. Hers is the way of a *tortuga*, not our way. Look how her little ones already crawl along, happy to be free. They carry their homes on their backs—all the protection they need. Lupe has done her work. Now the babies will do their own."

Each was one a perfect copy of Lupe, but greener and wet with newness. Even Tito was quiet as he laid the lettuce he brought at Lupe's feet. Ceci leaned against Rafaela's side, wanting to cry. The old woman put her arm around her, patting her shoulder. Could it really be that such tiny things could grow up to be as big as their mother?

Could it be that someday she would be as old as Daddy—and, someday, Rafaela? Ceci could not believe she'd ever get that old. Would Tito become a bent old man someday? Then Ceci tried to imagine her mama's face old and crinkled with joy like Rafaela's. Mama wore the Frownies to keep wrinkles away, but everything would get old, Ceci decided, even Mama. Everything!

"Ceci!" Tito shook her arm. "That big one in the front is mine. Which do you want? Which *tortuga* will you take home?"

Ceci turned and ran into the house before Tito could see her crying.

☆　☆　☆　☆

"Eat all your dinner, Cecilita—not just tortillas. Then we can break the piñata."

"She's doing her best, Pilar. That's a big plate." Grandma Katy took away half of Ceci's enchilada with her fork. "Let Grandma finish this. I need to fatten up a little."

"Wish I had that problem." Pilar sighed and pulled at the waist of her skirt. "Your cooking's too good, Rafaela. I'll have to let out all my clothes." She pushed away her plate.

"Tomorrow you'll be home again. You'll have all your housework and gardening to slim you down. Today you are celebrating! Forget about your *panza*, Pilar. I made a special dessert."

Tito straightened. "*Churros?*"

Rafaela narrowed her eyes. "What makes you think I made *churros*?"

"I smell cinnamon!"

Adelita rolled her eyes. "You always smell cinnamon."

"No *churros!*" Her hand on the refrigerator door, Rafaela chuckled. "Please, don't pout, Tito *mio*—I made *buñuelos*. I thought we'd have some with our café before we break the piñata. You see, Tito, we old people get tired; we need to rest after eating."

"Then why are we having dessert? If you're so tired—"

"You don't want *buñuelos, nieto*?"

"I do! I do!"

Rafaela slid the pan of crisp, puffy rounds of sugar and cinnamon-sprinkled cakes onto the table. Tito grabbed three at once, dropping one on the floor, and Carmen cleaned the mess, while Pilar told them about one of her Bingo friends who ended up in the hospital after trying to lose weight by eating only grapefruit and hardboiled eggs.

While the adults talked and Tito had his second *buñuelo*, Ceci slipped into the living room to take a last long look at Rafaela's altar. In the thin summer dark the candlelit walls were almost purple. As she had so often seen Rafaela do, Ceci knelt before the altar, trying to remember a prayer—any prayer—for the adventure ahead.

She whispered her goodbyes to the little saints: to Francis who held the bird on his finger, to Mary in her blue party dress and golden crown, and to the little brass deer that Rafaela had put there the day she had begun to pray for Mama.

"Cecilita!" Saint Francis waved to her. "Take me outdoors!"

The little brass deer galloped up to him; the pigeon fluttered into the air and landed on the roof of Lady Guadalupe's wooden house. Guadalupe in her starry green veil leaned out from her little arched box. "Do I hear a dove?"

"You do," cooed the bird. "You do, you do."

"*¡Dios mio!*" Guadalupe stretched her brown arms. "I've been standing here praying forever. If I could just smell one rose growing on a bush outdoors, how it would bless me!"

"Please, please, take us outside, Cecilita!" The saints sang out as one.

"I'll get in trouble."

"Silly Cecilita! Trust us. We've been in the business of getting people out of trouble for years." Guadalupe lifted her hand to her ear. "Listen, they're laughing. Tito is keeping them entertained. It's now, or never!"

No one had taught her how say no to the saints. So, Ceci made her skirt into a basket to carry them out Rafaela's front door. She waited on the front stoop until her eyes got used to the night, the sweat on the back of her neck cooling in the breeze. At the side of the house she stopped and laid the saints on the ground, because they were clunking against each other in her skirt. One at a time, she carried each saint into Rafaela's garden. She found a place for Lady Guadalupe in the rose bed and then put Francis and the deer in the wooly thyme.

"It's my favorite," she told them. "Like a carpet."

"Look at her!" Francis looked up. "I haven't seen her for years! Sister Moon, like a lantern in the delicious air—"

Some of their stories Ceci knew; others she just had to guess—she put Saint Martin by the chicken pen, the candle of Saint Barbara next to Mary in the rose bed, and the Virgin Guadalupe she set down near her namesake, Lupe the tortoise. Ceci worked until the garden looked like a world of small people in long robes, lit by giant candles. She stood back to take it all in. It was the best thing she had ever played, or made—she'd never been so proud of anything.

Then she heard a horrible sound: not quite a cough, like someone swallowing a caterpillar. She swung around to see her old tía, waving her arms like a windmill. "Ceci! Stop! What are you doing with Doña Rafaela's *santos*? Such disrespect! Sacrilege!"

"What's going on, Pilar? Why are you yelling?" Rafaela leaned out the screen door. "What mischief? Why is Cecilita crying? Tonight of all nights!"

"Oh, Rafaela, I am so sorry. The child has gone *completamente loca*, bringing all your saints out into the yard."

Biting the tip of her thumb, Ceci watched Rafaela step down into the garden. The *curandera* lifted a candle from the path for light, taking Ceci's hand. "Come, show me where you have put them all."

Pilar grabbed Saint Francis from the wooly thyme. "Look, his feet are all dirty!"

Taking the saint from Pilar, Rafaela wiped his feet on her apron. "Who else did you bring?"

Ceci showed Rafaela Mary and Barbara under the moonlit roses, the Lady Guadalupe in Lupe's pen, the little brass deer, Saint Martin, and all the candles she'd used to light up the garden. Rafaela let go her hand. Even in the dark Ceci could tell the *curandera* was crying. She pulled a red bandana from her apron pocket and blew her nose. Pilar put her arm around her friend.

"I'm so sorry, *amiga*. If my niece has done any damage to the *santos*, I will pay for them." She picked up a candle and blew it out. "She could have started a fire with these votives. It's a wonder she—"

"Indeed it is a wonder, Pilar. A great wonder!"

"A wonder she didn't burn herself, as well as the house. I'm so ashamed. Don't know what got into her."

"No!" Rafaela hugged Ceci to her. "Do not be ashamed. Cecilita has brought the saints outside into the darkness. Don't you see the wonder?"

"I see mischief. That's what happens when a child grows up without church."

"Please, Pilar, look." Rafaela tugged Tía's sleeve. "Look, how beautiful: each saint in a place according to his heart—Francis in the thyme with the moths fluttering around his candles, the Virgin in the roses." Her hands on her cheeks, Pilar walked the path, stopping at each saint. She started to giggle, first softly, then louder and louder. "*San Martin de Porres* in the chicken pen!"

"He wanted to be with the chickens." Ceci picked up *San Martin*. "Should I put him back in the house?"

"No, no, child! Go and get your *abuela,* and your *papá.* Get everybody. I want them to see this!"

Back in the kitchen, Ceci took her grandma by the hand. "Come with me! Everybody come out to the garden!"

"So, what is it we're going to see, macushla?"

"Just come, Grandma. It's a surprise."

Daddy laughed. "Whoa, slow down a little, Ceci. Your grandma is not as spry as Tito. Mind you don't pull her over."

"I'm as spry as I want to be, Barry. You just mind yourself."

Carmen, Adelita, and Tito soon were the garden with them.

"It's so pretty to see the candles at night. Yes, I think I will always keep some candles out here now." Rafaela nodded.

"What about rain?" Tito picked up a candle. "It'll go out."

"You just put that down, Tito *mio,*" Carmen took the candle. "It's not going to rain tonight."

"Well, what do you think, Barry?" Rafaela smiled, "Isn't it a miracle?"

"It's swell, Rafaela, just swell." Daddy shook his head slowly. "Even so, I need to talk to Ceci about monkeying with your things. Ceci, you should always ask permission." His green eyes grayed as he looked into hers. "Always!"

"Permission!" Rafaela's hand swept at the air. "God's surprises come unbidden. We must greet them as they come." She pulled Ceci to her side. "If she had asked me could she play with my altar, I would have said no. I am old and have less imagination than a child." She tapped her forehead. "This is a teaching for the old *curandera,* a very good teaching."

"Now, Rafaela, I don't want my daughter to become a spoiled brat."

"There is no danger of that, *amigo.* The entire time Ceci has been here, she has been a delight. I can't remember one time I spoke to her crossly."

"She isn't so good. She crossed the stree—"

"Tito!" Adelita's hand flew over Tito's mouth. She pressed him against her belly.

Rafaela took Ceci's hand, and they walked the garden together. "Tell me why have you put Our Lady of Guadalupe here?"

"She wanted to smell real roses, live ones, growing."

"And this one?"

"Saint Francis said he knew you wouldn't mind."

"Oh he did, did he now?"

Ceci looked up at the *curandera,* feeling very sure of what he'd said to her. "Yes, he did, because he likes it outside!"

"How does a little girl like you have conversations with the saints?"

"I dunno." Ceci wasn't sure she knew what a conversation was.

"I mean—they tell you things, the saints?" Rafaela straightened the ribbon in Ceci's hair.

"When I play with them, and in dreams."

"I know about the dreams. This play is news to me." She closed her eyes, a smile lit by the moon spreading across her face. She kissed the top of Ceci's head. "Remember this, and you will always be happy, *chiquita.* The saints talk to you when you play. They will come when you call them, too."

That last morning, the goodbyes were short and simple. Rafaela had a sick man coming for a *limpia,* and no time to chat. Tito and Adelita had spent the night, all of the children sleeping on the back porch and telling stories—not too scary this time, but with enough ghosts to keep them awake until the grownups, having taken a long time with their *café con leche,* remembered to tuck them in for the night. After breakfast, Adelita and Tito took the streetcar to school. Tito hung out the window, waving his notebook, until Adelita yanked him back by his belt. "Goodbye, Ceci!" Ceci waved until the streetcar pulled out of sight.

Barry told her they would drop off Tía Pilar at the Greyhound Station on the way to the freeway. After that, they'd head east onto Route 66. Grandma had spent the night, too. She woke up early to dress up for the trip, her thin cheeks glowing under her black straw hat with the red cherries on it.

As they said their final goodbyes to Carmen, Grandma and Pilar sat together in the back seat of the Mercury, talking. Daddy leaned out the driver's window to say goodbye one more time. Ceci hoped they wouldn't cry, because if they did, she would.

"I have to go, Barry. I'll be late for work!"

"Let me just look at you a bit."

Carmen laughed. "Whatever for?"

"I like the view—"

"Are you going to kiss her, Daddy?"

The old women's chatter stopped suddenly. Daddy's neck turned pink. Ceci looked back at Pilar and Grandma. "Is it all right if he kisses her?"

"'Tis!" Grandma grinned.

"And, you, Tía Pilar? Would you get mad?"

"You don't understand, child!" Tía Pilar's hands came together under her chin. "He's still married."

"Nonsense!" Grandma Katy patted her friend's hand. "Not in the eyes of the church. Dora and he eloped! It's perfectly all right. Kiss away, boyo!"

Daddy reached for Carmen's hand through the car window.

Grandma tapped his back. "Kiss her, then!"

"No!" Pilar elbowed Grandma. "Let him be."

Daddy opened the car door and pulled Carmen to him. Their kiss was nothing like anything in the movies. Carmen bumped her head on the door and Daddy kissed her nose.

Tears sliding down her cheeks, Carmen shut the car door. "Now, I really have to go! Goodbye! Goodbye, all my dears. It has been such a time!"

As she waved them on, Daddy called, "I'm coming back, you know!" He started the car. "I'm coming back to get you!"

"Sure, and I will make you!" Grandma said.

Ceci watched Carmen grow smaller and smaller, until they turned the corner, and she could no longer see her waving goodbye.

They'd been driving most of the day, stopping for snacks at roadside diners and filling up the gas tank in towns with names like Needles and Flagstaff. Route 66 was lined with dust, rock, and neon signs. Daddy had sung his way through Arizona:

Travel my way, the highway, that's best.
Get your kicks on Route 66!

After the paintbox sundown, it got dark. There was nothing more than neon signs to look at, and they were getting fewer. The moon came out, like a great big silver dollar following alongside their car. Ceci loved that it came all that way with them.

Unlike other friends, the moon didn't have to stay behind. Rafaela had promised Ceci the moon would follow her all the way to Ireland and back. It would disappear sometimes, so it could tell the *curandera* how Ceci and her family were doing, but it would come right back, at first very thin from its journey, and then grow fat again.

Daddy's eyes blinked slowly, like an owl's.

"Are you sleepy, Daddy?"

"Yeah, maybe. Better find us a place—call it a night."

"A hotel?"

"A motel, I guess they call them around here. I see a sign up ahead—Sage Brush Inn. Doesn't look like much, but we'll give it a try."

The Mercury's headlights lit up the side of a rusty pickup truck, the only car parked there, and the only light in the office came from the TV. Daddy looked over the seat. "Ready to turn in, Ma? I am!"

"Been turned in for hours. But I'd love to lie down." Grandma rolled down her window and shivered. "I thought it'd be hot."

"Desert's cold at night. Nothing to hold in the warmth in."

Grandma pulled on her sweater. "Have they a vacancy?"

"Sign's burnt out. Stay in the car, where it's warm. Ceci and I'll go check."

The bell that hung from the dirty glass door announced them. Dusty boots on the desk, a man slept with a cowboy hat over his face. Daddy waited a while, then pushed the knob of the round silver bell on the desk. The man snored on. Daddy pressed the bell again, coughing. The cowboy hat bobbed just a bit.

"Okay, Ceci Bean, it's up to you to wake him up."

Ceci stood on her tiptoes and pushed the bell over and over, until the man pulled off his cowboy hat. "Hold your horses, Zelma." His voice was dry as the air outside. "Uh, sorry folks. Thought you were my old lady. Y'all want a room?"

"We'll need two beds, and a cot for my daughter. Just us—and my ma."

"For seven bucks we can fix you up with two double beds, but we're clean out of cots." The man pushed Daddy the key. "Room six, just behind the office. You won't hear the trucks back there." He pulled the hat back over his eyes.

When they got to the car, they found Grandma had fallen back asleep.

"We'll get settled in the room, and I'll come get her." Daddy handed Ceci the little suitcase Grandma had given her. "You take yours, and I'll carry the others."

Sand had blown over the walkway to their room. It snuck into her shoe and made hard lumps under the new white socks with the lace around the tops. Ceci stopped to empty out her shoe.

"Sorry, sweetheart, this place is kind of a dump, but it's home for tonight."

"It's a lucky room—number six, like me!"

Daddy unlocked the door. Ceci liked the room—a cowboy room, cared for and clean as the outside was messy and ugly. Roy Rogers would have slept in beds like these—wagon wheel headboards and Indian blankets laid over them. The wood floors and the Indian rugs were clean as the desert air.

"Surprise! Surprise! Not bad, eh? Why don't you unpack your pajamas and toothbrush while I get your Grandma?"

Ceci opened her suitcase. Another surprise. There were presents on top, wrapped in white tissue tied with red string. She laid them on the bed—three packages. She opened the biggest first—a pink flannel nightgown with little hearts all over it. There was a card with cursive writing she couldn't read, a picture of a baby owl on the front. It must be from Tía Pilar, she decided, and laid the nightgown on the bed. As she smoothed the ruffles on the front, she counted six rose-colored heart buttons.

The next present was the Lady Guadalupe that had watched over Ceci all the time she'd slept in Rafaela's house. She kissed the dear little face, knowing it was from Rafaela.

Grandma and Barry stood in the door. "What have you there, macushla?"

"They gave me presents. A new nightgown, and—"

Daddy picked up the owl card. "From your Tía Pilar."

"Yes, I know. And—look what Rafaela gave me!"

"Isn't that the prettiest little thing? Very special."

"This one's from Carmen, Tito, and Adelita." Daddy read the writing on the tissue paper. 'Happy travels in Ireland. We love you very much!"

Ceci tore the tissue paper open—a velvet pouch about the size of a wallet, with a photo of Ceci with Lupe, the tortoise. As she laid the photo on the nightstand, something fell out of the pouch. It was a green stone turtle, only a little smaller than Lupe's babies, on a red ribbon. Ceci handed it to Grandma. "What's it for?"

"A necklace, I think. Looks like it might be made out of turquoise. How nice of them to give you presents! You'll miss them, won't you?"

Ceci nodded, wiping her eyes.

"Soon you will meet great-aunts and cousins in Ireland. It won't keep us from missing our friends, but it sure will help us feel better." Grandma hugged her and wiped at Ceci's cheek with her thumb. "Child, you're gritty! Is that just from the sand in the parking lot? You'd best take a shower before getting into that new nightgown." She yawned, "Oh, I'm the worse for wear. Can you wash up all by your lone? Your hair, there's something sticky in it."

Daddy tried to pick the stickiness out of Ceci's curls. "She doesn't much like hair washing, Ma—nor showers."

"I can wash my hair by myself now, Daddy. Rafaela taught me how. I can take a shower, too—I think. I'm not scared to try."

"Will wonders never cease?" Daddy kissed Ceci's cheek. "All right then, Ceci. You take the first shower and I'll tuck you in."

Ceci opened the bathroom door; it was all bright turquoise and yellow tiles, polished to a shine. For a long time, she stared at the shower handles: *H* must be hot and *C* for cold. Rafaela once told her if she turned on the cold water first, no matter how hot the water was, it could never burn her. So Ceci turned on the cold, and then turned the *H* knob until the water ran warm and soft onto her hand. She slipped out of her dusty clothes, humming to herself.

The water's deep and the water's wide—

Under the shower, the water wetting the stone turtle she had forgotten to take off, Ceci remembered Rafaela washing Lupe in the garden. Rafaela always laid the hose out in the sun before Lupe's shower to warm the water. If there weren't enough sun to warm the water, Lupe would pull back into her shell. When the water was just right, she stretched her wrinkly neck out to enjoy the shower.

Ceci let the water play on her head. It was a great feeling: the tapping of the droplets, her body soft, friendly, and warm. Accidentally, she breathed in a little water. It stung her throat, and she remembered how the Lady Guadalupe had lifted her from the ocean. Who were those other saints who'd warned, whispered, and played with her?

"I forget. Maybe later I'll remember—but I forget."

Like Lupe, *la tortuga*, Ceci had come very far, and she might have gotten lost, but she didn't. Now that she was found, all was well. All there was to do now was to be happy.

No more fears of devils, of hungry waves. Daddy would take care of that. Like the tortoise, like the snails, like a bean in its own shiny pod, Ceci was home—at home, no matter where she'd go in the world. She unwrapped a little bar of motel soap and washed herself clean.

Acknowledgments

Many people have blessed my life, and many have made this book possible. I hope you know who you are. You are the *curanderos* and *curanderas* who fill my world with friendship, laughter, and wisdom. You made this book possible, just by being you.

First, thank you to my beloved husband, Jim Nail. He encouraged me to publish now, instead of waiting forever for a perfect convergence of agent, editor, and commercial publisher. You always stood behind me, in front of me—anywhere I needed you—supporting and cheering me onward. A gifted musician and songwriter, my Saint James is an inspiration every day. Thank you to my sons Brendan and Devin, who taught me about the bridge from heaven across which parents must lead their children—and the pleasure of doing so.

Thanks to my friends Sally Gillette, Mike Huber, Jean Lee, Leslie Logan, April Vanderwal, Merrily Weidner, and Annie Witherspoon, who read drafts, listened long, prayed right, and shone light on things. Thank you, Ruba Byrd, for your loving editorial eye. Thank you also to Peg Edera, my spiritual director; because of you there is a deeper meaning. Thank you, dear Melanie Weidner, for the cover and interior art. When I wanted to pack it all in, you sent me the gorgeous cover painting, and I knew the book must be, if only for that cover. (Check out more of Melanie's art at: listenforjoy.com.) And thank you, Mark Pratt-Russum, for the author photo.

Last, but not least, thank you Señor Gonzalo Flores, *curandero.* Thank you for letting me study the medicine with you. You helped make it all true.

Author's Note

Regarding language: I deleted many Spanish and Nahuatl words in the editing process, but some had to stay. I attempted to translate by use in context. Most Spanish words are italicized for your convenience. With the ease of Internet translation, a glossary is unnecessary. If you can't find the proper translations, try to enjoy the music of language like notes of jazz, with an easy mind. You can still understand the story.

Curanderismo differs from practitioner to practitioner. Rafaela's style is the compilation of several years of research, but it is not meant to represent all forms of this complex and multifaceted folk medicine.

There are bound to be errors I couldn't catch with the nets of all my research, revisions, and editing. I hope you'll treat those like jazz as well. Sometimes, as jazzman Thelonious Monk once quipped, "I played the wrong, wrong notes!"

About the Author

A fifth-generation Californian, Claire Germain Nail now lives in Portland, Oregon. When not writing, Claire works as a multimedia artist and spiritual director. She offers this novel in gratitude to her Celtic and Hispanic ancestors, as a testimony to their ancient wisdom. Her father, John Maddock, inspired her love of jazz; her mother, Geraldine Girard, taught her the consequences of its chaos. She met her first *curandera*, a Mexican healer, as a youngster in California. Later, while teaching English as a Second Language, she witnessed the soul-ripping losses immigrant families experience to assimilate into homogeneous culture. Caught between worlds, they never feel fully at home in either. Claire studied Mexican folk medicine alongside *curandero* Gonzalo Flores to research this book. She urges you to cherish your unique heritage, wherever it originated.